Descent of Humanity

Book 2 in the Dusk of Humanity Series

M.K. Dawn

ISBN: 9781077271456

CHAPTER ONE

"Okay," Britney yelled from the top of the stairs as she pulled her red hair into a loose bun and fluffed her thick bangs, "if we leave in the next five minutes, we won't be late for church." Then she added under her breath, "Again."

The front door swung open and John, her husband of ten years, strolled toward the stairs still wearing his filthy work clothes. "You look nice, babe."

Britney stuck a hand on her jutted hip. "What are you doin'? I thought you came in an hour ago to get dressed?" Her country accent always sounded more pronounced when irritated.

"I did." He removed his grungy baseball cap and ran a hand through his even grungier dark, thinning hair. "But then I remembered I had to check on the calf in the back pen."

She closed her eyes and let out a weighted breath, trying to slow her quickened pulse. "Can you please go get ready? Pastor Beachem asked me to hand out flyers this morning for the church festival next Saturday."

"Screw 'em. I'm sure that busybody Susan will gladly step up to help."

She groaned. "Yeah, and hold it over my head for the rest of my life."

He gave her a light pat on the butt and jogged up the stairs. "A quick shower and I'll be ready to go."

"What? No!" Britney followed him, slower in her heels. "We don't have time. Just throw on some clothes so we can leave."

"I'll be fast," he hollered as he started the water.

Britney dropped her head back. "Lord, help me."

As fast as John thought he was at getting ready, she could dry her hair, put on makeup and try on five different outfits before he got out of the shower. His excuse: being a six-foot-five hefty man meant he had a lot of area to clean, unlike her "bite-size self."

At five-foot-four, she wasn't exactly short, but compared to him....

She glanced at the grandfather clock as she headed downstairs to check on the kids—ten o'clock, and church started at ten thirty. The drive into town took thirty minutes. Longer if they got behind a slow driver, or God bless, a tractor.

"Hey, boys." Her sons sat on the couch playing on their tablets, thankfully dressed. In wrinkled button-up shirts and scuffed boots, but at this point she'd take what she could get. "Where's Molly?"

Blake, Molly's twin brother, shrugged. "How should I know?"

"Watch your tone, kid." And they said two-year-olds were bad. Five going on fifteen wore on her nerves faster than any age. So far. She remembered how mouthy she was as a teenager and dreaded when her kids reached those years.

"Carson?" Britney pressed her nine-year-old.

He didn't bother looking up from his tablet. "She said something about her dress being itchy."

"Son of a bitch."

Two sets of hazel eyes gawked at her. Britney was a country girl through and through. She had her daddy's mouth and little self-control over her tongue, a combination that earned her a lot of wayward glances from the uppity women in town. Not that she gave a rat's ass what they thought.

"Umm," Blake scolded with a big smile, "Mommy said a bad word."

"Don't judge me." She shot them a little wink and went to check on Molly, who was probably in her room, rifling through the closet.

Britney left her heels at the bottom of the stairs and headed up.

Before dealing with Molly, she needed to check on the man-child she called a husband. "John, are you almost ready?"

"Yep." At least he was out of the shower.

An audible groan left her lips when she entered Molly's room. Dresses lay scattered on the floor, and in the middle of the mess stood a very pissed-off five-year-old. "I see you changed."

"My dress was itchy."

Britney wanted to say, "The same dress you wore and refused to take off the entire week before school?" but she opted for a more motherly approach. "So I've heard. Do you think you can put somethin' else on? We're late for church."

"Can I wear my *Brave* dress?" Molly narrowed her hazel eyes.

While Britney had green eyes and John had blue, all their kids' eyes matched those of Britney's younger sister, Sloan. "Your *Brave* dress?"

"We're twins. We have the same hair."

At this point she could wear her pajamas, as long as she had clothes to cover her body. "Sure, honey."

Molly cocked her head and, with a victorious smile, asked, "And the heels to match?"

"I'll make you a deal." Britney crouched in front of her fiery mini-me. "You can wear both if you can get them on by the time I count to sixty."

Thirty seconds later, they headed down the stairs, Molly dressed with a bulging purse slung on her shoulder. They were in trouble with that one.

John waited for them with the front door open. "Ladies, you look lovely."

Molly beamed and rushed outside. "Thanks, Daddy."

Britney slipped her shoes on and did a quick sweep around the house. "Where are the boys?"

"In the truck." John ushered her out and locked the door. "We've been waiting for the two of you."

Britney shoved his arm and tried not to laugh. "You're such an ass."

John kissed her on the cheek. "You know you love me."

***

The church bells donged as they entered town. Britney sank in her seat and groaned. "I'll never hear the end of this."

John gave her a sideways glance. "What's the big deal? You don't care what those women think anyway."

"No. But what they'll say behind my back, that sh—" She peered back at her three snickering kids. "Crap drives me up the wall."

John parked the car in front of the little white church. "I thought you loved gossip."

"Not when it's about me." She helped the twins out of the truck while Carson climbed out of the driver side.

"Look." John pointed as they rounded the truck. "We're not the only ones late."

"Good Lord." Britney couldn't believe who headed toward the church. "That can't be the Anthonys."

"You know any other elderly African American couple who attends our church?"

Britney swatted his arm. "Don't say that."

John cocked his head, genuinely confused. "What did I say?"

"Never mind." Britney knew John meant no disrespect. "I can't believe they're here. Just last month he was on his deathbed."

"Shh." John grabbed her hand, and they hurried inside just before the door closed.

Nobody noticed the Campbell family as Britney shoved them in the last pew. The Anthonys being back was bigger news than their reoccurring tardiness. This week, at least.

Pastor Christopher Beachem silenced the room with his lanky arms. "Patty and Thomas Anthony. The Lord has heard our prayers. Welcome back. Come, sit up front. I insist."

He waved them down the aisle, forcing Susan and her family to move a few rows back.

Britney snickered, though not loud enough for anyone but John to hear.

He shook his head, an amused grin splashed across his face.

Pastor Beachem strolled down the stairs and grasped each of the Anthonys' hands. "It is so good to see you both back here, in the house of our Lord. And for Thomas to appear so healthy."

"We are so blessed." Patty choked on the words and dabbed under her eyes with her white handkerchief. "God has answered our prayers. Thomas has been cured."

The congregation gasped. Not six months ago, the doctor had diagnosed Thomas with stage-four pancreatic cancer.

"How is that possible?" Britney whispered in John's ear.

"Cured?" Pastor Beachem's eyes widened. "Praise the Lord Jesus."

People applauded. Some wept.

Lost in her own thoughts, Britney didn't do either. She wanted to know how. As much as she believed in God, breast cancer had taken her mother when she was sixteen. She had spent months in this very church, praying for a miracle that never came. Breast cancer had a pretty good survival rate. Pancreatic cancer did not.

Thomas twisted around and gave the group a small nod and wave.

Though he appeared significantly better than he did the last time she'd seen him, there was still something off about his appearance. His ebony skin, usually so rich with a healthy glow, lacked the luster that had been there before.

"His skin is different." She kept her voice low so only John could hear. "Almost like there's a hint of gray to his colorin'."

"Brit," John said in the stern tone he used when her mouth was getting the best of her.

"What?" Her eyes flickered over at the kids, who sat in the pew playing with the small cars the boys must have stuffed in their pockets, and the ponies Molly had in her purse. At least they were quiet. "I'm not tryin' to be mean. I love Thomas. He and Patty were some of my parents' closest friends."

Pastor Beachem stood and silenced the congregation. "We prayed for a cure, and the Lord answered our prayers. Amen."

"Amen," they replied in unison.

The service continued till well past noon, when it usually let out at eleven thirty. They could thank Susan for that. As head of the fall festival committee, she wanted to make sure everything was in order for the following weekend. A conversation that could have waited until Monday evening when the committee met, but then Pastor Beachem wouldn't have been there to hear all the "hard work" she'd put into making this festival the "best ever." Unlike the festival Britney headed up last year, where half the town ended up with food poisoning. Like she had any control over the rancid turkey legs.

Not that Britney expected any less. She and Susan had been at each other's throats since elementary school. Britney caught Susan kissing her boyfriend on the playground—and broke her nose. A little blip in her past she wasn't exactly proud of, but it still brought a smile to her face.

By the time Pastor Beachem dismissed the service, the kids had all but lost their minds. Molly had said no less than thirty times in the last half hour she was starving, like Britney could do anything about it sitting in church. The boys couldn't stay still to save their lives. Their quiet car play had turned into a monster truck rally halfway through Beachem's second reading. Even though both Britney and John had scolded them through clenched teeth, they continued to get louder.

She had to hand it to the kids, as they knew what they could get away with and where. Church being one of them. God forbid she lost her temper in front of everybody. Like none of them ever yelled at their kids. *Please*. Some of them made her kids look like saints. Susan's youngest—that boy sent shivers down Britney's spine when he glanced her way.

They needed to get out of there before Britney's debutante smile slipped and the snarky side of her let loose. Her sanity hung on by a thread, and her kids held the scissors.

Britney understood their restlessness; as an adult, she struggled to sit still for longer than an hour. That's probably why ranching turned out to be a perfect fit. Not that she'd ever admit that to Sloan. After their father passed, Britney had to drop out of school and return home to take care of her younger sister and the farm he'd left behind. Not long after, Sloan left for college and never looked back. For years Britney resented her sister for leaving, but that dwindled after Carson was born. These days their relationship consisted of missed phone calls and postponed visits.

"So, Cracker Barrel for lunch?" John asked as they headed for the truck.

"Sure." Brittney scanned the parking lot in search of Patty and Thomas. His recovery had kept her mind reeling the entire service. As happy as she was for him, the curious side of her needed to know how the doctors had healed him. Last she heard, there was nothing left to do for him but make the most of what little time he had left.

***

Cracker Barrel was packed. There were two churches in the small town of Myrefall, Montana: the First Baptist Church and their nondenominational church, Gracepoint. Both started at ten thirty and ran about an hour. Go over that hour mark and the congregations grew antsy, partially because no one wanted to be stuck on the waiting list for lunch.

Typical small-town USA, the Cracker Barrel was the only restaurant open on Sundays. It was a race to see which congregation would get their first. First Baptist won today.

"There's a thirty-minute wait," John said, coming back from the hostess stand. "Want to go home and eat there?"

"No." Molly tugged on Britney's dress and whined, "I'm starving."

Britney brushed the fallen strands of hair out of her daughter's eyes. "Let's wait. By the time we get home and cook somethin'—"

"And I have to go to the bathroom," Molly interrupted.

"Okay." Britney watched the boys, who were eying the toy section of the country store attached to the restaurant. "Blake, Carson, you guys need to go to the bathroom too?"

Both shook their head.

Britney grabbed Molly's hand and led her through the restaurant.

On the way back, they passed Patty and Thomas.

"Hello, dear," Patty said with a tilt of her head. "How are you and your family doing?"

"Pretty good." Britney smiled. "Just waitin' for a table."

"Join us," Thomas offered. "We have plenty of room."

Britney scanned the four empty seats, surprised they'd sit the couple at such a big table. "Well there are five of us. And we wouldn't want to intrude. Are you expectin' others to join you?"

"Makayla canceled. Again. That daughter of ours." Patty tapped the tabletop with her index finger. "We'll pull up another chair. It's been ages. Go get John and the boys. You want to wait here with us, Molly?"

She nodded and slid in the chair next to Patty.

"I'll be right back, kid." Britney found John and the boys outside. "Come on. Let's go eat."

John checked his watch. "They called us already? It's only been ten minutes."

"Patty and Thomas invited us to sit with them."

"Oh." John hollered at the boys to come inside. "That was nice of them."

"Guess they want to catch up. It's been a while."

Carson grabbed the sleeve of Blake's shirt. "This way."

They hurried off inside while Britney and John trailed not too far behind.

"Maybe"—John focused on the floor—"don't mention him being better."

"Why on Earth not?"

John cleared his throat. "You're not the most tactful person in the world."

"Ugh." Britney's mouth fell open. "You think I'm going to offend them?"

"It's just…."

Britney scowled. "Just what?"

He pinched the bridge of his nose. "Nothing, dear."

"Fine." She rolled her eyes. "I won't bring it up unless they do. Happy?"

"Yes." He kissed the top of her head. "Looks like they've ordered drinks."

She squeezed John's hand as he pulled out her chair. "Thank you."

Patty and Thomas smiled and greeted John as they sat.

“I ordered the kids chocolate milk,” Patty said, “and the both of you sweet tea. I hope that’s okay. I know that’s what your mama always ordered.”

Britney sipped her drink. “That’s perfect. Mama loved her sweet tea. Said it was a southern thing.” Her mother was from Georgia. Britney had picked up on her mother’s drawl as a kid, which was why she now spoke with a southern twang.

“I’m hungry,” Molly growled. Again.

“We’re about to order.” Britney redirected Molly’s attention to the food listed on the kid’s menu. “Decide what you want.”

Thomas turned and lifted a finger. “Tammy, we’re ready.”

Tammy strolled over, the waitress’s voluptuous hips swaying, and pulled out her notepad. “Let’s start with the kids.”

Carson pointed at the menu. “Fried shrimp, please.”

Blake scrunched his nose and groaned. “I guess a hamburger.” John lifted an eyebrow and Blake added, “Please.”

Molly straightened and did her best adult impression. “I will take the mac and cheese, please.”

“Sweetie”—John patted her hand—“wouldn’t you like something other than mac and cheese? Something with meat?”

“But, Daddy,” Molly huffed, “I don’t like the other food. Only the mac and cheese.”

John looked to Britney for help, but this was a battle she didn’t feel like fighting. “It’s not worth it.”

“Fine.” John slumped in his chair. “I guess it’s mac and cheese for the princess.”

Molly beamed, and Britney had to bite her tongue to keep from laughing. Poor John. The boys he understood, but Molly? She tested his patience like no other.

The rest of the table ordered, and the waitress left, promising to be back in a few minutes to refill their drinks.

"You have to be wondering"—Patty grinned at Thomas—"how this all happened."

Britney's eyes danced to John. "I didn't want to pry."

Patty waved a dismissive hand. "The whole town has been talking about it since we got home a week ago. If it were bad news, I would be irate, but since my dear Thomas is all better, I don't mind answering all their questions."

Now that Britney had the go-ahead to talk about Thomas's recovery, she wouldn't hold back. "What I don't understand is how they cured the cancer in such a short time. I knew you had been accepted into some sort of medical trial. Through NATO, right? But I heard from Makayla it wasn't workin'."

"God gave us one child." Patty leaned back in her chair. "And bless her heart, she can't keep her mouth shut."

Makayla had a reputation for being a gossip, and as one of Britney's closest friends, they talked a lot. "It terrified her to think she might lose her father and knew I would understand."

Patty's eyes softened. "We were all scared. A week after the initial treatment, we went back for his follow-up and found out Thomas had been given the placebo. Heartbroken isn't a strong enough word."

Britney faced Thomas. "The experimental treatment didn't work?"

"It did work!" Patty nearly jumped out of her seat. "It worked so well that all the placebo patients received a dose. We go back in a month for a follow-up."

"That's crazy." Britney knew a little about drug testing since her sister was a surgeon. "A week seems pretty fast to determine if a drug is safe or not."

Patty cupped Thomas's cheek. "I'm so grateful. God has smiled down on the world with this amazing gift."

Britney opened her mouth to ask about side effects when John's firm hand grasped her leg.

She looked up at him and he shook his head. "Let it go."

"Who's hungry?" Tammy arrived with a tray of food in hand.

"Meeee!" Molly squealed.

"Toys away," John told the kids. "Should I take them to wash their hands?"

"No point." All three of them had already dug into their food. "A few germs never hurt anyone."

John snorted. "If Sloan heard you say that…."

"That would require her to visit, which I doubt will happen anytime soon."

A raspy cough broke through Thomas's belly laugh. He pounded on his chest for a second and cleared his throat. "Sorry about that. Food must have gone down the wrong pipe."

"Does that happen—" Before Britney could finish her sentence, boisterous laughter filled the room.

The entire dining room turned to stare at a group of bikers being taken to the back party room.

"Those guys are awesome. Their leather jackets are so cool." Carson's eyes widened. "I wonder what kind of motorcycles they ride."

"Fast ones," Blake said with the same awe. "Can we go see them?"

One man in particular caught Britney's eye, younger than the rest with jet-black hair and a five-o'clock shadow. A few tables over, a group of ladies swooned as he walked by. Britney didn't see the appeal. He scared her; they all did. Maybe it was her overactive imagination, but there was something about bikers that sent a chill down her spine.

"Mom!" Carson shouted, drawing her attention away from the group. "I'm done. Can we go check out their motorcycles?"

"Yeah!" Blake pointed out the window. "There are so many of them. I like the one with the flames."

Molly scrunched her nose. "I hate motorcycles."

"That's because you're a girl." Blake stuck out his tongue. "And motorcycles are for boys."

"Is that so?" a woman said.

The kids froze, and Britney turned around. A tall woman, head shaved and covered in countless tattoos, stood behind her.

Britney's breath hitched. "I'm so sorry, ma'am. They meant nothin' by it."

The woman smiled. "You don't get many of our kind in these parts, do ya?"

"Um." Britney turned to John, but he was on his phone talking about cattle, oblivious to what was happening a foot away. "Mostly just people passin' through. There's not much to do around here."

The woman took in the room. "It shows."

Britney hadn't noticed before, but everyone in the dining hall had halted their conversations and were staring at them. It was this sort of thing that gave small towns a bad name.

"Can I help you guys with somethin'?" Britney barked at the room. "No? Then mind your own business."

Heads snapped away and conversations picked up. Probably all about her, but at least they stopped staring.

The woman snorted. “Thanks. You happen to know of a hotel around here that can handle our group?”

They were staying the night? Interesting. “There’s a motel off Main Street. Few blocks over, right at the streetlight. Can’t miss it.”

“Thanks again. And you, little lady,” the biker addressed Molly. “There ain’t a damn thing in this world that’s just for boys. Excuse my language.”

“That’s okay.” Molly beamed. “Our mommy says lots of bad words.”

Britney glared at the pint-size traitor. “Molly.”

“My kind of people.” The woman patted Britney’s back. “Have a good one, folks.”

“Same to you.” John waved as she walked off.

“Oh, now you can speak. Where were you when I needed help?”

John laughed, a hardy sound that warmed her heart. “Honey, we all know you can take care of yourself.”

CHAPTER TWO

Axel tossed back the remainder of his beer and set the mug back on the counter.

"Want another?" The bartender, Jed, continued drying the glasses that had just come out of the dishwasher.

"Nah." Axel pulled a twenty from his wallet and tossed it on the bar.

Jed rotated around with a grin. "Only two beers today? Did I do something wrong?"

Axel chuckled and scratched at the stubble on his chin. "Day drinking isn't a sport I play too often these days. It takes a toll on this old man."

Jed threw the dish towel over his broad shoulder. The man looked more like a linebacker than a barkeep. "Old? Your ID says you're thirty-five."

"There are different types of old, my friend." Axel shook Jeb's hand. "Thanks for the hospitality."

"You guys heading out already? Dammit. Going to be losing my best customers in years."

"Not till Sunday morning."

“Well then.” Jed took back his hand. “It’s only Friday afternoon. Chances are good I’ll see you back here tomorrow.”

Axel and the other bikers had been stuck in this small town nearly a week. The meteorologist said the rainfall had been record-breaking. And even though the storms had moved out early yesterday morning, the flood waters hadn’t receded enough for them to get the hell out of this place.

“The others, maybe. Not me. Riding while hungover isn’t my idea of fun.”

“I hear ya, man.” Jed went back to drying the dishes. “Have a safe trip.”

“Thanks.” Axel left the bar and squinted as the harsh sunlight hit his eyes. After five days of clouds and rain, the sun, while welcomed, hurt like hell.

He dropped his glasses from his head to the bridge of his nose and took in the small town. The locals were out in full force, strolling the streets, having lunch, grocery shopping. They were everywhere but the bar, which was why he’d spent the past few days there throwing back a couple of cold ones and watching ESPN. The barkeep didn’t ask questions like the others around these parts.

Across the street, the white church was setting up for some kind of festival. In the middle of the dozens of women was the hot redhead from the restaurant last Sunday. She’d put the entire place in check when she caught them gawking at Queenie. Most people in the small towns they’d passed through wouldn’t have bothered. It meant a lot to Queenie and the others that the woman spoke up in their defense. Least he could do was say thanks.

Axel checked the streets for traffic, which he had yet to see since arriving, and jogged across. A few ladies smiled as he passed. Most turned away, their cheeks flushed.

He wasn't a hundred yards from the redhead when a woman stepped in front of him.

"Hello there, stranger," the bleached-blond cooed. "How can I help you? I'm Susan Boyd. I'm the one in charge here."

"I'm just checking things out." He peered over Susan, who stood way too close for comfort. "Actually, I wanted to speak to that woman over there. The one with the red hair."

Susan threw back her head and huffed. "Britney Campbell? Do you know her or something?"

Axel took a step back. "No."

"Then why do you want to talk to her?" Susan tapped her foot.

"Uh—"

"Susan," a woman called from across the parking lot, "we have a hayride issue over here."

The vein in Susan's neck pulsated. "Imbeciles." Then she plastered a smile on her face and squeezed Axel's arm. "Come by tomorrow, honey, won't you? We'd love to have you."

Axel had no words. All he could do was nod and watch the crazy woman storm off.

"That's what we call bein' Susaned," a southern woman said. "Washin' the ickiness off is the hard part."

"What?" Axel jerked his head toward the sound of the voice. The redhead, Britney, stood a few feet away, brush in hand and white paint all over her jean overalls.

"The way you were standin' there, all confused. She has that effect on everyone."

Axel blinked a few times. "What the hell's wrong with that lady?"

"She's a ragin' bitch."

He couldn't help but laugh. "So it's not just gawking at outsiders in restaurants that excites people here?"

"Excuse me?"

"Sunday." He'd expected her to remember. Everyone else in this town seemed to know who he and his friends were. "You were talking to my friend, Queenie."

"Oh." Her eyes widened. "I didn't recognize you without the...."

"The what?"

She brushed at her lips, smearing white paint all over her mouth and cheek.

He reached out to wipe the paint away, but she flinched back. "What are you doin'?"

"Sorry." He pulled his hands back and held them palms toward her. "Not trying to grope you, but you have paint all over your mouth and cheeks."

Her face flushed. "Shit. I have to go." She ran off in the direction of the church.

Axel followed, feeling bad for embarrassing her, but stopped just outside the entrance when he noticed how big of an audience he had attracted. He should go back to the motel. Small towns like this loved gossip, and a stranger talking to a clearly married woman would probably cause a stir. On the other hand, he should apologize for reaching out to touch her face. The last thing he wanted was to be labeled a creeper.

Britney came out a few minutes later, clean-faced and rubbing her brow. "Why are you still here?"

"I'm Axel, by the way."

"Axel?" She cocked her head. "What the hell kind of name is that?"

He shrugged. "What can I say? My parents were both bikers. And an axle is a—"

"I know what an axle is."

"Sorry. You're Britney Campbell, right?"

She brushed past him and headed down the stairs. “I’m married.”

“That’s great for you.” He trailed close behind. “And I’m sure your husband is real proud.”

She whirled around. “What the hell is that supposed to mean?”

“Nothing.” Were all the women in this town crazy? “I mean, you’re a lovely person and all—”

“Why are you here?” She waved her hands outward. “Here. In our town. You and your little biker gang.”

“Biker gang?” He chuckled. “Is that what you and this insane town think of us?”

“We’re not insane! But you have to understand, the majority of this town has been here for generations. We all know each other. Strangers who look like you and your friends are….”

“Care to finish that sentence?”

She peered over her shoulder, her face flushed. “I have to get back to work. The rain has screwed everything up. We have to set up in the parkin’ lot because it’s too muddy. The booths, which of course are my job, aren’t even out of storage yet. Susan is already runnin’ her mouth about that. What was I supposed to do, set up the wooden booths in the pourin’ rain?”

Axel scanned the area. “Where are all the men?”

Britney’s brow furrowed. “Why?”

“I’m guessing the wooden booths are heavy.”

“Listen.” She held up a finger. “I run a cattle ranch. Carryin’ a couple of booths is nothin’ compared to what I do on a daily basis.”

“I believe you. I just thought if you were running behind, you might need some help.”

She fiddled with her bangs which sat just above her green eyes. “Why? Are you offerin’?”

"Uh." Was he offering? That wasn't why he'd come over, but he had nothing else to do. "Yeah. Sure. Direct me to the storage building and tell me where you want them."

"Around the back. It's open. Taped lines on the asphalt mark where they go. All you have to do is line them up."

"No problem."

Her eyes fell on him, and then she quickly turned her head with a frown. "Uh… thank you."

"See?" he called out to her as she walked away. "Bikers can be nice guys too."

***

The sun was long gone before Axel finished setting up all the booths. Not only were they heavy as hell, there were a shit-ton of them. After the third, he ran back to the hotel to grab some of his buddies to help. It would have taken him all night to get those things out of there if he did it alone.

He found a bench and plopped down, laying his head back on his weary shoulders and closed his eyes.

"Axel?"

"Hey." He rubbed his eyes and straightened as Britney approached.

She handed him a beer. "Where are the others?"

"Thanks." He grabbed the bottle and pointed across the street. "They hit the bar."

"You didn't go with them?"

"Noooo." He took a drink. "I can't keep up."

She sat beside him and crossed her legs. "Seriously? How old are you?"

"Why is everyone around here so focused on a damn number? There are other ways to age besides a birthday."

"Yes, there are." She took a long drink of her beer. "I'm sorry about earlier. Susan's been on my ass for weeks about this fall festival. And she's been tellin' the other women in the congregation how bad I've been screwin' up. They already look down on me. I don't know why I even care."

"Why do they look down on you?" From what he could see, she was by far the hottest of the bunch.

"They all went to college, partied, slept around, got fancy degrees while I came home, got married and started ranchin'."

"Couldn't hack it?" He smirked.

"My father died."

Axel bent over on his knees. "Fuck. Sorry."

"It's fine. I dropped out of college and came home, because my sister was still too young to live alone, and the farm couldn't run itself."

"What about your mom?"

"She died when I was sixteen. Breast cancer."

He hung his head, knowing all too well the pain cancer caused. "I'm so sorry to hear that."

"A year later, Sloan, my sister, left for college. I was pissed. After all I sacrificed, she just up and left. But it worked out for the best. John and I got married shortly after, had a few kids." She took another pull on her beer. "I don't know why I'm tellin' you all this. I just came over to give you the beer and say thank you for all your help."

"You're very welcome." He tapped his beer to hers, leaned back and draped his arms over the back of the bench. "I've also been told I'm an excellent listener."

She stood and drained her drink. "I'm goin' to go."

"Should you be driving? I mean, you just told a stranger your life story."

"After one beer?" She tossed the bottle in the nearby trash can. "I'm not drunk, just don't know when to shut my mouth. I'll see ya around, Axel."

"Hey," he called out to her as she walked away. "We aren't a biker gang. We're on a charity ride."

"What's that?" She moved closer.

He didn't know why he felt the need to explain, but he didn't want her to think they were a bunch of criminals. "People donate money based on how many miles we ride."

"Oh." Her eyes brightened. "What's the cause?"

He swallowed hard. "A little girl who died of leukemia a few weeks back."

"Jesus. That's awful. Were you close to her?"

"Yeah." His chest tightened. "She was a great kid."

Tears filled her eyes. "I'm sorry to hear that."

He couldn't help but smile. "We've been saying that—'I'm sorry'—a lot."

"I blame my mother." The corner of her mouth twitched. "Anyway, I need to get going. The kids are probably starving."

"I'll walk you to your car." He stuck his hands in his pocket. "Since it's dark."

"Truck." Britney laughed as she made her way toward the line of vehicles parked in the back. "You're in Myrefall, Montana. The safest damn place in the entire world. Nothin' excitin' ever happens around here. This is me."

He held open her truck door. "My mother taught me if it's dark, you walk the woman to her car."

She climbed in and started the engine. "Too bad I don't have any single friends."

He sucked in a sharp, audible breath through his teeth. "I'm pretty sure I'm not a small-town kind of guy."

"Never underestimate the length you'd go for the love of the right woman." Britney slammed the door. "Have a good night, Axel."

He stood there and watched her drive out of sight, his mind spinning. For a second, he considered what it would be like to live in a place like this. With a woman like that. A ridiculous notion he would have never thought twice about until now.

***

Axel wrapped a towel around his waist and stepped out of the bathroom. The local news played silently on the TV. He'd fallen asleep with it on.

The news switched over to traffic, and Axel turned on the sound.

"Good news for those who are traveling this weekend," the anchor with an awful spray tan said. "The rivers have receded, and all roads are now open."

They could finally get out of this town.

"In other news, a mysterious virus—" He switched off the TV, not caring what else the anchors had to say.

They'd planned on waiting until Sunday to leave because of the flooding, but since that wasn't an issue anymore, he saw no reason why they couldn't head out this morning.

He threw on a pair of jeans, a black T-shirt, a leather jacket and boots and walked to the diner attached to the motel where he met the others each morning.

Fifteen of the twenty riders he traveled with sat at mismatched tables pulled together in the center of the dining room, eating breakfast and cracking jokes. A couple other diners sat scattered around the room, their eyes darting to the bikers from time to time.

Axel dragged a chair over from an empty table and sat next to Queenie. "Did you watch the weather this morning?"

Queenie buttered her toast. "More rain? Because let me tell you, I'd love to spend a few more days in this hick town."

Axel ordered a coffee from the waitress. "Nope, rain is gone and the rivers have receded. Time to get the hell out of here and back on the road."

"Today?" Gunner nearly spit out his eggs, his round cheeks flushed. "I thought we were leaving tomorrow?"

The table laughed, except for Axel, who didn't get the joke. "What am I missing?"

"Gunner made a lady friend last night." Mac shoved the grinning man's arm.

Axel suppressed a groan. Nothing good ever followed those words. "Did you? Who?"

"The bar's weekend waitress." Gunner beamed. "She's a beaut. I'm supposed to be seeing her again tonight. Promised I'd take her to the church festival."

Mac laughed, his deep brown skin wrinkling around his eyes. "And she promised something in return."

There it was. The reason they would stay another night.

Axel didn't argue; it was pointless. Instead, he laughed while they ragged on Gunner and finished his breakfast without another word. As the youngest of The Gravel Saints, his late father's motorcycle group, he didn't have much of a say in the happenings of the club.

After another round of coffee, Axel headed for his room, not sure what to do with the day. It wasn't like there was much to do in this town. He could head to the bar, even though he said he wouldn't. Day drinking on a Saturday wouldn't be a bad way to pass the time, but he'd risk being hungover tomorrow. He liked the outdoors, and the countryside was nice, but he didn't really have the shoes for a hike.

Maybe he'd take in a movie and kill a couple of hours. Or go for a ride by himself, explore the area before they moved on.

The hectic church grounds caught his attention. People rushing around, finishing the last of the setup. Sometime last night, the carneys came to town and assembled some kiddie rides. The smell of fried food and barbecue hit his nose, bringing back memories he wasn't ready to relive.

"Axel?" The sound of Britney's voice caught him by surprise.

He turned to find her coming up behind him, dragging a beach wagon full of cases of beer. "Wouldn't it be easier if you brought your truck over?"

She pressed her lips together. "My husband dropped me off this morning before heading to the feed store. And it seems no one else here had a vehicle to spare."

Trucks lined the streets. "I thought the people in small towns helped their neighbors?"

"Well"—she tugged on the wagon and headed toward the road—"when the queen bee herself threatens to outcast anyone who helps me, the Good Samaritan in people goes out the window."

"Need some help? I can handle a few stones thrown in my direction."

She checked the street for cars. "If you wouldn't mind makin' sure nothing falls off the back as I cross, that would be great."

"Sure." He followed close behind, keeping an eye on the wobbling cargo. "How many more of these trips do you need to make?"

"This is it." She navigated her way around the parking lot to the booth with the beer and wine sign.

He gaped down at the twenty cases. “Not a lot of big drinkers in this town?”

Britney laughed. “Sam’s Bar donated these. There’s already a ton on ice and more ready to take their place. Not to worry, we haven’t run out in the ten years this event has been held.”

Case by case, he handed her the beer while she stacked them behind the booth. “Any of the other years did you host a group of twenty bikers?”

“Can’t say we have.” She paused. “You guys are staying? I thought since the waters receded….”

“We’re heading out tomorrow. One of my buddies met a girl last night and promised to take her here. The weekend waitress at Sam’s.”

“Mary Ann? That makes sense. She has a reputation.” Britney gestured for another case. “Tell your friend to be careful. She can be a bit clingy.”

“Good to know.” He passed her the last of the beer. “That’s all of them.”

She folded the wagon and tucked it behind the booth. “Thanks for the help. So, all of you will be here tonight?”

Axel studied her face, trying to get a read on how she felt about that. “Is that okay? Wait, is your husband some jealous, crazy mountain man who’ll kill me just for looking at you?”

“Lord, no.” She chuckled. “He doesn’t have a jealous bone in his body.”

“That’s a relief.” Not that he’d thought they’d done anything wrong, but some guys took offense when another man talked to their woman. “You need help with anything else?”

“I don’t think so.” A mischievous grin tugged at her lips. “Unless you want to volunteer for the dunk tank?

Judgin' by the way the women of this town are talkin', we'd make a fortune."

Axel ran a hand through his hair. "You can't be serious."

"Let's just say your friend isn't the only one who has a shot at gettin' lucky tonight. Whether you're into a one-night stand or love at first sight."

His mouth dropped. "What?"

"Yeah, you have a fifty-fifty shot around here."

"Britney!" Susan yelled from the other side of the parking lot.

She hung her head. "The queen bee beckons. I have to go, but I'll see you later."

"Um, yeah. And maybe explain?"

"If you have questions on what girl falls under what category," she said as she took off, "come find me."

"Thanks," he muttered, checking out the crowd. He counted ten sets of eyes on him, all women and all staring at him like they wanted a taste.

He shuddered and headed back to his motel room. He wasn't much of a one-night-stand or love-at-first-sight kind of guy. Definitely didn't want to get caught up in the town gossip. Maybe he should stay in tonight, get some rest. The drive tomorrow would be long and, with the winds, exhausting. Staying in would be the smart thing to do. The responsible thing to do.

He kicked off his shoes and flipped on the TV. He would stay in, order a pizza and call it a night. He wouldn't let the others pressure him into going out. Tomorrow, this whole town and the crazy people in it would be nothing more than a memory.

CHAPTER THREE

"One more ride," Molly begged. "Please, Mommy. It's my favorite. I love it so much."

Britney looked to John. "What do you think? It's already ten and past their bedtime."

"It's Saturday." John dug through his pockets and pulled out another ribbon of tickets. "Plus, we have all these left. Don't want them to go to waste."

"Yes!" Carson reached for the tickets. "I'm so close to winning the monster truck."

John held them out of his reach. "These are for all three of you and will be split equally."

Carson scrunched his nose. "Yes, sir."

He handed the tickets to their oldest. "Keep an eye on the twins. We'll meet you by the picnic tables when you're done."

The kids ran off, and though Britney knew just about everyone in this town, she kept her eyes on them as they darted from ride to ride, game to game.

"Let's get a beer." John wrapped his arm around her waist and led her to the drinks booth.

The line stretched ten people deep but moved quickly. John ordered a beer while Britney opted for a glass of pinot grigio. They found an empty picnic table close to the festival to keep tabs on the kids.

"So, you're gettin' up with the kids in the mornin', right?" She took a sip of her wine. "Makin' breakfast? Playin' referee?"

"Maybe they'll sleep in."

"Wishful thinkin'." Britney shivered as a cool breeze swept through the grounds. "Cold front's movin' in."

"Remember when I asked if you wanted me to grab you a jacket?" John draped his jacket over her shoulders. "And you said no."

"Thanks. It wasn't cold when I was settin' up. And I didn't think we would stay so long." She scrutinized his thin long-sleeve shirt. "Aren't you cold?"

"Nah. I've got a couple extra layers keeping me warm."

Robust laughter drew their attention to the back corner of the tables.

Axel sat on the edge of the group of bikers, sipping a longneck. His eyes met hers, and he lifted his beer in acknowledgment.

Britney smiled back and waved.

"That the new boyfriend?" John teased.

She rotated back around to face her husband. "That's the guy I told you about. The one who helped move all the booths."

"Oh. You mean the one all the girls in town are swooning about?"

Britney took a drink of her wine. "That's the one. I tried to talk him into sittin' for the dunk tank this mornin', but he didn't seem interested."

"You talked to him this morning too?" John raised a brow and grinned.

"He helped me bring over the donated beer from Sam's, since *someone* took the truck. He's probably bored; small-town life must not be excitin' enough for him."

John took a pull of his beer. "So you're telling me two days in a row, he's come over and helped you out? Meaning I didn't have to come in town and do it?" He waved Axel over. "I owe the man a beer."

Axel hesitated but jogged over, his eyes darting to the nearby tables. He seemed a little nervous, which Britney understood. Even though John was as mellow as they came, he had the appearance of a man who'd shoot you just for the hell of it.

Not that Axel looked any tamer. He had a roughness about him that oozed danger.

John stood as Axel approached the table, then shook his hand. "Hey, man. John Campbell. Nice to meet you."

"Axel Mordecai."

"Have a seat, man. Let me buy you a beer."

Axel sat and jiggled his bottle. "Thanks, but I just got a cold one."

"Okay. But next round's on me."

Britney glared at John. "Next round?" If he started that, they'd never get out of there.

"I just want to thank your friend here for helping you these past couple of days." John smiled—a genuine smile, though by the look on Axel's face, he didn't know that.

She should reassure him that John didn't care, but letting him squirm turned out to be more entertaining.

Axel took a long drink of his beer. "No problem. I had nothing else to do."

"Well, you saved me a trip and countless hours."

"Ugh," Britney groaned. "I would have found a way to set them up."

Axel glanced at her, then at John and smiled. “She always this stubborn?”

“Man, you don’t know the half of it.” John nudged her arm. “When Brit makes her mind up about something or someone, there ain’t nothing going to change it.”

“I am not that bad.”

John coughed, “Bullshit,” and both men laughed.

Britney rolled her eyes. “Are you done?”

“What about you, Axel?” John sputtered, finally getting his laughter under control. “Where are you guys headed?”

“Canada.”

John nodded. “Where did you start?”

“New Mexico.”

“And that’s where you’re from?” Britney asked.

Axel drained his beer. “Nah, that’s just where my parents settled down after they retired. I’m an army brat. Moved all over as a kid, then enlisted right out of high school and got shipped from base to base.”

“That’s sad,” Britney said, feeling sorry for his unstable life.

“Brit.” John used his warning tone.

Axel waved him off. “It’s fine. I guess it’s kind of depressing in a way, but I’ve also seen the world on the government’s dime, so I’m not complaining.”

“Mom!” Blake put an end to the awkward silence as he flew his foam airplane between them. “Look what Carson won for me with his tickets!”

“He did?” Britney beamed at her oldest son. “That was nice of him.”

Carson grinned. “I already won the monster truck, and he used all his tickets on rides.”

"And Carson won me this unicorn!" Molly squealed, hugging the stuffed animal tight. "I love it so much. She's so cute. I'm going to call her Rainbow."

"I'm proud of you, son." John patted him on the back.

"What did you ride?" Britney asked as Molly climbed in her lap.

"The teacups. Three times! I almost threw up, but I didn't care because it was so fun."

"Sounds like you had a good time." Britney laughed. "Axel, these are the kids, if you hadn't guessed. Carson, Blake and Molly. Kids, this is Mr. Axel."

Carson gaped at Axel for a moment. "Are you an actual biker? Like you belong to a biker gang?"

Axel laughed. "No gang. But I do belong to a biker club called The Gravel Saints."

Carson's eyes widened. "And you have a real motorcycle? Like a Harley Davidson?"

"I do." Axel pointed out to the parking lot. "Last one on the right."

"Cool! Can I have a ride?"

"No," John and Britney said in unison.

Carson dropped his head. "Fine."

"How old are you, kid?" Axel asked.

"Nine," he mumbled.

Axel winked at Britney. "Your parents are right. You're too young to ride, not because they don't want you to but because of the law."

Carson's mouth gaped as he faced his parents. "When I get older? I mean, I already drive a four-wheeler."

"Um…." Britney had no idea how to answer that. "I—"

A panicked scream silenced the fair.

"Who was that?" Britney rose from her seat and searched the area. "Is that Thomas?"

John ran over to help Patty, who struggled to keep her husband on his feet.

"Shit," Axel muttered. "What happened?"

"He's been sick." Britney watched as John threw Thomas's arm over his neck.

Thomas thrashed his head in every direction.

"He looks delirious." Axel took a few steps closer. "Does John need some help?"

"I don't think so." Britney gathered her children. "Come on. Let's check on your dad and head for the truck."

"Be careful," Axel called out to her.

Britney turned around. "I'm sorry. I forget you're leavin' tomorrow. You guys have a safe trip, and if you find your way back to Myrefall, we're about thirty miles north of town. Name's on the mailbox. Stop by and say hi."

"Thanks." Axel smiled. "But you just told a stranger where you live."

"Don't you worry." Britney grinned. "I know how to use a gun."

***

"When's Dad coming?" Carson asked as Britney tucked him into bed. "And how is he going to get home when we took the truck?"

Britney kissed him on the forehead. "He'll be home in a little while. He needed to help Miss Patty get Mr. Thomas home."

"What's wrong with Mr. Thomas?" he asked through a yawn. Unlike the twins, he hadn't fallen asleep on the ride home. "He looked a little scary."

She sat on the edge of his full bed. “Scary? How’s that?”

Carson yawned again. “His face was funny. Kind of mean, like he was trying to bite people. Is Dad going to be okay?”

“Why wouldn’t he be okay?”

“I don’t know.” He rolled to his side and closed his eyes. “What if Mr. Thomas hurts him?”

“Your daddy is a strong man. He’ll be just fine.” She flipped off the light. “Get some sleep, and try not wake up too early.”

Carson smiled. “Seven’s not early.”

“Good night.”

Britney peeked in on the twins before heading downstairs to check her phone. Patty and Thomas lived in town not two miles from the church. The plan was John would drive them home and help get Thomas inside and in bed, then drive Patty’s car home. Tomorrow they’d drop it off at the Anthonys’ house before church and check in on Thomas.

With no missed calls or texts, she sat on the couch to read. She liked to wait up for John when he stayed out late. The dangerous road leading to their house had caused its share of accidents.

Thirty minutes passed without a word, and Britney began to worry. John said he’d be right behind them. Him being a talker, it wasn’t unusual for his goodbyes to turn into a full-blown conversation, but with Thomas being sick, Patty would have sent him on his way as soon as they got settled.

At the hour mark, Britney called John’s cell. The familiar George Strait ringtone went off in the house, and she found his cell on the table where they kept the keys. *Late and no cell phone. Way to go, John.* She would give him an earful when he got home. He knew how she worried.

As a child, when her father was late coming home from being out with his buddies, her mother would call all their houses, trying to put a timeline together to know whether to go looking for him. It didn't happen often, but a few times Britney could tell her mother was scared. Thankfully, he'd always found his way home. To a very pissed-off wife, but at least he was safe.

Cell phones helped ease some of the worry, when John remembered his. She swore he forgot it on purpose sometimes. He denied it, but the twinkle in his eyes didn't lie.

At midnight, Britney started to pace around the room, cell phone in hand, contemplating a call to Patty. After everything the woman had gone through tonight, Britney didn't want to wake them, but she also needed to know where her husband was.

She scrolled through her contacts and selected Patty's number. With a trembling finger hovering over the Call button, she grappled with whether to call. She tended to overreact, her mind fixating on the worst-case scenario.

The faint sound of dogs barking drew her to the window. She yanked back the curtain and watched as a set of headlights pulled up to the house.

John slammed the door of Thomas's '57 Chevy and lumbered toward the house.

Britney plopped back on the couch, e-reader in hand, focusing on the book she hadn't read in a week.

"Hey." John rubbed his brow as he came inside. "You didn't have to wait up."

Her eyes drifted to the clock. "Wow. Is it that late already? I didn't even notice the time."

"Really?" John picked up his phone from the table. "I have a missed call from you."

"Butt dial." She batted her eyelashes.

"You know, you're pretty cute when you're trying to pretend like you're not mad." He slung off his jacket and hung it on the rustic coatrack.

Britney swung her feet off the couch and rushed over to John. "What the hell happened to your arm?"

"Oh, this." He pointed to the bloodied bandage around his left forearm. "Hildebrand said it's nothing to worry about."

Dr. James Hildebrand was Patty and Thomas's son-in-law.

"You went to see him at this time of night?" Britney followed him into the kitchen.

John poured himself a whiskey and Coke. "Patty ended up having to call him to check on Thomas. He was out of control."

"What do you mean, out of control?" She had watched John help the elderly man into his car. He couldn't even stand without support.

"I don't know what happened." John drained the glass and mixed another. "Never seen anything like it. Got him in the house and into bed. Patty went to the kitchen to make him some hot lemon water, and then out of nowhere, he jumped on top of me, snapping his jaw like a damn alligator or something."

Her mouth fell open. "Are you serious?"

"He was so strong, like…." John drained his second drink. If she hadn't seen the sweat beading on his forehead, she would have thought he was joking. "Thomas is sixty-five years old, and I could barely overpower him. Bastard bit me. I had to kick him to get him off."

Britney snatched a wineglass from behind John's head and poured herself a glass of red. "Holy shit. Did he finally just settle down or somethin'?"

John skipped the Coke and just poured himself a shot. "Patty heard the struggle and called Hildebrand. He rushed over. By that point, I had Thomas pinned to the bed. Hildebrand shot him with a sedative and called an ambulance. He cleaned my bite before heading to the hospital, and then I came home."

"What does he think it is?" She went to take another drink, but the glass was empty. When had that happened?

"Have you heard about this new virus going around? Apparently it's been all over the news."

"News?" Britney snorted. "I can't remember the last time the news was on TV for more than a couple of minutes. And that was because the kids couldn't find the remote."

"Sounds like it's bad. Flu-like symptoms along with hallucinations and aggression."

"God. How do they think he got it?" Her gaze fell to John's blood-soaked bandage. "Did he say if it was contagious? Or how it's spread?"

"He didn't say much of anything." John twisted his arm around. "But I'm fine, though a little sore and in need of a new bandage."

"Come on." She led him up the stairs. "I'll get the first aid kit and get you cleaned up."

John didn't make it to the bathroom. She found him stretched out on the bed stripped down to his underwear, flipping through his phone.

"I really don't want blood on the bed."

"Sorry." He yawned. "I'm tired. It's been a long-ass day."

"You're tired?" Britney sat beside him and unwrapped the soiled bandage. "I've been at the church since eight this mornin' settin' up. Didn't get home until after dark last night after a full day."

"And I picked up your slack around here while you were flirting with that beefy biker." He grinned, knowing exactly how to get a rise out of her.

"Beefy?" She couldn't help but laugh. "Who says 'beefy' anymore?"

"Hey, it's not like I have experience in describing men. But you have to admit"—he rubbed her leg with his free hand—"he's a good-looking guy."

"Aww," Britney cooed, "are you jealous?"

"Nah." He lay back as she finished unwrapping the wound. "More like flattered. I know my wife is hot, but when a guy like that hits on her, and I'm the one who gets to take her home… makes a country boy like me feel pretty damn good."

"What the hell is this?" Britney stared down at John's arm. "I thought you said it was a bad bite?"

"It is."

She shoved his arm away. "Is this some kind of joke? Did any of what you told me even happen?"

"You think I'm lying?" He lifted his arm and paled. "What the fuck?"

"That barely counts as a scratch, John." She shoved the first aid supplies back into the kit. "Did Hildebrand put you up to this? Tryin' to get me back for last year's April Fools prank? Because I didn't even come up with the stunt. Makayla is the one—"

"Brit." He hurried to a sitting position and ran a finger over his skin. "This isn't a joke. There was a bite on my arm. A nasty bite deep enough that James thought I should get stitches. You saw the blood."

The panic in his voice caught her off guard. “That doesn’t make any sense. These are barely even puncture wounds. Are you sure you heard him right? Maybe he was talking about Thomas.”

“I washed the bite myself.”

Britney examined his arm. “What are those black lines? Bruises?”

“What black lines?”

“Right here.” She followed the line with her fingertip. “They kind of look like veins. Do veins bruise?”

John shrugged. “Not that I know of. But I’m not the expert.”

“I’ll call Sloan.”

As she reached for her phone, John grabbed hold of her arm. “It’s almost 2:00 a.m. Call her in the morning. Let’s go to bed. I don’t even want to think about how many hours we have left before the kids wake up.”

“You’re right. She’s at a conference or somethin’ this weekend anyway.” Britney headed for the bathroom to change into her pajamas.

“You talk to her lately?”

Britney threw on an old nightgown before turning off the light and getting into bed. “She left me a couple of messages on Thursday sayin’ she’d be unreachable until Sunday.”

“There you go.” John draped his arm over her body and pulled her close. “Call her tomorrow.”

Britney wiggled, trying to get comfortable with his heavy arm pinning her down. “You know I can’t sleep like this.”

He removed his arm and rolled over. “Good night.”

“Are you feeling okay? You didn’t even grab my ass.”

“Yeah,” he mumbled, “just tired.”

Britney buried herself under the covers and closed her eyes, hoping tomorrow would be a little less eventful than today.

CHAPTER FOUR

Axel took one last look at the sleepy town before mounting his motorcycle. The sun had barely peeked over the horizon, and as far as he could tell, not a single store had opened. Must have been that old-school Sunday mentality.

Maybe he'd come back one day, check out the scenery. In the week they'd been stuck here, the town had grown on him. Not in a 'pack up all his belongings and move' kind of way, more like 'it was a nice place to visit but wouldn't take long to get bored' kind of way.

Twenty motorcycle engines roared to life, and the group headed west out of town.

He hadn't mapped out their route, didn't even know how many miles they had left. Shutting out the world was one of the many reasons he had agreed to come along, to get lost in the drive and forget everything that happened this past year. All the pain and sorrow. The pity.

He shook off the memories and focused on the road. The rush of extreme acceleration. The bite of the drop in temperature. The outdoorsy smell only found this far removed from the city.

They took the scenic route through the mountains. He'd seen some stunning sights on the trip, and this was no exception. The snow-tipped peaks and blue lakes brought about a sense of serenity he hadn't felt in a while.

The group slowed, pulled onto the shoulder and parked, everyone dismounting to stretch their legs.

"I didn't see any signs for a rest stop. Guess I'll just have to make my own ladies' room behind a tree." Queenie headed off into the forest.

"Shouldn't someone go with her?" Axel watched her disappear. "Bears are common in these parts and she doesn't have a weapon"

Gunner waved. "Nah, she can handle herself. Though someone might want to protect the bears."

Everyone laughed except Axel. He kept his eyes on the tree line. Granted, he didn't know much about the mountains, but he'd spent a year in the Boy Scouts as a kid. He didn't remember much except to always stay with your buddy. Now, that could have been because they were eight years old, but in the middle of nowhere, that might not be a bad idea since she was unarmed.

A few minutes passed, and the biker grew restless.

"What the hell is taking her so long?" Mac growled. "The way we're going, we won't make the next stop until well after dark. We're already a week behind."

A shadow caught Axel's eye, and he took a few steps closer. "Did anyone else see that?"

No one responded. Hell, none of them were even looking at the trees.

As Axel moved closer to get a better look, an agonizing scream cut through the mindless chatter.

For a split second, no one moved, all eyes trained on the forest.

Axel darted back to his bike and retrieved the gun he kept in his side satchel.

"That wasn't Queenie, right?" Rainey, a forty-year-old former schoolteacher, asked. "That scream. It didn't even sound human."

"I'll go check it out." As far as he knew, Axel was the only one who carried a sidearm, a habit he couldn't bear to let go of after the war. With a gun in hand, he knew he could defend himself from whatever danger crossed his path.

"You want us to go with you?" Gunner asked.

Axel gave him a dismissive wave. "Unless you have a firearm, stay here."

He didn't wait for a response before disappearing into the woods. Queenie couldn't have gone too far or they wouldn't have heard her scream. If only he could figure out which way she went.

Soft gurgling from his left sent him running. He slid to a stop and fell to his knees beside Queenie. Blooded covered her from throat to chest, so much that he couldn't find the worst of the wounds.

Axel tossed his leather jacket aside and removed his T-shirt. It was filthy but would have to do.

He wiped away the blood the best he could. On her neck, he found what appeared to be a bite or deep claw marks. Wrapping the shirt around the wound slowed the bleeding, but if she had any chance of making it, he needed to her get out of these woods and to a hospital.

"I found her!" he called out, not wanting to leave her alone but needing help to carry her. "Call for help!"

Leaves rustled and Axel whirled around, gun in hand. No way they could have gotten to him that fast.

Shadows danced in the distance, making it difficult to tell if there was something out there or if his eyes were playing tricks on him. Chances were good whatever attacked Queenie was still out there. A predator didn't stray far from its downed prey.

A branch snapped, closer that time. Axel rose to his feet, hoping an increase in his size would scare the animal away.

"Get out of here!" he screamed, scanning the trees.

The creature answered with a low growl.

Goose bumps prickled his skin. He'd never heard anything quite like the menacing sound.

Bushes swished to his right. He readied his gun.

Hidden behind the trees, masked in the shadows, stood what looked to be a man.

Axel dropped his weapon. "It's okay. You can come out."

Footsteps crashed through the brush, and the man jerked his head.

"Those are my friends. Come with us and we can get you some help." Axel moved closer, gun tucked in the back of his jeans to show the man he meant no harm. "Sir?"

The man crouched and growled. The same growl he had heard moments ago.

"Axel?" Gunner screamed. "Where are you?"

The man jumped back, startled by the new voice. A thin stream of sunlight hit his gray skin, and then he was gone, back into the shadows.

"What the fuck?" Axel rubbed his eyes.

"Jesus, Queenie!" Mac yelled. "What the hell happened to her?"

"Grab Queenie and get her back to the bikes," Gunner ordered. "The park ranger said he could have a chopper here in a few minutes if need be."

Axel heard them as they lifted Queenie from the ground but couldn't take his eyes off the spot where the man had stood.

"Hey." Gunner grabbed Axel's arm. "Didn't you hear me calling out for you?"

Axel tore his eyes from the trees. "Yes, sorry. There was something out there."

"What was it?" Gunner inspected the area. "The animal that attacked her?"

"I'm not sure." He ran a hand over his temple. "As crazy as it sounds, I think it was a man."

"A man?" Gunner picked up Axel's jacket from the ground and threw it at him.

"Thanks." He slipped it on, thankful he had a clean T-shirt in his bag.

"Like a serial killer hiding out in the woods?"

"I don't know." Even now his mind was trying to rationalize what he had seen. "You said something about a park ranger?"

"Yeah. He drove by not ten minutes after you left. Told him we didn't know what happened, but we heard a scream. He's ready to call for a medevac, said there are lots of bears in these woods."

"Good. She needs to get to a hospital. Her wounds are bad."

As they headed out of the forest, a sudden chill ran up Axel's spine. They were being watched. Or stalked. Either way, he picked up the pace, needing to get the hell out of there and away from whatever it was he saw.

***

"How is she?" Axel asked the trauma nurse as they wheeled Queenie away.

The slender woman with a messy ponytail flipped through the chart clutched in her hand. "And who might you be?"

"Her nephew," Axel said without hesitation. He'd been around enough hospitals to know the staff could only give out information on a patient to family. "I came in with her on the chopper."

She rubbed her neck. "I'm going on an eighteen-hour shift with no end in sight, so I'm going to take your word for it. Patient lost a lot of blood, but we were able to close the wounds. Multiple lacerations across the neck and arms. We had to give her a second dose of sedative. Do you know if she takes stimulants?"

"Drugs? No. And what do you mean, a second dose? She's been unconscious since the attack in the woods."

"Well, she wasn't unconscious about twenty minutes ago. Started thrashing around, bit one of our interns."

Axel narrowed his eyes. "She bit somebody? That's crazy."

"The crazy part is—" Her gaze flickered around the room before she leaned in closer. "—she's not the only one. We've had five incidents in the past hour alone."

"I'm going to go out on a ledge and say that isn't normal."

"No." She checked her pager. "I've got to go. Another patient is being rerouted to us. Like we have space."

She rushed off, leaving Axel standing in the middle of the emergency room, unsure what to do next. As far as he knew, Queenie had no relatives, and the rest of their group wouldn't make it back here for a few more hours.

The park ranger had graciously offered to drop off his and Queenie's motorcycles after his shift when he found out what hospital they'd taken her to. One less thing to worry about. If Queenie woke and he didn't have an exact location of her bike, she'd probably have a heart attack. That ten-year-old Harley was her baby.

He took a seat in the packed waiting room and watched the news playing on the corner TV. The sound was off, but he could read the headlines that scrolled along the bottom.

The usual tiresome news passed: a B-list celebrity death, box office numbers, weather. He almost turned away until one headline caught his attention.

A new flu-like virus sweeping the nation. The infected's erratic behavior baffle doctors around the world.

Axel rose from his chair and moved closer, hoping to turn up the volume as the headline became the top story. Behind the anchors, a video of a man on a stretcher biting at the EMTs trying to strap him down played on a constant loop.

"Family of Queenie St. James?"

Axel snapped his head in the door's direction, where a nurse impatiently tapped her foot. "Yes."

"Come with me. I'll show you to her room." She didn't wait for a response before walking away.

He took one last look at the news broadcast and threaded a hand through his hair. This whole day had him paranoid. For a second he almost considered the possibility that the whole flu story was a cover-up for something more sinister. *Maybe I should get my head examined while I'm here.*

The sprightly nurse had already made if halfway down the hall when Axel stepped out of the waiting room. Either she hadn't noticed or didn't care. By the looks of the other doctors and nurses sprinting down the hall, the latter seemed more probable.

He picked up the pace, dodging those who were too consumed in their work to notice his presence. For a small-town hospital, they had a ton of patients. Each room he passed appeared occupied, and several had patients strapped to the bed. Armed security guards walked the halls.

The news he'd been watching in the waiting room was national. Maybe a local disaster happened? That would explain why they were so busy.

The nurse stopped at the last door. "She's in here. Unconscious. Bed by the window. Push the red button if you need something, though it might be awhile. We're swamped."

"Thanks," he said as she walked off.

Two other unconscious patients occupied the room besides Queenie.

The first man couldn't have been over twenty. With no obvious signs of physical injury, he looked like he'd just stumbled in here to take a nap. The only thing off Axel saw were half a dozen black streaks running up his neck from underneath his gown. For all he knew, those could have been from a tattoo.

The second man was a different story. His ebony skin had a gray tint to it that Axel had never seen before. Bald spots speckled his head as if the hair had been pulled out by the handfuls.

But the most disturbing thing about his appearance was his nails. Axel never considered himself refined. After his stint in the military, he'd taken up construction work. He spent his day outdoors, and it showed. Even as dirty as he got, a quick shower with a washrag and an off-brand bar of soap did the job. But as little as he cared about his outward appearance, he never let his nails get as long as this poor man's. Even more strange, they grew to a point and appeared to be sharp as hell. They reminded him of claws, as ridiculous as that sounded.

Maybe he cut them like that on purpose, but this man must have been pushing seventy. What purpose would they serve?

Blowing out his cheeks, Axel moved to Queenie's bed and drew the curtains, determined to focus on his friend.

He dragged a chair beside her bed and sat on the edge, taking her hand in his. Unlike most of the other bikers he rode with, he'd known Queenie for years. As one of his father's oldest friends and army buddies, she was like family. Seeing her laying in this bed, throat wrapped in bandages—

The phone in his pocket vibrated, putting an end to the depressing train of thought. "Hello?"

"It's Gunner." A tightness in his voice replaced his usual light tone. "What hospital are you at?"

"County General, in the town of—" The young man groaned at the sounds of Axel's voice. "Give me a second to step out of the room. I know it's just outside of Myrefall."

"Myrefall? Why the hell didn't they take her to the closest hospital?"

Axel pushed open the door to the stairwell to get away from the noise. "Yeah, they called in to several closer hospitals on the way, but none of them could handle any more trauma patients."

"What the hell kind of rinky-dink hospital system does this state have?"

Axel stepped to the side as two men in bloodied scrubs flew up the stairs and bolted through the doors. "I don't think it's the hospitals. There's some new crazy flu going around. Queenie's forced to share a room with two other guys."

"How's she doing?"

"Okay, I guess. The nurse didn't really tell me much. Haven't seen a doctor yet. They stopped the bleeding and closed the wounds. She's not hooked on any crazy machines or anything, which is good."

"You hanging in there?" A softness laced his voice. "You know, after everything?"

Axel's breathing quickened. "Fine. How long before you get here?"

Gunner repeated the question to one of the others before answering. "Three hours. Try to get some rest, you hear me?"

"Yeah. See you then."

Axel hung up the phone and returned to the chair next to Queenie's bed. He popped up the footrest and leaned back, closing his eyes. The stress of the day had taken a toll. A quick nap until the others arrived would help clear his head. Maybe when he woke up, Queenie could tell him what attacked her.

***

The sound of a screaming monitor and sneakers slapping the tile floor jolted Axel awake. He sat up and rubbed his eyes, the dim hospital room blurring in and out of focus.

It took him a second to remember how he'd found himself back in this room, sleeping in the familiar but uncomfortable chair.

Old memories faded as the new came back. Queenie had been attacked, and he was waiting for the others to get here.

He looked at the digital clock, which read 7:00 a.m. He rubbed his eyes again. "That can't be right."

"Hold him down!" a man screamed over the noise that woke him. "I need to give him a sedative."

Axel pulled back the curtain. The elderly man in the middle bed thrashed about, clawing and snapping at anything that moved.

One man got tossed to the ground as three others struggled to keep the patient still enough so the doctor could get the needle in his arm.

Axel rushed to the doctor's side. “What can I do?”

“Step back!” he ordered.

“You need help.” Axel grabbed hold of the flailing man’s wrist. “I can hold his arm still. Let the others take care of the body.”

“Fine.” The doctor removed the cap of the needle. “Just try not to get bit.”

Axel tightened his grip as the other four held the man’s legs and shoulders still. “Doesn’t this bed have some sort of straps?”

“We ran out of those last night.” The doctor wrapped a tourniquet around the man’s arm and stuck the needle into the bulging vein. “It should only take a second to kick in.”

Two minutes and a second round of sedatives later, the patient was out.

“Anyone hurt?” the doctor demanded. “Bit? Any sort of injury?”

The four orderlies shook their heads.

“Good.” The doctor leaned against the bed. “Go see if there are any open beds in the secure rooms. He can’t stay in here.”

They hurried off without a word.

“You okay there, Doc?” Axel asked.

Sweat beaded across his forehead. “James Hildebrand.”

“Axel.” He found a clean cup and filled it with cold water. “Here, drink this. You look like you’re about to pass out. You’re not hurt, are you?”

James took a sip. “Thank you. And no, I’m one of the lucky ones who haven’t been attacked.”

Axel studied the sickly man. “What’s wrong with him?”

“My father is a sick man.” James covered his eyes with his hands. “The CDC is saying it's similar to the flu virus.”

“That’s one hell of a flu.”

James set the cup on the table. “If it’s even the flu.”

“What else would it be?”

“That’s what we’re trying to figure out.” He straightened his jacket. “Last night I admitted my father with these symptoms. He was the only one. Today there are over fifty.”

“Jesus.” The man looked familiar. “Is he the one who got sick at the Myrefall church festival?”

“Yes. How did you know?”

“Britney’s husband.” Axel snapped his fingers. “What’s his name? John. He helped your father home.”

“That’s right.” James narrowed his eyes. “I need to call her.”

“Everything okay?”

James blew out a weighted breath. “I hope so.”

Axel looked back at Queenie. “What about my friend? I haven’t seen a doctor, unless they came in while I slept. I know she’s not sick with this virus, but a wild animal attacked her, and her wounds were severe.”

James peered around the curtain. “You sure she wasn’t sick before she got attacked?”

“Not that I know of, and she’s not one to keep stuff like that to herself.”

An orderly returned. “Found a spot for him.”

“Thank you, Abel. I’ll be right behind you.”

Abel wheeled the unconscious man out of the room.

"I need to go. I have a lot more patients who need looking after." James took one more look at Queenie. "She's sick. It's hard to tell how far along the virus is, but it'll only get worse before it gets better."

"Do they get better?"

"We're still waiting on lab work to determine exactly what we're dealing with. Anyway, thanks for your help." James reached out his hand but yanked it back again. "On second thought, maybe we should keep physical contact to a minimum."

Axel studied James's hand. A drop of blood bubbled from a small puncture wound on the side of his finger. "You okay there, Doc?"

He rushed to the sink and ran his hand under a steaming stream of water. "This is nothing. I caught my hand on an exposed bolt on the bed rail."

"Oh." Axel had only seen his hands on the patient.

"It happens. I should get going. Take care."

"You too," Axel mumbled as James hurried out of the room. He didn't want to be paranoid, but the way James's face had sobered when he saw the mark chilled him to the core. Sure, the flu sucked, and this strain had some shitty side effects, but James's reaction still felt off somehow.

Axel shook off the uneasiness nagging at his brain and headed into the bathroom. After a quick use of the facilities and a splash of cold water on his face, he didn't feel any better about the situation but could push his concerns aside for now. There were more important things to worry about. Like why the rest of the bikers hadn't shown up.

He found his phone stuffed in the side of the chair and checked it for messages, but got nothing but a black screen. In his exhaustion he hadn't even thought to stick it on the charger he had in his bag.

Still didn't explain why the others hadn't shown up. Wasn't like them to not check in on one of their own.

He found a spare outlet and plugged in his phone. A couple minutes and he'd have enough power to check for missed messages.

The phone came to life and the notifications began, one after another, echoing off the bare walls. A dozen text messages. Double the missed calls. And a voice mail, which he would check first, as it was the most recent.

A very annoyed Gus rambled off a slew of swear words before getting to the reason they hadn't shown up. They'd arrived early yesterday evening, well within the hours of the posted visitor times, but had been denied access, as the hospital had implemented a family-only policy for visitors.

Axel had heard nothing about that, but he'd also told the staff he was Queenie's nephew.

He sent a quick text to Gus asking where they were and when they wanted to meet up.

Gus replied almost immediately: the motel across the street, and they'd meet him outside the hospital in five minutes.

A diner would have been better—he hadn't eaten since yesterday morning—but he guessed that could wait.

He took one last look at Queenie and his heart clenched. James had said she'd contracted the virus going around, but Axel hadn't noticed her symptoms until that moment. Her once tan skin now had the same ashy tint as the other men in the room.

Strange how fast the infection took over. She'd acted fine before they left Myrefall, her normal exuberant self. But he also knew all too well how these sorts of things didn't manifest symptoms right away either.

The question remained on how she got infected. James had warned them not to get bit, which, until being attacked in the woods, Queenie hadn't been. If a random person had bitten her, they all would have heard about it a hundred times over.

Was it possible this virus was airborne and the doctors just didn't know it yet? The thought turned his stomach. He'd been in this room, in this hospital, since yesterday.

"Shit," he muttered as he left the room, taking the stairs down to the first floor.

He opened the door and checked the handle. As he suspected, the door needed a keycard to open it from the outside. He stuck a small rock between the door and the frame, careful to not make it obvious the door stood open but enough so he wouldn't be locked out.

The atmosphere outside could only be described as chaotic. Dozens of people had gathered, lingering around the front entrance. Most were huddled in their individual groups, but there were a few who'd taken up screaming at the poor orderly.

He was glad he'd propped open the stairwell door. The last thing he wanted to do was deal with that mess.

As he scanned the grounds, he spotted Gus and a few others sprinting across the street in his direction.

Axel gestured to the front entrance and then headed to the back of the hospital, where a crowd had also formed. Two security guards stood watch, preventing people from blocking the emergency entrance.

He'd never seen anything like this. Whatever was going on in this town, it was time to get the hell out.

CHAPTER FIVE

"Are you sure you're feelin' okay?" Britney watched as her stubborn husband sipped his coffee. He hadn't even attempted to scrounge up some breakfast or asked if she planned on making anything.

"Fine," he mumbled.

Britney snorted. "Well, you look like shit."

Molly snickered. "Mommy said s-h-i-t."

Britney whirled around. "What have we told you about spellin' bad words?"

"Sorry," Molly said with a sly grin.

"Hurry and eat your breakfast before you miss the bus."

"Can't you just take us?" Blake whined. "I hate the bus. It's so slow and takes *forever* to get to school."

Britney studied John. As much as she needed to run a few errands in town, she didn't want to leave him alone. Even if he agreed to stay in bed until she got back, chances were good he wouldn't. Not on purpose, but while lying around, he would remember something he needed to do. Something quick. And one quick chore would lead to another and another until resting was the furthest thing from his mind.

"I have things to do around here." Britney gathered their bowls and dumped them in the sink. "So you're ridin' the bus."

"Hey," Carson complained, "I wasn't done."

"Then you should have gotten dressed faster." The alarm on Britney's phone went off, a ten-minute warnin' before the bus reached their gate. "Grab your backpacks and get to the truck."

The kids didn't move.

"Now!"

They slung themselves out of the chairs and lumbered toward the door.

"I'll be right back." Britney brushed the back of her hand against John's forehead. "You're burnin' up. Go back to bed."

"Yeah, yeah. As soon as I check on the calf." He stood and stretched.

"I'll do that when I get back. You need to rest."

"Nah." John waved her off. "I've been sicker than this, and it never stopped me before. Not going to stop me now."

The truck horn blared, and Britney checked the clock. "Shit. I got to go."

She ran for the door and hopped in the driver side of the already-running diesel. "How many times do I have to tell you not to start the truck? And don't honk at me! That's just rude."

She sped down the dirt road until they reached the gate. Carson jumped out, unlocked and opened it so she could pull through.

The bus was nowhere in sight, which meant either the driver was running late or they had missed it—again.

"Can you take us to school now?" Molly asked.

"Give it a few more minutes. It's a little foggy this mornin', and he might just be runnin' behind."

"Mom," Carson huffed. "The bus always comes at 7:00 and it's 7:02."

"Which is what runnin' behind means." She tapped her fingers on the steering wheel. "Come on, bus."

"Mommy?" Molly leaned forward. "Is Daddy going to be okay?"

Britney brushed the fallen red strands of hair out of her daughter's face and kissed her on the forehead. "Daddy's goin' to be fine. He just has a cold or the flu or somethin'."

"Is that what's wrong with Mr. Thomas?"

"Um…." She didn't know how to answer. He had attacked John and bit his arm. Not that the kids knew what happened, but still, their little town thrived on gossip. More times than she could count, one of the kids had come home telling her things about the people they knew that they had no business knowing. "I'm not sure what's wrong with Mr. Thomas."

"Look, here comes the bus." Carson threw open his door.

"Thank God." Britney helped Molly and Blake down from the lifted truck, then hugged and kissed the twins. "Have a wonderful day. Carson, you at least goin' to tell me bye?"

He shuffled to her side and wrapped a limp arm around her waist. "Bye."

"Love you guys."

They rushed to the open door of the bus and climbed in with Britney close on their heels. She peered inside and waved at the substitute bus driver she knew from church. "Mornin', Sally. Where's Jerry today?" In the five years her kids had been riding the bus, the man had never missed a day.

"Sick. Caught the nasty bug going around."

"Oh." Britney's eyes wandered to the side of the bus. Molly and Blake waved their little hands out of the window. "When did he come down with it?"

"Sometime this weekend." Sally grabbed the handle of the door. "I need to get going. Have a nice day."

Britney took a step back, and the door closed.

"Bye, Mommy!" Molly called as the bus drove away.

Britney waved back, her heart pounding. The virus going around seemed to have some horrible side effects. And if her kids found themselves near someone with those symptoms?

She pushed away the thought as she climbed back into the truck. If the virus affected the school, they'd better let the parents know. Maybe she'd call when she got home and see if Jerry's case was an isolated incident or if others were sick. As important as school was, she didn't want to risk her kids' safety if this virus became an epidemic. It was bad enough that John started displaying symptoms yesterday, and he looked even worse today. She should probably separate him from her and the kids until he felt better, in case it was airborne.

Or she could call Sloan and ask if she knew anything about this virus. Because of her status in the medical community, the doctors she knew kept her updated on the latest happenings.

Pulling up to the house, Britney let out an audible sigh. As she predicted, John had given up on resting. Instead, he had saddled their horse, Mabel, and had a rifle strapped across his body.

"Just what in the hell do you think you're doin'?" Britney asked over the dogs that jumped and barked at Mabel's heels. Thank God the poor horse grew up with the hounds or John would have been thrown off by now, adding numerous broken bones to his already weakened state.

"Daddy called; said he saw bear droppings this morning just outside his fence line. I'm going to check things out."

"Keepin' bears out was the main reason we installed the high fence."

John mounted the horse. "But my parents don't have a high fence, which leaves their livestock vulnerable."

"They could have. The fence guys would have given them a hell of a deal."

John's family ranch butted up against her family's land. As an only child, John's parents relied on him to help out when the stresses of ranching became too much. Many times she had tried to convince John to hire a few ranch hands to help his father—Lord knew his family could afford it—but her suggestion had fallen on deaf ears.

"Campbells take care of their own." A stupid motto, if she were being honest. Not that she would ever tell John that. Family was everything to him.

"You know Daddy's old school when it comes to things like that." John removed his baseball cap and wiped his brow. "I won't be gone too long."

Britney noticed how discolored his skin had grown in the fifteen minutes it had taken to get the kids on the bus. "I don't think you should be goin' anywhere. Have you looked in the mirror this mornin'?"

"I know I look like shit, as you've already told me, but honestly I don't feel too bad. A little worn out, I suppose, but it's nothing I can't handle."

Britney watched as the two black lab-pit mutts wrestled in the dirt. They had wandered up to the house a few years ago. Skin and bones, she didn't think the puppies would last through the night, let alone become some of the best dogs she'd ever own.

"Those two going with you, right?" The dogs were good at scaring predators away.

"Like I could stop them." John rubbed Mabel's mane. "Let's go, girl."

Britney threw her head back and groaned. "You have your cell phone?"

John patted the front pocket of his shirt. "Got it right here."

"Be careful, please." She didn't like the idea of him wandering the ranch alone. "And don't stay out too long. You need to get some rest."

He waved as Mabel headed down the path she knew all too well. "I'll be back in an hour."

***

Two hours passed and still John hadn't returned home. She'd tried his cell half a dozen times with no luck. Reception was spotty out in the fields, but for her to call six times and him not answer?

Most days she wouldn't worry—it wasn't uncommon for him to leave at dawn and not come home until dusk without a word all day—but with him being sick….

She swung open the screen door of the house and headed to the gate leading into the fields. There was no sign of him, only cattle. She'd check the hay barns next, praying she'd find him piddling around with God knew what, his phone on vibrate and forgotten.

"John?" she called out in the noiseless barn. In the back he had what Britney had dubbed his man cave with a small cot, TV and a beer fridge—everything he needed. She peeked inside and found it empty. And a freaking mess. Where the hell was his trash can?

"Dammit, John. Stay in bed and rest. Why is that so hard?" She quickly checked the livestock barn and their multitude of sheds with no luck.

The only other option would be to take the four-wheeler out and check the pastures.

Britney ran inside to change into boots. Grabbing a jacket, she jumped on the four-wheeler and headed out. The downside of taking it was the noise it made. Damn thing was loud, and it was nearly impossible to hear over the rumble of the engine.

She drove along the fence line, the way John normally went when checking for any issues. The drive went on for a good while through the flat farmlands, making it easier to see for a good distance. About halfway into the first pasture, Britney cut the engine and listened, afraid John would call out for help but she'd be unable to hear him. Grass rustled in the cool breeze, but she heard nothing else.

"John!" Growing up in the country, she'd learned to yell loud. Back then, without cell phones, it was the only way to call someone in from the fields.

The distant sound of dogs barking caught her attention. Not unusual, as the dogs barked all the damn time, but they knew to stay close by. If she could pinpoint where the sound came from, it would lead her to John.

She fired up the four-wheeler and headed across the pasture toward the back acres that butted up to her in-laws' land.

"John!" she called out again as Mabel came into view, her saddle hanging off to the side.

Britney hit the throttle before skidding to a stop a few feet from the oblivious horse. "Get home." She patted Mabel on the back and the horse took off.

Scanning the area, Britney found John lying on his back not twenty yards away, the dogs nestled beside him.

"Jesus." She rushed to him and fell to her knees. "John, can you hear me?"

The rise and fall of his chest gave her some comfort. He was unconscious but alive. She retrieved the phone from her back pocket and dialed 911. A busy signal greeted her from the other end.

"What the hell?" She disconnected and tried again, her eyes trained on John.

Three attempts later, the line finally rang.

A woman answered, her voice bordering on the edge of frantic. "Nine-one-one, what's your emergency?"

"Yes, my husband's sick and fell off his horse. He's unconscious and unresponsive. We're out in a pasture. I need help!"

"I can try to get someone out to you, but it might be quicker if you can bring him to the hospital yourself. And only if necessary."

"What do you mean? If I could get him to the hospital myself, I wouldn't have called you."

"I'm so sorry"—the woman's voice cracked—"but we're overloaded with calls."

"How is that possible?" They lived in a small town in a small county where most people didn't believe in going to the doctor, let alone the hospital. "Can you call another county?"

"There are so many sick. Even our EMS drivers are coming down with the virus, collapsing while responding to calls. And it's not just us. It's everywhere."

Britney fell backward, landing hard on her butt. "What is this?"

"Nobody knows. But it's spreading fast. My advice to you is stay home if you can."

"What about my husband?"

The woman sniffled. "I'm so sorry. I've put in your request, but I don't know when or if someone will respond."

"Have there been any fatalities?" She stared down at John. "I mean… will he get better on his own?"

"I don't know…." The dispatcher's voice trailed off.

"Cancel the request." The phone slipped in Britney's trembling fingers. The woman called out for her, but Britney hung up.

John couldn't wait for the possibility of an ambulance showing up. He needed to see a doctor, and not just because of the virus; unconscious after falling off the horse, he could have a concussion.

"Honey, I'm goin' to be right back." She turned to the dogs. "Stay."

She climbed on the four-wheeler and took off back to the house at full speed, the wind prickling her skin. As fast as she drove, it wasn't near fast enough. Leaving John hurt and alone broke her heart in more ways than she thought possible.

Back at the house, she sprinted upstairs and into the kids' bathroom. In the linen closet was a first aid kit her sister had given her after Carson's birth, a little welcome home present from the doctor in the family.

Britney had laughed at some of the items. Bandages, Neosporin, and children's ibuprofen she understood, but smelling salts for a child's first aid kit?

Sloan had said they might come in handy one day. Britney hated when she was right.

With the kit in hand, Britney grabbed the truck keys and bolted out the door, back to John.

The cows had moved closer to the house, which meant Britney would have to close the gate behind her as she went through. An annoying task even when she wasn't in a hurry, but the last thing they needed when they got back home was the cows running loose.

The drive back to John felt like an eternity. She pulled up so the passenger door opened to him and jumped out, smelling salts in hand. If he didn't wake up with this, she'd be screwed. There was no way she could get him into the truck by herself.

"I'm back." She kneeled beside him and ran the smelling salts under his nose while shaking him. "John, can you hear me? Wake up! Wake up!"

His eyelids fluttered, and he groaned.

"John, can you hear me?" Tears welled in Britney's eyes. "John?"

"Yep. What the hell happened?"

Britney exhaled a shaky breath. "You fell off the horse, that's what happened. Because you're sick and should have been restin'."

"My head is killing me."

"That's because you probably have a concussion. I need to get you to the hospital. Can you stand?"

John waved her off as he attempted to sit up. "No hospitals. I'm fine."

"Are you?" She backed away. "Then get up by yourself. Show me you're fine."

He managed to get to a sitting position, but not to his feet. "Give me a minute."

"See, you can't even stand by yourself." She hooked her arm under his shoulder. "Let me help you."

Him being twice her weight and a foot taller than her made helping him up a challenge, but she steadied him enough that he climbed in the truck.

"See?" He lay back against the headrest. "I'm already getting better."

Britney took off through the pasture toward the house. "Sure you are."

"Can you not drive through the crops?"

"I'm not." Even with a concussion, he couldn't help himself, but she'd let it go until he got better. "We're in the front pasture closest to the house."

"Can you fix up the couch for me? I don't think I can make it up the stairs."

Britney got out of the truck without responding to open the gate. Once through, she closed it again, cursing under her breath. They'd been meaning to install the solar gates John had stored in one of his sheds but hadn't gotten around to it.

"Buckle your seat belt."

Britney went through the whole routine again with the front gate.

"I said no hospital," John said when she climbed back into the truck. "I feel better."

His eyes had perked up a little, but his skin still had an ashy tint.

"Too bad. I have no idea how long you were unconscious." Her gaze met John's. "Please get checked out."

The corner of John's mouth twitched. "Well, since you said 'please.'"

***

"Good God." Britney pulled over when they reached the packed little hospital. Dozens of people stood outside, including a couple of security guards at the emergency entrance. "This is crazy. There's no way all of these people can be sick."

"We should go home. It's not worth it."

Britney glared at him. The whole way here—the entire forty-five minutes—all he did was complain about having to go to the hospital. “I found you unconscious in a field. You need to see a doctor.”

“We could have stopped at the med clinic in Myrefall.”

“Are you serious?” Britney scrunched her nose. “They can’t even handle a splinter, let alone a concussion.”

John chuckled, then proceeded to hack for a solid minute.

“And you don’t need a hospital?”

“Just a little tickle in my throat.”

Britney refrained from rolling her eyes. “Maybe they’ll let me drive through the emergency lane and drop you off at the door. That way you don’t have to walk.”

“I doubt it.” John leaned his head back. “Just find a parking spot. My legs aren’t broken.”

He might be awake, but he still looked horrible. “Broken legs or not, I’m not sure you can make it from the overflow lot across the street. And I don’t see anything closer.”

“Brit, if I say I can make it, I can make it. Like I told you, I’m feeling much better.”

She eyeballed the main parking lot and the distance to the hospital. “And if you fall? There’s no way I’ll be able to get you off the ground.”

“*If* I fall, which I won’t, I’m sure you can find someone to come help me up.”

Reverse lights caught her attention as a car backed out of a parking spot. “There!” She made a sharp U-turn, foot heavy on the gas.

The unexpected movement threw John against the window. “Jesus, woman. Slow down. You’re driving like a crazy person.”

"I didn't want anyone to steal this spot."

"There's no one around."

Britney eased the truck into the small space. "This is the only one not across the street. If I didn't hurry to park here, someone would have. It's like twice the distance."

"Distance isn't going to matter if you knock me out."

She put the truck into Park. "Do you want me to go in first while you wait here? I can check how long the wait is and sign you in."

"If the wait's too long, do we get to go home?"

"No."

John opened the door, careful not to hit the car next to them. "Then I might as well go in with you and wait. At least in there I can get a crappy cup of coffee."

"John." She was sick of his flippant attitude. "You're actin' like I'm doin' this to piss you off or punish you. Do you know how scared I was to find you lyin' in the field? I thought you were dead."

His face softened. "You're right. I'm sorry. If you think I need to see a doctor, then I'll sit in the waiting room, mouth shut, and see the doctor."

"It's not just me." She exited the truck and hurried to the passenger side to help John out. "Your mother agrees with me."

"Of course she does. She's a worrier too."

Britney had called John's parents on the way, not knowing how long they'd be here. Someone needed to be at the house when the kids got off the bus.

"Let me help you."

John brushed her off. "I can do it myself. Besides, there's not enough room for both of us."

Britney watched as he wobbled alongside the truck. "Are you sure you don't need some help? I can see if I can find a wheelchair. And an orderly to push you."

"Funny." He tottered beside her as they headed for the emergency entrance.

The short walk took an excruciating amount of time, and each of his unsteady steps put her more on edge. John wasn't what most would consider athletic, but he'd spent his entire life working on a farm. The manual labor kept him strong. Seeing him struggle to just put one foot in front of the other scared the shit out of her.

"See." John paused for a breather as they reached the security guards. "I made it and didn't fall."

"It only took you ten minutes to do so."

"Can I help you?" A gruff security guard named Max, according to his nameplate, crossed his arms, accenting his bulging biceps that clashed with his round belly.

"My husband fell off his horse this mornin'. I found him unconscious, called 911, but the operator said it would be quicker if I drove him myself." Her eyes darted to the approaching ambulance—the third one since they'd arrived. "And I can see why. You guys are swamped."

"We're not allowing visitors due to the influx of patients. Lots of people been trying to lie their way in." Max took a moment to inspect John. "But you look like hell. Better head inside. Got to warn you, it'll be awhile."

John huffed. "Wonderful."

"Inside." Britney tugged at his arm. "The sooner we sign in, the sooner you'll be seen and we can go home."

He dragged his feet but followed her inside. "Holy shit."

"This is insane." She knew it would be busy from the number of cars outside, but this? There were people everywhere, taking up all the chairs and most floor space. Finding a path to the nurses' station would require a certain amount of coordination that John did not possess at the moment. “Wait here. I’ll sign you in.”

John slumped against the nearby wall. “Yep.”

Britney navigated through the crowd, careful not to step on any toes or fingers. A few people attempted to scoot out of the way, but most didn’t even acknowledge her as she passed.

“Hi,” she greeted the nurse, who didn’t bother to look up as she approached. “I need to sign in my husband.”

The nurse—Chloe, according to her name badge—tapped the clipboard on the counter.

“I see the sign-in sheet, but it’s full.”

“Try the next page.”

Britney flipped through all three sheets—a total of sixty people—and her heart sank. “They’re all full.”

Chloe glanced up from the chart in her hand and sighed. “What’s wrong with… who did you say you brought in?”

“My husband. He fell off his horse, and I found him unconscious.”

She glanced past Britney. “Is he unconscious now?”

Britney raised an eyebrow. “No, but—”

“Is there vomiting? Confusion? Dizziness? Ringing in the ears? Any other concerning symptom?”

“He’s weak and struggled with the walk from the parkin’ lot to here.”

Chloe tapped a pen against the desk. “Look around, lady. All these people struggled to get in here. If the only thing wrong with your husband is a little bump on the head, I suggest you go home.”

“But he’s also sick. It’s why he fell from the horse.” She couldn’t believe the hospital was turning them away.

“Sick how?”

“He’s—”

“Brit,” John’s voice cut her off.

She whirled around to find him edging toward the door. “What are you doin’?”

“We should go,” he said over the soft whispers. “Let the doctors focus on the more serious patients.”

Tears filled her eyes. “But I found you unconscious.”

“He’s walking. Talking.” Chloe’s said with a flat, uncaring tone. “He needs rest which you won’t find here. I can give you a list of symptoms to look for that would indicate a more serious issue.”

“Britney,” John urged. “Come on.”

“Don’t bother.” She stormed through the crowd and burst out the door, leaving John behind.

“Honey,” he called out, “wait up!”

As angry as she felt at the moment, she stopped and let him catch up, but kept her back to him for good measure.

“Thanks.” He wrapped an arm around her shoulder and pulled her close.

They walked side by side back to the truck, Britney no longer fuming but hurt he would go back on his word. “Why did you do that? After you said you’d see the doctor.”

“I overheard the security guards talking. They’re about to quarantine the hospital and not allow anyone showing signs of the virus and those exposed to leave.”

Britney peered back at the hospital. “Why would they do that?”

“The virus is causing violent outbursts, and they don’t how it’s spreading.”

“What about you?” Britney whispered. “You’re sick.”

They stopped at the truck, and he spun her around so she faced him. “Yes, but it’s been a couple of days and I haven’t experienced any violent behavior.”

“And if you do? What about the kids?”

“I’ll go upstairs, lock myself in the bedroom until it passes. Deal?”

She nodded. “I guess.”

He leaned in and pressed his lips to her cheek—a sweet gesture at first until she felt the brush of his teeth against her skin.

She jumped back out of his reach, wiping her cheek. “What are you doin’? We don’t know how this thing spreads.”

“I doubt it’s by a quick peck on the cheek.” He climbed in the truck and slammed the door.

A wave of goose bumps spread over her body as she lifted herself into the driver seat and started the truck. “Your teeth touched my skin.”

John laughed. “You’re just being paranoid.”

“Are you sure about that?” Britney watched as they locked the hospital entrance. Those inside banged on the doors, their faces begging to be freed.

CHAPTER SIX

Axel left Sam's diner and headed back to the hospital. Breakfast with Gus and the other riders who'd stayed had been interesting.

In the couple of hours they were there, eating breakfast and drinking a couple pots of coffee, two people had collapsed. The 911 operator had said all ambulances were tied up by other, more serious calls. The woman had hit her head on the edge of the table, leaving a two-inch gash on her forehead. The man never regained consciousness. Instead of waiting on an ambulance, their friends had taken them to the hospital themselves.

He suspected the tie-up in ambulances had to do with the mysterious virus going around. The violent outburst he'd witnessed in Queenie's room scared the shit out of him, but he hadn't heard how long the side effects lasted, or how long it took for the virus to leave the infected's system.

The craziness of this virus was the reason five of their riders had left that morning. After the hospital had denied them visitation, they'd all settled in the motel across the street and called to check on their families. Turned out the same madness going on there was happening all over the country.

Gus hadn't said if any of their families were infected, and Axel didn't have the heart to ask.

The news had called it an epidemic, and doctors were puzzled by how quickly it spread. The origin had yet to be discovered—or just wasn't announced to the public. Death toll unknown.

And that was it. The entire story summed up in a short two-minute segment. Not that it mattered. People were scared, and who could blame them?

Right before their group left the diner, local officials had announced schools in the surrounding areas would be released after lunch and classes suspended until further notice.

Yesterday, Axel would have thought the decision to be a bit of an overkill, but after what he'd seen that poor man go through in the hospital, it was probably for the best. Keeping people isolated could help get the virus under control.

He crossed the street toward the hospital, where even more people had gathered. Gus and the others had gone back to the motel to pack and would meet Axel in an hour. After much debate, they'd decided the best thing to do was get Queenie out of this town and head back home, with the doctor's permission or not.

Of course, they hadn't seen her yet. Axel tried to argue that moving her would be dangerous, but each of them had families of their own. They'd stayed out of respect for their fallen rider but were eager to get home.

Axel's situation was different. The only family he had left wasn't really family. More like a soon-to-be ex-wife.

They'd separated a few months back and hadn't spoken since then. He heard through mutual friends that she'd moved to New York, but not much else. He didn't even know if she'd filed the divorce papers yet, like she said she would before he'd slammed the door and left.

The memory brought with it a bout of guilt that turned his stomach. He hated himself for the way he'd left, but he couldn't stay. The pain surrounding that life ate away at him to the point he couldn't feel anything else.

He pushed away the memories and picked up the pace, jogging past the crowds toward the door he'd left propped open. Trying to act as inconspicuous as possible, he slipped through the door and pulled it closed. The last thing the hospital needed was a bunch of people stampeding up the stairs. The staff had enough to deal with.

Taking the stairs two at a time, Axel rushed up to the second floor. He cracked the door and surveyed the hall, checking for watchful eyes.

If someone caught him using the stairs, it would ruin their entire plan. No way he'd be able to get back down and let a group of bikers inside, let alone sneak out a patient.

When he was positive no one was looking, he crept into the hall and back into Queenie's room

The first patient, the young man, had been moved, and no one had replaced the older man he had helped the doctor sedate.

He expected both spots to be full considering the insane amount of people who not only waited outside, insisting to see their loved ones, but the number of patients he'd seen as he came down the hall yesterday. And now with the ambulances swamped, he couldn't imagine what the emergency room looked like today.

If a small town like this could have so many sick, he couldn't fathom what the big city hospitals was like.

The little voice in the back of his head whispered, *If you would call Lane, she could tell you. Ex or not, she's still family.*

He fiddled with the phone in his pocket before deciding against calling her right then. Maybe later, after they hit the road—which was another challenge.

Queenie wouldn't be able to ride her motorcycle, and leaving it behind… well, they might as well her leave her too.

Gus said he'd check with the motel manager to see if he could get the name of a local car rental place. A truck with an extra-long bed might work. If they rented out trailers, that would be even better.

Queenie groaned from the other side of the drawn curtain. Axel rushed to her side, cursing himself for not checking on her as soon as he got back into the room. "Queenie? You okay?"

The poor woman's condition had worsened in the few hours he'd been gone. Her skin especially. The gray tint now dominated her pigment, and black lines spread outward from her injuries.

He'd never seen anything like it. A doctor once told him infections could cause red streaks as it advanced through the body, but he'd never heard of them turning black.

Queenie groaned again; the sound more feral than pain stricken. He checked her IV bag and found it empty.

How long had it been since a doctor or nurse came to check on her? He understood the place was overflowing with patients, probably many sicker than her, but failing to check her IV bag? Unacceptable. The lack of pain medication, not to mention the fluids and antibiotics—no wonder she looked so bad.

"Hold on, Queenie. I'll go grab a nurse and get your meds going again." He brushed his hand over her head and clumps of hair fell onto her pillow.

Queenie's head snapped at the sound of his voice, ripping the unchanged bandage from her neck.

The air whooshed from Axel's lungs. The deep gashes along her throat had healed to the point that he couldn't even pinpoint their exact locations.

A scream echoed down the hall, and Queenie's eyes flew open. Axel stumbled backward at the blackness staring back at him. No white just solid black.

"Holy shit." He struggled to regain his footing.

A low growl passed her lips, revealing her now-serrated teeth.

"Queenie?" He couldn't think of anything else to say, the reality of the situation fighting against what he knew of the world. "It's Axel. I'm going to grab a doctor and get you some help."

Her head jerked again. A quick twitch of her nose and she growled, lunging toward him.

He fell to the ground, bringing the curtain down with him. Throwing it aside, he jumped to his feet, reaching for the gun he didn't have.

Queenie snapped her teeth, tugging at the wrist and ankle restraints hidden beneath her blankets. The metal attachments stretched as she struggled to break free.

He rushed from the room toward the nurses' station in the middle of the hall.

"I need a sedative!" he screamed as he skidded to a stop.

The nurse's head fell back as she attempted to look up at him. "What?"

"Shit. You're sick too?" Axel whirled around, trying to find someone to help. How had he not noticed it before? Collapsed doctors, nurses and orderlies lined the hall. Most were unconscious, but there were a few trying to get back to their feet.

He fell to his knees beside the nurse who had shown him to Queenie's room. "What can I do?"

"Leave," she croaked, handing him her badge, "before it's too late."

"Too late for what?"

Her eyes darted to the door to her left. "They've locked us in, but they're so strong. It won't be long."

"Who's strong?"

"Inside." She tilted her head to the door.

Axel rose to his feet and stared inside the room. "I don't see any—shit! What the hell is that?" The person—though unrecognizable as such except for the shape of its body—scratched at the window and slammed its shoulders against the door, growling.

"A woman admitted with the virus two days ago."

"What?" Axel kept his eyes on the room. "What did it do to her?"

"Killed her."

"She's not dead," Axel whispered.

The nurse coughed. "Not anymore. Go. Now. The National Guard has been called and will be here any minute. They're going to make it look like an accident. They'll do anything to contain this."

"Come with me." He reached out to her. "And anyone else who's still alive."

She lifted her hand, showing him a small bite mark. "I'm already dead. So is everyone else here."

"A bite mark?"

"Go." She bared her teeth.

Axel took a step back. "I—"

"Go. Now." She snapped her jaw in his direction. "I can't control it."

"I'm sorry." Axel took off running down the hall toward the stairwell. He paused at Queenie's door and peered inside the empty room. "Shit."

A door slammed and Axel jumped, whirling around. He couldn't be sure, but he swore he heard footsteps coming down the hall.

He threw open the stairwell doors and sprinted down, the sound of his boots echoing off the walls. He didn't stop, didn't dare look back, afraid what might be behind him. The exit sign came into view a second later, the light blinking an ominous red. He shoved the panic bar on the door and nearly knocked himself to the ground.

"Son of a bitch." In a rush, he'd forgotten he needed the keycard to get out.

He reached in his back left pocket and then the right; both were empty. He knew he'd put the keycard in one of them.

He turned to go back up the stairs and search for the damn thing when the door above him creaked open and then slammed closed.

Axel froze. Part of him wanted to call out, hope someone responded and eased his fears. The other part screamed to get the hell out of there.

He scanned the area in search of the fallen keycard; chances were it fell out of his pocket when he ran down the stairs. Seconds felt like hours as footsteps scraped against metal. He couldn't tell if whoever—whatever—had moved from the second floor, and he didn't want to find out.

A hint of light reflecting off metal drew his attention upward to the corner landing of the stairwell. The key card lay there teasing him, his freedom only a few steps away.

He didn't hesitate, bolting up the stairs and snatching the key card from the ground.

A terrifying growl echoed off the walls. Axel snapped his head upward, his heart thrashing in his chest. For a second he stood there motionless as the monster sniffed the air.

On its left arm was the outline of a familiar tattoo—angel wings surrounding the name Lea, the love of Queenie's life.

"Queenie?" Axel called out, more instinctively than anything else.

The monster jerked its head, not in recognition but like a predator recognizing the sounds of its prey. Then it bolted down the stairs, bouncing off the walls as if it couldn't see.

Axel didn't miss a beat, flying down the stairs and slapping the keycard against the reader. It beeped and he slammed on the handle, but the door didn't budge.

He swiped the card repeatedly, each time hitting the panic bar harder, to no avail.

Behind him the scrape of nails against metal grew closer. He hadn't dared look to see how close Queenie—the monster—had gotten.

He had seconds left before it attacked.

Why the nurse's badge didn't work when she thought it would, he didn't know and didn't have time to analyze. Getting out of there was the only thing that mattered.

He took a step back and kicked the door with as much strength as he could muster.

The monster growled again, this time so close the hairs on his neck stood up. Axel turned and ducked as the creature lunged, knocking its head into the steel door.

The impact did nothing to slow its hunt. It was up on its feet faster than he'd ever seen anything move before.

Axel scurried backward, keeping as far away from the mouth of the creature as he could. The nurse had said she'd been bitten. He'd be damned if he let that happen to him.

The creature lunged at him again, its aim horrible, but there wasn't much space in the tiny area. Axel didn't dodge this time, instead landing his foot in its sternum.

That seemed to do some damage, or at least stunned the monster enough that he could try the door again.

A quick swipe of the keycard and he pushed the door open, stumbling to the ground. He kicked the door for good measure, evoking another ear-piercing howl.

Fear coursed through him as claws ground against metal.

He needed to warn someone, *anyone,* of the monsters lurking behind these walls.

The nurse had said the National Guard was on their way. If he could just get to them in time, before the monsters escaped….

He managed a few feet before being thrown to the ground, a massive explosion rocking the small town to its core.

***

Axel's ears rang, muffling the sounds of sirens. Every breath he took hurt; every muscle he moved ached.

"Axel!" a voice screamed over the commotion. He lifted his head for a heartbeat and then laid it back on the ground as Gus came into view. "What the fuck, man? Were you in there?"

"Almost," Axel groaned as Gus helped him to his feet.

"Do you know what happened?"

Axel scanned the area, but smoke and debris offered limited visibility. "Where's the National Guard?"

"National Guard?" Gus helped guide Axel across the street. "The explosion just happened, man. No way they could get here that quickly."

"The nurse." Axel wanted to explain but found it hard to articulate the words. "She said they were coming, told me to get out."

"Jesus." Angie hurried up to them. "Should I get someone to look at him?"

Axel glanced over his shoulder. "I'm not sure there's anyone left."

She sucked in a sharp breath. "You think the explosion killed everyone?"

"I can't imagine how anyone could have survived." Axel's legs wobbled. "I think I need to sit down."

"Come on." Angie jogged toward the motel. "You can rest in my room, but no sleeping."

"My head feels fine." Axel lumbered behind her with Gus by his side. "It's everything else that hurts like a bitch."

"The others went to get lunch." Angie opened the unlocked door. "They should be back soon. Can I get you something, Axel? Ice pack? Painkillers? A stiff drink?"

Axel fell to the bed. "Yes."

Angie paused. "Yes to what?"

"All of them."

Gus laughed. "Maybe start with the ice and painkillers, Angie."

"I think I need the drink more." After everything Axel had seen, his nerves were shot.

"You're bleeding." Gus threw him a towel. "From multiple spots. Alcohol is a blood thinner."

Axel caught the towel and gave himself a quick once-over. As much pain as he was in, he hadn't noticed the deep gash along his left upper arm or the multitude of cuts, scrapes and bruises on the rest of his arms. Too bad he hadn't been wearing his leather jacket.

"Dammit." Axel shot up, the room spinning at the sudden movement. Maybe he had hit his head.

The door flew open and Angie came bursting in. "What's wrong?"

Axel narrowed his eyes. "Where did you go?" How did he not know she left?

She set the ice bucket on the nightstand and rubbed her eyes. "I really think you need to get checked out."

"I'm fine. Where's Gus?"

"Really?" Angie went to the bathroom and brought back a washcloth. "Not five minutes ago, I told you I was going out for ice. Gus went to go find the others and left at the same time I did. Don't you remember?"

"Shit." Axel kneaded the heels of his hands on his temples. "I guess not. Did I respond?"

She placed some ice in the washcloth and handed it to him. "Come to think of it, you didn't. Not really. Maybe a little grunt."

Axel pressed the ice pack to his head and lay back down.

Angie sat down beside him, fiddling with her hands. "Gus didn't want to talk about it, but I have to ask. Was Queenie… do you think… I mean, she was in there…."

The sadness in her voice resonated with him on so many levels. "She was, but—"

The door opened, and Gus and the other eleven who remained pushed inside, food bags in hand. All wore somber looks on their faces, their heads hung low. It was hard to believe twenty-four hours ago they had been such a happy, fun-loving group.

"The National Guard just showed up." Gus took a seat in the only chair in the room. "The fire department has the flames under control. There's going to do a press conference later this evening, according to the police officer I ran into."

"Any word on survivors?" Angie asked.

Gus frowned. "They're not optimistic. The temperature of the fire alone…."

Axel studied each of their faces. None of them openly sobbed—it wasn't their way—but many had tears streaming down their cheeks. He needed to tell them what he saw inside, what the nurse had said, what happened before he escaped.

"Guys." He cleared his throat, unsure how to start, or if they would even believe him. "There's something you should know. I don't think the explosion was an accident."

All eyes shot to him, but it was Gus who spoke. "That's a damn serious accusation. Got any evidence to back it up?"

Axel thought about standing and throwing his shoulders back as he addressed the group, like his father always did. It showed confidence, his father said, and that what you had to say held importance.

Too bad his legs screamed in protest when he sat up. No way he'd be able to stand. Falling would only show weakness and cause doubt, which was already going to be an uphill battle.

"I forgot the pain meds." Angie jumped from the bed and hurried into the bathroom, returning a second later with a bottle of pills. "Sorry."

He took four brown tablets and washed them down with a bottle of water. "Thanks."

"Back to the explosion." Shifter ran a hand over his waist-long white beard. "And why someone would blow up a damn hospital."

"Not someone." His gaze met Shifter's. "The National Guard."

Gus snorted. "Kid, I think you hit your head harder than you think you did."

Axel ignored him and continued. "When I snuck back into the hospital to check on Queenie—"

"How is she?" Angie's voice cracked. "Was she…?"

Axel patted her knee. "She had gotten so much worse. Had changed."

"Changed how?" Gus asked.

"Her skin had turned gray, and when she opened her eyes…." The memories flooded back, knocking the air from his lungs. "They were black."

"Black eyes?" Gus paced the room. "I don't get your point. Her eyes have always been dark."

"Not just her pupils, the entire eye. There was no white left. The whole thing was black. She growled at me. Attacked me in the stairwell."

Gus sank back into his chair. "What did the doctor say?"

"I went to go find someone, but everyone was sick." Axel swallowed. "There were others locked in their rooms who had the same look as Queenie. I spoke with a nurse, the only one who I found conscious. She told me to get out, that the National Guard was coming."

"Why didn't you get her out?" Gunner asked.

"I tried, but she refused." Guilt burned his stomach. "Said she'd been bitten by a patient, and it wouldn't be long before it killed her—" He paused, not sure if he could get the last of the sentence out. "—and she became one of them."

Gus jumped from his chair. "What the hell is that supposed to mean? You're talking crazy. If she's dead, how can she become one of them?"

Axel stood, his legs wobbling, but he kept himself steady. "I don't know what any of it means. And I agree, if any of you were telling me this story, I would think you're crazy too. Hell, I barely believe it and I was inside that hospital. I was attacked by one of them… by Queenie."

"No way." Gunner slammed a fist into the wall. "Just yesterday she nearly died. There's no way she could have the strength—"

"Her injuries were gone," Axel interrupted. "I saw it with my own eyes. And she attacked me in the stairwell when I was trying to get out. They had locked the whole hospital down. The nurse gave me her keycard so I could leave, but it didn't work right away. Queenie came down the stairs at a speed I've never seen before and jumped at me, hitting her head against the door. It didn't even faze her. She lunged at me again until I kicked her in the chest. That slowed her down enough that I could try the keycard again and get out."

"You're sure it was her?" Angie asked. "I mean, you recognized her?"

"Recognized her, no. She didn't even look human anymore."

Gunner marched up to Axel and got into his face. "Then how do you know?"

"The tattoo on her arm." Axel dropped back to the bed and leaned forward, elbows on his knees. "She would have killed me. She had serrated teeth and razor claws. What the hell is going on here?"

Angie rubbed his back. "I believe you."

"You can't be serious." Gunner threw up his arms. "Gus?"

"Why would he lie?" Gus asked.

"Because he's a coward and saved himself, leaving Queenie there to die."

Axel balled his hands into fists, trying to calm the rage. "She was already dead. They all were. And this explosion was a way to keep whatever the hell those things were from getting out."

The room stayed quiet for a couple of minutes until Gus spoke up. "We should leave. There's no point in waiting around. Everyone, go get your things and meet by the bikes in fifteen minutes."

A few grumbled, "Okay," as they left the room. None could look Axel in the eyes.

They probably didn't believe him, not that he gave a fuck. Whatever had caused those people to change, he feared the hospital was only the beginning.

***

"What should we do with Queenie's bike?" Angie brushed her hand over the seat. "We can't just leave it here."

Axel looked to Gus. "Is there a storage place around here? I'll gladly pay the monthly fee until we figure out how to get it home." He patted his back pocket for his wallet. It was the only thing he had left; all his other belongings had been in the bag he'd left the hospital room.

"Even if there is a storage place, I'm not sure anyone would be there." Gus pointed to the town square. "Looks like everyone is waiting for the press conference."

"Should we stay?" Rainey left the group, moving closer to the town square. "It might be nice to know what happened."

"You mean the official report? Or the bullshit lies they're going to tell everyone to cover up the truth?"

Mac mounted his bike. "Let's get on the road. The farther we get away from this town, the better."

Axel agreed. "We only have a few hours until it gets dark. Better make the most of it."

"Maybe Rainey's right," Angie said. "Someone's going onstage now, and he looks pretty official. What's a few more minutes?"

"Press conferences can last for hours if they allow for questions." Gunner crossed his arms. "There's no point in waiting around. What caused the explosion doesn't really matter. It happened. Not a damn thing we can do to change that."

"What about Queenie?" Rainey asked. "Don't you want to know why this happened?"

Axel grabbed his helmet. "I told you what happened. Whatever they're going to say will be some bullshit story to hide the truth. Let's go."

"Good afternoon, ladies and gentlemen," the voice boomed over the loudspeaker. "For those who don't know me, I'm Mayor Croger. In just a moment, Caption Boyer of the Montana National Guard will come up and speak with you on what happened at the hospital earlier today. Before he does, I want to offer my deepest sympathies to those who lost a loved one, friend or neighbor in this tragic accident. Our small town is a close-knit community, and those who lost their lives will be missed but never forgotten."

A light applause filtered through the crowd, but it was the sound of sobbing that dominated.

"Caption Boyer"—the mayor held out his hand—"if you would please tell us what you know."

The older man wearing army fatigues climbed the stairs and joined the mayor onstage. His somber face reflected the emotions of the town, but in his eyes Axel saw defeat.

"Good afternoon. First, I would like to take a moment to offer my condolences. Tragedies such as these are never easy, especially in tight-knit communities. My team has been hard at work since arriving on the scene. With the quick work of the fire department, we were able to enter the parts of the building which is still standing and conduct a search and rescue. Unfortunately, we have found no survivors."

He paused, knowing the reaction such news would evoke from the crowd.

Once they settled, he continued, "The cause of the explosion was a combination of faulty wiring and a gas leak."

Axel joined the others who had each, in their own time, moved closer.

"What about the virus?" a woman called from the crowd.

Capitan Boyer glanced to his left at another, older man, who nodded, before addressing the crowd. "The virus, though a separate incident, is also a great concern of ours. We have brought with us our own doctors and mobile clinic. Those exhibiting symptoms must report to the clinic immediately."

"Why?" a man yelled.

Boyer's face tightened. "So they can be treated. Which comes to the next order of business. We are implementing a town-wide curfew following this press conference. Everyone will return to their homes, and my men will go house by house to check for those who are exhibiting symptoms of the virus."

"Shit," Axel mumbled. "We need to get out of here now or they aren't going to let us leave."

"All roads coming in and out of town have been closed until we can ensure all those infected have been quarantined. If you live on the outskirts of town, you are to report to the school's gymnasium until cleared to return home."

Axel tugged on Gus's jacket and leaned in to whisper, "Do you think we can make it out?"

Gus shook his head. "We can try, but we're probably stuck here for another day or two."

"I will not be taking questions at this time," Boyer said over the enraged crowd. "If those who are healthy could all return to your homes, and those who are sick, please follow my men to the left of the stage. They'll take real good care of you."

"We should have left!" Mac mounted his motorcycle. "I think we should try to leave anyway. We can find some small side road, go through some fields."

"No." Gus had always been the unofficial leader of the group. People had a tendency to look to him when decisions needed to be made. "We need to go back to the room and cooperate. None of us are sick, so there should be nothing holding us here after they have cleared us."

Axel stared down at his arms, at the deep gash in particular. "Son of a bitch. What if they think my injuries have to do with the virus?"

"Why would they think that?" Rainey asked.

"Because they know what was in that hospital. What this virus turns people into."

"If what you say is true." Gunner's tone screamed disbelief.

"Every word." Axel ground his teeth.

"Whatever." Gunner rolled his neck. "The virus turns people into a monster. Could you be infected?"

Axel scanned the group. "The nurse said it had bitten her, which I wasn't. But she was also sick and could have been delusional."

Mac took a step back. “You were around them. Stayed in the hospital last night. If it’s airborne, you could be sick.”

Gus moved closer to Axel. “Remember breakfast? Two people collapsed; others looked like shit. If it’s airborne, we’re already sick.”

Mac ran his hand over his short black hair.

“And none of the National Guard are wearing any protective gear.” Axel glanced over his shoulder. “They would be in full-on quarantine getup if they thought just interaction with people could get them infected.”

“So they know what this is?” Angie let out a weighted breath. “Maybe they have a cure.”

Axel’s eyes met Gus’s. He didn’t have the heart to tell the woman that if they had a cure, they wouldn’t have blown up an entire hospital.

“Let’s get moving, folks.” A couple of men with rifles and military attire strolled up to the group. “Do you need a ride home?”

“We’re not from around here, sir,” Gus said. “We’re staying at this motel and will head inside now.”

“We appreciate your cooperation.”

Gus smiled. “You’re here to protect. We understand. Most of us have been in your shoes once or twice in our lives.”

The younger soldier’s body relaxed. “You’ve served. Good to know.”

“Yes, sir, and are here to help if need be.”

“Thank you, but that shouldn’t be necessary.”

Axel wanted to ask how long it would be before someone could clear them but kept his mouth shut, allowing Gus to work his magic.

“Have you heard how other towns around the country are doing?” Gus asked. “Being so far away from our families, it's been difficult.”

"I've heard a little, but I'll see what I can find out." He studied Axel's face, then down to his arm. "Can you tell me how you got that injury, sir?"

Axel didn't hesitate. "Flying debris sliced my arm."

The soldier cocked his head. "What were you doing so close to the hospital?"

"Trying to visit a friend, in which they denied me access."

"I see." The soldier pressed a button on his walkie-talkie. "Yes, I need a medic at the motel across the street from the hospital for a wound check."

Axel clenched his jaw. "Got to tell you, I don't enjoy being called a liar."

"It's standard procedure, sir." The older soldier's grip tightened around his gun.

Mac moved closer to Axel. "What does a scratch have to do with a damn flu virus?"

"Nothing." The older soldier's nostrils flared. "Back to your rooms. A medic will be here shortly."

Gus moved in front of Mac. "We'll be waiting in room 108."

The soldier watched as Gus guided them into the motel room.

Axel peeked out the window fifteen minutes later. "They're still there."

"Did you expect them to leave?" Gus flipped through the TV channels. "Strange how none of the national news stations are reporting on the hospital explosion. Seems right up their alley."

Axel knew he should probably keep his mouth shut, but he couldn't help himself. "Kind of adds a little credulity to my story, doesn't it?"

A light rap at the door prevented any comebacks.

"Come in," Gus called out as no one else bothered to get up.

A young woman opened the door and entered. The two soldiers who'd called in Axel's injury waited outside the door.

"Hi. I'm Dr. Tina Cabinal and am here to do a symptom check. Though I didn't realize there were so many of you."

"Fourteen," Axel told her as she silently counted the people in the room.

"Thanks. If I would have known there were so many, I would have brought some help."

Gunner glared. "You need help to check one scratch?"

Dr. Cabinal placed her bag on the nightstand. "No, but since I'm here, I planned on examining and hopefully clearing everyone. Unless you'd like to wait until someone else comes available? I heard it could take days."

"That won't be necessary." Gus patted Mac on the shoulder. "We'll all cooperate and hopefully make your job a little easier."

"Thank you." She looked at Axel. "Am I to assume you're the one I was called here to check?"

Axel rolled up his sleeve to reveal the entire gash. "Yes. You want me to sit on the bed?"

"No, I'll do all the exams in the bathroom so each of you can have some privacy." She grabbed her bag and headed that way. "If you would please strip down to your undergarments."

"What?" Axel paused. "It's my arm that's hurt."

"I see that, but I have to make sure you have no other wounds or any physical symptoms of the virus."

"Fine." Axel followed her into the bathroom and slammed the door. "You at least going to turn around while I take my clothes off?"

She turned around. "I'm a medical professional, Mister…."

"Axel. Just Axel."

"Axel. Trust me when I say there isn't anything under your clothing I haven't seen before."

He tossed his clothes on the counter, leaving him standing in the cold room in his boxers. "All stripped down ready to be examined."

She chuckled as she turned back around. "I'll take your vitals, do a quick skin check, and then tend to your cut."

"Whatever." He'd let her do whatever she wanted if it would get him out of this town.

After his temperature, blood pressure and breathing all came back normal, she started on the visual exam.

"If you could please bend over so I can check your head."

He complied, holding back the inappropriate remarks that popped in his head.

"Everything looks good so far. Now if you would please pull down your boxers."

"Do the physical symptoms normally start in the genital area? Or is this more personal curiosity?"

The corner of her mouth twitched. "Have to say, I haven't heard that one before."

"I can't tell if you're being sarcastic or not."

"Please, your boxer shorts."

He dropped them to the ground as she crouched before him and then behind.

"Everything looks good. You can pull them back up."

He didn't bother with a witty comment. "Can I get dressed?"

"Not yet. If you could take a seat on the edge of the tub, I'll inspect your arm."

"The toilet too high?" He straddled the narrow edge.

"There's no room for me to move next to the toilet." She bent over and examined his arm with a pair of tweezers. "How did you say this happened?"

"Debris." He winced as she poked and pinched at the already tender skin. "What are you doing?"

"See this?" She showed him the tweezers. "It's a splinter I pulled from the skin."

"Okay. What does that mean?"

She grabbed a few more supplies from her bag and cleaned his wound. "It means a piece of wood caused this injury. I can stitch it if you want."

"Do you have something to numb it?" He hated needles.

"Sorry."

"I'll pass."

She dug in her bag again. "Most men do. You aren't allergic to penicillin, are you?"

"Nope."

"Good." She tossed him a bottle. "Take this twice a day for ten days."

He shook the bottle. "This is ten days' worth of pills?"

"Closer to three weeks. Just in case you need them."

"Thanks."

"No problem. You can get dressed now."

He slipped on his clothes and stuffed the bottle in his pocket. "Does this mean I've been cleared to leave?"

"Yes, when they open the roads again."

"Any idea when that will be?"

"Sorry. Your arm, please." She snapped a green band on his wrist. "This will be your 'get out of jail free' card."

"Seems a little simplistic. What's stopping someone from taking this off and giving it to someone else?"

"The only way this comes off is if it's cut. Now if you don't mind, I need to check the rest of your group."

"Sure." He went back into the main room and pointed at Gunner. "You're up."

Gunner grumbled but didn't argue.

"Everything okay?" Gus asked Axel.

Axel held up the wrist with the green band. "Ready to get the hell out of here."

CHAPTER SEVEN

"Mom," Blake screamed from the living room, "what channel are the cartoons on?"

Britney took a drink of her cold coffee and sighed. One hour into the canceled school day and already she prayed for a miraculous reopening.

"Mom," Blake whined again. "There's only the stupid news on. Can you come fix it?"

"Comin'." She stuck her mug in the microwave and hit thirty seconds. Maybe she'd get to drink it hot this time.

"Look." Blake pointed the remote at the TV and flipped through the channels. "I can't find the cartoons."

It wasn't like they had cable. Most of the time, they streamed everything, but for some reason, Blake loved the PBS cartoons and spent most of the mornings when he didn't have school glued to the TV.

"If there aren't any cartoons on, why don't you just turn on Netflix?"

"No!" He flipped through the channels again. "They don't have my favorite."

"How do you even know if you're on PBS? You haven't stopped long enough on a channel to see what's on."

"Ugh," he groaned, "didn't you see! It's the same thing on every channel. Stupid news."

"Are you sure?" Britney held out her hand. "Give me the remote and let me look."

He slammed it in her hand more forcefully than necessary, and she glared. "Why don't you go play."

"But—"

"Don't." Nine o'clock and she'd already heard enough backtalk. "Go upstairs or outside, or I'll find you somethin' to do."

"Fine." Blake rolled his eyes, and Britney forced herself not to notice. "I'll just go play on my tablet."

"No," Britney snapped. "Toys or outside. Carson is shootin' baskets. Why don't you go play with him? It's a pretty mornin'. Before long it's goin' to be cold and snowin', and you'll wish you had played outside more."

"I guess." Blake headed outside, the screen door slamming behind him.

Britney went to turn off the TV when she noticed the news reporter standing in front of a burning building. She upped the volume and sank to the couch as she realized where they were.

"Oh my God." Less than twenty-four hours ago, they'd been sitting in that hospital's waiting room. What if they had seen John? Or admitted him?

"Britney?" Debra, her mother-in-law, came down the stairs, wet washrag in hand. "What's going on there?"

"The hospital I took John to." Her words cracked. "There was a gas leak, and it exploded."

"Exploded?" Debra sat down beside her. "What do you mean?"

"Exploded," Britney repeated. "All the patients, the staff… they're all dead."

"You're kidding." Debra rubbed Britney's back. "When did it happen?"

"Hours after we left." Britney leaned into her surrogate mother. Debra had been a godsend after her mother died, taking care of Britney and Sloan's womanly needs when their father didn't know what to do. "Can you believe that? A few hours. We could have been there."

"God works in mysterious ways." Debra kissed her on the top of the head. "John's resting peacefully now. I'm going to go home and check on Martin. Lord knows what he's been up to since I've been gone."

"Haven't you spoken to him since yesterday?" Debra had brought the kids home from the bus stop. One look at John when they got home and she stayed overnight to help Britney take care of him.

Debra's main concern, as was hers, was keeping the kids away from John so they wouldn't become ill.

"I spoke with him last night but not this morning." She grabbed her purse and keys from the table. "I'm sure it's nothing. Most likely he's out checking cows, but with that virus going around, I want to make sure he's all right."

"Oh." Britney rose from the couch to walk Debra out. "I didn't know he was sick."

"He's not. At least he wasn't when I left yesterday."

"How about you?" Britney followed Debra until she reached her beat-up truck. "You feelin' okay after spending so much time with John?"

"I am. A little tired, but that's nothing more than age."

"Thanks again, Debra." Britney closed the driver door for her mother-in-law.

"Call if you need me to come back." She started the diesel truck. "Oh, and John mentioned something about filling up the gas cans. Something about the generators."

"The generators?" They had several but hadn't used them in years. "Why would he mention those? He just had the tank filled up."

"I don't know. I guess all the craziness going on has gotten him worked up."

"What do you think?"

Debra brushed Britney's cheek in true motherly fashion. "Maybe it wouldn't hurt. With the schools closed and the nearest hospital destroyed… you know how crazy the world can be when scared."

Britney spotted the kids in the tree house her father had built in the ancient tree out front. "There's half a dozen gas cans in the barn I can get filled up." She needed to stop by the store anyway. "What about John? I'm not sure I should leave him alone."

"He'll be out for a while. I gave him a mild sedative."

"Debra!" Britney couldn't believe she would so such a thing. "Why would you do that?"

"He was being aggressive, snapping at me like a wild animal. It's not safe."

"Did he bite you?"

Debra waved a dismissive hand. "Nothing to worry about."

Britney sighed. *Stubborn woman.* "I'll call you when I get home. Do you need anythin' from town?"

Debra pulled out a twenty from her wallet. "I don't, but get the kids some treats on me."

Britney took the money, knowing better not to enter an argument she'd never win. "Thank you. And leave the gate open. We'll be right behind you." She waved as Debra drove off.

"Go get some shoes on!" Britney yelled at the kids, who pretended not to hear her. "Grandma gave me money for snacks."

That got them out of the tree. They rushed in the house and were back before Britney loaded the last gas can.

"Are we going to leave Daddy all alone?" Molly asked. "What if he needs us?"

"Grandma gave him some medicine that will help him sleep while we're gone."

Molly climbed in the back, followed by the boys. "Should we get him some chicken noodle soup, Mommy? That's what you always give us when we're sick."

"Sure, baby." She checked to make sure they were all buckled before heading off. "I think chicken noodle soup will make him feel much better."

***

"Why are there so many cars?" Molly said with an exaggerated whine. "Can't we go back home? This is taking forever."

Britney glared at her daughter from the rearview mirror even though she had just been thinking the same thing. Too bad she had to be the adult of the family. "It hasn't been that long, sweetie. Besides, if we go home, you won't get any special snacks."

"I don't care. I'm bored and squished." She kicked the back of Britney's seat. "I have no room,"

"You have more room than me!" Carson knocked his knees into the back of the passenger seat.

"Enough. Both of you have plenty of room." Britney's eye twitched. It was bad enough that she'd hardly slept last night, but to sit here in traffic with the kids bickering? She'd be lucky if she made it home without having a nervous breakdown.

"How long until we get there?" Molly and her damn whine. It grated on Britney's nerves.

"Can you please talk like a big girl?" Britney tapped on the steering wheel, praying they would move again soon. In her entire life, she never remembered the road into town being so backed up.

"Maybe there's an accident." Blake leaned forward. "Do you see any dead bodies lying in the road?"

All three of the kids busted up laughing.

Britney swatted at her son. "Knock it off. That is not funny."

"I'm just kidding. Gosh, Mom. Take a joke."

"Ugh." Britney dropped her head on the steering wheel. "You guys are drivin' me crazy."

The kids laughed again. They loved getting under her skin.

"Can't you find somethin' to do? There are colorin' books back there, word searches and God knows what else."

"Why can't we just go home?" Carson asked. "We can get snacks another day."

Britney looked over her shoulder. "I have to fill the gas cans."

"Why?" Molly's favorite question.

"In case we need to run the generators."

Molly scrunched her nose. "What's a gentorator?"

"Generator," Carson corrected.

"That's what I said." Molly stuck out her tongue. "Stop correcting me all the time."

The car in front of them moved forward a few feet. "That's it? What the hell is going on in town?"

Carson lifted himself off his seat. "All I can see is a lot of cars. Where do you think everyone is going?"

"Maybe there's a parade." Molly's eyes grew wide. "Or a carnival! Or a petting zoo. Can we stop, Mommy, pleeeease?"

"Sure, honey. If there are any of those three things, we'll stop."

"Yay!" She bounced in her seat. "I hope they have pony rides. No, elephant rides. Or the best would be unicorn rides."

Carson snickered. "You're so dumb."

Britney whirled around. "And you're so grounded if you don't apologize to your sister right this minute."

"Fine," Carson sighed. "Sorry."

"Apology not accepted." Molly crossed her arms.

"Looks like Blake is goin' to be the only one gettin' a treat at the store."

Molly and Carson whipped their heads at Blake, who was busy doing a word search. As the quieter one of the three, she could usually count on him to set a good example.

"I'm being good, Mommy." Molly pulled out her favorite coloring book and crayons. "See? I'm going to color a picture for Daddy to make him feel better."

"I think he would like that very much."

Carson, being the oldest, wasn't as easy to manipulate. "Can I play on your phone? I need to check one of my games."

"No." They moved another few inches forward. "Why don't you play with your Legos or draw?"

Carson threw back his head and closed his eyes. "I'll just take a nap."

Even better. Not that she dared say that out loud. "If you feel like it."

The line of cars moved again, this time far enough in town that Britney could sort of see what was going on. "Is this a line to get into the med clinic?"

"I thought you hated that place, Mommy." Molly remembered every word Britney said, especially if it was negative.

"I don't hate that place. I just don't think they're very good at their jobs."

"Yeah." Carson crossed his arms with a huff. "Like when I had a sore throat and they said it was just allergies, but really I had strep throat."

One of the many examples of their incompetence. The first time, Britney had played off the miss as an innocent mistake. When it happened again and Blake had ended up in the hospital with pneumonia, it took everything she had not to go back to that place and wring somebody's neck.

"So we have to sit here and wait in line even though we aren't going to that stupid place?"

"Don't say 'stupid,' Carson." Britney maneuvered the truck enough to the left so she stayed in her lane but could look around the traffic. There was no way she could drive around with the line of cars spanning twenty deep and visibility of oncoming traffic limited.

"Go around. Go around," the kids chanted in unison.

"Please stop." Her request came out more like a groan. Sitting in traffic for the past thirty minutes had fried what little patience she had left. "I can't go around. It's not safe."

But she could go through the neighborhood, an advantage of living here her entire life. Checking for cars, she veered left.

"Where are we going now?" Molly threw up her hands. "Can't we just go home?"

"I'm taking the back way. And no, we're already in town. I'm not going home and coming back later. Just settle down. We'll be there in a few minutes." More like fifteen, but she wasn't telling them that. Whoever designed this neighborhood knew what they were doing. There were only two ways in and out, a deterrent to keep people from doing exactly what she was doing.

It had been years since she'd driven from one entrance to the other. Many of the houses she'd once used as directional markers had been updated, making it hard for her to remember the turns she needed to take. The neighborhood reminded her of a fall corn maze—one wrong turn and you'd be stuck going in circles for hours.

Molly screamed, not her dramatic scream but a soul-piercing one.

Britney slammed on the brakes and whirled around meeting the faces of three terrified kids. "What happened, Molly? Are you okay?"

Her little body trembled. "I saw a monster."

"What the hell?" Britney threw her head back. "A monster? Are you freaking kidding me?"

"I did, Mommy." Her voice cracked and tears rolled down her cheeks. "I promise."

As dramatic as Molly could be, real tears were never part of the act.

"I'm sorry, sweetie." Britney reached back and squeezed her hand. "Tell me what you saw?"

"I… I…," Molly stammered and then sobbed.

"Boys, did you see anything?"

Both shook their heads.

Britney scanned the surrounding area but saw nothing. "Maybe it wasn't a monster. Maybe just person in a costume."

"A costume?" Tears shone in her big eyes. "A monster costume?"

"Yep. It's gettin' close to Halloween. Someone was probably just trying their costume on."

"And their makeup?"

"Makeup?" Britney forced a smile. "What kind of makeup?"

"The monster had gray skin and blood all over his mouth and chest."

Britney forced a smile, but inside her pulse raced. When she had suggested a costume, she thought more on the lines of a mask, but full-blown makeup?

"Mommy?" Molly pressed. "Do you think it was a monster?"

"No." Britney started back down the road. "There are no such things as monsters. It was probably just someone playin' a trick on their friends."

"There it is!" Carson yelled.

Britney whipped her head to the right and caught a glimpse of something running behind a house.

"Was it a monster?" Blake screamed.

"No. It looked like a person." She pressed on the gas, ready to get the hell out of there. "I saw shoes on his feet."

"Then why are you going so fast?" Carson asked.

Britney took a sharp right. "Because I remembered the way and don't want to forget."

Whether or not they believed her, they didn't say, but by the fear splashed across the twins' faces, she hadn't done enough to convince them that she didn't believe they'd seen a monster.

"So," Britney said as she turned back onto the main road, "what does everyone want from the store?"

No answer, which scared her more than Molly's scream. She checked on them in the rearview mirror. "You guys okay?"

"I want to go home." Molly sniffled. "I'm scared."

The fear in her voice broke Britney's heart. "I know there's a lot of craziness goin' on right now, but there's nothin' to be scared of."

Carson's eyes locked with hers for a brief second. "Then why did they cancel school?"

Britney took a shaky breath. She'd expected the question, but finding the right words to explain the situation without scaring them… she had no clue what to say.

Growing up, her mother always told them the truth, even if that truth wasn't pleasant. She opted for somewhere in between.

"Well, lots of people in town are sick, so to stop them from gettin' everyone else sick, they closed the schools."

"Oh." Carson scrunched his face. "I thought it was because they didn't want anyone else to get hurt?"

Britney slowed the truck. The line to the gas station wasn't nearly as long as the med clinic. She took a second to comprehend what Carson had said. "Hurt? Who got hurt?"

Carson shrugged. "I don't know. A couple of kids in Mr. Sabinal's class had to go to the nurse."

"What did they do? Fall on the playground or somethin'?" Britney tried to sound aloof but heard her voice crack just a little.

"Nah. They were on the playground before school and a kindergartener bit them."

Britney froze. "Bit them? Are you sure?"

Their small school system only had two kindergarten classes. They had placed the twins in the same classroom at Britney's request. One classroom party, field trip, parent-teacher conference was much easier to attend than two.

The truck behind her laid on the horn. Britney startled and pulled up.

"Why are they honking?" Blake asked.

"Because they're impatient." Her gaze flicked back to the kids. "So this kindergartener who bit some kids, was it someone in your class?"

Molly beamed. "Yes! Blake's friend the meanie Ian who always gets sent to the principal."

Britney swallowed hard. "Did you play with him that mornin', Blake? Was he in class … after he bit the other kids?"

"Nope." Carson grinned. "Our bus was late, remember? I saw them taking him to the office when we got there. He was acting all crazy, pretending to be a wolf or something."

"A wolf?" Britney's heart clenched. Blake and Ian were inseparable. If their bus would have been on time yesterday, Blake could have been one of the kids who was bitten.

"Yeah. He kept trying to bite the principal. It was hilarious."

Molly crossed her arms and rolled her eyes. "I didn't think it was very funny."

The line of cars pulled up, putting them in line next for the pump. "Now I see what's takin' so long. The card readers aren't workin'."

"What does that mean?" Carson asked.

Britney grabbed for her wallet to see how much cash she had. "It means everyone is havin' to go inside and pay for their gas." Chances were good if the outside card readers weren't working, the inside one wasn't either.

"Good thing I had to go inside anyway." She pulled a hundred from her wallet. They had farm diesel back home, so she wouldn't worry about filling up the truck, which meant she had plenty of cash to fill up the gas cans. "Speakin' of goin' inside, what does everyone want?"

"Can't we just go in?" Blake did a little bounce in his seat. "That way we can pick."

Britney eyed the line of people waiting to pay. Several of them didn't look well. "No. You guys will stay in the truck."

"Ugh," Molly groaned. "That's boring."

"It'll be more borin' waitin' in that long line." And aggravating for Britney. Three kids in a store full of candy and junk food never ended well. "I'll leave it runnin' so you can listen to music."

"I call Taylor Swift!" Molly shouted before the boys had a chance to speak.

"No," Blake and Carson shouted in unison.

Britney scrolled through her phone's playlists and connected it to Bluetooth. "This will play a variety of music each of you like. The car in front of me is almost done. Tell me what you want."

They each rattled off their favorite Icee, candy and chips.

Britney made a quick note on a scrap of paper and parked the truck next to the pump. "Looks like I have to pay first. Carson, climb in the passenger seat and lock the doors after I get out."

Carson cocked his head. "Lock the doors?"

Living in such a tight-knit community, most people didn't bother locking doors to their vehicles, especially when they'd only be a few feet away.

"Lock the doors and stay in the truck. There are lots of people around here. Most I've never seen before." She didn't want to scare them but didn't want to put them in danger either. "Please listen."

The kids nodded, and Britney got out of the car. Hearing the familiar click of the lock, she headed inside.

The small convenience store had never been so busy. Most of the shelves lay bare, including the chips the kids asked for. She settled for an assortment of cookies and donuts before pouring each of them an Icee. As she headed toward the line, she passed the small wine section and picked out a cheap bottle of white for herself. After the past few days, a tall chilled glass tonight sounded like heaven.

The line to check out stood fifteen people deep. From the end, Britney could keep an eye on the kids, who appeared content jamming out to whatever song was playing.

"Excuse me?" a soft voice said from behind.

Britney peered over her shoulder to find an elderly woman no more than four feet tall standing in line. "Hi."

"Oh, never mind, dear." The woman caught sight of Britney's full arms. "I needed help getting something off a high shelf, but you don't seem to have any free hands."

Britney laughed. "I'm sorry."

"Honey." A woman in front of them tapped her husband. She must have been listening. "Why don't you help the woman? I'll hold our place."

The man turned around, his skin pale and gray. "Of course."

Britney moved out of his way with a forced smile.

"He's such a wonderful guy, my husband," the woman gushed.

"Is he feeling okay?"

The woman blinked before answering. "This damn virus. It's getting the best of everyone."

"I know what…." Britney trailed off as she glanced back out the window. "What are they doin'?"

The woman moved closer to Britney. "Who?"

"My kids. I think they're talkin' to someone."

"That white truck yours? With the three kids? Yeah, there's a man on the driver side. And it looks like the window is rolled down."

Britney’s heart raced. “I told them to stay in the truck with the doors locked.”

“Technically, they seem to be doing both,” the woman said with a chuckle. “Sorry. I’m a teacher, so I know how kids are. I’m sure they’re fine. Probably someone they know. I mean, that’s the good thing about small towns, right?”

Britney shuffled to take a better look. “Yeah, I think you’re right.” She let out a heavy breath. It was just Dr. Hildebrand. “Still, it would have been nice if they would have listened.”

“That’s the way kids are. Give them an inch—oh God.”

“What?” The snacks fell from Britney’s arm, smashing to the ground. “He’s takin’ my truck!”

She bolted from the store, chasing after the truck and screaming, “He’s stealin’ my truck! My kids!”

People stopped and gawked, though a couple of men ran after her. With every step she gained significant ground on the vehicle stuck in traffic trying to exit the parking lot.

The kids' screams could be heard even through the window, their tiny fists pounding on the door, begging to be let out.

Every muscle in her legs burned as she gasped for air, but she kept pushing. A few more feet and she’d be there.

Hildebrand slammed on the gas and the truck jerked forward, pushing the smaller truck in front of him out of the way in a matter of seconds.

“No!”

As he pulled out onto the street, a motorcycle swerved in front of her truck. Hildebrand slammed on the brakes.

The man on the motorcycle dropped his bike and threw open the truck door, pulling Hildebrand to the ground. Then the biker peeked inside the truck. "Are you okay?" she heard him ask the kids.

Britney shoved him out of the way and climbed inside, touching each of her sobbing kids' faces. "It's okay. I'm here. Mommy's here."

"Get out of here," the biker ordered. "Now!"

Britney turned to thank him and gasped. "Axel?"

"Good timing, right?" His eyes fell to the ground. "You need to go home."

"But the police—"

"I'll take care of it." He slammed the truck door. "Go now. This is just the beginning."

"Mommy," Molly sobbed. "I don't want to wait for the police. I want to go home. I want to go home. He tried to bite Carson."

Britney threw the truck in gear and sped away, but not before she heard a gunshot and saw Axel standing over Dr. Hildebrand with a gun.

CHAPTER EIGHT

"Axel." The muffled voice broke through the sound of panic ringing in his ears.

He'd shot someone. In the middle of the street. In small-town America. There were families around. Children watching. What the fuck was he thinking?

The gun slipped from his fingers as his entire body shook. His knees buckled as black spots danced before his eyes.

Years of suppressed memories came flooding back. The horrors he'd seen. The lives lost—ones he'd taken and ones he'd watched slip away.

"Axel." A strong hand seized his arm. "Come on. We have to go."

"Go?" Axel squeezed his lips closed, forcing the bile back down his throat. "I can't go. The police. I need to tell the police what happened."

"You will." Gus tugged on Axel's arm. "But not here."

Axel pulled his arm away. "I can't leave."

"That's not what I'm—"

A low growl cut him off. People screamed.

Axel scanned the area, trying to find the source of the hysteria.

"What the fuck!" Gus yanked Axel backward.

He stared at the ground. Dr. Hildebrand's limbs twitched, the stream of blood from his forehead now black. "What's wrong with him?"

It was a stupid question. Axel had killed him. Pulled out his gun and shot him in the head before he could hurt anyone else, though the poor woman Hildebrand had pounced on after Axel threw him from the truck had a large gash across her face.

"He was dead," Gus whispered. "I watched him take his last breath."

Axel moved closer and nudged Hildebrand's foot with his boot. "Maybe it's just a death spasm?"

"I have a bad feeling about this. We need to get out of here." Angie seized both their arms. "Come on."

Hildebrand's body twitched again and his mouth opened, revealing serrated teeth just like Queenie. The nurse said the patients had died and come back in the form of these monsters, but how the hell did a direct shot to the brain not kill them? *What the fuck is going on?*

"She's right. We need to go." Axel looked at the crowd. "Everyone needs to go!"

"We're not leaving!" a man in a cowboy hat shouted. "And neither are you! The cops are on their way."

Hildebrand lifted his nose to the air. Time was up.

Axel snatched his gun from Gus and pointed it at the crowd of people. "Leave! Now! Before it's too late!"

People screamed and rushed back to their vehicles.

"Jesus, Axel." Gus mounted his bike. "What the fuck are you doing?"

Axel stuffed his gun in the back of jeans—his damn holster had burned with the hospital—and got on his bike. "Trying to save their lives."

Before Gus or any of the other bikers could ask what he meant, the answer presented itself.

Hildebrand jumped to his feet, his skin more ashen than black. A growl ripped from his lips, sending terror pulsating through Axel's veins.

"Go!" Axel sped away. Hildebrand—or whatever the man had become—jerked his head to the sound of engines roaring to life. Vehicles went in every direction, causing the bikes to swerve to avoid being hit.

Axel checked over his shoulder to see where Hildebrand had gone but couldn't find him, which probably wasn't a good thing.

They needed to regroup, find a safe place to get their bearings about the situation and make a plan on how to get home. But first he had to go to the police, explain his side of the story. Someone had called them after he'd shot Hildebrand in the head. More than one person. Why they hadn't shown up yet, he didn't know, but the last thing he needed was to be caught fleeing the scene and looking as if he'd gone on the run.

He moved to the front of the group and motioned for them to pull over in the empty parking lot across from the police station.

Angie removed her helmet and hung it on her handlebars. "For a second there, I thought you were going to do something stupid like turn yourself in."

"I am." Axel averted his eyes. "I killed a guy. Pulled a gun and shot him in the head."

"He was stealing those kids," Shifter said. "Attacked a woman. You did what needed to be done."

"No." Guilt weighted heavily on his chest. "I could have wrestled him to the ground, held him until the police arrived. Hell, I could have shot him in the leg to keep him from running off. But I didn't."

"This is bullshit." Gunner kicked a stray rock. "That was no man you killed—it was a monster. And I can't even say you killed him because he got back up off the fucking ground and growled. Growled! Like a damn animal. We need to get as far away from this place as possible. Leave and never look back."

"You should all go. If this is happening all over the country, you need to be with your families."

"Axel." Gus moved to his side. "You know I would never advise you to do something against the law, but this… what's happening… it's not normal. And the witnesses, all they'll be able to tell the police is a tatted-up biker did this."

"The woman knows me."

"Woman?" Gus asked. "What woman?"

"The kids' mom, the truck owner. Her name's Britney. She's a local. She's the one we helped with the booths for the church festival."

"Shit," Gunner grumbled. "So she can identify you?"

He didn't care if she could or not—either way, he was turning himself in—but if it helped them accept his decision…. "Yes. She said my name when I removed the doctor from the truck." He held up his hand before anyone else could argue. "I know none of you agree, but who would I be if I walked away? He has a family that will want to know what happened to him. Plus, he was a really nice guy."

"You've met him before?" Rainey asked.

"In the hospital. He was a doctor and his father a patient in Queenie's room. What happened to him… it happened because he gave his life trying to save people. It's not his fault."

"It's not your fault either." Gus patted him on the shoulder. "But if this is what you feel is right, know you have my full support."

The others nodded in agreement.

"Thank you." Their understanding made him feel a little better.

"But remember, you were trying to—no, you *did* save lives. You shouldn't be punished for that," Gus said.

Axel mounted his bike and started the engine. "I'll call when I can. Head home. Be with your families."

He didn't wait for a response before speeding off across the street and parking in front of the police station. With a quick wave goodbye, he went inside, ready to get this over with.

A plump receptionist glared when he entered, purse on her shoulder and a sour look on her face. "What do you need?"

Axel started through the glass door leading toward the back, surprised the place wasn't busier. "I need to speak with an officer."

"Why?" the receptionist—Betty, according to her nameplate—snapped.

"Um. I want to report a crime."

Betty planted a hand on her full hips. "Have you been outside? This entire town has turned into one big crime scene."

"A murder." Axel cleared his throat. "I need to speak to someone about a murder."

Betty took a step back. "And who did the murdering?"

"I did." Then he quickly added, "Self-defense. A man tried to drive off with a stolen truck. The woman's three kids were still in the back."

Betty smacked on her gum. "Sheriff's in the back. The other three officers who work here have been called out, so the sheriff's in no sort of mood for games. Phones have been ringing off the hook. Now I'm having to leave because my mama's sick."

"I understand."

Betty removed her jacket from the back of her office chair and slung it over her arm. "What kind of man turns himself in for committing a murder when the world is ending?"

The question caught Axel off guard. "I didn't realize this was the end. Plus, it's the right thing to do."

"You said this man tried to kidnap three kids?"

Axel's eyes locked on hers. "Yes, in the gas station parking lot."

Betty slipped her hand under the desk and the door buzzed. "I'm not saying you have to go through, or that I think you should…."

Axel reached for the handle and yanked the door open. "I hope your mother feels better."

"Thank you." She shuffled toward the door. "First door on the left. You can't miss it."

"Be careful out there." Axel let the door slam behind him. "Hello?" he called out.

This had to be the smallest police office he'd ever seen. To the right, three desks were in the center of the room, each empty except for a computer and a ringing phone.

The back wall had two doors, one a bathroom and must lead to the jail. On the left was a single office, the door closed and shades pulled down.

Axel knocked, and when the sheriff didn't respond, he cracked open the door.

A gray-haired man sat at his desk, headphones on, staring at a silent TV.

Axel waved, catching the man's attention.

He removed his headphones and turned off the TV. "What the hell are you doing back here?"

Axel hooked his thumb toward the entrance. "Betty let me in."

He narrowed his eyes. "Betty's gone."

"Just left. Said her mother was sick." When he didn't respond, Axel continued. "I'm Axel, and I'm here to turn myself in. You must be Sheriff...."

"Cornhill." He leaned back in his chair. "Turn yourself in for what, son?"

Axel sucked in air through his nose. "I killed a man, sir. Dr. James Hildebrand, I believe was his name."

"And you killed him? With what?"

Axel raised both hands in front of him and slowly turned around. "The gun I have in the back of my jeans."

"Hands on your head," Cornhill ordered, his boots slapping against the tile floor. "Don't move. I'm going to seize the gun. Do you have a wallet?"

"Back pocket."

Cornhill removed his gun and wallet. "Any other weapons I should know about?"

"No, sir."

"Have a seat." Cornhill paused. "Wait. Before you sit, close the door. That damn ringing is driving me insane."

"Shouldn't you be answering the calls? There's a lot of crazy shit going on outside." Axel took a seat across from the sheriff. "How do you want to do this?"

Cornhill leaned back in his chair. "By this, do you mean your confession?"

"Yes." Axel had a sneaking suspicion this man had no intention of taking him seriously. "I can write it down if you'd like."

"Here's the thing"—Cornhill pulled out a bottle of whiskey from his bottom drawer and poured a glass—"I can't figure out. Why would you, a proclaimed murderer, come here and confess when you could have left? No one would have been the wiser."

"I would have."

Cornhill laughed. "A guilty conscience versus life in prison. Seems like a no-brainer."

Axel didn't like the sheriff's condescending tone. "I said I killed someone, not murdered."

"What's the difference?" Cornhill gulped down his whiskey. "You took a life."

"And I saved several others." Axel leaned closer. "Do you know what's happening outside these walls? What's happening to the victims of this so-called virus?"

"It does something to their mind. Causes delusions. Violent outbursts."

Axel dropped his head. He couldn't believe what he was about to say next. "At first, yes, but the virus… it's killing people. Changing them into—"

"Into what?" Cornhill poured himself another drink.

"Monsters." The word rolled off his tongue easier than Axel ever expected it to.

Cornhill laughed. "Monsters? You're fucking nuts. Is that why you're here? Knew if you turned yourself in with this ridiculous notion, you'd get off by pleading insanity?"

Axel slammed his fist on the desk. "Dr. Hildebrand stole a truck with three kids inside. After I pulled him from the truck, he jumped on a lady and nearly ripped her arm off with his teeth. So I put a bullet in his head. A few minutes later, he was back on his feet, the bullet wound healing at an impossible pace."

"Get up." Cornhill rose to his feet. "You're under arrest for the murder of Dr. James Hildebrand."

Axel didn't resist. "I would like to speak to a lawyer."

"You don't have much experience with this sort of thing, do you?" Cornhill rounded the desk. "Most ask to speak with a lawyer before they confess."

"Does that change anything?"

Cornhill led him out of the office and toward the back. "I'll have to lock you up. Not sure when the judge will be able to set your bail."

"And a lawyer?"

Cornhill stopped at the first cell. "I'll make a few calls, see who I can get a hold of. As for now, you just need to sit tight."

Axel stared at the only other prisoner being housed. "He looks sick."

"He's drunk."

Axel backed away from the cell. "I'm not staying in there with him. Look at his skin. The color's off."

"Still sticking with this story, huh?"

Axel whipped his head around as anger boiled from within. "It's not a story. This is how it starts. I'll bet everything I have that someone—a very sick someone—bit him."

Cornhill's face dropped. "How did you know that?"

All the pieces were falling in place. "It's how the virus spreads. After being bitten, they start displaying symptoms of their own. Become violent. Their skin turns gray. Mark my words, this man will die. And when he does, I don't want to be in the same fucking cell with the thing he comes back as."

Cornhill stayed quiet for a moment, probably thinking about the next course of action. "My first instinct is to lock you in the cell with this man just to prove to you how crazy your theory really is."

Axel's heart thrashed in his chest. He'd run before he allowed that to happened.

"But," Cornhill continued, "the state is always on my ass about being more sensitive to the needs of our prisoners. Last thing I need is some PC lawyer in here lecturing me about following protocol and shit." He unlocked the next cell. "In you go."

"Thank you." Axel entered the small space.

Cornhill turned the lock. "Never thought I'd see the day when a man thanked me for locking him up."

"Yeah, well"—Axel took a seat on the squeaky bed—"never thought I'd see the day when a dead man came back to life."

CHAPTER NINE

Britney sped down the old winding road faster than she'd ever driven before.

Molly and Blake sobbed quietly in the back, but it was Carson's reaction that concerned her the most. His blank face focused out the window, watching the world fly by, scared her more than the other two's crying.

"Carson? You doin' okay, honey?"

His head bobbed, but he didn't reply.

"Do you want to talk about it?" Not that she wanted to talk about it—she never wanted to think about the awful incident again—but if they needed to….

"I don't understand, Mommy." Molly sniffled. "Dr. Hildebrand, he was a nice man. Why would he hurt Carson?"

"Hurt Carson? What do you mean?" Her eyes flicked to the rearview mirror. "Are you hurt?"

Carson lifted a trembling arm, revealing bloody marks.

Britney swerved off the road and slammed on her brakes. "Come here! Let me see your arm."

"It's fine, Mom." Carson didn't move.

Britney threw off her seat belt and climbed in the back grabbing his arm. “Did he bite you?”

“What?” Carson yanked back his arm. “Why would he bite me?”

“Then how did you get these marks?” Britney tried to keep her voice calm, but inside she was shaking.

“He scratched me with his creepy long nails.”

Britney’s heart sank. She didn’t know what to do or if the virus spread through a scratch. “You might need to see a doctor.”

“No.” Carson went back to staring at the window. “I just want to go home.”

“Me too, Mommy.” Molly reached for her hand.

Blake dropped his head in his hands and continued to cry. “I want to go home too.”

They had been through such trauma, and the last thing she wanted to do was add any more. “Okay. We’ll go home. But, Carson, we are goin’ to get you cleaned up, and if I even think you look a little sick, it’s straight to the doctor.”

“Whatever.” He leaned his head against the window. “Can we just go?”

“Sure.” Britney climbed into the front seat and merged back onto the road. “We should do something fun later. How does homemade pizza and game night sound? Buy a new movie? We’ll pop some popcorn. Sound like fun?”

They didn’t answer, their silence breaking her heart even more. Movie-game night was their favorite.

She pulled up to their locked gate and parked. “Carson? Can you open the gate?”

His eyes widened. “I don’t want to.”

Any other time he refused to open the gate, she would have gotten pissed and ordered him out of the truck. This time was different; the fear in his eyes told her not to press. “Never mind, honey. I’ll get the gate.”

Carson sniffled a quiet “Thanks.”

Britney quickly unlocked and drove through the gate, checking the lock twice before heading toward the house.

“Anyone hungry for lunch?” She parked the truck in front of the house and turned off the engine, leaving the keys in the ignition. “I can make grilled cheese or mac and cheese or whatever you feel like.”

“I’m not hungry.” Carson unbuckled his seat belt. “Can I play on my tablet?”

“Yes.” She eyed her three children. “In your room. Take the twins with you, please. I need to check on Dad, and then I’ll come in with the first aid kit and get your arm cleaned up.”

The kids left the truck without arguing, which was unusual. Carson usually put up a fight when told to play with the twins. Most of the time he and Blake got along okay, but both at one time didn’t go over so well.

She lumbered out of the truck and into the quiet house. Setting her things on the table, she headed up the stairs and peeked into their dark room. “John?”

When he didn’t answer, she flipped on the light and found the bed empty, the bathroom too.

“Let’s play with our tablets in the tree house,” Carson yelled out as three sets of footsteps pounded the stairs.

For a heartbeat she considered calling out to them and ordering them back into the bedroom. There she knew they’d be safe, close. But outside….

She forced the thoughts away, not wanting to get caught up in her usual paranoid thinking. Her main concern at the moment needed to be hunting down John and forcing him back to bed. The last thing they needed was for John to have a violent outburst in front of the kids. They'd been through enough for one day.

"John?" Britney called out, her voice echoing through the house. "Honey?"

Out of nowhere, a terrifying scream ripped through the silence.

Britney burst through her closet door without thinking. A mother knew the types of screams that came from her children, and whatever had caused Molly's had scared her to her core. She pressed her hand on the gun safe's scanner, the lock clicking with recognition. She grabbed the shotgun they kept loaded, then bolted down the stairs and out the door.

"What's wrong?" she shouted up at the kids in the treehouse, gun ready.

"There." Carson pointed toward the barn. "We saw something."

Her shoulders slumped. "Like an animal? A snake?"

Molly peeked over the side railing. "A monster."

Britney cocked her head and stared off in the direction of the barn. "A monster? Are you sure it wasn't your dad walkin' around? He's not in the house."

"It had claws and sharp teeth."

The hairs on Britney's arm stood up. "Stay up there. I'll go check it out."

"No, Mommy!" Molly pleaded. "Don't go."

Britney showed her the gun. "It's okay. I have protection. Just stay here until I get back."

She jogged toward the barn, making sure her feet slapped the ground. If there *was* something out there and she made enough noise, hopefully it would scare whatever it was away. Or alert her husband—though he should have come when Molly screamed.

She went barn by barn, shed by shed, checking each of them for the monster the kids swore they saw. By the time she finished, sweat dripped from her brow, and she was convinced the monster the kids saw was nothing more than a figment of their overactive imaginations. After the morning they had, who could blame them? She couldn't go a couple of seconds without thinking about what could have happened if Axel hadn't shown up.

Pulling her phone from her pocket, she dialed John's cell. He must have felt better and gone out to work on something. Idiot. At least he could have called and let her know.

The line rang a couple of times, and in the distance, she could hear the faint sound of his ringer coming from the front of the house.

She made her way toward the sound, ready to put this whole ordeal behind them. What she wouldn't give to have his arms wrapped around her as she sobbed about the horrors of the day.

She spotted him squatting in the small pasture to the right of the house they used for animals that needed to be keep separated from the others for various reasons. From this distance she couldn't tell what he was doing—the position was a difficult one to get up from considering his size.

"John?" The closer she got to the open fence, the better she could see just how bad her husband looked. "You need to get back inside and in bed. Did you even look in the mirror before you came out here?"

John flinched at the sound of her voice and hunched his shoulders, digging his fingers into the ground.

A chill ran down Britney's spine at the strange reaction. Even on his worst days, she'd never seen him act so hostile.

"Honey?" Britney kept her distance, remembering how violent John said Thomas had become. "Go back inside. I'll finish up out here."

"Mommy!" Molly shouted from the tree house. "Look what we're making."

Britney snapped her head toward the sound of Molly's voice. "That's awesome. Why don't you come down—"

A menacing growl cut her off. Britney whipped her head around and screamed at the creature dressed in John's clothes.

Its bald head and serrated teeth dripping with blood. The overall body shape was John's, but there was nothing else connecting him to what stood ten feet away. With gray skin and solid black eyes, he looked like… a monster.

She rotated her head so she could check the tree house and still keep an eye on the creature, which had returned to the dead calf it was eating.

Her gut told her she needed to run, get as far away from this thing as possible, but her heart held her in place.

Whatever had caused her husband to transform into this, he was still her husband, and she longed to help him however she could.

As long as her children weren't in any immediate danger.

People didn't just turn into monsters. If she could get him someplace secure and call the doctor, maybe wait until they found a cure….

"Mommy!" Molly yelled. "I'm hungry."

Britney turned around and found Molly making her way down the stairs. "Wait! Stay there. I'll bring—"

John—the creature—sprinted past her at speeds her eyes could only make out as a blur of gray flesh.

"Back up!" Britney shouted as she darted after John. "Stay up there!"

Molly started climbing back up, but her little foot slipped on the makeshift ladder. “Mommy, help!”

Britney couldn’t get there fast enough. John had already reached the bottom of the tree, jumping and clawing in the direction of Molly’s screams.

“I got you.” Carson reached through the door and grabbed his sister’s hand, pulling her through the hole in the floor.

“Close it!” Britney ordered, gun pointed at John.

“Mommy!” Blake sobbed.

“It’s okay, honey.” Britney aimed the gun at what used to be her husband. “Get away from the kids.”

If he recognized her voice, it didn’t show. Clawing at the bottom of the tree, he acted more like a rabid animal than a person.

She didn’t know what to do. The kids couldn’t stay up there forever; she feared he’d eventually figure out the ladder. She needed to get him away from the kids and find somewhere to keep him locked up. In a barn, maybe.

“John!” she shouted.

He jerked his head and then whirled around. Britney froze as his eyes locked on to her, but he didn’t move. Instead he jutted his chin and sniffed the air. He must have caught on to her scent; crouching down, he let out a horrendous growl and charged in her direction.

Britney took off running toward the barns. The kids cried out for her, but she didn’t dare look back. She could hear he was following her. That was all that mattered.

Bursting through the doors of the hay barn, she darted up the ladder to the top rafters. John entered a second later, pausing in the middle of the barn, sniffing the air and locking on to her scent.

Another growl left his lips as he ran into a post trying to find a way up. The rafters shook, and Britney crawled along the wall, trying to see if she could get back down without being noticed. Then she could lock him inside.

Britney froze, suddenly aware of how quiet the barn had grown. Popping up, she leaned over the edge, afraid he'd left in search of more active prey.

Her gaze darted around the room. *Where the hell did he go?*

She opened her mouth to call out his name when the now familiar growl came from behind her.

Britney whirled around. John stood not five feet away, baring teeth that resembled fangs.

"Please stop." She took a step back, her heel brushing the edge of the rafter. "John, if you're in there, it's me, Britney. Your wife."

He moved closer, shoulders hunched and black goo dripping from his teeth. If he hadn't been wearing John's clothes, she would have never guessed it was him.

"Please." She held up the gun in another desperate attempt to stop his attack. If he hurt her… killed her… she couldn't bear the thought of leaving her children alone. "I don't want to hurt you."

He lunged.

Britney lost her footing and toppled over the edge, landing with a thud on the thin pile of hay. Air whooshed from her lungs as the room blurred.

The gun had slipped from her hands and landed a good twenty feet away.

She struggled to her feet and then spun in a circle, looking for her attacker.

Had he gone over the edge? Was he hiding in the shadows, waiting to pounce?

She wouldn't stick around to find out. She sprinted toward the gun but wasn't fast enough, letting out a piercing scream as sharp claws dug into her ankle, yanking her to the ground.

Britney rolled to her back and kicked her heel into the face of the monster, who snapped his teeth. The shock of the impact caused him to release her ankle.

She scurried on her hands and knees, grabbed the gun and aimed it at her attacker. Done with warnings, she pulled the trigger, hitting him square in the shoulder. A black inky substance oozed from the wound.

The monster howled but barely slowed down.

Britney fired again, shattering his kneecap. That time he slowed as more of the black substance leaked down his leg.

Britney took a few quick breaths, hoping the two bullet wounds had been enough to drop him.

Back on her feet, she hurried for the door. As she passed, the monster snapped his head up and reached for her legs with the arm she'd shot.

"No." She gaped at the healing wound. Seconds. That was all it had taken for him to regain the use of his arm.

The monster rose to his feet and hissed.

Without thinking, Britney aimed at his chest and fired.

Black oozed from the wound as he fell to the ground.

Britney didn't wait to find out if that shot had done the trick. She sprinted out the door and threw the lock.

Leaning against the old barn door, she slid to the ground and sobbed.

Her husband, the love her life, had tried to kill her and their children, and she had shot him in the heart.

***

Britney regained her composure and peeked back into the barn. John—or whatever he had become—still lay motionless in the middle of the barn floor, the black liquid pooling around his abdomen.

She slammed the door closed and snapped the padlock. She didn't want the kids wandering inside and finding their father this way. His death would be hard enough. And by her hands….

She shuddered and sprinted toward the tree house desperate to check on her kids.

"Hello? Molly, Blake, Carson?" She paused at the bottom of the tree house ladder. "Are you up there?" As hard as she tried to keep her voice steady, it trembled as she spoke. "You're safe now. Come down. Please."

The floor door opened, and Carson stuck his head through. "Was that Dad?"

"Come inside. Bring the twins." Tears clogged her throat. "We need to talk. And we need to clean your arm still."

Carson's eyes swept the area. "How do we know there aren't more of them?"

Britney forced a smile. "It's just us."

"Where's Daddy?" Molly pushed Carson aside, her little cheeks red and eyes puffy. "I want my Daddy!"

"Come on." Britney waved them down.

Molly shook her head. "There's a monster."

"Not anymore, baby. Not anymore." She couldn't hold back her tears. "Come on. We need to go inside. Where's Blake?"

"Right here." Blake started down the ladder but paused halfway. "You won't leave again, right?"

His words shattered her already broken heart. "I'm so sorry." She helped him down and pulled him into a tight hug.

Molly came down next, followed by Carson. With each of them as close as they could get to her and still walk, she ushered them inside and onto the couch. "I have to make a few phone calls and then we'll talk, okay?"

Carson dropped his head and sniffled. As the oldest, he always tried to put on a brave face for his younger siblings, even though he was just a kid himself. "We heard the gunshots."

Britney swallowed hard. "Yes."

"That thing." Carson's eyes locked with hers. "Was that Dad?"

It took every ounce of strength she had left just to nod. Hot tears rolled down her cheeks. "I'm so sorry."

Molly eyes widened. "You shot Daddy?"

Britney threw her hand over her mouth, ready to break. "I… he tried… I have to make a phone call."

Rushing to the kitchen, she grabbed the landline phone, not sure where she left her cell. She found Sheriff Cornhill's business card hanging on the corkboard and dialed his number.

It rang half a dozen times before he picked up. "Cornhill here."

"Hi. It's Britney Campbell, John's wife." She didn't know the man well, but John had played on a couple of bowling leagues with him.

"Yes, ma'am. How can I help you?"

With her bottom lip between her teeth, she tried to hold back the tears. Her voice shook when she finally got the nerve to speak, "It's John. I… I…."

"Is he okay?" The sheriff spoke with a cautious edge.

"No." Britney peeked around the corner to check on the kids, who were huddled together on the couch watching TV. "I shot him."

The line fell so silent she thought they might have been disconnected.

"Sheriff?"

"I'm here."

Her voice quivered. "Did you hear what I said?"

"You shot your husband. He dead?"

Britney bobbed her head as if he could see her through the line.

"Mrs. Campbell? Is he dead?"

"Yes." The word came out as a rushed whisper. "He attacked me. Threatened my children. I had no choice."

"This behavior normal for him?"

"Behavior?" Britney couldn't believe he would ask her such a thing. "You knew John. He was a kind man and a loving husband and father, but he got sick. And it changed him."

"Changed him how?"

Britney bit back the bile burning her throat. "I don't know how to explain. You'll have to see for yourself. There's no way to describe it over the phone."

"Where is the body, ma'am? Have you moved him?"

"I left him locked in the barn."

The sheriff clicked his tongue. "That necessary?"

"I didn't want to take a chance." She left it at that. It would be better to tell him—show him—in person. "Can you come over? I don't know what to with his… his body."

"I'll come straight over. Do you have someone to take the kids for a few days?"

"What? Why? I did nothin' wrong." She'd called for help, not to be arrested for a crime.

"You just confessed to killing your husband."

Britney ground her teeth. "To protect myself and my children. You'll see when you get here."

"Ma'am, self-defense or not, I'll still have to take your statement here, at the station."

"Fine. I'll call my in-laws. Can you please hurry? I don't want my children seein' their father this way. Not after…."

"I'll be on the road in five."

"Thank you." Britney hung up the phone and quickly dialed her in-laws. The phone rang until the voice mail picked up. She hung up; this wasn't the kind of news to leave in a message.

Putting the handset down, she turned to go back into the living room.

"Jesus." She jumped back, grasping her chest. "Molly, sweetie. I didn't hear you come."

"Mommy." She stuck her arms in the air. "Can you hold me?"

Britney lifted her off the ground and held her tight, not able to remember the last time Molly wanted to be picked up. "Let's go back into the livin' room. Carson, can you please turn off the TV? We need to have a little family meetin'."

"How can we have a family meeting without Dad?" Blake scooted over to give Britney and Molly room to sit.

Tears stung her eyes. There was no way she was getting through this without breaking down. "It's about Daddy."

"Is he going to be okay?" Molly blinked through tears. "Can't we take him to the hospital?"

Britney brushed the fallen strands of hair from her daughter's face. "There's nothin' the hospital could do for him. He… he got sick. Very sick. And somethin' happened to him. He changed."

"He looked like a monster." Blake moved closer to her side.

As much as she wanted to argue, ‘monster’ was what she had thought when John—what was left of him—first faced her.

“Did he turn into a monster, Mommy?” Molly sniffled.

“I….” Tears clogged her throat. “I’m not sure what happened to him. He was sick. Lots of people in town have been sick.”

“Wait.” Carson shot up. “There are more people like Dad?”

“What if they come here?” Blake shrieked.

Britney’s heart pounded in her ears. Their fears pulsated through her veins.

Lie, the protective voice in her head pleaded. But what good would that do? If there were others out there like John, they all needed to be prepared.

Jumping off the couch, she bolted to the front door and locked it. “I need to check the back door and the windows. Just in case.”

“What? Why?” Molly grabbed a blanket from the back of the couch and buried under it up to her neck. “Does that mean there are more monsters outside?”

“I don’t know.” Britney peered out as she checked the living room window. “Maybe Daddy was the only one who acted that way when he got sick, but I’m not sure. Dr. Hildebrand was actin’ weird too.”

Pain etched on each of their faces at the mention of his name.

She dropped to her knees in front of them. “I’m so sorry. I can’t… I tried to stop him. He was going to ki—”

“You don’t know that!” Carson jumped to his feet. “You could have knocked him out. But you shot him! You killed our dad!”

"Wait! Your scratch!"

Carson ignored her as he ran up the stairs and slammed his bedroom door.

Britney's body shook, knowing all too well the pain of losing a parent at such a young age.

"I'm going upstairs." Molly put on her best angry face, but in her eyes there was so much pain that Britney's stomach turned.

"Me too," Blake said with a sadness that tore her in two. Out of the three, he was the worst at masking his feelings.

Britney sucked in a sharp breath. "Okay. I'll call you when it's time to eat."

They lumbered up the stairs and closed their doors, leaving her alone.

The weight of the day pulled her to the floor, and for a second she considered allowing herself to break.

Instead, she forced herself to her feet. Grief would have to wait. What happened to Thomas, to John, to the hospital—it couldn't be a coincidence.

There was something terrible lurking in the shadows, and she had to find a way to protect her children. No matter the cost.

CHAPTER TEN

"Lunch." The sound of Cornhill's voice startled Axel awake.

He sat up on the squeaky cot they called a bed and stretched his achy muscles. His caught sight of the metal tray Cornhill had left on the small open slot of the door. He crossed the cell and grabbed the sandwich, the bread crumbled in his hand. "You call this food?"

"It's the best we got." The sheriff tapped the first cell with his nightstick. "Rise and shine."

Axel stuck a piece of stale bread in his mouth. "How long has he been out? I mean, before I got here."

Cornhill shrugged. "I've been a little preoccupied. A drunk sleeping isn't top on the list."

"You sure he's just drunk?" Axel leaned against the bars separating the two cells.

"Like I said, I got better things to concern myself with."

"How are things out there?"

"The world's gone to shit." Cornhill removed his cowboy hat and wiped his brow. "I got to go take care of some business. Ugly, ugly business."

The way he spoke, his words drawn out and full of sorrow, caught Axel off guard. "What happened?"

Cornhill straightened his shoulders and stuck his hat back on his head. "Nothing that concerns you. I'll be back in time for dinner."

"Wait!" Axel called out as Cornhill turned for the door. "What about my lawyer?"

"Lawyer?" The sheriff shook his head. "The damn lawyer can't be bothered to return my calls."

"Isn't there someone else you can call? What about the judge? Isn't he the one who'll set bail?"

Cornhill rotated around. "You sure know a lot about this. You been in trouble before, son?"

Axel stooped his shoulders and covered his face with his hands, frustrated with the lack of answers. "No, sir. But I know my rights."

"Well, we only got the one lawyer, and the county judge won't set bail until he hears from the lawyer."

Axel shoved his hands through his hair. "Son of a bitch."

"There's no need for language. You're the one who murdered a man and turned yourself in."

Axel cocked an eyebrow. "Sounds like you're saying I should have gotten the hell out of Dodge. Left the man's family wondering what happened."

"What I'm saying is to be patient. There's a lot of crazy shit going on right now. We should expect a certain level of delay."

"Fine." Axel leaned his head against the wall behind him. "Can I at least make a phone call?"

"Sure, kid." The sheriff opened the door to leave. "When I get back."

The door slammed behind him with a clang. The unconscious man in the cell next to him stirred. Axel watched as the man writhed around, moaning a slew of strange noises.

"Sir, are you okay?" Axel moved to get a better look. He hadn't really paid much attention to the man, hadn't noticed how gray his exposed skin had grown.

"Shit." Axel quietly backed away, trying not to draw any unwanted attention to himself. He needed to get the sheriff back in here if he hadn't already left.

Scanning the small room, he spotted a camera in the corner and waved at it, hoping the thing was on and being monitored.

Minutes ticked by as Axel continued to signal the sheriff, all the while keeping a close eye on the other cell.

The man had fallen so still that Axel wasn't sure he was even breathing. He didn't know if that was a good thing or not, but he really didn't want to stick around to find out.

A good five minutes passed before the door swung open and Cornhill burst through the door. "What the hell is going on in here? You look like a damn bird waving your arms around like that. I told you I was about to head out."

Axel pointed to the motionless man in the cell next to him. "Something's wrong with him. Do you see his skin, how gray it is? That's what happens to the people who are sick, before they become violent."

Cornhill moved closer to the first cell and peered inside. "Shit! I don't think he's breathing." He fumbled with his keys and unlocked the cell.

"Wait!" Axel sprinted to his door. "You can't go in there."

Anger spread across Cornhill's face. "What the hell is the matter with you? The man needs medical attention if it's not already too late."

"You don't understand." Axel moved alongside the sheriff as he rushed to the man while calling for an ambulance on his shoulder radio. "If died and comes back to life—"

"What are you talking about?" Cornhill kneeled beside the other prisoner and pressed two fingers against his neck. "No pulse. I'm going to start CPR."

Axel watched in horror as hair fell from the man's head with each chest compression, leaving behind a gray scalp with inky black streaks. "I think you need to get out of there, Sheriff."

"Shut the fuck up." He continued the chest compressions. "The ambulance will be here any minute."

The man's fingers twitched, his long nails reminding Axel of something out of a monster movie. "Seriously, Sheriff, you need to get the hell out of there and lock him inside."

Cornhill snapped his head in Axel's direction. "I told you to shut the fu—"

A menacing growl cut him off.

"Get out of there now!" Axel screamed, but it was too late.

The man—if Axel could even call him that—sprang from the bed and pounced on Cornhill, knocking him on his back.

Axel banged against the bars, trying to get the monster's attention and buy the sheriff time to retrieve his gun, but it was too late.

The monster overpowered Cornhill in a matter of seconds and sank its teeth into the sheriff's throat, ripping it open with a single jerk of its head.

"No!" Axel screamed, stumbling backward.

Blood gushed from the massive wound, Cornhill's dead eyes locked in terror.

The infected lapped up the pooled blood from the floor before turning its attention to Axel's cell.

He couldn't be sure, but the creature didn't seem to be able to see him.

With its nose in the air, it sniffed and sprinted in Axel's direction running straight into the bars. A fierce growl escaped its lips as it staggered backwards. A thin line of black goo seeped from the wound on its head before healing in a matter of seconds.

Axel sucked in a sharp breath. His surveyed the sheriff's body, the wound on his throat significantly smaller.

Fear ran through his blood like ice. He was in some serious shit here.

The infected growled and eased back toward the bars, wrapping each of its gray hands around a pole. The movies depicted the undead as mindless creatures, but this thing just proved that wasn't their reality.

The simple action had scared the shit out of Axel more than any horror movie he had ever seen in his life.

Sniffing the air, the infected let out another growl, then swiped its sharp claws between the bars in Axel's direction.

Axel scooted toward the bed and hid underneath, hoping the old, musty sheets would mask his smell.

The infected lumbered along, making its way out of the cell and around the room. It was like it could sense its prey lingered close by.

***

Axel's eyes grew heavy with sleep, but he didn't dare give in to the exhaustion. In the hours since the infected had killed Cornhill, it had been roaming the jail room. Every time Axel shifted, it would cock its nose in the air and growl like it was trying to figure out his location.

And the bastard was strong. Twice it had bent the bars enough that it could stick its head between them. Axel feared if it pinpointed his location, it wouldn't stop until it made its way into his cell. Then he'd be screwed.

His eyes drooped again, and he rubbed them in a poor attempt to keep himself awake. Lack of food, water and sleep had sucked the energy right out of him. He didn't know how much longer he could hold sleep at bay.

A muffled shout snapped him awake. If the infected hadn't jerked its head toward the door, he might have thought it was a dream. But it too had heard the sound and was trying to figure out where it came from.

If someone was out there, Axel needed to signal them like he did the sheriff. Which hadn't ended well, but could have if the man would have listened. There wasn't anything he could do about that now, but he could try to save whoever was out there. Maybe if he did, that person would get him the hell out.

Axel crept out from under the bed, careful not to make a sound. If the infected really couldn't see—which seemed to be the case—then he didn't want to draw any attention to himself.

Positioning himself in the middle of the room, he waved his hands around again as he did to get the sheriff's attention. The problem was he didn't know how to convey to whoever was out there that they couldn't just come barreling in.

Which was exactly what the deputy did.

The door flew open, but before Axel could warn him, the infected bolted across the room faster than anything Axel had ever seen.

The deputy didn't even have a chance to pull his gun from its holster before the infected sank its teeth into his neck.

That time the bite was more methodical, more precise, like the infected had learned to control its hunger or whatever it was that drove it to attack.

Axel didn't hesitate, diving back under the bed while the infected was occupied. Nothing could be done for the deputy now.

The attack lasted less than a minute, leaving the dead deputy lying in the doorway, his lifeless body propping open the door.

The infected didn't hesitate or look back before exiting the room, leaving Axel alone with two dead officers and no way out.

He only thought he was screwed before. He couldn't remember how many officers the department had, though it probably wasn't many. Two of them lay dead in this room. There might be a few who'd stop by the office to check in. Or he could get lucky and the secretary might come back. Neither sounded likely. He'd have better odds digging his way out with a plastic spoon if past luck was any indication.

His gaze drifted to the dead sheriff, the wound on his neck nearly healed.

A set of keys hung off his belt—Axel's last hope of freedom. Axel couldn't be sure, not knowing enough about the infected, but he feared as soon as the sheriff was completely healed, he'd wake up as the same kind of monster that took his life.

Axel would need to work fast. Not only would he have to keep a close eye on the sheriff but the deputy too. The infected didn't do near the damage to him as it did on the sheriff. Chances were good he'd wake up soon, and then it wouldn't matter whether or not Axel had the keys.

Slipping out from under the bed, Axel crawled toward the cells' shared bars. He stretched his arm between the bars and grabbed hold of the sheriff's boot. He gave the stiff leg a quick tug and inched the body closer. Bastard was heavier than he looked.

Axel yanked on the leg again and the hand twitched. He froze and held his breath, watching to see if he could spot any other signs that the sheriff had reanimated.

Seconds ticked by and the sheriff's body remained still.

It was possible Axel had imagined the hand twitch or caused the motion when he moved the body. Either way, it reminded him that he needed to keep a close eye not only on the infected in front of him but the one at the door who no longer sported any signs of trauma. Axel yanked on the leg again, his shoulder screaming in pain. He didn't care what sort of damage he inflicted; all that mattered was getting the keys and getting out before—

Axel snapped his head toward the door. He could have sworn he heard a noise, a movement, clothes dragging against the floor or a slight shift. The deputy still lay motionless, but that didn't mean he hadn't made the sound. For all Axel knew, the reanimation process happened in stages.

He needed to get the keys and get the hell out of there before he was trapped in the room with two infected.

Turning back to the sheriff, Axel gave him another tug, his shoulder through the bars as he reached for the keys. His fingertips brushed against the metal. So close, yet het still couldn't wrap his hand around them. Just a little farther and he'd have them.

He leaned back to pull his arm in so he could rotate his shoulder before trying again when he realized he couldn't.

"No, no, no!" He heaved himself back only to be held in place by his stuck shoulder blade. "Come on. Son of a bitch."

Movement out of the corner of his eye caught his attention. Axel froze and watched the sheriff's entire body twitch.

He was fucked if he couldn't get his arm free. Probably fucked either way, but he refused to go down like this, without a fight.

The former sheriff, now one of the infected, let out a ferocious growl.

Axel planted his feet on the bars and grabbed one with his free hand, hoping the extra leverage would be enough.

Another hard thrust backward and his shoulder budged. Just an inch, but better than nothing.

The infected rose to its feet and stuck its nose in the air. It had Axel's scent in a heartbeat and turned to face him.

Razor-sharp teeth dripped with a black goo-like substance. With every step it took, hair fell from its head until it was bald.

Why it hadn't lunged, Axel didn't know, but he was grateful for the extra seconds.

He almost had his shoulder through; just one more hard yank and he'd be free.

The infected paused and sniffed the air. It couldn't see—he was sure of that now—but its nose and ears were exceptional.

Axel held his bottom lip between his teeth and forced himself silent.

The infected crouched like a predator ready to attack its prey.

He was out of time.

It lunged forward. Axel whipped his arm up and out of the way and kicked it in the face, careful not to stick his leg too far between the bars.

The infected released the most high-pitched shriek he'd ever heard, then shook its head and prepared to attack again.

Axel sucked in a breath and threw his entire body weight backward just as the infected jumped, teeth ready to sink into his exposed flesh.

His arm slid through the bar with an agonizing pop. A scream ripped past his lips as he fell back on the ground, his arm hanging limp by his side.

The second infected—the former deputy—shuddered and woke then. It was much faster, much livelier than the sheriff, and found its footing in a matter of seconds.

Both attacked at once, claws and nails scratching at the metal bars, trying to find their way in.

Axel climbed on his bed and pulled his knees to his chest. He needed a plan.

All he had to defend himself were his cheap metal food tray and rusty bed. By the look of the infected's strength, the bed might buy him a couple of seconds at best. Not that he had the keys to get out.

He was fucked. Royally fucked.

Leaning his head against the wall, he closed his eyes and tried to block out the sounds of his impending death. What he wouldn't give for a gun. Or a knife. Hell, any sharp object would be a godsend.

The room fell silent then, and for a moment, Axel thought he must have drifted off.

He forced his eyes open, not ready to face reality but also not wanting to be surprised by what was coming next.

The infected had stopped attacking the cell and instead turned to the door, which had closed when the deputy came back from the dead.

Whatever was on the other side held their attention, but Axel had no intention of getting his hopes up. The last person who could have rescued him ended up dead. If only the guy had been prepared, had his gun ready.

A thought struck him then. Creeping off the bed, Axel positioned himself in front of the camera. As stupid as he felt, he made a gun with his fingers and showed it the camera.

"Gun," he mouthed over and over. "Gun."

God, there better be someone on the other side watching this.

The infected moved closer to the door. Someone had to be on the other side to keep their attention; he just prayed they'd gotten his message and came ready.

The door inched open, and the infected lunged.

A gun popped twice, and one after the other fell to the ground, black goo oozing from their heads.

Axel fell to his knees. "Help! I'm in here!"

Gunner's familiar face poked past the doorframe, his eyes on the two infected.

"What's wrong?" Axel watched in horror as the two infected clambered back to their feet. "Holy shit."

Gunner raised his gun and shot both of them in the chest.

This time when they fell, they didn't get back up even after a full five minutes of waiting.

Axel had counted every second.

"I guess that settles that." Gunner swung the door open and made his way around the two dead infected, removing the keys from the sheriff's belt.

"Settles what?" Axel stood on wobbly legs.

"Head shot doesn't kill them. Got to hit them in the chest. Guess the bastards have never seen a horror movie before." Gunner unlocked the cell door.

"What are you doing here?" Axel nearly collapsed against Gunner as he left the cell. "Where are the others?"

"They're waiting by the door, keeping an eye on things."

"I thought you all were hitting the road?" Axel cautiously stepped around the dead bodies, not trusting that they wouldn't come back to life and take a bite out of his leg.

"Many did. A few of us planned to stay back a few days to make sure this Podunk town provided you with a decent lawyer and got you in front of a judge."

Axel took a weighted breath and slammed the jail door behind them. "Apparently he couldn't get a hold of anyone."

"Yeah, well, that's not a surprise." Gunner waved the others in from where they waited by the receptionist desk. "The world's gone to shit. These things…."

"The infected?" Axel asked.

Gunner nodded. "Yeah. They're everywhere, killing anyone who crosses their path and turning them into whatever they are."

Axel dropped into a chair close to the window. Nothing appeared too out of the ordinary until he really took in all in. Parked cars were actually abandoned. Empty streets were no longer a sign of small-town living but that people had gone into hiding or were dead.

"What are you saying? This is some kind of apocalypse?"

Gunner snorted. "Yeah. A fucking zombie apocalypse."

CHAPTER ELEVEN

Axel sat in the same chair of the sheriff's office for hours, staring out the window. The urge to debunk Gunner's term 'zombie apocalypse' pulsed through his veins.

Zombies didn't exist. They were fictional monsters made up by someone with a wicked imagination. And they sure as hell didn't act the way the infected did. No rotting flesh, aimless lumbering about. What they were dealing with, what the world was dealing with, was something different.

"Fucking parasites," he mumbled.

"What?" Mac paced, his massive frame seeming to fill up the small room.

"Nothing." Axel stood and stretched his good arm. Rainey had found him a sling for his other arm to keep it still after they had put the damn thing back in its socket. "Just thinking about this whole zombie thing and how ridiculous it is."

Gus fiddled with his black mustache. "It's a figure of speech. People die, come back to life and try to eat people. What the hell would you call them?"

Six sets of eyes fell on him: Gus, Gunner, Rainey, Angie, Shifter and Mac. The others had left. How far they had gotten, no one knew or dared to speculate.

"I've been calling them the infected. Zombies are dead bodies walking around eating flesh. This… this is something different, like something takes over the body."

"Body snatchers." Mac chuckled, but there was no amusement in his voice. "This is fucking nuts."

Angie yawned and flipped her thick black braids over her shoulder. "What now? We can't stay here. The fridge is empty, and what's left in the vending machine won't last us but a day or two."

"Do you think help is coming?" Rainey flipped through the TV channels and found nothing but static. "Maybe the army or air force? We can't be the only ones."

Shifter snatched the remote from her hand and turned off the TV. "Enough. You've been flipping channels for hours and nothing's changed."

At five-foot-nothing, Rainey looked like a child next to Shifter, but that didn't stop her from standing her ground. "Don't take things from my hand. I would have turned the damn thing off if you would have asked."

Gunner maneuvered himself between the two. "Fighting won't do us any good. We need a plan. Somewhere to go. Out of town would be best, away from people."

That gave Axel an idea. "Remember the redhead from the church? The chick with the three kids—"

"And the grass-fed husband who could probably kick all our asses," Gunner cut in.

Axel ignored him. "She mentioned they live on a farm or ranch or something outside of town."

Mac shuffled things around on the desk. “What’s your point?”

“She gave me the location and said to stop by next time I was in town.”

Angie snorted. “She gave you her address?”

“Well—” Axel ran his tongue along his teeth. “She gave me the general direction and told me to look for the mailbox with her name on it.”

“So, what’s the plan?” Shifter crossed his arms. “We just roll up on our bikes and ask for a place to crash?”

Axel shrugged. “Why not?”

“Because we’ll get our assess shot.” Gus patted Axel on his good shoulder. “With the world going to shit, ain’t no way they’ll trust a bunch of strangers on their land, with their kids.”

“I think….” He didn’t know how to explain to them why he thought Britney would welcome them into their home, but he believed she would.

Gunner sat on the edge of the desk. “You remember she’s married, right?”

“I do.” Axel glared at him. “And her husband is a hell of a nice guy. We had a beer.”

“You had a beer?” Mac shook his head. “So that makes you two bros?”

“That’s not what I’m saying.” Axel wished they would just shut up and let him explain. “It just that… they’re good people. Churchgoing, ‘help thy neighbor’ kind of people.”

Rainey twirled her brown hair around her finger. “How far is it from here?”

Angie scrunched her face. “You’re not seriously thinking we should go there, are you?”

“I don’t know.” Rainey scanned the room. “Like you said, we can’t stay here. And the town is a horror movie. Where else is there to go?”

“If we go there,” Gus said as he paced the room, “it’s a risk all the way around. We have a general direction but don’t know how long it will take to drive there. The motorcycles offer no protection. What if the”— he glanced at Axel—“infected are roaming around those parts? We’ve all seen how fast they move. If they come out of nowhere, we’re screwed.”

“Leave or stay here, it doesn’t matter.” Axel stared out the window at the night that had engulfed the town. “Those things are strong. If they figure out we’re in here, they’ll find a way in. The windows alone….”

Everyone took a collective step toward the middle of the room.

“If they get in….” Mac shook his head with a sigh. “I sure as hell don’t want to be trapped in this room with no way out.”

Gunner clapped his hands on his thighs before standing. “Should we vote?”

Axel scanned the room. “All in favor of leaving?”

Everyone raised their hands.

Gus stepped in the center of the group. “Does anyone else want to make a suggestion on where we go? Or are we all in agreement on heading to the redhead’s house?”

Angie clicked her tongue half a dozen times. “Axel, you really think she’ll let us stay?”

He didn’t want to bullshit her or any of them, didn’t want to lie. “I think it’s our best option. If she turns us away, we move on. If the carnage is as bad as you all say it is, we’re bound to find a vacant house.”

“Why don’t we just look for one of those?” Shifter tugged on his beard. “Why risk getting shot by some country folks?”

Axel could think of a dozen reasons why they needed to head to Britney’s house. “For starters, they live on a fucking farm. They probably have a garden, and I know they have cattle. First thing people will loot is food and water. If they have a well, we'll be golden."

"If they let us stay," Angie reminded them as if they'd somehow forgotten.

"We do whatever we can to convince them." A small surge of relief washed over him. "Now that we have a destination, we're going to need a vehicle."

"What do you suggest we do?" Angie stuck a hand on her hip. "Steal a minivan?"

Axel leaned against the wall next to the window. "That or an SUV or a truck. Anything will do, really."

Rainey dropped into the nearest chair. "Stealing? I don't know how I feel about that."

Axel hated it with every fiber of his being; it went against everything he stood for. "I understand how you feel, but we don't have much of a choice."

"Maybe if we call it borrowing…." Rainey shrugged.

Mac cracked his neck. "Well, we best get on it."

"How we going to do this?" Gunner rolled up the sleeves of his ratty old T-shirt. "Scout the area from the front window and pick out our best option?"

"First things first." Axel pushed off the wall. "We need to search the building for weapons, ammunition, and anything else that be useful."

Shifter tugged at his beard. "Extra clothing, vests. Stuff like that might come in handy."

"Let's get to it. We leave in ten." Axel didn't know how the others would take to him barking orders and didn't care. They needed to get out of there.

"I'll take the office." Mac headed that way.

Gunner eyed the jail. "What about the two dead in there? Both had uniforms on. Think they have anything good we could use?"

"They would each have a sidearm. Extra clips." Gus followed Gunner to the door and peeked inside. "And they still look dead. Might be worth checking out."

Axel would keep his mouth shut unless they asked for his opinion. They knew so little about the infected; he wasn't sure the reward outweighed the risk.

"I found a couple of backpacks." Angie tossed them on the desk. "They're big and should hold quite a bit of stuff."

Shifter had wandered toward the back and returned a few minutes later while the rest of them gathered stuff from around the office. "There's a safe back there. Probably where they keep the guns and other important shit. Anybody find a set of keys?"

"Keys." Axel snapped his fingers. "Gunner had the sheriff's keys. Maybe the one for the safe is on that. They're in there checking the bodies."

"Gunner!" Shifter called out.

"Yeah?" He came back into the room; both he and Gus had a police belt and gun in hand. "We got some good stuff from. May they rest in peace."

"You got the sheriff's keys?" Shifter asked.

Gunner laid the stuff on the desk and reached in his back pocket. "Here you go. You find something?"

"Possible gun safe." Shifter cocked his head toward the back. "Wanna give me a hand?"

Gunner and Gus followed Shifter while Axel checked in on Mac. "You find anything in here?"

Mac lifted a limp backpack from behind the desk. "Not much. A bottle of whiskey that might come in handy."

The corner of Axel's mouth twitched at the thought of a stiff drink. "Guard that with your life."

Mac chuckled and tossed Axel a clear Ziplock bag. "Here's your wallet and keys. And I found the sheriff's cell phone." Mac draped the backpack on his shoulder. "There's no signal."

"I'm not surprised." Axel left the room and tossed his wallet into a backpack. He left the motorcycle keys on the desk. He wouldn't need those anymore.

Angie and Rainey were huddled near the desk talking quietly when Axel and Mac joined them.

"We packed all the medical supplies." Rainey inspected Axel's arm. "How's your shoulder? I found some painkillers."

Axel winced as he rotated his arm. "Maybe when we get settled. Don't want them clouding my judgment."

Angie glanced to Rainey, then back to Axel. "Are you sure? Lord only knows what we'll face when we leave this building."

Axel removed the sling and grabbed a gun from the table. "I've had worse injuries under worse conditions. I'll be fine."

Gus, Shifter and Gunner returned with a smaller bag than Axel had hoped.

"Damn small towns." Shifter threw the bag on the table. "There wasn't much in the safe, but we took it all. See you already picked your weapon. Should we each take one?"

"That depends." Axel moved closer to the arsenal. "How many of you know how to use a gun?"

"I do." Gunner raised his hand.

Gus crossed his arms. "I'm retired military. Hand me a gun."

"Anyone else?" The others shook their heads. "Three out of seven. We can work with that."

"So the rest of us will go out there with no protection?" Mac ground his teeth. "No way. I want a gun."

Axel didn't blame him. He wouldn't want to go outside without a weapon either. "You ever shot a gun before? Held one?"

Mac shook his head and picked the small handgun off the table. "Do video games count?"

Axel hated the idea of someone with no experience walking around with a loaded weapon, but what choice did they have? "The gun already has one in the chamber. You flip the safety off, aim and pull the trigger. Do not forget to flip the safety."

"Got it." Mac wrapped his fingers around the handle.

"Anyone else want a gun?" Axel asked.

The girls shook their heads.

Shifter pulled an axe from the bag. "Found this beauty hanging on the wall. Didn't even know they still did that. I think she'll make a damn fine weapon."

"All right. Are we ready to go?" No one answered, but they also didn't argue, so Axel took that as a yes. "Okay. Rainey, Angie, you two want to grab these backpacks?"

They each took one and secured them on their backs.

"I got the weapons bag." Gunner slung it across his body.

Mac patted the backpack he still wore. "And I have the stuff from the sheriff's office."

"Is there anything else we need to take?" Axel tucked his gun in the side of his jeans. He hated doing that, but with a bum arm, he didn't have much of a choice.

"I think we're good." Gus held his handgun by his side. "Let's go."

They followed Gus into the receptionist area and hovered close together, everyone on guard.

Axel scanned the parking lot and spotted a police SUV. "Gunner, there any car keys on the set you have?"

Gunner fished them out of his pocket. "Yep. There's a clicker. Want me to try it?"

Axel blew out a breath. "The infected are attracted to sound. If you hit that button and it beeps… well, it's like ringing a dinner bell."

"Maybe it's already unlocked?" Rainey suggested. "It is a small town."

"Yeah." Axel continued to scan the dark area; the moon wasn't even out to offer light. "But with all the equipment in there, I doubt it."

"What do we do?" Angie asked. "Take a chance and go out there, hope those are the right keys?"

Axel turned to look at them. "We need to decide together. We can try to unlock it now, but if that draws their attention to us, I'm not sure we can keep them out of here."

"I say we go for it." Mac moved closer to the door. "Run for the vehicle, unlock it when we get there."

"And if it doesn't unlock?" Angie huffed.

"Let's worry about that if it happens." Shifter patted her on the back. "I'll drive. Everyone else needs to call out where they're sitting too. Don't want people fighting over seats."

Axel hadn't thought of that. "I'll get in the back. The trunk. Cargo area. Whatever it's called."

"Me too," Mac said.

Gunner called shotgun.

"Guess that leaves the girls and Gus in the middle. That'll also give us a gun at each point." Axel looked over at the three who didn't get to pick. "That okay?"

"Let's get this over with." Rainey shook out her hands. "Before my nerves get the best of me."

Mac wrapped his hand around the doorknob. "Clear?"

Axel took in the parking lot one final time. "It's dark, but I don't see anything. Girls—"

"Women or ladies," Angie corrected.

Axel furrowed his brow. "My apologies. Ladies, since you don't have weapons, stay in the middle. We need to move fast but as quietly as possible. It doesn't take much noise to alert them. If we're…." He hesitated, trying to find the right word that wouldn't cause any panic, but couldn't think of any. "If we're attacked, aim for the chest. That seems like the only way to take them down."

"Huddle up," Gus ordered. "Weapons ready. Mac, you got the door."

"Yep." He twisted the knob, opened the door and peered out. "Nothing. Let's go."

Axel's heart raced as they rushed out the door. It was hard to move fast and keep their group together, but they managed. The SUV couldn't have been more than a hundred feet away, but it felt like miles.

They all kept their heads moving and their mouths quiet. Bringing up the rear, Axel took up jogging backward to make sure nothing came up from behind.

"Unlock it," Gus ordered as they approached the SUV.

"I'm trying," Gunner mumbled. "I don't think these are the right keys."

"What?" Rainey whimpered.

"It's locked," Shifter said, tugging on the door handle. "Try the key again?"

"It's not doing anything." Gunner shoved the keys at Shifter. "Maybe the battery's dead. Try the actual key."

"Wait!" Axel reached out, but it was too late. Shifter had already stuck the key in the hole, setting off the alarm.

A chorus of roars filled the night air.

"Fuck!" Axel shouted. "They're coming!"

"What now?" Angie screamed.

Gunner started for the police station. "We have to go back."

"No." Shifter slammed the butt of his axe in the passenger-side window and hit the lock. "Get in."

Everyone piled into the vehicle just as a group of infected scrambled down the street. There were so many of them—no way they had enough bullets.

"What now?" Axel called from the back. "We don't have any keys!"

"Give me a second," Shifter yelled back. "I almost got it."

The infected barreled into the SUV, rocking it to the point that Axel thought for sure they'd knock it over.

"Hurry!" Gunner screamed, firing his gun at the infected swiping at him from his broken window.

The back glass shattered as the infected tried to claw their way in.

With no open shot to the chest, Axel saved his bullets and slammed his foot into the infected's faces, knocking them back.

"Got it!" The engine roared to life. "Hold on." Shifter threw it into Reverse, plowing into the infected at their rear. "Which way?"

"That way." Axel pointed, trying to catch his breath. "Then east. Out of town. The way we came in."

Shifter floored it, the SUV jerking and then hauling ass down the road. "Looks like they aren't that fast."

Axel lay back next to Mac, his heart pounding. "You okay?"

Mac swallowed. "Yeah. You?"

Axel nodded. "Everyone okay up there? Gunner?" He was that most exposed.

"I'm okay," Gunner replied. "Did you see how many there were? And their teeth and claws. What the fuck is going on?"

Bile burned Axel's throat, but he forced it back. Whatever it was that caused these people to turn had consumed an entire town so quickly. He couldn't imagine what the rest of the world looked like.

CHAPTER TWELVE

"Come on, kids." Britney drew back the curtains of her front window and checked for the sheriff. "Turn off the TV. It's time for dinner."

The movie continued to play, and Britney rotated around. She didn't have the heart to get after them, but it was getting late, and after the trauma of the day, they needed some sleep.

And she needed time alone to grieve.

"You guys have to be hungry." She crouched beside the TV and hit Stop on the DVD player. "I made your favorite."

Most days the simple act of turning off their movie would cause mass hysteria, but today wasn't most days. They didn't react, didn't say a word, just lay on the couch, their eyes still focused on the black screen.

Britney moved closer and ran her hand across each of their cheeks. "I know how hard this is, how much it hurts, but Daddy wouldn't want to see you like this. He wants you to be happy."

Carson's eyes locked with hers, and he ran his fingers over his still-red scratch. "Am I going to be like him?"

"What?" Britney cupped his face. "Why would you even ask that?"

"Because Dr. Hildebrand was sick, and he scratched me. That's how Dad got sick."

Tears welled in Britney's eyes. "No. Your dad got… bit, and it healed really fast. Your scratches still look the same."

She didn't know if that was really how John had gotten sick, but it seemed to ease some of his fears.

"I'm scared, Mommy." Molly wrapped her arms around Britney's neck.

"I know, baby. But I won't let anythin' happen to you." She kissed her cheek and patted Blake on the leg. "You okay there, kid?"

He bobbed his head.

"Good. Let's go to the kitchen and eat. I made mac and cheese and chicken nuggets. Then for dessert, we'll have a bowl of ice cream."

Molly's eyes lit up. Dessert always lightened her mood. "With sprinkles?"

"Sure." She guided the kids to the table. "And chocolate syrup and cherries."

"Yummy." Molly licked her lips.

Britney fixed them all a plate and sat down with them at the table. They ate in silence, which never happened; Molly alone could keep the conversation going even if no one joined in.

Britney popped a chicken nugget in her mouth and chewed it slowly, trying to keep it down. Her eyes bounced from the kids to the empty spot at the table John sat at just a few days ago. Tears clogged her throat, making it hard to swallow.

She needed a distraction—they all did—but for the life of her she couldn't think of anything to say.

Weekdays they'd talk about what happened at school. John had a knack for storytelling, captivating the kids with tales about ranch life. Most nights he'd have them in stitches.

Britney forced the memories away and focused on the present.

"You're not hungry?" The kids had barely touched their food.

Molly pushed the noodles around with her fork while Blake played with his dinosaur chicken nuggets. Neither answered.

Carson stood suddenly, nearly knocking his chair backward. "Can I be excused?"

"You want some ice cream first?"

"No." He shook his head. "I want to go to bed."

Britney checked the kitchen clock. Seven o'clock. Never had any of her kids asked to go to bed so early. "There's no school tomorrow. You can stay up for a little while if you want."

"I'm tired." Carson pushed in his chair.

"Me too." Molly stood, rubbing her eyes.

Blake yawned. "Yep."

"No ice cream for you either?"

"Can we have it tomorrow?" Molly asked.

Britney forced a smile and got up from her seat. "Sure, honey. It's not goin' anywhere. Let's go upstairs and get your pajamas on and your teeth brushed."

Carson paused at the bottom of the stairs. The twins stopped behind him.

"What's wrong?" Britney asked. "Why did everybody stop?"

"I don't want to sleep in my room." Carson took a step back.

"That's fine." Britney moved in front of them and crouched down. "Why don't we all sleep in my room tonight?"

Molly and Blake smiled, but Carson shook his head. "No. There're windows in there. What if there are more like Dad and they break in?"

"On the second floor?" Britney asked. "I don't think we have to worry about that."

"You don't know that for sure." Carson backed away from the stairs. "I don't want to sleep up there."

"Me either," Blake and Molly said in unison.

Britney bit her bottom lip, trying to come up with the best way to handle this. She didn't want to give in to their fears, but after everything they'd gone through today…. "Carson, I know you're scared, but if we all sleep in my room together, we'll be safe."

"No." His body trembled. "I want to sleep downstairs."

"Okay." Britney smiled. "We can sleep on the couch, have a slumber party."

Carson shook his head. "I meant the basement. There are no windows down there."

"Oh." Years ago they'd remodeled the basement and turned half of it into a guest room. The other they used as a pantry for the fruits and vegetables she canned. "Um, I don't know about that." She didn't like the idea of them sleeping so far away.

"Please, Mommy," Molly begged. "I don't want to sleep by the windows."

"Okay." She rarely gave in to them so easily, but she didn't want to argue about it. "You guys head down there, and I'll go get your stuff."

She went upstairs and collected their toothbrushes, pajamas, favorite blankets and stuffed animals, hauling them down to the basement.

The kids were already under the comforter together and not fighting, a sight she'd never seen before. The king-sized bed allowed them each plenty of room, but they snuggled together, Carson in the middle with an arm around each of the twins.

More surprising than that, they were already asleep.

She draped each of their blankets on top of them and placed their favorite stuffed animal above their heads.

With a quick kiss on each of their foreheads, she told them how much she loved them.

Before leaving, she did a quick check of the basement, making sure everything was in order. The last thing they needed was more surprises.

Satisfied the room was safe, she headed back upstairs.

She stopped by the window and checked for the sheriff. It'd been hours since she'd called him; he should have been there by now.

After cleaning the kitchen, she checked outside again. *Where the hell is he?*

She hated to call him a second time, but what choice did she have?

His cell went voice mail. No one answered at the police station.

Exhaustion washed over her. She needed rest, but as tired as she was, she didn't think she could fall asleep with everything going on.

Running upstairs, she grabbed a shotgun from the safe and a box of ammo. When she went back downstairs, she dragged a chair next to the front window and tied back the blinds to wait.

The sheriff would show eventually. She had to believe that.

Until then, she would keep watch, guard the farm and her family.

She'd keep her children safe.

***

Britney's eyes flew open. The horrors she witnessed in her dreams overwhelmed her unconscious, making it difficult to distinguish reality from the nightmares. She rubbed the sleep from her eyes and checked the time—1:55 a.m. Exhaustion must have gotten the best of her to fall asleep in the old wooden chair.

After running downstairs to check on the kids, she headed for the kitchen to make a pot of coffee. She hadn't meant to fall asleep, hated the idea that she'd left the kids without someone watching over them. And even though she was a light sleeper, had been since bringing Carson home from the hospital, it terrified her to think someone or something could have snuck past her and gotten to the children while she slept.

She knew she couldn't go without sleep forever, but she would feel better if, when she did sleep, it was feet away, not a floor.

The sweet aroma of coffee hit her nose, and her heart contracted. She hadn't even realized she'd brewed John's favorite blend.

Her legs gave out and she collapsed, the reality of the situation too much to bear.

Just as she was about to let the grief take over, the dogs began to bark.

Britney pulled herself off the floor and sprinted toward the front window, praying the sheriff had finally shown up.

Tearing back the curtains, she let out a small sob of relief when she spotted the familiar white SUV with the gold lettering.

"Finally," she mumbled.

Britney paused at the door and looked at the gun propped against the wall. After all she'd witnessed today, she didn't want to go outside in the dead of night without protection. But greeting a sheriff with a loaded shotgun, no matter how well John knew him, was stupid.

Still, something in the back of her mind urged her to grab it. When she'd called the sheriff to report the shooting, she'd explained the situation. Not that he believed her, but she had proof—John's body was the proof. There was no way Cornhill could look at his body and not agree she'd acted out of self-defense. His lack of hair, the gray color of his skin, the serrated teeth and claws for nails—everything about him screamed predator.

Chances were good he wasn't the only one, couldn't be. Not after what happened with Dr. Hildebrand.

Grabbing the gun, she opened the door and headed toward the sheriff, who'd parked in the horseshoe drive. She kept the gun visible so as to not be perceived as a threat.

"Hello?" Britney called out as she made her way to the beat-up SUV. The passenger window, which she had first thought had been rolled down, had been shattered. Scratches, dents and what could be claw marks covered the side of the SUV.

"Sheriff Cornhill?" Britney slowed as she approached. *Why hasn't he gotten out of the vehicle?*

The cloudy night made it difficult for her to see inside the SUV. How many times had she asked John to wire in lights for the gravel driveway?

The passenger door swung open, startling her backward a few steps. The other doors followed, including the back of the SUV.

Britney held up her gun as seven people made their way out of the vehicle and huddled together near the back.

In the dark, it was hard to make out their faces, but she had a feeling she'd seen them before. They definitely weren't part of the sheriff's small department, that was for sure.

"Who are you, and what are you doin' with the sheriff's SUV?"

"Britney?" a familiar voice called out in the dark.

She snapped her head as the biker stepped into the moonlight. "Axel? What the hell are you doin' here? Where's Sheriff Cornhill?"

Light reflecting off his waist drew her eyes downward. Tucked in his jeans was the handle of a gun. She scanned the others, figuring if one of them showed up armed, the rest probably did too.

Britney took another step back, the shotgun aimed at the man she almost considered a friend. "You need to go. Now."

"Wait." Axel held up his hands. "If you would just listen."

"No."

Axel moved closer. "Britney, please. We need your help."

"Where's Sheriff Cornhill?" she asked again, this time through clenched teeth. "And why do you have his patrol car?"

"The sheriff is dead," Axel said matter-of-factly. "Bitten."

Britney narrowed her eyes. "What do you mean, bitten? Bitten by what?"

"One of the infected." Axel lowered his hands. "Him and one of his deputies. Both of them are dead."

"Did they turn into somethin'?" Britney asked in a low whisper.

Axel nodded. "Yeah. They turned into whatever the hell it is people are turning into after being bitten and dying."

Britney lowered the gun, no longer aiming it at Axel's head. She had no idea where to go from here. But no way was she going to let these strangers stay at her house. "If he's dead, I guess I need to call the highway patrol."

Axel looked to his friends and back to her. "Haven't you seen the news?"

"Not since this mornin'." Britney pressed her lips together. "Why?"

"Your town… there isn't anything left."

Britney's heart thrashed in her chest. "What do you mean, nothin' left? What happened?"

Axel rubbed at the scruff on his chin. "The town's been overrun by the monsters, the infected."

"Impossible. We were just there." Britney raised her gun. "Get off my property. Now!"

Axel's face fell. "We have nowhere else to go."

"That's not my problem." Britney's voice shook. "Leave. And never come back."

The looks on his friends' faces—angry, scared, defeated—broke her heart, but she had more important people to worry about. "Just go, please."

"Where's John?" Axel asked.

Tears stung her eyes. She couldn't believe he was asking for her husband. "Get off my land. Now."

"What are you going to do, shoot me?" Axel challenged. "Shoot all of us?"

If he thought she didn't have the guts to shoot him, all of them, he had another thing coming. "Do you really want to test me? Do you?"

"I don't have to. I know you won't shoot seven innocent people in cold blood. It's not who you are."

"You don't know a damn thin' about me," Britney snapped.

"I know you're a kind, God-fearing woman who helps in her community. People like that, people like you, don't kill people."

Britney ground her teeth. "I might be all of those things, but I'm a mother first. If the world is fallin' apart, I will do anythin', and I mean *anythin'*, to protect my children."

Axel moved closer. "Really? Anything?"

Britney aimed the gun just above his head and pulled the trigger. All seven of the intruders fell to the ground.

Axel lifted his head first. With a smirk on his face, he said, "You missed."

"I don't miss." Britney returned the smirk. "That was just a warnin'."

She headed back into the house and slammed the door. With a heavy sigh, she collapsed on the floor.

What the hell was she going to do? Axel was right—she couldn't shoot people who sought her out for help.

A multitude of emotions flowed through her, fear being the strongest.

Axel had said the town had been taken over by those things. How was that even possible?

Her mama always said when life got tough and you didn't know which way to turn, look to God for guidance. It had tested her faith to have both her parents pass at such a young age. Sure, she still went through the motions of going to church, but most days her heart wasn't in it. After the tragedy her family had lived through and now this? What kind of God would allow people to turn into monsters?

A deep yawn pulled tears from her eyes. Forcing herself off the floor, she checked on the kids and then lumbered to the couch. As much as she wanted the intruders to leave, she found comfort in knowing other armed adults kept watch just outside her front door.

With another heavy yawn, she lay down on the couch. A couple of minutes of sleep wouldn't hurt. She'd just been outside and saw nothing out of the ordinary. Maybe the world wasn't as bad as Axel said.

CHAPTER THIRTEEN

"Axel, man. What the fuck?" Shifter spat through a clenched jaw. "You told us you were friends with this chick, that she would take us in. Fuck. She nearly took your head off with a shotgun."

Axel had to admit he didn't expect her to pull a gun on them. The good news was she didn't shoot any of them. If she wanted them dead, they wouldn't be standing there discussing what could have happened. "She's scared. Something's wrong."

"Of course something's wrong." Angie made her way back to the back seat of the SUV. "The world's gone to shit, and you're expecting some stranger to take us in. I don't blame her for shooting at us. She's got three kids, a farm to protect. I would have shot at us too, probably taken out a kneecap just to prove a point."

Axel stared at the house. "Something's not right."

"Yeah, you said that." The vein in Gus's neck throbbed.

Axel turned to face them. "No, I mean really wrong. Like with her family. Where the hell is her husband?

What kind of man lets his wife greet strangers in the middle of the night alone?"

"Maybe he's not home," Rainey suggested.

Axel remembered the conversation he'd had with the sheriff. "I don't think so. The sheriff mentioned he'd gotten a call. Seemed real upset about it. Maybe he was talking about Britney and something awful that happened here."

"You can't know that." Gunner ran his fingers through his beard. "Bad shit is happening everywhere."

"She was expecting the sheriff," Axel surmised. "Wasn't surprised to see his SUV in front of her house."

Rainey licked her lips. "Maybe they're friends?"

"Friends don't show up in the middle of the night." Axel kicked around the loose pebbles on the driveway. "Something happened here, and she called the sheriff for help."

"Do you think it has to do with her husband?" Rainey asked.

Axel frowned. "God, I hope he's not sick."

"Shit." Mac ran a hand over his bald, sweaty head. "If he's sick like all those other people are sick and turns, hell, I don't want to be here for that."

"I don't want to be around those things any more than you do." Axel's throat constricted. "But she's got three kids in there—young kids. Are we just going to leave her alone and hope she can take care of him herself?"

"Wait a minute." Angie crossed her arm over her chest. "We don't even know if he *is* sick. And if he is, I'm not sure I want to get involved."

Axel cracked his neck from side to side. "I mean… I don't know… aren't we sort of involved already?"

He'd never forgive himself if they left and something happened to the family.

"Aren't you forgetting something?" Gus leaned against the SUV. "She doesn't want us here. Told us to leave."

"Because she's scared," Axel reminded them. "For God's sake, her kids were nearly kidnapped this morning, and now strangers show up in the middle of the night. And we're not exactly the most clean-cut-looking people."

Shifter headed for the SUV. "Which is why we should leave. Like you said, she's scared, and scared people do stupid things. Like shoot at people."

Angie nodded in agreement.

"Hey," Axel adopted a challenging tone, "this isn't some 'all for one and one for all' *Three Musketeers* bullshit. If you want to leave, no one's stopping you."

The others glanced at each other.

Axel didn't wait for them to answer. "Seriously, take the SUV and go. But I'm staying. Even if her husband is well, they're going to need some help."

"You got much farm experience?" Angie asked.

"No," Axel snapped. "But by the look of the town, we have little choice."

Rainey chewed on her bottom lip. "Other parts of the country, maybe even the state, could be fine."

"You're right," Axel agreed, "but until we get some kind of confirmation, I'm staying. I'd rather be stuck on some farm than in the city. You saw how many infected were at the police station. The population of the town and the surrounding area couldn't be more than a thousand. Can you imagine what the big cities look like? At least here there's a fence, food, probably a well. Here we can survive."

Angie snorted. "Yeah, if she doesn't shoot us first."

"Then we need to prove that she needs us and we can be trusted. Unless anybody has a better suggestion?"

"Say we stay, against the lady's wishes," Max said. "What are we going to do? It's not like we can live in the stolen police car. The busted windows alone make that impossible."

Axel surveyed the area the best he could in the dark night. "There are a lot of barns. Maybe we can talk her into letting us take one of those."

Gunner chuckled. "You really think she's going to give up one of her barns to let us sleep in? And even if she does, how do we know it'll be safe?"

Axel's face tightened. "I'll take being in a wooden barn over standing out here in the open exposed."

Rainey's face paled as she frantically searched the area. "I didn't even think of that."

Axel patted her on the shoulder. "I don't think it's anything we have to worry about right now. Once we got out of the city, we didn't see any of the infected roaming around."

"Doesn't mean they're not hiding in the bushes," Gus grumbled.

"That's it." Angie threw up her hands. "I'm getting back in the car."

"Me too." Rainey followed her into the back seat and slammed the door.

Axel mumbled a slew of curses under his breath. "I'm sorry." He didn't know what else to say. Never in a million years did he think Britney would react the way she did. "I just… didn't know what else to do. Where else to go."

Gus's shoulders slumped. "We didn't think this through. I mean, you don't just show up at someone's house and expect them to take you in. Not when the fucking world is ending. Supplies are limited. Whatever they have, they aren't going to share them with us. Family, maybe, but not strangers."

As much as Axel hated to admit it, Gus was right. If they wanted something from her, they needed to offer something in return. "I saw a general store on the way out of town."

"Excuse me?" Mac's mouth went slack. "You are not suggesting what I think you are. We nearly got ourselves killed getting out of that police station."

"We also made a whole hell of a lot of noise," Axel reminded him. "Car alarm, remember? If we could get into town without drawing too much attention to ourselves—"

"An SUV driving around when nothing else is moving will definitely draw some attention," Mac cut in.

"I'm not suggesting we all go." A plan started forming in Axel's head. "Maybe a few of us. A quick in and out. Back the SUV to the entrance, grab as much crap as we can and get out. We have guns and know how to kill them. Gunner, Gus and I both have decent aim."

Shifter scratched at his jaw. "What you're saying is you're going to take the SUV and leave the rest of us here with the crazy, gun-wielding chick. Are you fucking nuts?"

"No one said you have to stay here." Axel glared. "You want to come, come. The more hands, the more shit we can get and the faster we can get out of there."

"Hey, this ain't some bullshit zombie apocalypse, end-of-the-world TV show." Gunner's nostrils flared.

Axel raked his hands through his hair. "Not a TV show. Reality. The world is gone. How long do you think we'll survive without supplies? The electricity is on now, but how long will that last? Water, food, medical supplies? We're in fucking Montana. The weather might be okay now, but what about winter? No electricity when the temperatures drop below freezing.

The infected will be the last of our worries when we have no way to cook or stay warm."

"You're talking about months from now." Mac shook his head. "We have no idea what the world will be like then. Hell, as far as we know, the military might be fighting them off right now. A week or two, this could all just be a bad dream."

Gus turned to Mac. "You really believe that?"

He hung his head. "Better than believing the world's over."

"No, you're right, Mac," Axel said "In a week this could be over with. There could be some crazy shit going down we don't know about. Hell, they could already have a vaccine and be handing it out. But what if there isn't? We have to prepare for the worst. If we don't, we'll all be dead."

Gunner let out a weighted breath. "I'm in. When you want to head out?"

It surprised Axel that Gunner volunteered so quickly. He thought he'd have to do a lot more convincing. "I say we leave at first light. Get a few hours of shut-eye. That way we'll be able to see what's coming."

"I'd feel a whole hell of a lot better if I could see what's coming," Gunner said.

"Agreed." Axel looked to other three men. "What about you?"

"I'm in," Shifter said. "I can't stand waiting around."

"If Shifter is going, I think the two of you should stay here," Axel addressed Mac and Gus.

Mac yawned. "I wasn't planning on volunteering. Suicide ain't my thing."

"We're not planning on dying out there." Shifter puffed out his chest.

"No one ever does." Mac's face softened. "Gus and I will stay here, keep an eye on the girls. Maybe they can convince the crazy lady to let us stay."

"Guess we have a plan." Axel's insides turned. "Okay. Let's get some rest." He checked his watch. "Only have a few hours before we head out."

They climbed back into the SUV. It didn't take but a few minutes before everyone was out. Everyone but Axel. He had silently volunteered to keep the first and only watch. With the windows busted out, they were exposed in the worst kind of way.

If all went well tomorrow, they'd come back with a shitload of supplies and hopefully convince Britney they were worth keeping around.

CHAPTER FOURTEEN

Britney woke early the next morning to the sound of tires against gravel. She popped off the couch and rushed to the window.

They were leaving, thank God. Axel seemed like a nice guy from the few encounters she'd had with him, but that didn't mean she'd just automatically allow them to stay on her farm. Now that it was just her and the kids, there was no such thing as being too cautious.

The sight of them leaving relieved her and made her tense all in the same breath.

"Mommy?" Molly called out.

Britney jumped and turned around to find all three kids standing behind her. How long had they been there?

Carson moved closer to the window. "Was someone here?"

"No," Britney said too quickly.

"You're lying," Carson spat. "I saw a white car driving away."

"Fine." She couldn't continue to lie to them when they had already spotted the truth. "Yes, a few people showed up, but I sent them away."

"You're still lying!" Blake shouted.

Britney bent down so they were face-to-face. "That's not nice, and I'm not lyin'. They showed up last night, and I told them they had to leave."

Blake pointed out the window. "I can see four people out there!"

"What?" Britney popped up and her jaw dropped. "Why are they still here?"

"They look weird." Molly cocked her head. "Who are they?"

Carson leaned against the window. "They look like those bikers!"

Britney grabbed her shotgun. "Stay inside. I need to go talk to them."

"Mommy?" Molly whimpered.

"Stay here." She slammed the door behind her and marched over to where the four stood huddled underneath the tree. "I thought I told you to get off my property!"

"Hold your horses." The African American woman with braids down to her waist held up her hands in defense. "We had nowhere else to go."

"Nowhere else to go?" Britney bordered on hysterics. "How about anywhere else but here? Each town, whichever direction you go, has a hotel. What's wrong with one of those?"

The large and intimidating African American man gawked. "I can't tell if you're being serious."

Britney raised the shotgun. "I'm serious."

"Listen." An older man with a black beard stepped forward. "I think we got off on the wrong foot here. I'm Gus. This is Mac, Angie and the woman who's kept her mouth shut is Rainey."

Britney didn't reply.

"And you're Britney, right?" Gus continued, not bothered by her silence.

"Yes." She gave each of them a once-over. "Now answer my question. Why here?"

Rainey moved in front of the group. "The town—your town—it's gone."

"What do you mean, gone?" Sweat dampened her hands.

"Those things—Axel calls them the infected—they've taken over." Gus yawned.

Britney lowered the gun. Even though Axel had told her the same thing last night, she still had a hard time believing it. "That's impossible. We were just in town yesterday mornin'."

"Hey." Gus lowered himself to the ground and leaned against the trunk of the tree. "I'm not saying everyone is dead, or has turned into one of those things. I'm just saying, when we left, there wasn't a live person in sight."

Britney's body trembled. "This can't be happenin'."

Mac glanced over Britney's shoulder and smiled. "Looks like we have company."

Britney whirled around and glared at all three kids running toward them. "I told you to stay in the house!"

"But—" Molly started, but Carson silenced her with a hand across her mouth.

"Let me. You don't know how to say it right." She'd never seen Carson so adult-like. "The electricity went out."

"What?" Britney peered back at the house. "Are you sure?"

Molly stepped forward. "The TV won't turn on."

"And there's no internet," Blake added.

Britney sighed. "That doesn't mean the electricity is out."

"Mom." Carson rolled his eyes. "The lights won't turn on either. And the microwave isn't working."

She threw back her head and groaned. "Go back inside. I'll be right in."

They didn't move.

Carson pointed to Gus. "Hey, aren't you those bikers? Axel's friends?"

Britney couldn't believe Carson remembered his name.

"That's right, kid."

Blake spun around. "Where's your bike?"

Gus's eyes met Britney's. "You better do what your mama said. Head back inside and maybe, if your mama says it's okay, we can talk bikes later."

Carson threw back his shoulders. "That would awesome. I mean, I would like that very much. Come on." He placed a hand on each of Molly's and Blake's shoulders. "Let's go inside. I'll get you both a bowl of cereal."

"Those are some kids you have there." Mac's face lit up. "That older one taking care of the younger ones, that's real mature."

Britney spun back around. "Please leave my children out of this."

Mac's eyes widened. "You think we want to hurt your children?"

"I don't know what to think," Britney snapped. "I don't know you."

Mac puffed up his chest. "I'm the proud father of two girls—eighteen and twenty-one—both in college and getting straight As."

Gus patted Mac on the shoulder. "I have five grandchildren."

"I'm a former elementary school teacher," Rainey said. "Taught for fifteen years until my daddy passed away. I left teaching to run his motorcycle shop."

Angie squeezed Rainey's hand. "I have no kids, but I ran the youth group at my church. Loved those kids like my own."

Britney didn't expect these bikers with their many tattoos and leather vests to be so… family oriented.

"Then why are you here?" She couldn't help herself. They still hadn't explained how they ended up on her farm. "Why not go home?"

Mac clenched his jaw. "You think we want to be here? That we haven't been trying for days to contact our families?"

Britney's heart contracted. "You can't get a hold of them?"

Rainey sniffled and turned away. "Not a single one answered."

"Don't mean nothing." Angie pulled Rainey into a tight hug. "Just means the phone lines are down."

"The roads have gone to shit," Gus explained. "Abandoned cars everywhere. Stores, gas stations, all closed. Those things—the infected—coming out of nowhere. It's not safe."

"But Axel and the two others, they left, didn't they?"

"They went into town to get supplies," Mac said. "For you."

"For me?" Britney huffed. "Why would they do that?"

Angie released Rainey. "We thought that, after your reaction to us showing up unannounced last night, maybe coming here empty-handed wasn't the smartest idea. And that maybe if we had something to offer, you'd let us stay."

Britney rubbed at her eyes. "That is the stupidest damn thing I've ever heard. If things are as bad as you say they are—"

"Probably worse," Mac interrupted.

"What a fuckin' idiot," she mumbled and then headed back toward the house. "Goin, to get himself killed."

Before she got too far, she paused and turned back around to face four confused bikers. Damn her mother's southern hospitality she'd instilled in them growing up. "I'm going to make some coffee and then some breakfast if anyone is interested."

"Um"—Angie cocked her head—"I thought the kid said the electricity was out?"

"I have an old-ass gas stove, one I've tried talkin' my husband into gettin' rid of for years. But if it still works, why get rid of it?"

Gus moved closer to her with a fatherly expression tugging at his eyes. "My dear, I have to ask, not only for our safety but that of your children. Is your husband sick? Is that why we haven't seen him?"

Britney knew the question would come up again. "He was sick and turned into one of those things. I did what I had to do to protect my children. Don't go in the big barn. I've locked the door, but he's already come back once."

She left them standing there with their mouths hung open and headed inside. Maybe now they believed her when she said she'd do anything to protect her family.

CHAPTER FIFTEEN

Axel didn't bother masking the yawn tugging at his lips. He'd spent the entire night awake and on guard, afraid of what might happen if he closed his eyes for even a second.

Every time the dogs barked or the leaves rustled, he'd readied his gun and prepared for the worst.

He had no idea how smart the infected were or what kind of fences surrounded Britney's property. From what he could tell when they drove up, the fencing couldn't keep a deer out.

"So, do we have a shopping list?" Shifter kept a close eye on the road as he drove toward town. "Or is it just a free-for-all?"

His training in the military had taught him more than just basic survival skills. In his twenties, if asked the same question, he could have rattled off a hundred different items and how many they'd need of each one per person, per day. But the fog clouding Axel's brain made it difficult to think in the moment.

"Maybe they have one of those survival guidebooks," Gunner suggested. "You know the ones:

'how to use household items in case of the end of the world.'"

"I hadn't thought of that." Axel considered the idea for a minute. "Maybe other books might be useful as well. Family medical guides, stuff like that."

"Books aren't going to keep us alive." Shifter never minced words and always said what was on his mind. Most of the time Axel didn't mind, but in times like this, he wished the man would keep his opinions to himself.

"Keep your eyes peeled," Axel changed the subject. "We're coming into town. And maybe keep the noise to a minimum. Their eyesight might be shit, but their hearing more than makes up for it."

Shifter slowed the SUV. "Fuck. Looks like a damn tornado went through here."

"Yeah." Axel stared out the window as Shifter maneuvered around the abandoned vehicles and other crap that lay scattered in the road. "What the hell happened here?"

Gunner leaned in from the back seat. "A whole bunch of people lost their damn minds."

Axel gave him a once-over. "After the gas station, where did you all go?"

"Back to the hotel to regroup," Gunner said. "The ones who left didn't stick around for more than an hour. The rest of us just hung out in our hotel rooms. We wanted to make sure you got out all right. We were about to walk over to the bar for dinner and saw people running around screaming and being chased. Gus decided to head over to the police station to check on you, and we followed."

Axel wanted to hug him. "Glad you did." Without them he would still be stuck in that cell, or worse.

"Back it up to the front?" Shifter pulled into the parking lot of the general store.

"Might as well." Axel kept a close eye on their surroundings. "Not like anyone's going to arrest us for breaking in."

"Nah," Gunner gaffed. "Probably more like shoot first, ask questions later."

Axel reached for the handle of the passenger door but paused when neither Shifter nor Gunner attempted to get out. "What's wrong?" Hadn't they just discussed getting in and out as quickly as possible? "Do you see something?"

"That's the problem," Shifter said. "I don't see anything. There's nobody roaming the streets or driving around or trying to flag us down for help. There aren't even any dead bodies."

Gunner sucked in a sharp breath. "You want to see dead bodies?"

Shifter looked at him from over his shoulder. "Better than the alternative. Dead bodies mean not everyone has turned into one of those monsters. No dead bodies, lots more monsters."

Axel's stomach rolled. "All the more reason to get the shit we need and get out."

"Which we still haven't decided on." Shifter tapped his thumb against the steering wheel. They could probably use nearly everything in this store, but no way the back of the SUV would hold that much. Essentials would have to do for now.

"Nonperishable food items and water. Batteries, all sizes. Flashlights and matches. Anything for camping. Medical supplies." Axel leaned closer, trying to get a better look inside. "Whatever you can grab and fit in here."

"What if…?" Gunner's voice trailed off.

Axel knew exactly where Gunner's train of thought was headed. "First we need to scope the place out, make sure none of the infected are inside. Then we check all the exits. Once we're certain the place is secure, we start loading the SUV."

"Let's get this over with." Shifter hit the button to unlock the doors. "Jesus, I hope we don't have to break down the front door."

Axel climbed out of the SUV and scanned the area. "Whatever we have to do, we do it quietly."

Gunner moved close to his side. "God, I hate this."

Axel patted him on the back. "So do I. Once inside, we'll be less at risk."

"Well, lookie there." Shifter opened the front door. "Looks like lady luck is on our side."

Axel followed him inside, gun held in front of him, ready for whatever waited. "I wouldn't go that far."

Gunner stayed close behind, keeping his eyes toward the outside. "See anything?"

"Nope." Axel broke from the group and headed right. "I'll take these aisles. Shifter, take the left. Gunner, you got the door?"

"Yep."

Aisle by aisle they searched the small store, then circled back to the front.

"Well?" Gunner asked.

Axel lowered his gun. "Good news is there's no infected."

Gunner lifted a brow. "And the bad news?"

Shifter pulled a handkerchief from his back pocket and wiped the sweat off his forehead. "Someone's already been here."

"Fuck," Gunner groaned. "What'd they get?"

"A shit ton." Shifter tugged at his beard. "There ain't a whole hell of a lot left, unless Axel's side looks any different."

"I saw a few things." Meaning two boxes of rice and some toilet paper. "Guess we should gather up everything we can and—"

"What about the back?" Gunner interrupted.

It took a second for Axel to realize where he was going with this. "You mean like a storage room?"

A smile tugged the corner of Shifter's mouth. "That's a damn fine idea. They got to keep extra stuff somewhere to restock."

Axel wasn't as excited as the other two. Whoever had raided the place knew what they were doing. Chances were good they'd hit up the back as well. "I saw an 'employee's only' door. It's locked, so I didn't check it out."

Shifter lifted his ax. "I think we can take care of that."

"Maybe we can find a key, try not to draw any attention to ourselves?" Metal hitting against metal would make a hell of a lot of noise.

"Maybe I can use the axe to pry it open, not hit it." Shifter headed toward the back.

"You want to stay here, keep an eye out?" Axel asked Gunner.

"Yep." Gunner returned to his previous position. "Yell if you need help."

"Thanks." Axel jogged to the back and found Shifter. "Any luck?"

Shifter stepped aside. "I can wedge the blade between the door and frame. If I tug on the handle a little"—Shifter pulled on the ax—"the door should just pop open."

Axel watched in silence as Shifter tried his hardest to pry open the door. "Must be one hell of a lock."

“Screw this.” Shifter yanked the axe out of the doorframe. “Let’s just bust this open so we can get the hell out of here.”

“I don’t know if that’s such—”

Shifter slammed the butt of the axe into the door handle, knocking it loose. “Now we’re getting somewhere.”

“Wait a minute, man.” Axel moved closer. He could have sworn he heard something. “We don’t know what’s behind that door or why they kept it locked.”

“They locked it “because they didn’t want anybody taking what’s in there.” Shifter hit the handle again.

Axel readied his gun. Shifter was a hardheaded son of a bitch. Nothing Axel said would get him to stop trying to break open the door. Being ready for whatever waited on the other side was his only option.

“One more hard hit and we’re in.”

Axel took a step back to give him some room. “Maybe don’t kick the door in until we know what we’re dealing with.”

The clang of the metal handle hitting the floor reverberated in Axel’s ears. The door swung on its hinges for a moment, then stilled.

Shifter dropped the axe to his side. “See. Nothing. Feel better?”

“I’ll feel better once we’re sure the room’s clear.” Axel inched forward, still unsure if he’d heard something on the other side or if his ears were playing tricks on him. “Do you hear that?”

“Nope.” Shifter rested his hand on the door. “When you’re ready, chief.”

Axel’s heartbeat thrashed in his ears. “After everything we’ve seen, we can’t be too careful.”

“On three?” Shifter smirked.

Axel didn't understand how he could stand there so calm. "Just ease it open."

Shifter pushed on the door and it creaked.

A soft growl emanated from the room.

"Shit," Axel muttered. "Get ready."

"Where's the fucking light?" Shifter raised his axe.

They waited for the infected to burst through the door, but it never did.

"Why isn't it coming?" Shifter gritted through his teeth. "What is it waiting for?"

"Dammit." Axel moved closer. "We need some damn light. Did you see any flashlights left on the shelf?"

"Some shitty ones, maybe."

"Get them."

Shifter didn't move. "And leave you alone? You sure about that? It could figure a way out."

"Then I suggest you hurry the hell back." They didn't have time to argue. If they were going to get whatever was left in this storage room, they needed to make it safe.

"Fine." Shifter jogged back into the main store.

Axel waited, gun pointed at the black open space, for what felt like hours. Each sound, no matter where it came from, sent his adrenaline into overdrive.

How long did it take to grab some damn flashlights?

Footsteps pounded the floor, and Axel chanced a quick glance. Shifter and Gunner rounded the corner, each with their weapons in hand.

"I thought for sure we'd find you in a shootout." Shifter stopped beside Axel. "It never showed its face?"

"It didn't." Axel looked to Gunner. "Why aren't you watching the front door?"

Gunner lifted his head and smiled. "We barricaded it."

Axel didn't know what irritated him more: that they had blocked the door—their only exit—or the pride Gunner displayed. "Why the hell would you do that?"

Gunner scrunched his brow. "So none of those things would get in while we're dealing with the one back here."

"What about us?" Axel snapped. "What if we need to get out in a hurry?"

"Um." Gunner's face fell. "We didn't think of that."

Axel needed to remember they weren't soldiers, never had been. "In situations like this, always have a way out. You never want to get backed into a corner."

"Want me to go move the blockade?" Gunner asked.

Axel shook his head. "No. We need to deal with whatever is in this room. Shifter, you find us some flashlights?"

"A few." Shifter lifted his chin to Gunner. "He found a damn good one."

"Behind the checkout counter." Gunner held up the flashlight in his hand. "It's damn bright."

"Good." Axel moved toward the door and gestured for them to follow. "We need to stay together and keep our eyes peeled. There's at least one in there. Might be more. We need to be ready for an attack."

Shifter handed him a red plastic flashlight. "Want this?"

The two men hovered close behind him but made no effort to take point.

"Give it here." Axel turned the flashlight on. "Guess I'm going in first?"

"We've got your back." Gunner flipped his on too. The damn thing nearly lit the entire front part of the storage room.

“That’s one hell of a flashlight.” Axel inched his way into the storage room. “Keep it pointed ahead of us. The infected is close.”

They entered the room at a snail's pace, checking each crevice.

“There it is.” Gunner pointed the light to the left. “Underneath a fallen shelf.”

Axel kneeled down to get a closer look. “This one’s not moving.”

“What do you mean?” Shifter took a step back. “Do you think there are more?”

Gunner flicked his light in the direction of Shifter. “Look out!”

Shifter screamed. “Get it off!”

Axel jumped to his feet and spun around to find an infected pinned under a second fallen shelf. It was still alive, stretching its free arm in their direction. “There’s the ones making all that noise.”

“Fuck!” Shifter fell face first on the floor as the infected swept his feet from under him. Flipping over to his back, he kicked his legs frantically, trying to release the claws that had hold of his pants.

“In the chest!” Axel screamed.

Shifter didn’t hesitate before swinging his axe, burying his blade deep in the infected’s chest. “Son of a bitch. Did you see that thing?”

“Is that it?” Gunner spun around. “Do you still hear something?”

“Shh.” Axel pressed a finger to his lips. “I can’t hear shit.”

Both men fell silent, and for a brief second, Axel thought that might be the end.

“I think I hear another one.” Gunner moved deeper into the room, shining his flashlight from side to side. “Do you see anything?”

Axel and Shifter both used their less powerful flashlights to fill in the gaps Gunner's didn't reach.

"I don't hear anything." Shifter paused. "Maybe we should start loading this shit up."

"No." Gunner pressed forward. "I heard something. We need to make sure the room is clear."

"Agreed." Axel had heard nothing else but, like Gunner, knew it was better to be sure than dead.

"It would be nice if we could turn on the damn lights," Shifter said. "What kind of store doesn't have a backup generator?"

"Maybe it needs to be switched on?" Axel thought most generators were automatic nowadays, but this town seemed to resist change.

"Good thinking." Shifter slapped Axel on the back. "I'll look around, see if I can find it."

"Wait!" Axel called out, but it was too late. Shifter was already gone.

Gunner shone the light toward the door. "I'm not sure he understands how dangerous the situation is."

"Or he doesn't care." Axel rubbed his temples. "Should we wait in the hall until he gets back?"

"Yeah." Gunner started that way. "Then if he screams, we're that much closer."

Axel hoped it didn't come to that. "What about the sounds you heard in here?"

"If there are any more, maybe they're trapped like the others. Judging by how they attacked last night, if they haven't made a move yet, we're good."

"I wouldn't go that far." Axel peered over his shoulder. "Maybe we should—"

The lights flickered and came on, cut him off.

"Holy shit." Gunner shut off the flashlight. "He did it."

Axel couldn't believe it either. "I guess we can load things up now." He did a quick inventory. "There's not a whole hell of a lot in here either, but it's better than there was out front."

Gunner stuck his head out the door. "Should we go check on Shifter? I thought he'd be back by now."

"If he was in trouble, we'd have heard something." Axel stopped next to the infected Shifter had killed with his ax. "It's crazy how you can still see the human side underneath all the changes."

"Scary's more like it." Gunner came up beside him. "How do teeth change like that? Ours are flat, but theirs look like a shark or alligator or something."

The last thing Axel wanted to do was stand around speculating. "Let's get to work."

"Wait." Gunner cocked his head. "I heard the sound again. This way."

Axel stayed far enough behind to keep an eye out on the rest of the stockroom as Gunner took a hard left down the last aisle.

"Oh my fucking God!"

The horror in Gunner's voice sent Axel sprinting after him

before skidding to a stop. "Jesus Christ. Is that…?" His brain couldn't comprehend the state of the infected trapped in the corner.

"Is that a dog kennel?" Gunner sputtered.

"Yeah." Bile burned Axel's throat.

"And the infected…." Gunner turned his back to cage. "Was that a ch-child?"

Axel's hands trembled. "I… I think so."

"What the fuck!" Shifter had come out of nowhere. "What the fuck! Jesus. Why? Why?"

"I can't see this." Gunner started down the aisle. "I'll grab some boxes on my way out. I just can't… a damn kid locked in a fucking dog kennel."

"Why would someone do this to a child?" Shifter's voice cracked.

Axel had been so caught up in his horror that he hadn't notice the racket it was making.

"Can you believe this shit?" Shifter asked when Axel didn't answer.

"No. Those two… the two infected trapped under the fallen shelves. If I had to guess, they were the child's parents." Axel pointed to the kennel. "They either put her in there for her protection or theirs."

"Her?"

Tears clogged Axel's throat. "There's a doll in there with her. And pink bows."

Shifter rubbed at his mouth. "Fuck. What do we do now?"

"Load the SUV with the stuff we talked about. Batteries, camping supplies, flashlights, matches."

"What about…?" Shifter jerked his chin toward the cage.

"I'll take care of it." Axel swallowed hard.

"Are you sure?"

"Yeah."

Shifter lowered his eyes and walked away.

Every fiber in his soul screamed at him to get the hell out of there, but he couldn't leave her—it—this way.

Kneeling next to the cage, he didn't hesitate, didn't think, just aimed for the chest and pulled the trigger.

***

The taste of bile still lingered in Axel's mouth as they closed the back of the SUV.

Shifter inspected their haul through the busted-out window. “We got a lot of crap. More than I thought we’d bring back.”

They had packed the trunk of the SUV with as much as they could, though it didn’t hold near as much as Axel had hoped. There were still things they could have used that they had to leave behind.

Gunner pulled the store doors closed. “I found a set of keys behind the counter. Maybe we can lock the place up? Come back to get the rest of the stuff another time?”

Axel didn’t think a locked door would keep people out for long but kept his opinion to himself. “Might as well. Maybe we’ll get lucky.”

Snifter grunted and headed for the driver side. “Let’s get out of here.”

Axel pulled the back door closed, careful not to slam it.

Gunner glanced over his shoulder at Axel. “Sure you don’t want the front seat?”

Axel yawned. “Nah. If Shifter thinks he can find his way back, I’m going to close my eyes for a while. I didn’t sleep at all last night.”

Shifter hot-wired the SUV. “We just keep on this road until we hit her gate.”

“A small-town perk.” Axel laid his head on the sleeping bags stacked beside him and closed his eyes. A short nap would do him wonders.

“Son of a bitch!” Shifter slammed on the brakes, jolting Axel awake.

Axel sat up and scanned the area. “What happened?” They hadn’t even made it out of town yet.

“A woman just ran in front of us.” Gunner stuck his head out of the SUV.

“Where?” Axel rolled down his window to get a better look. “I don’t see anything. Did you hit her?”

"No." Shifter put the SUV in Park. "I think she might have ducked in front of us."

"Dammit." Axel scanned the area. He really didn't want to get out. Even though he didn't see any infected, they could be on top of their little group faster than they could react. "Back up. Maybe she took off."

Shifter eased the SUV backward a few feet until the woman came into view.

"What the hell is she doing?" Gunner asked.

She sat on the ground, her arms wrapped around her knees as she rocked back and forth.

"She's in shock." Axel reached for the door handle but paused. Even though his instincts were to help the woman, he knew it wasn't safe. "What should we do?"

"I don't know," Gunner said. "She's the only person we've seen. What if she's not sick? I don't know if I can handle leaving her here knowing we could have helped."

"What if she's infected?" Shifter snapped. "We can't risk it."

A quick movement drew Axel's attention away from the impending argument. "Did you see that?"

"What?" Shifter and Gunner jerked their heads in unison, both in the opposite direction.

"I don't—" Shifter started to roll up his window. "Fuck! They're coming. We have to go."

Gunner leaned away from his busted-out window. "Now I remember why you didn't want to sit up front."

"That's not why…." Axel's eyes fell on the woman still huddled on the ground. "I'll be right back."

He busted through the door and rushed around the car. "Lady, grab my hand. We need to get into the SUV and get out of here."

Her entire body shook. "I… I—"

"Come on!" He scooped her in his arms. They didn't have time to discuss their options. The infected had caught on to their location and were running for them.

Axel tossed her into the back seat and climbed in. "Go, go, go!"

Shifter hit the gas, and they sped out of town.

Once in the clear, Shifter slowed, and Axel turned his attention back to the borderline hysterical woman. He wiped her matted hair away from her face. "Susan?"

"Who?" Shifter looked back at them in the rearview mirror.

"From the church. She was in charge of the festival."

Gunner rotated around in his seat. "And how do you know all that? I thought you were just friends with the rancher chick?"

"Susan." Axel ignored Gunner, instead focusing on the poor woman trembling beside him. He cupped her chin and forced her to face him. "Can you tell me what happened?"

"I-I," she stuttered. "I…."

"You're safe now," Axel reassured her. "We're taking you somewhere safe."

She raised a trembling hand to her lips, and he caught a glimpse of a bite on the side.

"Shit," Axel mumbled. "She's been bitten."

Shifter skidded off the road and threw the SUV in Park. "Get her out."

"What?" Gunner scrunched his face. "You want to leave her out here? Alone? To die?"

Axel kept his eyes trained on Susan. The rational part of his brain knew exactly how dangerous this woman was, but the other side—the human side—couldn't fathom kicking her out of the SUV to die alone.

"She's already dead," Shifter said with a coldness Axel had never heard before.

"No." Gunner hooked his thumb over his shoulder. "That woman is still alive."

"Not for long," Shifter barked.

"Axel?" Gunner glared. "Want to weigh in on this?"

He knew taking her back to the ranch was stupid, but he couldn't bring himself to open the door. "I don't think I can do it."

"Do what?" Shifter gritted through his teeth. "She's dangerous. We can't bring her back. You want that rancher chick—"

"Britney," Axel corrected.

"You want to earn Britney's trust? Convince her to let us stay? Bringing back an infected ain't the way to do that."

"I know." He thought back to the infected child he had to put down just a while ago. "It's just—"

"Please don't leave me!" Susan grabbed Axel's sleeve. "Please."

"Fuck," Shifter grumbled. "Should have kicked her out before she spoke."

"Jesus," Gunner spat. "What the hell is wrong with you? She's sitting right there."

"Susan?" Axel kept a close eye on her mouth, watching for any signs of aggression. "How long ago were you bitten?"

Tears burst from her eyes. "Thank you. Those… those… things. They were after me."

"Answer the damn question, lady," Shifter snapped.

Susan jumped.

"Take it down a notch, man." Gunner leaned back and patted Susan on the leg. "You're safe now."

Her lips trembled as she went to speak.

"Take your time." Axel grasped her hand.

Shifter snorted.

"And ignore him," Axel added.

Her head bobbed and voice cracked as she spoke. "What was your question?"

"When were you bitten?" Axel asked again.

"This morning," she sobbed. "I went to check on my youngest son—my husband took the other two to his parents'. My son's been sick, and… and… I don't know what changed overnight."

Axel's heart ached for the woman. He didn't think he could hear any more. "He bit you?"

"Yes. Got my finger as I pushed him away. And then I ran. I left my boy sick and alone," she wailed.

"No." Axel wanted to pull her into a hug but thought better of it, instead squeezing her hands in his. "The thing that bit you wasn't your son. Your son is at peace."

Gunner swallowed hard. "Shifter, let's get going."

"With her? Hell no."

Susan gasped for air. "Please don't leave me here alone. Please. I won't survive."

"You're already dead," Shifter said through clenched teeth.

"What?" Susan's eyes widened.

"Enough!" Axel snapped. "Britney knows this woman. We will not leave her alone to die. We'll deal with what comes next back at the farm."

"Britney Campbell?" Susan inspected Axel's face then. "I know you. You're that biker."

"Yeah." Axel patted the back of Shifter's seat. "Let's go. I'll deal with Britney."

Shifter threw the SUV into Drive. "Don't unpack."

CHAPTER SIXTEEN

"Mommy!" Molly shrieked. "I'm bored!"

Britney threw back her head and swore. The kids hadn't even gone five hours without electricity and they were already complaining. She didn't have the heart to tell them it might never come back on again.

"Mommy!" Molly screamed again. "Where are you!"

"Comin'!" she hollered back and then headed down the basement stairs. The kids had decided that the upstairs was no longer safe, and that the basement, because it had no windows, was best place to hang out. Of course, they had no electricity and no windows, which one would think would put a hindrance on their plan. Not her kids. They had pulled out all the lanterns they could find and placed them around the room.

Britney knew she shouldn't let them waste batteries that way, but after everything they'd been through, she didn't want to upset them even further. After a few more hours of hanging out down there, they would tire of being cooped up anyway.

"There you are!" Molly planted her hands on her hips and did her best teenager impression. "I've been calling you!"

"Settle down there, girl. You called twice." Britney patted Molly on the head before taking a seat on the bed. "What's goin' on?"

"We're bored." Seemed Molly had designated herself the spokesperson for the group. Though the boys looked content sitting on the floor playing with their Legos.

"You are?" Britney eyed the pile of Barbies and ponies Molly had carried down after breakfast. "Why? You have plenty of toys to play with."

Molly rolled her eyes. "These are *all* I have. And I've been playing with them *forever*."

"What about all the toys you have in your room? Why don't you go upstairs and play with those?"

"Upstairs?" Molly huffed. "By myself? With a window in my room?"

"You're on the second floor." Trying to reason with a stubborn five-year-old made her head hurt. "Nothin' can get in your window from that high up."

"Carson said *they* could."

Britney glared at her oldest son. "And how would Carson know what *they* can and cannot do?"

He ignored them.

"Yeah!" Molly turned her annoyance on her big brother. "How do you know what *they* can do? You're just a big dummy!"

"Okay." Britney grabbed Molly's hand and guided her up the stairs before the war of insults started. "Why don't you come with me and leave the boys alone."

"They won't let me play." Molly sniffled. Damn, she was getting good at flipping her emotions.

Britney squeezed her hand. "We can do somethin'."

"Like what?" Molly grumbled. "Something boring."

"Enough." Britney hated having to bring out the stern mommy voice, but the child's attitude was grating on her last nerve. "I understand you're upset, and there is a lot of scary stuff goin' on, but that doesn't give you the right to be rude to everyone. We're all sad. And scared. And confused."

Fat tears filled Molly's eyes. "I miss Daddy."

Britney's nose tingled and her eyes blurred. She kneeled down in front of Molly and pulled her into a hug. "Me too, baby. So much. I'm so sorry all of this is happenin'."

"Is he still in the barn?" Her little voice trembled. "Can I see him? I want to tell him bye and I love him."

Tears rolled down Britney's cheeks. She didn't know what to say. The last thing she wanted was for her kids to remember John as the monster he'd become.

"Please, Mommy."

Britney cupped Molly's chin. "Baby… I know you want to see Daddy again, but—" The sound of dogs barking cut her off.

Molly's eyes widened. "Why are they barking? Is there a monster out there?"

"I don't think so. It's probably just the people outside." Britney grabbed her shotgun off the mantel as she headed for the door. "Stay in here. I'm goin' to check things out."

"Don't go, Mommy." Molly seized the hem of Britney's shirt. "I don't want you to die too."

"Shh." Britney brushed the fallen strands of hair out of Molly's face. "I'm not goin' to die. I have a gun for protection. Stay in the house with your brothers, okay?"

She bobbed her head.

"I'll be right back." Britney headed outside and spotted the sheriff's SUV parked near the tree where the bikers hung out. Axel stood among them, as did two other men whose names she didn't know. Inside the SUV, she could sort of make out the silhouette of someone else, though with the sun reflecting off the windshield, she couldn't be sure.

"Axel," she called out. "Can I speak with you?"

He finished the conversation she had interrupted and jogged over. "Hey. What's up?"

"What's up?" Anger coursed through her. "That's all you have to say?"

"Good morning." The corner of his mouth twitched. "Or should I say good afternoon?"

"This isn't a joke. I told you and your friends I wanted you gone." She waved her hands around. "And you're still here. Why?"

Axel's face softened. "Gus told me about your husband. I'm so sorry, Britney. I can't imagine how you and the kids are dealing with such a loss."

The genuine sorrow in his voice caught her off guard. The anger she'd felt just a moment ago faded. "I did what I had to do to protect my kids."

"I get that."

She pushed away the pain eating at her chest.

"I want to apologize for last night," Axel continued. "We showed up unannounced in the middle of the night, expecting you to take us in with nothing to offer in return. It was stupid, and we're lucky you just fired a warning shot."

"Why did you come here?" Britney still didn't understand why they'd chosen her house of all places.

Axel shrugged. "We had nowhere else to go. Don't know anybody around here. And you were kind to us when all the rest of your town wanted to do was gossip and stare. Plus, you kind of told me where you lived."

Britney pinched her lips together, trying not to laugh. "Yeah, well, I won't be makin' that mistake again."

Axel chuckled. "Anyway, I know we had no right showing up here empty-handed and expecting a handout. That's why we went into town this morning for supplies."

"I thought everything in town was closed down?" Britney pinched the bridge of her nose. "That those things overran it?"

"It is, and they have."

"So, what?" Britney's nostrils flared. "You looted a store?"

Axel held his chin high. "'Looted' is kind of harsh considering the situation, don't you think?"

"What store did you break into?" she snapped.

"The general store."

Britney averted her eyes. She'd grown up with Bob, the owner, and his wife, Sandy. They'd worked hard keeping that store going after Bob's father died last year. "Well, that was a stupid place to go. Bob never keeps the place fully stocked."

"That would have been good to know." Axel glanced back at the SUV. "I mean, we still got a trunkful, but it was slim pickings."

"You could have asked!" Britney didn't know why she yelled at him, but she couldn't help it. "I would have told you not to bother."

"We need supplies."

"We!" she shouted. "We? There is no *we*. There is us and there is you. We're not together."

Axel eyed the gun she held firmly by her side. "You mind putting the gun down? You're angry, and it's making me nervous."

"You think I'm goin' to shoot you? Really?" Her muscles quivered. "I just… it's just… you should have talked to me first before runnin' into town and stealin' supplies. You don't even know what I have here or what we might need. For all I know, you just brought back junk."

"Junk? I'm not an idiot. We didn't risk our lives stealing TVs and candy canes."

Britney couldn't help but laugh at the ridiculousness of what he'd just said. "Candy canes? Really?"

Axel rubbed his eyes with the heels of his hands. "I don't know where that came from."

"What did you get?"

"Batteries, bags of rice, a couple of boxes of canned food. Flashlights and matches. And some camping supplies: a few tents, sleeping bags, a small grill."

"We have a grill, so that was a waste of space."

"Sorry," Axel mimicked her bitchy tone. "Maybe next time you can make a list."

She didn't even want to think about there being a next time. "You did well on the rest of the stuff."

Axel smiled. "Was that a compliment?"

"Don't get used to it." She headed off toward the SUV.

"Wait a second." Axel wrapped a hand around her wrist and spun her back to him. "Does that mean you'll let us stay?"

She snatched her arm away. "You don't have to grab me."

He raised his hands in defeat. "Sorry. Won't happen again."

"Thank you. Now I want to see how much stuff you brought back so I can figure out where to put it all."

"Before you go over there"—Axel moved in front of her—"there's something else I need to tell you."

"What is it?" Britney tapped her foot. She wanted to get back inside and check on the kids.

Axel scratched at his five o'clock shadow. "The thing is, we saw no one in town. At least nobody who wasn't infected and turned. That is until we left. A woman ran out in front of the SUV, scared and hyperventilating. And these things, the infected, they're attracted to noise. They came out of nowhere. I couldn't leave her out there."

"So you brought her back here? Another stranger?"

"It's Susan." Axel rubbed the back of his neck. "I know you two don't like each other very much—"

"What?" She pushed past him and sprinted toward the SUV. Gus shifted in front of the back door as Britney reached for the handle. "What are you doin'? Let her out."

"Wait," Axel called out from behind her. "She's been bitten."

Britney whirled around. "Are you fuckin' kidding me!"

"We didn't know when we saved her. It wasn't until we were halfway here that I noticed the bite mark on her hand."

"I told Axel to leave him," one man said.

"Shut the fuck up, Shifter," Axel barked before turning his attention back to Britney. "She was terrified. And lucid. I couldn't leave her out in the middle of nowhere to die. What was I supposed to do?"

Britney peered over her shoulder at Susan, who sat in the back seat sobbing into her hands. "You shouldn't have brought her here. You don't know when or how fast she'll turn. You've put my children—this whole farm—in danger."

"I didn't know what else to do," Axel whispered.

"You have a gun." Britney stormed past him. "Kill her before she kills us all."

***

"We want to go outside and play," Carson whined. "We have nothing to do in here."

Britney took another long swig of her wine. It was early, and probably not the best idea to be drinking with everything going on outside, but she needed something to calm her nerves before she did something stupid.

"Mom!" Carson waved in front of her face. "Are you even listening?"

"You're not goin' outside. Not right now. So please, just go upstairs and play in your room."

"But the window!" Blake yelled from the other room.

Britney glared at Carson. They wanted to go outside but wouldn't go into a damn room with a window? "You need to go convince the twins that your rooms are safe."

"But—"

She held up her index finger. "No buts. No arguin'. There is no way anything is gettin' into your rooms from the window. There is no ledge on the outside. Nothin' to grab hold of or pull up on. Check the windows, make sure they're locked, and go play."

"Fine. But if we get eaten, you're going to feel really bad."

"Go!" Britney pointed to the stairs.

Carson spun around and stomped his feet all the way into the living room. "Come on, you two. Mom said upstairs."

"But the windows!" Blake said again.

"Don't be such a baby. They can't get in the window."

Molly gasped. "You said they could. You're such a liar."

Most of the time when the kids argued, Britney would try to intervene. Right now, she didn't care. As long as they did it upstairs.

She sat in the kitchen alone for a while, sipping on her wine and contemplating what to do next. With everything going on, she hadn't checked on or fed the animals that morning. Plus, John's body was still locked in the barn. And she hadn't been able to get a hold of his parents. It wouldn't take but thirty minutes to drive over there and speak with them in person, but that would mean leaving the house. Leaving the kids. Or taking them with her. She wasn't sure which was worse.

Being out in the open seemed risky. Even if she went armed, if more than a couple of—what had Axel called them?—the *infected* came after her, she'd be screwed.

"Fuck." She propped her elbows on the table and covered her face. The lack of sleep clouded her judgment, and worse, put her on edge to the point that she felt like she might snap any minute.

She needed a nap. With the kids upstairs and the bikers outside, this would be the perfect opportunity. She didn't need anyone in the house to watch the kids, just someone to keep an eye out for danger lurking around the property.

Danger like Susan. Jesus, what was Axel thinking bringing her here? They had to be smarter if they were to survive. Emotions needed to take a back seat to reason. One infected, fully turned or not, could wipe them all out in a matter of days, maybe even hours. She wouldn't let that happen.

Britney threw back the rest of the wine, grabbed her gun and headed outside. This ended now.

"What are you doing?" Axel asked as Britney sprinted past him.

Her eyes locked on Susan, who was still in the back seat of the police SUV sobbing.

"Britney!" Axel yelled. "Stop!"

Once again Gus blocked the door of the SUV.

"Get out of my way." She aimed the gun at him. "We have to end this before someone else gets infected."

Gus didn't hesitate before stepping aside. "If you think you can do it."

Britney yanked open the back door and pointed the gun at Susan. "Get out. Now!"

Susan's blotchy face trembled. "Please."

"Out! Don't make me tell you again."

Susan held up her hands and slid out. "Okay."

"On your knees!" Britney followed her every movement with the barrel of the gun, afraid that any minute she might try to attack them.

"Get back!" Axel yelled to the others. He came up beside Britney and whispered, "You don't want to do this."

"I don't." Britney's voice cracked. "But what choice do we have? Her bite is a death sentence. She might be lucid now, but for how long?"

"Kill me," Susan croaked. "Just do it. I know what I'm turning into. I don't want to be a monster. I don't want to hurt anybody. So kill me before it's too late."

Britney swallowed hard and blinked away the tears clouding her vision. She looked down at Susan, a woman she'd known her entire life, and her finger twitched over the trigger. "I… I—"

"Mommy! No!" The sound of Blake's cries sliced through her heart.

Britney's legs buckled and she collapsed, the gun slipping from her hand.

Axel caught the gun before it hit the ground.

Angie rushed to Britney's side and pulled her close. "It's going to be okay. We got this. It's going to be okay."

Britney sobbed into her chest like a child with her mother. "I would have killed her. My babies almost saw me kill someone."

"Shh." Angie rubbed her back. "They saw you put down the gun. That's all that matters."

"Where are they?" Britney pulled out of Angie's embrace. Rainey had Molly tucked in her arms while she guided the boys into the house.

"Rainey's great with kids. She'll calm them down and keep an eye on them until you're ready. They're in good hands."

Britney turned to face Susan, who was now on her feet next to Axel. "I'm sorry. I just want to protect my kids from all of this."

"I would have done the same thing, but I wouldn't have hesitated to pull the trigger." Susan straightened her filthy dress and threw back her shoulders.

Britney lowered her eyes, feeling like a failure even though she'd just spared a life.

Axel cocked his head. "What are you trying to say? You're ready to die now?"

"Of course not." Susan ran her index fingers under her eyes, wiping away the stray tears that still lingered. "Just that I wish I wouldn't have been so passive when it came to protecting my son."

"Did he…?" Britney could hardly form the words. "Did he turn?"

Susan sucked in a sharp breath. "And attacked me. I left him locked in our house. Alone."

Britney stood, wiping the dirt from her jeans. "Well, I think I killed John. Bullet straight through the heart."

"I'm so sorry." Susan lowered her eyes. "We should get this over with. I don't want to risk harming your children. I actually *like* them."

Britney laughed. After all these years of hating each other, Britney wanted nothing more than to pull the woman into a tight hug. "There's a small house in the back. My great-grandparents built it when they first bought this land. There's not much to it, but you'll be comfortable in there until…."

"We're just going to leave her loose?" Axel asked. "No offense."

"None taken." Susan swallowed hard. "You're right. I would be better if I got as far away from here as possible."

"There's a bed." Britney could tell by the way Susan fidgeted that she was terrified of being alone. "It's handmade and heavy. We can secure you to it and keep you comfortable. If you want."

Susan dropped her head and nodded. Teardrops splattered on the ground at her feet as they led her away.

***

"Good mornin'." Britney peeked her head inside her great-grandparents' old house. Even though they had tied Susan's hands and feet to the bed, she always checked first. "How are you feelin'?"

Sweat beaded across Susan's graying skin. "I can't do this anymore. I tried to bite Angie yesterday and don't even remember doing it. Whatever this is inside of me, it's trying to take over."

"You think somethin' is inside of you?" Britney took a seat in the chair next to the bed. Two days had passed since Susan had been bitten, and she was fading fast. "Like you can feel the virus?"

"Virus? Do you still think that's what this is?" Susan's eyes fell on the bowl in Britney's hand. "Is that for me?"

"Yes. Sorry." She'd forgotten about the food. "I hope you like oatmeal."

"Not particularly." Susan opened her mouth for a bite. Britney stuck the spoon in Susan's mouth, careful to keep her fingers as far away as possible.

Susan gagged and spit the oatmeal out. "I can't. It's awful."

"I can make you somethin' else. Eggs, maybe?" Britney may have spent the last twentysomething years at war with the woman, but she didn't hate her. Not really.

"You're not listening." Susan wiggled her fingers.

Britney took her hand and squeezed tight. "I'm listenin'."

"I'm ready to die. This, being tied to the bed, is not how I want to spend the little time I have left. And I sure as hell don't want to turn into one of those monsters. Please, Brit, let me go."

Tears clogged Britney's throat. The thought of someone killing Susan or her taking her own life made her sick. "I understand and will help in any way I can."

Susan let out a weighted breath. "Thank you."

"Do you know how you want to go?" Britney couldn't believe she was asking such a question.

"How do you kill those things, the infected?"

Britney pressed her lips together, trying not to think about John. "Through the chest."

Susan closed her eyes. "Will you do it? Shoot me in the chest, I mean."

"You want me to do it?" Britney dropped Susan's hand. "I don't know if I can."

A hacking laugh slash cough escaped Susan's lips. "You always said I didn't have a heart. Guess now I get to prove you wrong."

"I shouldn't have broken your nose in elementary school." Britney hung her head and let the tears fall.

"I did kiss your boyfriend on the playground." Susan's voice cracked, making the whole situation even harder.

Britney forced a smile. "What ever happened to Billy Horner? I lost track of him after high school."

"You don't know?" Susan's eyes brightened. "After college he moved to California and got married. To a man."

"Oh my God. You're kidding!" Britney's hand flew to her mouth. "That explains so much."

"Right?" Susan giggled. "He's actually the one who helped pick out my senior prom dress."

Britney gasped. "No? The red one with the open back?"

"Yep."

"Damn, he has good taste. That dress was gorgeous." Britney leaned back in her chair. "Did you know he was gay in high school? You two were good friends, weren't you?"

"I had my suspicions, but he hadn't come out yet."

"That's crazy." Britney hadn't thought about Billy in years. "Though I can see it. He always had the best taste in clothes of any of the other boys in our school. I just can't believe I never noticed it sooner."

"It's not like you didn't have more important things to deal with." A pained expression washed over Susan's face. "I never told you how sorry I was to hear about your mother passing. And your father."

Britney didn't know what to say. "You sent flowers with a lovely card."

"I was a bitch." Susan focused on the ceiling. "I'm ready to go now. My jaw is killing me, and my entire body aches. I don't want to hurt anyone. And if we wait too much longer, I will."

"Um." Susan might have been ready, but Britney sure wasn't. Not now. Not yet.

"I've changed my mind," Susan said without looking at Britney. "I don't want you to kill me. Get someone else. Maybe that biker who wanted to leave me for dead. He'll probably jump at the chance."

Shifter had been against keeping Susan alive for this long, so she was probably right. "If you're sure you're ready."

Susan's eyes watered, but she smiled through the pain etched in the lines of her face. "Yes. The sooner the better."

Britney forced herself to stand. "Okay. I'll go get someone."

"Thank you."

Britney reached for the door handle.

"Do you think…?" Susan's voice was barely audible. "My son, even though he's been turned, do you think his soul is in heaven and he's waiting for me? I would hate to think he's stuck in some sort of limbo."

Turning around, Britney held back her tears and smiled. "There's no doubt in my mind that he's waitin' for you with open arms."

"Thank you." Susan bit down on her bottom lip. "Now hurry. I have somewhere to be."

Britney closed the door and hurried off to find Axel. Tears blurred her vision, but she forced herself not to succumb to the sorrow or guilt or whatever it was that ate away at her conscience.

All these years she'd talked shit about Susan behind her back. Even said some not-nice things about her son,

Colten. She'd never believed much in karma, but it sure seemed like it had come back to bite her in the ass.

"Britney." Axel rose to his feet. He and the other bikers had set up the tents they'd brought back under the big tree in her front yard. "What's wrong?"

"It's Susan," she addressed the group, who sat around a small campfire, a cold front having blown in the night before. "She's ready to die."

"What do you mean, ready?" Angie asked. "Like about to kick the bucket or pull the trigger?"

Gus turned to her and frowned. "Let's try to be more tactful. Susan is, after all, Britney's friend. This can't be easy on either of them."

"She wants to die before she hurts anyone. And she's goin' to need some help." Britney tried to keep her voice steady, but it came out uneven and whiny.

"Not you." Axel reached for his gun. "I can… help."

He sounded just as unsure as she did. "What about you, Shifter? You haven't shut up about endin' her life since she arrived."

"You think I *want* to kill her?" Shifter stood and moved toward Britney. "She's a threat. To me. To my friends. To your kids. And you're keeping her locked up like some kind of sick puppy. There's not a damn thing we can do for her now but put her out of her misery."

Britney shoved her pistol into his chest. "You're right. Let's get it over with."

Shifter took the gun slower than Britney expected. "Fine."

He headed toward the old shack with Britney and Axel trailing behind.

"Are you sure about this?" Axel asked.

"No." Britney pushed back the voice in her head that screamed to put an end to this craziness. "But Susan wants to die. She doesn't want to turn into one of the infected. I can't say I blame her for that."

"That I understand. But you really want Shifter to be the one to pull the trigger?"

Britney watched the determined biker slow his steps as he approached the small house. "How well do you know him?"

Axel shrugged. "He was a good friend of my dad's. A nice guy who would do anything for the ones he cares about."

Britney stopped. "Do you think we can trust him?"

"Yes." Axel glanced at Shifter and then back to Britney. "I know right now he seems a bit unruly, but he only wants to protect us. All of us."

"Are you coming in?" Shifter called out. "You want to say goodbye?"

"No." She couldn't go back inside or she'd never let him pull the trigger. "Tell her…."

"It's better this way, you know," Shifter said as Britney and Axel approached the house. "She'll die in peace knowing she won't become one of those things. Won't hurt the people she cares about."

Axel placed a hand on the small of Britney's back. "It's what I would want, if I were in Susan's position."

Shifter smiled at her in a way that made her feel slightly better. "You ready?"

Tears fell from her eyes, but she nodded anyway.

"Okay." Shifter entered the house and closed the door.

"How long do you think it—"

The gunshot reverberated in her ears, and her legs buckled. Axel caught her before she crumbled to the ground.

"It's okay," he whispered. "It's over. She's at peace."

The hinges of the door whined. Britney jumped to her feet and glared at Shifter. "You couldn't even give her a second before you pulled the trigger? What kind of heartless bastard are you?"

Shifter staggered toward them, the gun hanging at his side. "She was unconscious. Wore a smile as she slept. Probably dreaming about her boy. It was better that way. She didn't see it coming. There was no fear or second-guessing. She's free."

Britney watched as Shifter walked back to their makeshift camp, dumbfounded by his compassion.

"Are you okay?" Axel asked.

"I will be." She turned for the barn. "But first I need your help with somethin'."

***

"Why do we have to wear this?" Carson tugged at the jacket of his suit. "It's not Christmas. Or Easter."

Britney spun him around and crouched in front of him. "Because today we're layin' your daddy to rest. And Miss Susan."

She'd never taken the kids to a funeral before and wasn't sure how they would react, but it was important for them to say goodbye and hopefully find closure. If such a thing existed.

"But why do we have to wear this?" Carson made a big show out of his uncomfortableness. "It's so annoying. And it's not like Dad can see us."

Britney held her tongue as a multitude of emotions overwhelmed her. The last thing she wanted to do was say something out of anger and make Carson even more upset. "Because it's respectful. And we're all dressin' up."

"Even the bikers?" Carson cocked an eyebrow.

"Um, well…." Britney didn't know how to answer. She hadn't spoken to any of the bikers besides Axel since Shifter helped with Susan.

"They are coming, aren't they?"

Britney stood and straightened his jacket. "Probably not. They didn't know your dad or Susan."

"But they're our friends."

That surprised Britney. "Friends?"

"Yes." Carson plopped on the bed. "That's what Rainey said."

"I need to go get dressed." She gave him a quick kiss on the head and headed for her bedroom.

Over the past few days, the former teacher had spent a lot of time with the kids while Britney took care of Susan and the farm. Axel had volunteered to plan the funeral, including prepping the bodies. At first, she tried to argue, not wanting to put him in such a terrible position, but he had insisted. And after considering what prepping the bodies would entail, she accepted his offer. After everything, she didn't think she could handle seeing John as the monster he became.

In the master bathroom, she splashed cold water on her face and shivered. God, how she missed hot water already. Thankfully, the well ran on a windmill, so they didn't have to worry about getting water, but no electricity sucked. The house had a backup generator, but she hadn't turned it on yet. Probably wouldn't until necessary. They would need the house's heater in the winter. Nights could be brutal.

"Britney?" The sound of Axel's voice coming from such a close distance made her jump.

Her hand flew to her chest as she spun around to find him standing at the door of her bathroom. "What the hell are you doin'?"

Axel crossed his arms and leaned against the doorframe. "The kids let me in. You didn't hear me calling your name? Or the kids screaming at you that I was here?"

"Obviously not." Her heart thrashed in her chest. "What are you doin' in here anyway?"

"You said to meet you on the front porch at ten." He made a show of looking down at his watch. "It's ten thirty now. I wanted to make sure you and the kids were okay."

Britney propped herself up against the counter. "We're fine."

"Are you sure?" Axel asked. "Because you didn't even hear me come in, and I caught you staring at your bathtub."

Had she been staring at the tub that intently? "I was just thinkin'."

"About hygiene?"

Britney chuckled. "That and how much I miss soakin' in the bathtub. It's always been my way of unwindin' after a stressful day or week. Near-scaldin' water, candles, bubbles and a big glass of wine. John would keep the kids occupied, and I would just close my eyes and relax."

"I'm sorry."

Britney blinked away the unexpected tears. "For what?"

"For all you and your kids are going through."

"It's not like it's just us." Britney rotated around and scrunched her nose at her now-blotchy face. "We're all goin' through this shit."

"It's different. We only have ourselves to look after. You have three small kids." Axel handed her a tissue from the counter. "I think I can speak for everyone when

I say we'll do everything we can to keep your children safe."

Britney's chin trembled, but she didn't dare look up for fear of breaking down completely. "Thank you."

"Take your time. I'll meet you on the porch when you're ready."

"You're welcome to wait in the house," Britney said without a second thought. "If you want."

"Thanks. Do you mind if I hang with the kids? They had a pretty serious game of Go Fish going on down there."

Britney's eyes darted to him and then back to the mirror. She couldn't believe this burly, tattooed man wanted to spend time with her kids. "Sure. But I feel it's only fair to warn you, they'll kick your ass and laugh in your face while doin' it."

Axel snorted. "My kind of people. See you in a few."

After he left, Britney rummaged through her closet and settled for a knee-length black dress and matching cowboy boots. High heels weren't going to cut it today.

In the kitchen, she found Axel and the kids sitting around the breakfast table, each with a set of cards in their hands.

"Molly." Axel peeked over his cards and grinned. "Do you have any fours?"

"Go fish," she giggled.

"Son of a bi—" Axel paused and cleared his throat. "Sorry."

Blake snickered. "It's okay. Mommy says bad words all the time."

"Hey!" Britney playfully smacked him on the back of the head. "Stop tellin' people that."

"Mom." Carson drew out the word for emphasis. "You always tell us not to lie."

"And I also tell you not to be goin' around makin' me look bad." She kissed the top of his head. "Are we ready?"

Molly popped up from her chair. "Is Axel coming too?"

"Um…." She didn't know how to answer that. He'd planned the damn thing, but they never discussed if he wanted to attend.

"Of course I'm going," Axel said, grabbing his leather jacket. "We all are."

Britney's eyes met his. "Everyone?"

Axel cocked an eyebrow. "Why do you look so surprised?"

"It's just that, well," Britney started as she corralled the kids toward the door, "you guys didn't know John or Susan. And funerals are not exactly pleasant."

Axel held open the front door and gestured them to the porch where the rest of the bikers waited. "We take care of our own."

Tears clogged Britney's throat, but she forced them back. If she cried this early, she'd never stop. "Thank you all for comin'."

"Sorry we didn't dress up." Gus walked beside her as they headed for her family's cemetery past the main homestead.

Britney smiled but didn't reply. She had no words. Their kindness had pushed her to the edge of an emotional breakdown; she was afraid if she opened her mouth, she wouldn't be able to hold back the tears.

They walked in silence the rest of the way—an amazing feat for her children, since it took a good thirty minutes. She rarely visited the small cemetery where both her parents were buried, along with her dad's parents and grandparents. The place had always given her the creeps as a child. And after her mother died, it served as a constant reminder of the life she would never have.

"Britney?"

She glanced up at Axel, who had come up beside her. "Yes?"

"I hope you don't mind." His gaze shifted toward the cemetery. "I wrapped the bodies in sheets. I didn't think you wanted the kids seeing their father that way."

Britney's eyes fell on the two wrapped bodies lying beside two already dug graves. A wooden cross marked each one.

"I hope I didn't overstep," he continued.

"No." Britney blinked away the tears. "Thank you."

"Mommy!" Molly called from the rusty wrought iron gate. "Can we go in?"

"Sure, honey." Britney had only taken the kids up here a couple of times. A few months back, the twins had been obsessed with learning more about Britney's parents. Death was not a concept kids grasped easily.

Pausing at the gate, Britney scanned their surroundings, suddenly all too aware of how exposed they were out there in the open.

"I don't like this," she whispered under her breath.

Axel held open the gate. "Several of us brought guns. We'll keep an eye out for any sort of movement."

"We should make it quick," Britney said as she entered.

"Take all the time you need." Axel rounded her parents' grave.

"We won't need much." Britney headed for the kids, who moved amongst the headstones, taking a moment to listen to Carson as he read each one.

"Will Daddy have one of those big stone things with his name on it?" Blake asked as Britney came up beside them.

"One day, maybe." As hard as she tried to keep her attention on the grave before them, her eyes kept dancing toward John's wrapped body. "Come on now."

She guided them toward the two shallow openings. Each of them dragged their feet, but she didn't push. She knew how tough it was to say goodbye to a parent.

The bikers hung back, all except Axel and Angie.

"Where's the box?" Molly asked.

Carson glared. "That's mean."

Britney pulled them apart before a full-on brawl started. "I don't think she was askin' to be mean. Do you mean the coffin, honey?"

Molly bobbed her head. "Yes."

"Yeah, he needs a box," Blake chimed in, "or else the worms will eat him."

Britney's body shook, though with humiliation, anger or amusement, she couldn't tell. Maybe a little of them all. It wasn't like he was trying to be funny; the sadness in his eyes was obvious.

Angie kneeled in front of Blake and straightened his tie. "Don't you worry about that, sugar britches. Your daddy's body might be wrapped up in that blanket, but his soul is in heaven, smiling down on you."

Blake looked up and, as if on cue, a raindrop landed on his cheek.

"See." Angie wiped it away. "He's letting you know he's here."

Blake frowned. "By crying?"

"Happy tears." Angie rose to her feet, a bemused look on her face.

Molly waved at the sky. "Hi, Daddy. I love you. Say hi to Jesus for me."

Blake waved along with her.

Carson wasn't as obvious, but Britney caught him glance upward and smile.

"What about Ms. Susan?" Blake asked.

Britney rubbed his little shoulder. "I'm sure she's in heaven too."

"But, Mommy," Molly said in her all-knowing tone, "you've said lots of times that Miss Susan can go to hell."

Britney's face flushed while everyone else chuckled, except for Blake and Carson, who busted out laughing. "Molly, honey. I didn't mean literally *go to hell.*"

"What did you mean, Mommy?"

Axel cleared his throat. "Maybe we should begin? Britney, did you want to say a few words?"

Her eyes widened. She hadn't even thought to prepare something. "Um…."

"What if," Angie cut in, "I sing 'Amazing Grace'?"

Her heart broke at the thought, not because of the song but because of how much John would have loved it. "That would be lovely. Thank you."

CHAPTER SEVENTEEN

The sound of blocks crashing on the wood floors made Britney jump. She lived in a constant state of fear, always worrying something bad was about to happen.

She pushed away the knot in her stomach and focused on cooking the eggs, grateful John had the propane tank filled last month. Not that she'd used the stove much. They usually cooked most of their meals outside over an open flame, but it was a wet morning, and the fire refused to ignite.

A week had passed since the funerals, and Britney and the bikers had fallen into a good routine around the farm. Everyone had offered to pitch in with whatever she needed. The only obstacle was none of them knew a damn thing about farming, but they'd proved to be fast learners and hard workers, which made her life a whole hell of a lot easier.

She moved the eggs to the back burner and pulled out another frying pan for the bacon. The backup house generator was now being used to run the refrigerator and freezer. John had a knack for stockpiling meat from the animals he slaughtered or killed hunting. She used to give him a hard time for it, but now she couldn't be more grateful. They had enough meat to last through the winter, if not the spring if they portioned it correctly.

Carson strolled into the kitchen and opened the fridge. "I'm hungry. And so are the twins." Some habits were hard to break. Her kids were snackers. And their favor snack had run out two days ago.

"Breakfast will be ready soon."

"Ugh," he grumbled. "Can't we have something now?"

"No." She closed the fridge door and shooed him out of the room. "I'll call you when it's ready."

She went to open the bacon when she heard the scream followed by a gunshot. The package slipped from her fingers as she bolted for the front door, grabbing the shotgun she kept loaded on a high shelf out of the kids' reach.

"Downstairs!" she yelled at the kids as entered the living room. "Now!"

They didn't argue or hesitate before running for the basement.

Throwing open the front door, she readied her gun.

The bikers sprinted toward the house and up the porch stairs.

"Infected!" Axel screamed.

Britney moved from the doorway, allowing them to enter, and then locked the door behind them. "In the basement. Follow me."

"Where are the kids?" Rainey asked, her voice shaking.

"Already down there." She held open the door for them, making sure everyone made it inside.

Downstairs, the kids had already turned on the lanterns. They waited on the bed, the twins buried under the covers and Carson keeping watch.

"What's going on?" Carson sounded so much like an adult it was eerie.

Axel's eyes darted to Britney, and she nodded. There was no point in lying to them. This was the world they now lived in, and they all—her included—needed to accept that.

"We spotted some infected," Axel said.

"Spotted?" Angie's mouth went slack. "It attacked my tent!"

"Jesus." Britney gulped down a couple of breaths. "Are you okay? Was anyone bit?"

Gus took a seat on the floor and put his head between his knees. "It was a close call, but no, I don't think so."

Britney looked to each of them as they shook their heads.

"I'm so sorry. This is all my fault." Britney ran her fingers over her eyes. "I should have never let you stay in tents outside. I should have opened my home. There's plenty of room." They had helped so much, taken over so many of the daily responsibilities. It was the least she could do.

Axel rubbed her back. "I think plenty of room is a bit of an overstatement."

"What?" Britney gawked at him. "You want to stay outside in tents?"

"No." Mac crossed his bulging arms over his chest. "The tents suck, and it's cold outside."

"But we can't impose," Gus added. "There are children who must be considered."

Britney thought about it for a minute. "What about the hay barn?"

"Isn't that full of hay?" Gunner asked.

"Yes." Britney held back the smartass comeback tickling her tongue. "But there's a small room John used occasionally and a loft we can clear."

"That's not a bad id—" The horrendous cries of animals in distress cut Axel off. "What was that?"

"Shit." Britney grabbed her gun. "They're killin' the animals. We have to do something."

"Like what?" Shifter gaped the stairs. "Like go out there? We don't even know how many there are."

"We don't have a choice." Britney stared at the bikers. "They're killing our food supplies."

Axel stepped forward. "Gunner and I are the only ones with a decent shot besides Gus, whose heart isn't great. The others should stay back, keep the kids safe."

Britney turned to her trembling children.

Molly blinked away her tears. "Mommy, please don't go out there."

She moved to the bed and sat beside Carson. "I have to go. We can't let them kill all the animals."

"The others can do it," Blake cried. "We don't want you to die like Daddy."

As Britney was about to reassure them that she'd be back, Carson spoke up. "Mom will be fine. She has to protect the farm and the animals."

The twins both nodded, their faces racked with fear.

Britney squeezed Carson's knee. "When did you get so big?"

Carson threw back his shoulders. "I'm the man of the house now. It's my job to be strong."

Britney wasn't sure how she felt about that, but this wasn't the time to get into it. Another cow cried out, forcing her to her feet.

She kissed each of her children on the tops of their heads. If she made a big scene about leaving, it would only make it harder.

"Time to go," Britney said with as much muster as she could gather. "You have weapons?"

“We each have a Glock.” Axel removed the gun from his hip holster. “And a couple of bullets left.”

“That won’t work.” Britney jogged past them. “Luckily there’s a safe down here where John kept his extra guns.”

“*Extra* guns?” Shifter asked.

Britney entered the code, tossed them both a cartridge and grabbed one for herself. “I think these are fifteen-round magazines. Don’t waste them.” Before closing the safe, she turned to Gus. “I have another handgun in here if you need it.”

Gus shook his head. “Last thing we need to do is waste your bullets.”

Britney’s heart raced at the thought of leaving her kids down here without at least one of them carrying, but then more animals cried out. *Guess I don’t have much of a choice.* “Please keep them safe.”

Rainey had moved to the bed with the kids. “We’ll protect them with our lives.”

“Britney.” Axel seized her elbow. “We have to go before it’s too late.”

She knew they needed to hurry, that they had wasted too much time already, but her motherly instincts kept her feet planted in place. Leaving them felt like the worst form of torture imaginable.

“I love you.” She blew a kiss to each of her children and then headed up the stairs.

CHAPTER EIGHTEEN

"What's the plan?" Axel asked as he checked to make sure Gus locked the basement door.

"Kill the fuckers." Britney didn't bother slowing down as she raced for the front door.

Axel sprinted for her, wrapping his arms around her waist before she bolted out the door. "Hold on there. We can't just run outside shooting everything we see."

Britney pushed out of his arms. "The hell we can't."

"We have no idea what's out there or how many there are."

"He's right." Gunner peeked out the living room window. "We need to be smart about this."

She clenched her jaw but didn't argue. "What do you suggest?"

Axel opened the door, stuck his head out and listened. "Stay together. Take it slow. Do you know what animals they might have been attacking?"

"Probably the pen closest to the house," Britney said, "or we wouldn't have heard them."

"That's the one to left?" Made sense, as it was on the same side as the basement. "How many cows are in there?"

"Six," Gunner replied and then shrugged when both Axel and Britney openly stared at him. "What? I've been feeding them."

He didn't hear any more animals crying out, but that didn't mean much. "I suggest we check that area first. Everyone agree?"

Neither answered but didn't disagree, so he took that as they were all on the same page.

"Who's the better shot?" Gunner asked. "I'm decent."

"Does it matter?" Britney pulled her hair up into a ponytail.

Gunner rolled his neck. "Just thought the better shot might go first."

"I'll go first." Axel stepped outside and scanned the area.

Britney pushed past him and headed down the stairs. "Keep up."

"That girl is a firecracker," Gunner whispered as he and Axel followed Britney down the stairs.

Axel readied his gun. "Let's focus on the task at hand. Keep your eyes open. We all know how fast these fuckers can come out of know where."

Gunner rotated around and kept his eyes on their back.

"You see anything?" Axel asked as they approached the pen. There were several trees and bushes surrounding it, making it hard to get a good look inside.

Britney slowly approached the gate and crouched down. "Shit. There are two. They killed a cow."

"Are the others hurt?" Gunner asked.

Axel settled in next to Britney. "I don't think so."

"They're in the far corner." Britney leaned closer. "What now?"

"Draw them to us." Axel searched the ground for something he could use. "They're attracted to sound. If we bang on the railings, maybe they'll come check it out. When they get closer, we fire."

Britney picked up a rock that lay by her feet and handed one to Axel. "I hope this works."

"Gunner," Axel said, "keep an eye on our backs. Just in case there are others we haven't seen."

"Got it."

"Ready?" Axel asked Britney.

She nodded.

"Okay." Axel held his breath and slammed the rock into the metal post. The infected jerked their heads in the direction of the sound. "We got their attention. Now let's get them to come over."

Britney and Axel beat their rocks against the metal fencing, each hit drawing the infected closer. It didn't take but a minute for them to move close enough that Axel felt comfortable taking a shot.

"You keep hitting the fence and I'll shoot," he whispered to Britney as he kept his eyes on the infected. When she didn't reply, he took a second to look in direction. The rock slipped from her hand, and her entire body trembled. "Britney? What's wrong?"

Tears streamed down her face. "They're my in-laws."

Axel studied the two infected, who had their noses in the air, trying to figure out where the noise came from. Besides the clothes they still wore and the shape of their bodies, neither resembled a human anymore with their bald heads and gray skin. "How can you tell?"

"Her necklace." Britney fell to her backside and brought her knees to her chest. "I can't do this."

"Um, Axel?" Gunner said, raising his gun. "They're getting closer."

"Britney, do not freak out on me now." Axel aimed his gun and fired, missing. Damn things were so fast. "We need you."

She continued to shake beside him. "She was like a mother."

Axel and Gunner both fired, Gunner hitting the farther one in the pelvis, slowing it down.

"Britney," Axel said in a sharp tone. "Your in-laws are dead. These things killed them. Now get off your ass and help us take them down. Do you want your kids to lose their mother too?"

Her eyes narrowed. It had pissed her off, but she got up off the ground and fired. Her first shot hit the injured one in the leg, the second square in the chest, killing it. She was a damn good shot. Better than he'd expected.

"How the hell do they move so fast?" Gunner fired another round at the one still standing.

"Move." Britney shoved both men out of the way. "I need to get a better angle."

Axel fired off a couple more rounds, finally hitting the thing in the shoulder. It paused for a second, long enough for Britney to shoot it in the chest.

"Jesus." She collapsed to the ground, her back against the fence. "That was close."

Close was an understatement. The second infected had fallen not twenty feet away.

"Are you okay?" Gunner kneeled beside Britney.

She squeezed her eyes closed and nodded. "Sorry for freezin'. I don't know what came over me."

Axel sat down beside her and patted her thigh, dirt flying in all directions. "You've lost a lot these last few days."

Britney stood and dusted off her jeans. “I could have gotten us all killed.”

“You’re being too hard on yourself.” Gunner’s eyes went to Axel as if asking what they should do next.

Axel didn’t like self-pity. But she had screwed up, and he felt like maybe tough love might work better with Britney than coddling. “You’re right. You screwed up, and you could have gotten not only us but everyone inside killed.”

Her eyes bugged out and her nostrils flared. “What?”

“Axel. Man.” Gunner shuffled back. “That’s a little harsh.”

“This is a harsh world.” Axel moved closer to Britney. “Emotional attachment to the infected will get you killed. Freezing up when under attack will get you killed.”

Tears welled in her eyes, but she said nothing.

“You screwed up today.” Axel placed a hand on each of her shoulders. “But you also snapped out of it and saved us. We have to remember that once they turn, they are no longer the people we knew. Whatever is causing this takes over. I, for one, would want to know someone would shoot me instead of allowing me to become a killer.”

Britney dropped her chin to her chest. “I should have gone over there.”

“Over where?” Axel asked

“To my in-laws’ house.” Her voice cracked. “After John died—after I killed him—I tried to call them, but they never answered. I should have gone over there to tell them what happened to their son. If I did, this would have never happened.”

Axel cupped her chin and lifted her head. “Or you might have been killed. Your kids might have been killed.”

"Or they could still be alive. I could have warned them."

"You can't think like that." Axel pulled her into a hug. He hoped she didn't mind, but she looked like she needed some comforting. "All we can do is keep moving forward."

"I hate to break this up," Gunner said, "but shouldn't we check out the rest of the place and make sure there aren't any more?"

Britney wiggled out of Axel's arms and wiped her face with the back of her hand. "Agreed. They were the only two who lived on their ranch, but we have other neighbors. No one close, but I'm not sure that matters."

Axel peered back into the cattle pen. "What should we do about the bodies? The infected and the cattle?"

"Burn the cattle." Britney let out an audible sigh. "And bury my in-laws next to their son. But no funeral. And don't mention who it was in front of the kids. They were close to their grandparents. I'll tell them when I think they're ready."

"Of course." Axel turned to Gunner, who nodded.

"Thank you." Britney forced a smile. "I guess we should make sure the rest of the place is safe."

Axel gestured her onward. "Lead the way."

***

Tensions ran thick as they sat around the dining room table eating cold eggs and a slice of toast. Britney had offered to reheat them and cook the bacon she'd left on the counter, but everyone decided they were too hungry to wait. Plus, it was nearing lunchtime; no need to waste a perfectly good slab of bacon when they'd be eating again in the next few hours.

"Mommy." Molly ended the silence. "I'm done. Can I go upstairs and play?"

"Sure, honey." Britney pushed her untouched eggs around with her fork. "Carson? Blake? What about you two? I think there's a little left in the pan."

"I'm done." Carson took his plate to the kitchen and came back with an apple in hand.

Blake stuffed the last of his eggs in his mouth. "Me too."

"Go play, then," Britney said with a smile that was obviously forced. "Upstairs with your sister. No fightin'."

"Come on, Blake." Carson took his brother's hand and half guided, half dragged him upstairs.

When Axel was sure they were out of earshot, he turned to Britney. "Are you okay?"

She didn't look up. "I'm not a great liar."

"Kids are resilient," Rainy reassured her. "They'll be okay."

"They've been through so much." Britney kept her eyes on her plate. "Seen so much already. It kills me to know this is the world they're goin' to grow up in. I just want them to grow up in a place that's safe."

"Maybe it won't be." Angie, who sat to Britney's left, squeezed her hand. "We have no idea what's going on in the rest of the world. They could be fighting back, creating a vaccine. Or a cure. This might not be our forever."

Axel wished he held the same optimism Angie did. "I think we need to figure out how the infected got in. You have a fence surrounding the entire property, right?"

"A ten-foot electric one." Britney set down her fork. "Not that it does us any good now. Still, it's a damn good fence. We had it installed after a very aggressive bear attacked our cattle."

"You think the infected could get through it?" Shifter asked. "Their claws are ridiculous."

"I don't know. The steel is top-notch." Britney stared at her eggs. "I hate to waste these. Anyone want them?"

Mac raised his hand. "Yes, ma'am. I'll take them."

She passed him her plate. "Here you go."

Axel pushed his plate away and propped his elbows on the table. "So, Britney, should we go check out the fence situation?"

"Sure. Let me just get the kitchen cleaned up."

"I'll take care of the kitchen. Angie, do you mind boiling some water?" Rainey collected the empty plates.

"On the stove or over the firepit?" Angie asked.

Gus peeked out the window. "The sun's out. I'll start a fire. No use wasting propane if we don't have to."

Shifter stood and stretched. "I'll gather some firewood and make sure we have enough for the next few days."

"I'll go with you." Mac scooped what was left of Britney's eggs into his mouth. As the largest person in the group, the poor guy had to be hungry with the small portions they'd been living on.

"Oh." Rainey popped her head back into the dining room. "It goes without saying that I'll keep an eye on the kids.

Britney smiled. "Thank you."

"Sure thing." As quickly as she'd appeared, she was gone again.

"I guess the only thing left to do is clean up the cattle pen." She pressed her lips together.

Axel and Gunner had already wrapped and removed the bodies. Later this afternoon, Axel would go to the cemetery and dig the graves.

Gunner popped up from his chair. "On it."

"You really don't have to do that." Britney scratched her bottom lip. As much as she had been accepting their help, it was obvious she still felt bad relying on them for so much.

"I don't mind." Gunner wiped his mouth with his old rag and stuck it back into his pocket. "Really. I want to make sure the calf that lost its mama is doing okay." Gunner left with a smile on his face and a hitch in his step Axel couldn't believe.

"He's sure adapting to farm life, isn't he?" Angie asked with a chuckle. "Never in my life would I have pictured him all giddy over a bunch of cows."

"I'll go saddle the horses," Britney said over the uproar of laughter about Gunner's newfound hobby.

"Horses?" Maybe Axel heard wrong.

"Yep." Britney grabbed her gun and stuck it back into her holster. She insisted everyone remove their weapon while in the house and around the children. "Meet you outside in a few."

Mac grinned at Axel. "Didn't know you could ride a horse."

"I'm pretty sure I can't." Axel sank into his chair. "Doesn't she have a four-wheeler we could use?"

"Got to save the fuel for the generators," Gus said.

"True." Axel ran a hand over his damp forehead. He was nervous. After everything they'd been through, the thought of getting on a horse made him sweat. "Any of you know how to ride a horse?"

"Nope." Shifter draped his arm around Mac's shoulders. "Ready to go get that firewood?"

"Yes, sir." Mac's eyes danced with amusement. "Axel, you better be getting out there. Don't want to keep the missus waiting."

"Shut up," Axel snapped. He didn't like what the term *missus* implied. "And if any of you think you're going to sit out there and talk shit about my horse-riding abilities, I will throw you under the bus so hard…."

Gus, Gunner and Mac all laughed. Axel hated that none of them ever took him seriously.

"Ignore them," Angie said. "Not a single one of us can ride a damn horse. And we sure as hell aren't going to make fun of you for trying. Probably wouldn't be a bad idea for all of us to take a few lessons from Brit. Might come in handy."

Mac snorted. "It'll be a cold day in hell before you get me on top of a horse."

"We're three days away from October." Angie planted a stern hand on her hip. "And we're in Montana in the middle of a fucking zombie apocalypse. Hell's about to freeze over."

Even though Angie's anger wasn't directed at him, she still scared the hell out of him.

"Fine." Mac held up his hands in defeat. "I'll learn how to ride a damn horse. Hope she has one suited for an extra-large rider."

Angie narrowed her eyes. "Go get firewood so Gus can get the fire started. We got work to do."

The three men left the house, heads hung low.

She laughed. "That's all there is to it. Doesn't take much to put them in their place."

"Easy for you to say," Axel grumbled. "They respect you."

"Who said they don't respect you?"

Axel ground his teeth. "It's pretty damn obvious."

"Let's get one thing straight." Angie bent over so she could get right in his face. "After the hell you've been through, and how you managed to come out the side and still keep moving forward, there's not a person among us who doesn't have the utmost respect for you. They give you shit because you're like a son to them. Or maybe a baby brother, since none of us wants to admit we're old enough to have a kid your age. But we wouldn't be here—and they wouldn't have followed you here—if they didn't respect you. Your quick thinking saved us. If it weren't for you, God only knows where we might be."

"Thanks, Angie." Axel really wanted to hug her.

She must have seen the need in his eyes, because she opens her arms and waved him over. "Come here."

***

"Just stick your left foot in the stirrup," Britney directed, "and kick off the ground, throwin' your other leg over the horse."

Damn, could this be any more humiliating? Well, it could have been if Angie hadn't shooed Mac and Shifter away.

"You almost had it that time."

Axel could hear the amusement in Britney's voice. "This funny to you? I got a lot of weight to throw over this horse."

"Please." Britney laughed. "John was a lot bigger than you and didn't have any problems."

He planted his feet and glared. "I bet John had a *couple* more years' experience than I do."

Britney winked. "Just a few."

"Maybe I should just walk."

"Oh my God." Britney threw her head back. "Stop being such a baby and get on the horse."

Axel took a step back to catch his breath. "He doesn't like me."

"*Mabel* is the same horse all the kids learned how to ride on when they were three. She's as tame as they come. I think the problem is you. Have you really never been on a horse before?"

"One time," Axel huffed. "I don't like to talk about it."

"The horse threw you." It wasn't a question.

Axel's stomach tightened, but he didn't answer.

"How old were you?" Britney pressed.

"Ten." Axel pointed to his forehead. "Fifteen stitches. And a concussion. I spent two nights in the hospital."

Britney dismounted from her horse and made her way to Axel. "I'm sorry I laughed. That must have been a very traumatic experience. But I promise you, this mare will not kick you off. She's very gentle."

"Fine." Axel stuck his foot in the stirrup. "Let me try again." He pushed himself off the ground as hard as he could and threw his left leg over the horse's back.

"There you go!" Britney messed with his saddle as he got situated. "That wasn't so bad, was it?"

"After the twentieth try, no, not bad at all."

Britney mounted her horse with ease. "At least I didn't have to bring out the box."

"What's the box?" Axel asked.

"It's like a step stool." Britney tugged on the reins and headed toward the back pasture. "Come on, Mabel."

Axel's horse trotted along behind Britney. "There's a step stool? I might look like a badass, but I would have felt no shame in using the box to get on top of this beast."

Britney jumped off her horse to open the gate. "Who said you looked like a badass?" She whistled for the horses. "Let's go."

"Ouch." Axel clasped his chest. "That hurt."

"Please don't tell me Mr. Badass gets his ego bruised so easily?"

Axel chuckled. "Most of the time, no. But you pretty much just called me a wuss."

Britney closed the gate and mounted her horse, King. "I did not call you a wuss. I just don't know if badass is the right description."

"Are you fucking with me?" Axel gently kicked Mabel's side in hopes of catching up with her. "How do you make this thing go faster?"

Britney clicked her tongue. "Come on, girl."

Mabel picked up her pace.

"I think lessons might be in order."

"I'll have Carson give you a few pointers." Her smile was infectious. "And to answer your question, yes, I'm fucking with you. You're the most badass of all the badasses I've ever known."

"I appreciate the compliment." They took a right along the fence line. Neither spoke for a while, both checking for any signs of damage. "There's something I've been meaning to ask you."

"What's that?"

"The rest of the bikers and I, we don't scare you, do we?" Axel pressed his lips together. "It's just sometimes it seems like we might."

She hesitated before answering. "At first you did. I mean, look at you. Rode into town on your motorcycles wearin' leather jackets. Your tattoos alone…."

"You've never seen anybody with sleeve tattoos?" They were common in the circle he ran with.

"In the short time I was in college. From afar." A light blush touched her cheeks. "They weren't exactly the kind of people I hung out with."

"No offense taken." The corner of Axel's mouth twitched. "But that doesn't surprise me."

Her face tightened. "Why's that?"

"Most people who've never been around bikers find us intimidating."

"That's fair." Britney scratched her nails along her chapped bottom lip. "I just want to say… I'm glad you guys are here. With John gone…."

"How are you and the kids handling it? His death, I mean."

Britney rubbed at her eyes and sighed. "We have our moments. Good and bad. Nights are tough, but we've managed. It helps, you and the others being here."

"I wish I could tell you the pain disappears, but it tends to stick with you." He knew from experience.

Her eyes met his. "Who did you lose?"

Axel rubbed the back of his neck. He couldn't. Not now. Not when the pain was still so fresh. So he did what he always did when the topic came up and changed the subject. "You're right. This is one hell of a fence. I'm impressed."

If his avoidance of the question bothered Britney, she didn't show it. "Yeah, John was big on keepin' predators out and away from the livestock."

"I don't remember seeing this high a fence when we drove in."

Britney turned the horses around. "We were havin' the fence installed in stages and hadn't gotten that far. Plus, predators rarely use the main road."

"Depends on the predator's intelligence."

Britney's breath hitched. "Do you think they're intelligent? That they're more than mindless zombies?"

Axel shouldn't have said anything. The fear in her eyes alone put his stomach in knots. But at this point he wouldn't lie. That wasn't the kind of foundation he wanted their friendship to be built upon. "I don't think they're mindless. This morning they paused when we went silent. That requires some sort of intelligence."

"You think we should check the weakest point of the fence? The stretch along the main road?"

Axel stared at the well-built, sturdy fence. “How many acres do you have?”

“About two thousand.”

He didn’t even try to calculate how long that meant the fence would be. “Check it all. We can’t be too careful.”

“We should get goin’.”

They took the ride along the fence slow—for his benefit, no doubt, but also because they needed to be thorough. With the intelligence of the infected in question, any minor defect in the fence could spell trouble for the entire homestead.

“Everything looks good so far,” Britney said over the wind that had picked up not thirty minutes ago. “But I think a storm is movin’ in.”

Axel peered up at the sky. He’d been so focused on staying on his horse that he hadn’t bothered to check why the wind started to howl. “Do we need to do something with the cattle? Or the sheep?” They had passed both along the way.

“No, they’re used to the weather here.”

Thunder echoed off the mountain, resonating deep in his bones.

Mabel whined but thankfully didn’t rear up like King did.

Britney white-knuckled the reins. “The horses don’t like being out in the storms.”

“Should we go back?” Axel shouted over another rumble of thunder.

“We’re almost to the main road,” Britney yelled over the wind. “I think we have time before the actual rain hits.”

“Think?” Axel covered his face as the wind sent a cloud of dust in their direction. He really didn’t want to get stuck out here during a downpour. The dampness in the air had already seeped deep into his skin.

"We'll have to go faster than a trot." Britney whistled for the horses, who took off racin. down the fence line.

Axel held on tight as the horse slung his body in every direction. Obviously he was doing something wrong; Britney didn't seem to have a problem staying upright.

A light rain fell as they reached the main road. Britney slowed King, and Mabel followed suit.

This section of fence was as he remembered—three rows of barbed wire wrapped around a wood post for as far as the eyes could see. "Yeah, this isn't worth a shit."

Britney crossed her arms over her chest. "It keeps the livestock in."

Axel hadn't meant it as an insult. "Sorry. I meant for keeping out the infected."

"I know what you meant. I'm just frustrated that we never had the fence finished. We kept puttin' it off and puttin' it off."

"It's not like you knew the apocalypse was coming."

"*Always protect the homestead with as much as you can spare*." Britney sighed. "That's what my father always preached."

"You were more prepared than most." Axel managed to maneuver his horse beside her. "And you took us in when you didn't have to. You saved us."

"I want to save more." Her eyes went round. "I didn't even know I was goin' to say that."

"It's your farm." Axel understood her need to save those lost in the world, those who couldn't help themselves. That was the main reason he had joined the military.

"Our farm." The words came out so low he wasn't sure he'd heard her right.

"What did you say?"

Britney's eyes locked with his. "It's our farm. All of ours. Don't make me repeat it for a third time, or I might change my mind."

Axel didn't press, though he wanted to question her change of heart. "Thank you."

"This isn't a damn handout. You guys have been bustin' your asses helpin' around here. Of course, if that changes, I'll have to rethink some things."

A small chuckle escaped his lips. He didn't know what to say, so instead he focused on the task at hand. "You see any signs that the infected got through over here?"

One of the great things about Britney was she never seemed to mind changing the subject when conversation got too heavy.

"Damn wind throwin' dirt everywhere." She dismounted, handed Axel the reins and walked the fence line. "I couldn't see a thing from up there."

"Want me to jump down and help?"

Britney whirled around and shot him the most incredulous look. "Are you goin' to be able to get back up if you do?"

"Point taken. I'll just stay up here, keep an eye on things." Axel reached out and grabbed King's reins. "And hang on to the horses."

She continued along the fence line while he watched for anything out of the ordinary.

"I think I found something!"

And not a moment too soon. They were about to get wailed on by the impending storm. "What is it?"

She held up a piece of torn fabric. "This is the dress my mother-in-law was wearin'."

Axel squinted. “What else is hanging on the fence?”

“Skin.” Her face blanched. “Tore a big chunk off when it climbed over.”

Rain pelted Axel’s exposed skin. “We should head in.”

“What about this?” The fabric flapped in the wind.

He tossed her King’s reins and she mounted. “Nothing we can do about it right now.”

“They just climbed over.” Britney rubbed her hand against her soaked pant leg. “How are we supposed to keep them out when they can do that?”

“I don’t know.” Axel braced himself as a gust of wind nearly knocked him off the horse. “But we’ll figure something out. Right now we have to get back to the house.”

“What was that?” Britney whipped around. “Did you hear that?”

“What?” Axel was having a hard time hearing her, and she wasn’t even three feet away.

Britney’s lips trembled. “There’s somethin’ out there.”

Axel scanned the area. “I don’t see anything.”

“It’s out there.” She pointed a shaky finger toward the tree line across the road. “It’s not attackin’. Do you think it’s scared of the storm?”

“God, I hope so. But let's not stick around and find out.”

***

The rain didn’t stop for five days. As muddy, wet and cold as it was, Axel welcomed the gloomy weather. It gave them a chance to get settled into their new living spaces.

Britney had offered Rainey and Angie the basement. Rainey accepted. Angie did not. Unbeknownst to everyone else, she and Mac had become an item, and as a couple, they wanted their privacy. Which the basement and barn didn't really have much of. So Britney, being the saint she was, told them to take her grandparents' old house.

Axel cringed at the thought. It hadn't even been two weeks since Susan's death. But Angie and Mac didn't seem to mind. All they really cared about was having their own space. Not that Axel could blame them; they'd been living in close quarters for far too long.

That left Shifter, Gunner, Gus and Axel with the barn. The loft had three sections, one to the back and one on each side. It wouldn't take much to separate the three, but that still left two people who would have to share.

As they went back and forth on who would share, Britney popped by to see how things were going. And then she threw a wrench in mix.

John had a small room under the stairs, a man cave that he used on nights when he had to be up with a sick or birthing animal. Or when Britney was pissed at him. She said one of them could have it. The problem was deciding who in the fairest way possible.

Britney suggested they draw sticks, longest one wins.

And that's how Axel got his own room with a door and a small cot. He even had a TV and beer fridge, not that either worked.

But it was peaceful. And confined. And all his.

He closed his eyes and relished in the silence. What he wouldn't give for a solid night's sleep.

A light knock at the door forced him to open his eyes.

With a deep yawn, he called out, "Come in."

Britney peeked her head past the door. "Wow. You cleaned up. I hardly recognize the place."

Axel threw his legs off the bed. "I put all John's personal stuff in a box."

"You didn't put these." Britney ran her fingers along the photos of her and the kids.

"I didn't take anything off the walls." He almost had, but something about the way they all smiled made the world feel a little brighter. "I can if it's weird. Or if you want the pictures back."

She turned to him and forced a smile. "Whatever you want to do with them is fine with me."

"Maybe I'll keep them up." Axel watched her reaction closely. "You know, keep a little piece of John here, in the space he loved so much."

Britney's eyes softened. "Some days, when it was really hot out, I'd find him in here when I thought he was out workin'. Beer in hand, watchin' a game on TV. I used to get so mad at him for sneakin' off when I was stuck inside with a cryin' baby or rowdy kids. But then he would hand me a beer and pull me down beside him on the bed, and we'd hang out here for a bit until the kids hunted us down. It was nice."

"I don't have to stay in here if it's too weird." The more she talked about the room, the less comfortable he felt about using it.

"Don't be silly." Britney waved a dismissive hand. "It's just a room."

"Okay. Then I'll stay."

Britney beamed. "Great!"

"Great," he repeated because he didn't know what else to say. "Was there anything else you needed?"

"Oh!" She rubbed her temples. "Sorry. I haven't been sleepin' well."

"Everything okay?"

"You know…." Her smile dropped. "It's hard not to worry with these things on the loose and not knowin' when or where they'll show up. Or what they're capable of. I know the kids are upstairs, but what if the infected can open doors? Or climb walls? Break windows? We know they have no problem with barbed wire fencin' and don't care if they're injured."

"There's a lot of unknown. But now that the storms have passed, we can focus on security. I think the fence line along the road needs to come first."

"Any ideas?"

"Actually." Axel stood and stretched, trying to suppress a yawn. "Yes."

Britney pressed her lips together. "Sorry. It's late. You were about to go to bed, weren't you?"

Axel pulled back the dusty curtain of the small window. "It's not even dark outside."

"Still, it's been a long couple of weeks. We're all exhausted. We can talk about this tomorrow. Or whenever you have time." She turned for the door.

"Wait." Axel slipped on his boots. "There's something I saw and want to ask you about it."

"Ask away."

Axel grabbed his leather jacket from the hook beside the door. "I think it'll be easier to explain if we're looking at it."

"All right." Britney followed him out.

They weaved around barns and sheds in silence as Axel guided them out to the back corner of the acreage. "I noticed John kept a lot scrap metal and other discarded stuff out this way."

"You mean his junkyard where all things went to die. Yeah. He had a serious problem." Behind him he could hear Britney's boots sloshing through the mud.

"He might have been a hoarder before the apocalypse, but he left us a goldmine." Axel stopped at the first of twenty-plus piles of sheet metal. "What do you think of this?"

"All this corrugated metal? It used to be an old barn. John bought that at an auction a few years back. What about it?"

"You have a gas welder, right?"

Britney nodded. "Yes. Why?"

"I was thinking we could build a wall to replace the old fence along the road using all this." When she didn't reply, he asked, "What do you think?"

"A wall, huh?" A bright smile stretched across her face. "I think that might just work."

CHAPTER NINETEEN

"Why is it so fucking cold here!" Shifter howled.

Britney couldn't help but chuckle. "It's like thirty-eight degrees. Not even below freezin'. It's actually kind of nice for November."

Shifter tossed his hammer aside. "Where I come from, we wear shorts on Thanksgiving. Because it's hot."

Axel shut off the welder and removed the helmet he used to protect his face from the sparks. Sweat poured off his wet head. "You can take over for me? It's hot as fuck under this helmet."

"You think you'd be used to it by now after nearly two months," Britney teased.

They'd been working their asses off since the end of September, trying to get the wall built. Digging trenches, welding the pieces together. The learning curve didn't help—they ended up doing so much rework at one point that they nearly said screw it. But an infected sighting reminded them of why they'd started this project in the first place.

"You'd also think he'd be getting better after all that time." Gunner full-on belly laughed as tears ran down his face. "But he's still slow as hell."

"We should have been done by now," Shifter muttered.

"Excuse me?" Axel yanked off his gloves and tossed them to ground. "You want to talk about being slow? What about all the rework we had to do because you fucked up the plans?"

Axel and Shifter had been at each other's throats for weeks. Most of the time, Axel blew off Shifter's insults, but today he was pissed

Shifter took a menacing step toward Axel. "I'm not some fucking architect or engineer."

"And I'm not a fucking welder," Axel said with equal disdain.

"Well, I'm goin' to go." Britney didn't want to stick around and watch them come to blows. Plus, she wanted to check on Angie and Rainey. They had volunteered to inventory the freezers and the boxes in the storage building where Britney kept all the extra blankets and old clothes. "Try not to kill each other while I'm gone."

"No promises." Axel snatched his helmet and gloves off the ground and got back to work.

The walk from the road back to the house never used to bother Britney. On pretty days, she would walk instead of taking the truck to pick up the kids from the bus stop. The peacefulness of the country always had a way of soothing her soul. But now every time the leaves rustled or the wind howled, she reached for her gun. She hated the helplessness, the uncertainty.

Still, over the past few months, she had come to terms with the world they now lived in, even going so far as embracing the simple way of life. Her father had promised her that one day learning how to live off the land would come in handy. Sure, he probably didn't mean in the form of an apocalypse, but he was right. They were still alive because of her knowledge. She prayed that after they finished this wall, they would also be safe.

Britney walked into a quiet house, the last thing she expected. "Hello?"

The back door slammed, and Rainey strolled into the living room covered in dust. "Hey, Britney. How's the fence building going?"

"Shifter and Axel are at it again." Britney narrowed her eyes. "Where are the kids?"

"In the basement. Angie found a box of old board games and toys. They were so excited." Rainey froze, her eyes wide. "I hope that's okay."

"Of course. I told you, what's mine is yours. Stop worryin'."

Rainey wet her lips. "I just don't want to piss you off."

Britney laughed. "Oh my God, Rainey. Seriously. You might only weigh eighty pounds, but you could still kick my ass."

"Just because I can doesn't mean I want it to come to that." Rainey shot her a little wink. "Which is why I don't want to upset you."

"Please." Britney waved her off. "You're goin' to piss me off. But that's what family does. And then we get over it and move on."

Tears filled Rainey's eyes.

"What did I say?"

"Come here." Rainey beckoned her over. "I need to hug you."

"I didn't mean to upset you," Britney whispered in her ear as they embraced.

Rainey cupped Britney's cheeks. "Upset me? Have you lost your mind? Calling me—us—family means everything."

She couldn't have been over ten years older than Britney, but she had a motherly way about her that put Britney at ease.

"I meant it." And she did. With every ounce of her being. "I'm so glad you guys are here."

"Aww." Angie clapped her hands. How long had she been standing there? "Did I miss the group hug?"

Rainey rolled her eyes. "What's your man doing?"

"He and Gus are chopping firewood." Angie narrowed her eyes at Britney. "Because someone said we need a *butt load* more."

"I'm pretty sure I said *shit ton* more." Britney smirked. "Find anythin' good in the storage building?"

Angie grimaced. "Girl, it's not good."

"What do you mean?" It had only been a few months since she'd been in there, and everything appeared fine then.

"You ever have any kind of issue with mice or rats?" Angie asked.

Britney threw back her head and groaned. "They didn't."

"Never seen anything like it." Angie plopped down on the couch. "They chewed through the plastic totes. What the hell kind of rodent can do that?"

"Was there anything salvageable?" Britney couldn't believe it. They would need those extra blankets this winter. "Maybe if we wash them?"

Rainey shook her head. "They shredded them all."

"Yep. Those totes are full of dirty, stinky scraps of cloth," Angie added. "There ain't nothing we can do about them."

Britney dropped on to the couch next to Angie. "What about the clothes?"

"Your mama was a tiny woman, wasn't she?" Angie asked. "Because the only clothes I found will fit you and Rainey."

"There wasn't anything else?" Britney could have sworn there was more.

Angie patted her leg. "Nothing I could wear, but if you want to see if you can work your farm magic on it, be my guest."

Britney scrunched her nose. "I guess the mice got into those boxes too?"

"Sorry, sugar."

"Dammit." Britney grabbed a pillow, covered her face and screamed. No extra blankets, no extra clothes. They were screwed. So fucking screwed. "What about the freezers?"

"Rainey has the list," Angie said. "I think we're sitting pretty good. We took stock of the jars of food you have in the basement. You can all of those yourself?"

"Yep." Britney flopped her head to the side so she could face Angie. "And I'll teach you how to can crops too once our garden produces."

Angie cocked an eyebrow. "I'll have you know I've grown my fair share of tomatoes."

"Good. That's a great starter plant." Britney rubbed at her eyes. "Between the meat and the canned goods, we should be set for the winter?"

"We think so. You should still look over the inventory list, but I don't think we'll starve."

Some good news. Thank God.

"There's one other thing," Rainey said.

Britney leaned her head back so she could look at her. "What's that?"

“Well”—Rainey looked at Angie—“we found a frozen turkey. And we're thinking since Thanksgiving is two days away….”

Even though Britney knew they should focus on winter prep, her heart leaped at the thought of celebrating an actual holiday. It had crushed the kids when they found out they wouldn’t be able to trick-or-treat. Thanksgiving wasn’t their favorite, but celebrating something—anything—would do them all a world of good.

“It’s a great idea. Let's get started!”

***

An hour later, the new supply list had grown to over three pages long. That wasn’t even their biggest concern. Britney still had to ask Axel if he would be willing to go on another run. He never said what exactly happened last time, but she had heard Shifter and Gunner talking about a kid who’d been turned. She couldn’t even imagine seeing something so horrific.

“I’m goin’ to hunt down Axel,” Britney said, “see what he thinks about all this.”

Rainey kept her eyes on the Go Fish cards in her hand. “Sure. I’ve got the kids. Angie will start lunch.”

“Thanks.” It was such a comfort having these two women around to help. Didn’t hurt that the kids loved them too.

Britney left the house and was headed toward the main road when she spotted Axel jogging to the barn. She considered calling out to him, but they had all agreed to keep the place as quiet as possible since noise drew the infected in.

She knocked on the doorframe of Axel’s room, not wanting to intrude even though the door was open.

“Come in,” he said.

"Hey." Britney gave him a quick once-over, making sure he and Shifter didn't get into a fight after she left. "I don't see any blood. Guess you guys worked things out?"

He glanced up from a piece of paper his hands. "That was nothing."

"It didn't look like nothing."

Axel grinned. "Shifter has always been a hothead. And he loves to run his mouth."

"I can see that." Britney shifted from foot to foot. She always felt a little uncomfortable coming into Axel's room. It was such a small space, and she never knew where to stand or if she should sit.

"Did you need something?" Axel watched her with such intensity it made her cheeks burn. "What's that in your hand?"

"Right." Britney waved the paper around. How had the reason she'd come here slipped her mind? "The bad news. All the extra blankets and stuff I had packed away are ruined. Freakin' mice or rats chewed their way through the plastic storage containers and made themselves at home."

"That's not good."

Britney needed to bring up the supply run, but the words caught in her throat. "Not good at all." *What the hell is wrong with me today?*

"So...." A mischievous smile tugged at his lips. "Is that all? Or was there something else?"

"Um... I guess that's it." She turned to leave.

"Wait." Axel laughed. "Is everything okay?"

Britney ran her hands across her face. "Yes. No."

"Which is it?"

She rolled her eyes. "We need blankets. Actually," she said, handing him the supply list, "we need a lot more than that if we want to survive the winter."

Axel flipped through the papers. “Shit. That is a lot.”

“I’m sorry.” The words came out of nowhere.

“For what?”

Britney sighed. “I shouldn’t assume, shouldn’t be askin’ you to go out there. It’s too dangerous.”

“Here.” Axel handed her the paper he was looking over when she entered the room. “I was about to come and find you. We need some supplies to finish the wall. The gate in particular. Got to make sure it’s strong but also easy to open.”

“So you’ve already planned a supply run?”

Axel dropped to the bed. “Yep. Fun, fun. You coming this time?”

“What?” The question caught her off guard. “I didn’t even consider it an option.”

“We could use your help. Not to mention you’re the only one who knows this area.”

Britney tugged at her bottom lip. “What about the farm? The kids? I can’t leave them defenseless.”

“Speaking of that, the others need to learn how to shoot. I know they’ve been practicing on the kids’ BB guns.”

Carson’s idea, and a brilliant one at that. “They’ve gotten pretty good. Can even hit their target most of the time.”

“Good. But a BB gun is not the same as the real thing. The trigger alone….”

Britney leaned against the wall and pushed off again. Why was it so hard to find a comfortable place to stand in this room?

“Do you want to sit?” Axel patted the bed beside him. “I won’t bite.”

“Funny.” Britney took a seat and maneuvered her body so she could face him. “Anyway, yes, a real gun differs from a BB gun, but we only have so many bullets and shouldn't waste them on target practice. What we really need are practice weapons, like an air gun or somethin'."

"You have one of those?"

Britney shook her head. "Nope. But they might be easier to find since people can't use them for protection."

"Here's your list back. Add that gun and the bullets that go with it. Plus regular old guns and any kind of bullets we need for the ones you already have."

Britney did. "But you realize that should be a given, right? Find a weapon, pick it up, bring it home."

"I thought you would say, 'All day long you have good luck.'"

She chuckled. "I didn't realize you were funny."

"I have my moments." Axel propped himself against the wall and crossed his ankles. "So, where do you suggest we go to get all that shit you have on your list? And how do we bring it home? The SUV doesn't hold much."

"There's a Walmart a few towns over. And a Tractor Supply. Gun shops are everywhere."

Axel rubbed his nose. "A few towns over in which direction?"

"I have a map. I'll mark it all up for you, make sure you don't get lost."

"And what about hauling all this crap home? Any suggestion?"

"Ever driven a truck with a cattle trailer attached?"

"Can't say I have."

Britney smiled. "Do you think you can handle it?"

"Seriously?" Axel cocked his head. "Not like there's going to be any traffic for me to have to maneuver through."

“I just wanted to make sure you felt comfortable drivin’ somethin’ so big.” Britney nudged his arm before standing. Sitting still was making her antsy. “It can be challengin’.”

“We’ll manage.”

A small weight lifted from her shoulders. She came in here thinking it might be tough to convince him to go on another supply run, but he seemed fine. “Thank you for doing this.”

“Someone has to. And I’m not sure I would trust the others not to bail if things got dicey out there.”

She stared down at him. “That’s not a bad thing, you know. Gettin’ out of there if the danger is too great. Some might even say it would be selfish if you stayed. There are a lot of people here who depend on you.”

Axel’s eyes met hers. “Are you speaking on behalf of everyone or yourself?”

“Everyone,” she blurted. Too quickly. “We need you. So don’t do anythin’ stupid when you’re out there.”

“I’ll do my best to stay alive.” He shot her a wink.

“That’s all I ask.” Her heart pounded against her chest. What the hell was going on? She was around Axel all the time, and now, out of the blue, she felt nervous. “When do you think you’ll go? Who will go with you?”

“Gunner volunteered. As for the when, we haven’t decided. The sooner the better, I guess.”

“Plan for Friday.”

“We have something going on this week I don’t know about?”

“Thursday is Thanksgiving. Angie found a turkey in the freezer. We thought we would celebrate. And it’s important everyone’s here, together. As a family.”

“You think that’s the smartest thing to do?” Axel scratched at the scruff on his chin. “Are we talking a feast?”

"Not overboard, but yes. I think we deserve to splurge a little. We've been really good about portion control. I can't remember the last time any of us had dessert."

"But—"

Britney held up her hand to stop him from trying to talk her out of it. "No *buts*. Not to go all *Game of Thrones* on you, but winter is comin'. And winters here are a bitch. We need this. Not just the extra calories but the morale boost. Not celebratin' Halloween already broke the kids' hearts. I don't even want to think about Christmas. This will be good for them, for all of us. We've survived this long, and we should take the time to give thanks for all we still have."

"You're right. Though let's not get carried away. Last thing we want to do is waste food."

"Excuse me?" Britney pulled the waistband of her jeans a good two inches away from her skin. "These jeans haven't fit me since before the twins were born. I promise you, we will waste no food."

"All right. So we're celebrating Thanksgiving this year?"

A genuine smile spread across her face. "Yes, we are. Are you excited?"

"For a shit ton of food? Hell yes."

***

"How's the turkey doing?" Axel asked as he joined Britney at the barbecue pit.

It had been years since she'd done any of the grilling. That was the only kind of cooking John insisted on doing.

Britney stuck the thermometer into the breast and watched the temperature rise. "Give it another hour and it should be good to go."

"Perfect." Axel took a big whiff. "It smells amazing."

"Thanks. How's everything else comin' along?" Everyone had taken it upon themselves to make their favorite Thanksgiving dish.

"Not to brag"—Axel tugged at the collar of his leather jacket—"but my mashed potatoes are fucking awesome. Probably the best thing we'll eat all day."

Britney closed the lid of the pit and headed back toward the house. "You did pick the easiest thing to make."

Axel's mouth dropped open. "I can't believe you just said that. Knife in the heart, woman. Knife. In. The. Heart." He accented each word by thrusting his fist into his chest.

"I don't know what to tell you. Sometimes the truth hurts." The rest of the group huddled by the large fire, stirring pots and checking under foil covers. Her stomach growled. "I think you've all outdone yourself. Do I smell apple pie?"

"That would be my specialty." Angie beamed. "I can hardly wait until it's time to eat."

Gus closed the lid on his pot of green beans. "How's the turkey?"

"About an hour and it'll be perfect," Britney told them.

"Same for my sweet potatoes," Shifter said. "You really kept your pantry stocked up."

John used to give her a hard time about her food-hoarding tendencies, saying her garden was too big for just the five of them. But gardening wasn't about how much she grew so much as the process. She loved digging her fingers in the dirt and nurturing a seedling until it bloomed.

"That reminds me." Britney looked to Axel. "I need you to add a large greenhouse or lots of small greenhouses to the list. The kind we can build around my garden. That way my plants won't all die this winter."

Axel jotted it down. He had made it a habit the last few days of carrying the thing around with him. "What did you do before?"

"Buy new seeds and replant. But I don't want to risk not being able to find any."

"Adding fruit and vegetable seeds to the list," he said as he wrote.

She didn't argue. She'd never used a greenhouse before and wasn't sure how well the plants would survive even under its protection. "Thanks. I'm going to go check on the kids."

"Don't go in there," Angie told her. "You'll ruin the surprise."

Britney spun around. "What surprise?"

Angie jutted her hip out. "Now if I told you, it wouldn't be a surprise, would it?"

It went against every one of her motherly instincts, but she stayed outside. "Fine. I'm assumin' Rainey's with them?"

"You know she is." Angie went back to tending to her pie.

"Maybe you should sit down for a bit," Axel suggested. "Take a break."

How long had it been since she'd sat around doing nothing? Months, at least. "I'm sure there's somethin' that needs to be done. Firewood, maybe?"

Axel unfolded a chair and forced her to sit. "Gunner's taking care of that, and checking the animals. There's nothing else that needs your attention at the moment."

“I can set the table.”

“Nope.” Axel grabbed another chair and sat beside her. “Taken care of.”

“Fine.” Britney slouched down and crossed her arms. “I’ll just sit here and do nothin’.”

Axel tapped his foot. “I can go get you something from the house. A book, maybe? You like to read, right?”

“I love to read.” Britney groaned. “But my e-reader is dead. And I gave all my paperbacks to the church a few years back for their rummage sale.”

“Sorry.”

“It’s one thing’\ I miss the most. Gettin’ lost in a different world and forgettin’ about everything else.”

Axel poked at the fire. “What do you like to read? Harlequin romances?” He raised an eyebrow.

Britney laughed. “No. I like fantasy, paranormal.”

“Like ghosts?”

“Vampires, werewolves, shifters, stuff like that.”

“Like *Twilight*?”

“No.” Britney scrunched her nose. “Too much high school drama and love at first sight for me.”

“Gotcha.” Axel leaned back in his chair and closed his eyes. “Why don’t you just rest, like me? Block out the world for a little while and enjoy the peacefulness that surrounds us in this moment.”

“That doesn’t sound very relaxin’. Now, if I were in the house in my bathtub, *that* would be a different story.”

“We could use the generator to heat the water. I’m sure no one would mind a hot shower.”

What Britney wouldn’t give to stand under a heated waterfall. “As much as I would love that, we have to save the generators for winter.”

"I know, I know. What about football? That's a Thanksgiving tradition and would help you get out some of your restless energy. Pass the time."

"Hey, Brit!" Rainey called from the house. "Gunner said the turkey's ready! He's going to bring it inside and get it carved up."

Britney spun around. The turkey was her thing.

"Hey." Axel laid his hand on top of hers before she argued. "Let it go."

She turned to Axel. "But I'm doin' the turkey. That was my job."

"After all you've done for us, everyone here just wants the chance to do something for you. Please let them."

"It's been months. You guys have done plenty to repay me."

"Brit!" Rainey called out again. "Is that okay?"

Axel's eyes begged for her to agree. "Please."

"That's fine!" Britney called back. "Thank you. We'll bring the rest of the food in."

Before she had the chance to ask if she could carry something, they all headed back to the house, food in hand.

"At least let me get the door!" she shouted, running forward to hold it open.

The kids greeted them as they entered the house, each wearing a Pilgrim hat made of construction paper.

"You guys look so cute." Britney pulled them into a group hug. "Did Rainey help you make those?"

"Yep." Molly beamed. "She's great at crafts. "You have to see what else—"

"Hush," Carson hissed. "It's a surprise."

Britney's mouth curved into a smile. "I heard somethin' super-secret was goin' on in here. When do I get to find out what you've been up to?"

"Right now." Blake grabbed Britney's hand. "But close your eyes."

Molly took her other hand. "And no peeking. We'll make sure you don't run into anything."

"Okay." Britney closed her eyes. "I'm trustin' you."

She shuffled her feet as they guided her toward what she could only assume was the dining room.

"You can open your eyes!" Carson ordered.

Britney gasped at the sight before her. Brown, orange, yellow and red paper chains hung from the ceiling. Dozens of hand turkeys decorated the walls. A handmade cornucopia sat in the center the table, surrounded by the most delicious-looking food she'd ever seen. "This is amazin'."

Molly dragged Britney to the wall and pointed at one of the smaller turkeys. "I made this one for Daddy."

Tears stung Britney's eyes. "I'm sure he loves it."

"Come sit down, Mom." Carson pulled out the chair at the head of the table. John's chair. "Dad would want you to sit in his spot."

Her heart ached at the thought of John not being there to serve the turkey, but she sat down anyway. The kids were handling his absence so much better than she ever imagined. She could thank Angie for that. The way she spoke to the kids about heaven and the signs all around them that meant their dad was present had made all the difference in the world.

"Should we sit anywhere?" Axel asked.

Britney hadn't even noticed that the bikers were still standing. The boys were already in their normal chairs, Molly in the one where Britney used to sit.

"Axel should take the second head of the table," Carson said with an authoritative tone. "Everyone else can sit where they like."

Mac patted Carson on the back and took the seat next to him. "Thank you, sir. It honors us that you have invited us to your home and allowed us to join you for Thanksgiving dinner."

Molly giggled. "You're so silly, Mac. This is your home too."

He shot her a quick wink, and she giggled harder.

Funny how they had never discussed how Britney opened up their home to the bikers but Molly picked up on it all the same.

Britney took in the feast before everyone dug in. Turkey, mashed potatoes, sweet potatoes, stuffing and rolls. She'd never seen such an amazing meal in her life.

And with the good china being used, it almost felt like a regular Thanksgiving during any other year.

But there was one thing missing. "I'll be right back."

Britney hurried into the kitchen and returned with four bottles of wine. "We can't have a toast or celebrate without wine."

She opened two bottles and passed them around. Carson ran to the pantry and brought back a bottle of grape juice for the kids.

Britney raised her glass. "A toast—to friends who have become family."

"Cheers." Glasses clinked and long sips were taken.

"Now eat up." Britney gestured to the food. "And after we're done, I believe Axel mentioned somethin' about a football game?"

"Yay!" Carson and Blake cheered.

"I call cheerleader," Molly said with her mouth stuffed with bread.

"Cheerleader?" Axel feigned a gasp. "Oh, no, young lady. I need you on my team."

Molly eyes widened. "Really? Girls can play football too?"

Axel pointed at her with his fork. “Not only can they play, but I bet they can do some serious butt kicking.”

“You hear that, boys?” she sneered at her brothers. “I’m going to kick your butts.”

The room erupted in a mixture of trash talk and everyone trying to call who would be on what team.

Through the chaos, Britney’s gaze locked with Axel’s. She lifted her glass and mouthed, “Thank you.” Not just for Molly, but for everything he’d done for them. For everything he was about to risk.

CHAPTER TWENTY

Friday, Axel woke up to find half a foot of snow on the ground, and it was still snowing. Not having any experience driving in that weather, he delayed the supply run until Saturday. But then it snowed another three inches, so they pushed back the run again. But they couldn't push it back forever.

"Maybe wait another day," Britney said as she hooked the trailer to her pickup truck. "See if the snow lets up."

Axel was tired of waiting. "We have no idea when that might be. The longer we wait, the worse the roads will get."

"Or they could get better," she huffed. "You don't even know how to drive in the snow."

"Isn't that what the chains are for?" Axel kicked at the tires. He understood her concern, but with no weather app, they had no way of knowing when the snow would let up. If it ever did. Britney had said sometimes it started to snow in November and didn't stop till spring.

"You're comin' back tomorrow, right?" she asked for the tenth time.

"That's the plan."

Britney ground her teeth. "No, that's what will happen. We have no cell phones. If we don't have a time set when you're supposed to be back, how are we supposed to know if something bad happened? Or when to send a search party out?"

"Please, no search parties." Axel placed a firm hand on each of her shoulders. "Relax. We'll be fine."

"You have no idea what you're gettin' yourselves into." Britney blew out her cheeks. "What if the infected thrive in snowy weather? What if you skid off the road and land in a ditch somewhere? Without a set time, we would never know."

"We'll be back tomorrow evening. I promise."

Britney sucked in a shaky breath. "I'm sorry. I'm not tryin' to nag or act like a crazy worryin' woman, but we need you here. Both you and Gunner."

"Thanks for that," Gunner called out from the passenger seat.

"If it's too dangerous, we'll turn around and figure out another way to get the supplies we need," Axel told her.

"You have the list, right?"

"Yes. Everything in Walmart."

"That's not funny." Britney crossed her arms over her chest.

Axel had a sudden urge to pull her into a hug, to comfort her, but he resisted, not sure if their friendship had reached the point of unannounced embraces. "I've got the list and the map."

"Should we go over the route one more time?"

"Are you stalling?" Axel asked.

Britney threw back her head. “Fine. Go. Get on the road. The sooner you leave, the sooner you can get back.”

“You need us to do anything else before we leave?”

She pressed her lips together and shook her head. “Just be careful.”

“We will.” Axel climbed into the driver seat of the beat-up Ford before she changed her mind. “See you tomorrow.”

“Bye.” Britney waved.

Axel watched from the side mirror as she headed back to the house. He hated leaving as much as she hated for him to go.

“That’s cute,” Gunner said.

“What?” Axel stopped at the old gate they had yet to take down. The panels to the new gates were ready, they just needed some big-ass hinges to hang them up.

“I’ll get the gate.” Gunner jumped out of the truck and waited for Axel to drive through before climbing back into the cab. “Ready?”

Axel took a left onto the old county road heading in the opposite direction of Myrefall. Snow covered the roads, but they weren’t bad.

Gunner slumped down. “That’s a damn fine wall, if I say so myself.”

“I have to admit, I wasn’t sure we’d be able to pull it off.”

“But we did.” Gunner smacked Axel on the shoulder. “What’s your girl think about it?”

Axel shot him a sideways glance. “My girl?”

“Don’t play dumb with me.” Gunner furrowed his brow. “Wait. You’re not playing dumb, are you?”

“Nope.”

“Britney. You two have something going on, don’t you?”

Axel's muscles went rigid. "No. Wait does everyone think there's something going on between us?"

"I guess we all assumed there was. You two are always talking and laughing. Plus, she's freaking drop-dead gorgeous. And you're a good-looking kid. Got the ripped abs and tattoos going for you."

"Stop." Sure, Axel found her attractive, but the thought never crossed his mind. Well, it did, but not in any serious way. "She just buried her husband."

"Two months ago." Gunner let out a low whistle. "And let me tell you, two months living in the apocalypse is like two years."

"No." Axel swallowed hard. "It's not like that between the two of us. We're just friends. I doubt she has any feelings about me that go beyond that."

Gunner slapped his own forehead and shook his head. "Were you and I not just seeing the same thing back there? She nearly had a meltdown before you left."

"Over both us."

"No, sir. I was an afterthought. But you? She could barely stand the idea of you going off to war and never coming back."

Axel glanced at Gunner, unsure if he was being serious or just fucking with him. "You really believe that, don't you?"

"You're going to sit there and tell me there ain't nothing—no spark, nothing—between the two of you?"

"I mean…." Axel kept his focus on the road. This conversation distracted him from the task at hand, but not in a good way. "I don't know. There hasn't been much time to worry about stuff like that lately."

"Mac and Angie made time."

An opening to change the subject. "About that. How long do you think that's been going on? Before the trip, maybe? Or is this just a post-apocalypse romance?"

"I see what you're doing. And if you don't want to talk about Britney, we won't. Just keep an eye out for the signs. Don't want to go pissing off the only woman your age within a hundred-mile radius."

"Fine." Axel slowed as they approached a fork in the road. "Now if you don't mind, tell me which way we're going. I don't want to be away for any longer than we have to."

Gunner clicked his tongue. "I know you don't. You got a lot waiting for you back home."

***

Axel parked in front of Walmart and left the truck running.

"Guess we aren't the only ones who thought this would be a good place to rob." Gunner rubbed his forehead. The glass of the outer doors had been shattered.

"I'm not sure robbing is the right word. Makes us sound like criminals.

Gunner chuckled. "Always the good guy. You like 'looting' better?"

"Not really." Axel leaned against the steering wheel in an attempt to see past the first set of doors. "We should still look inside. Just because someone tried to break in doesn't mean they made it out."

"That's why we're here." Gunner swung open the door and got out. Axel shut off the truck and did the same. "Should we lock it?"

The old Ford didn't have a push-button lock. Axel didn't much care for the idea of having to stick the key in the lock to get in if being chased, but he also didn't want to come back and the truck be gone. Not that a locked door would hinder anyone from stealing it, but it might slow them down. "I guess we should. At least if it gets stolen, we can say we did what we could to prevent it from happening."

Axel checked to make sure he had his gun, the list and extra bullets.

"It's quiet out here," Gunner said as Axel rounded the front of the truck. "Do you find that even the least bit strange?"

"By quiet you mean we haven't seen any infected?"

Gunner maneuvered through the shattered glass door, careful to avoid the shards. Axel, being a lot trimmer than Gunner, didn't have to be as cautious.

"Damn. These doors aren't even broken." Gunner pointed to the inner set of doors. "Someone just left them open."

"We should grab two baskets each. I say we fill them up, bring them back and get more empty ones. Then we load the supplies at the same time."

"Sounds like a plan." Gunner yanked to get them apart from one another. "Son of a bitch. Some things never change." He rolled two Axel's way, then got two of his own.

"Should we stick together?" Axel asked as they crept into the store. Like outside, the silence was deafening. He could hear his heartbeat thrashing in his ears. "Keep an eye on each other's backs?"

"Fuck me." Gunner had made it farther in than Axel, which gave him a better vantage point to see the rest of the store.

"What's wrong?" Axel picked up the pace, eager to see what had stopped Gunner dead in his tracks.

"Look at all of them." Gunner blew out a weighted breath.

Dead bodies lay scattered about. Axel didn't count them, didn't want to know how many had fallen victim. "Hey, wait a minute." Axel moved closer to get a better look. "Most of these dead are infected. And they've been shot."

"So there are others survivors out there? Others like us?"

"Looks like it." Axel didn't know how he felt about that. On the one hand, other survivors meant potential allies. But it also meant there were people fighting for the same resources they came here to collect.

"How long ago do you think they were here?"

Axel kneeled down next to one of the bodies. "This black goo they have inside of them is dry."

"Good." Gunner cracked his neck. "Last thing I want to do is get into some kind of gunfight over what little is left in this store."

"Let's not be the type of people who start the gunfight, all right?"

Gunner grabbed each of his carts by the front and dragged them behind him. "I'm a lover, not a fighter. Where should we start? Back of the store first?"

"Might as well." Axel trailed close behind Gunner, keeping an eye out for movement. Whoever had come here before did a number on the store. From what he could see, there wasn't much left, which was impressive considering the number of infected they'd killed.

"Bastards. They took all the sleeping bags and most of the camping supplies. What else is on your list for this area?"

"Fishing poles. Britney said they have a nice-size pond on their property, and there's a river not far."

Gunner picked up a rod. "Got to admit, I don't know much about fishing."

"We'll take these." Axel grabbed the remaining four that already had reels attached and stuck them in his basket. "Let's hit hardware next, then the blankets. I don't see anything else in this section we need." The others who had come through wiped it clean.

The rest of the store was more of the same. The only thing they found in the hardware section was the hinges they needed. Blankets, towels, and comforters were all gone, and the clothing section was nonexistent. By the time they made it back to the front of the store, only two of the four carts had anything in them. One of them was filled with the last remaining dog food on the shelf. Britney had made it clear that the dogs needed to be fed; they were excellent guards and would bark if anything got near the house.

Gunner dropped to the ground. "What the fuck, man? How did they wipe out an entire Walmart?"

"It's been months." Axel took a seat beside him. "Who knows how many trips they've made. We should have come here a lot sooner."

"I don't want to go back empty-handed." Gunner kneaded the back of his neck. "What about the warehouse in the back?"

"We can look." Axel didn't want to go back with an empty trailer either. "Guess it doesn't matter if we leave these baskets unattended, does it?"

"You think someone's going to steal our fishing poles? Maybe the shampoo, bars of soaps and deodorant? Or the paperback books and board games you thought might come in handy?"

"Boredom can be deadly." Axel forced himself to get up off the floor. "Let's go check out the back. Maybe we'll get lucky."

They walked in silence, plucking a few random items off the shelf and throwing them into the empty cart they brought with them.

"You've got to be kidding." Gunner tugged at the lock securing a heavy-duty chain through the door handle. "Selfish bastards locked the rest of the stuff up like they own the whole goddamn store. I'm pretty sure I saw some bolt cutters in the hardware section. I'll grab them and cut this bitch open."

"Wait." Axel pressed his ear against the metal door. "I think we need to leave it locked."

"Why the fuck would we do that?"

Axel kicked the door with his steel-toe boot.

An uproar of growling cut through the silence. The infected on the other side scratched and slammed into the door.

"That's why. They didn't lock the doors to keep people out. They locked the doors to keep the infected in."

"I wonder how many they have trapped in there."

Axel took a step back as the doors cracked open and a set of clawed fingers pushed through. "Too many. We should go. Maybe they'll settle down if they can't hear us anymore."

Sprinting back to the front of the store, they took turns looking over their shoulders, making sure the infected hadn't broken free.

"Now what?" Gunner asked, leaning over with his heads on his knees as he tried to catch his breath.

"We load what little we have into the trailer and get the hell out of here." Axel pushed the basket loaded with dog food out of the store.

Gus followed with the other cart. "Should we keep searching? Maybe there are other stores in town that might have some stuff."

"The Tractor Supply store is down the street." Axel unlocked the back of the trailer and stacked the dog food bags. "We'll see if we can find anything in there. But if Walmart is any indication, we won't find much."

Gunner pushed his empty cart back on the sidewalk. “I put the rest of the stuff in the back seat. Need any help?”

Axel closed the trailer and locked it. “Nope. Doesn’t take much to load ten bags of dog food.”

They climbed back into the cab, and Axel started the engine. He was pissed. The others were counting on them, and right now they didn’t have jack-shit. What he wouldn’t give to have his cell phone right now to Google the nearest Walmart or any other store that might be useful. He hated driving around blind and without a backup plan.

“Ready?” Gus asked.

Axel put the truck in Drive and headed for the nearest exit.

“What are those?” Gunner pointed out the window as they drove past the edge of the store.

Axel followed Gunner’s finger and slammed on the brakes when he spotted the row of ten cargo containers. “Holy shit. Walmart uses those around the holidays to store overflow.”

“They don’t look like they’ve been opened.”

“Only one way to find out.” God, Axel hoped they’d found something.

He parked in front of the first container and both men got out.

Gunner pointed to the right. “I’ll start at this end if you want to start at the other. We’ll meet back in the middle?”

“Yep.” Axel tugged on each lock but none of them budged. “Still locked. That’s a good sign, right?”

“These are too,” Gunner said when they met back up. “Are there any bolt cutters in the back seat?”

"I'll check." Axel ran back to the truck and pulled out a rusty old toolbox. He found the bolt cutters at the bottom and hurried back with them. "Here you go."

Gunner cocked an eyebrow. "I get to do the honors?"

"I can do it if you think I'm stronger."

"Always the comedian." Gunner snatched the tool and cut the first lock. The sound of metal breaking echoed off the snow.

Axel reached for his gun and scanned the area. "That was loud."

"Do you hear them?" Gunner asked

"No. Keep going. I'll keep an eye out."

Three more cuts and Axel still heard nothing, though he did spot some movement off in the distance. He couldn't be sure what it was, but he wasn't taking any chances, keeping close to Gunner as he continued to cut each lock.

"That was the last of them." Gunner threw the bolt cutters into the back seat. "And no infected. That must be some kind of miracle."

"Speaking of miracles." Axel opened the first cargo container and nearly cried. "You've got to see this."

Gunner peeked his head inside and screamed, "Son of a bitch! I can't believe it. That's fucking food in there. Instant potatoes, canned veggies, and pie fillings."

And that was just the first row. The container looked to be completely full. "I wonder what's in the other ones."

Each container they opened was more exciting than the next. They found Christmas décor, including bedding, towels and blankets. Ugly sweaters, jackets, kids' jeans and sweaters. Boxes of warm pajamas. Gift sets including knives and tools and flashlights, half a dozen cases of wine, and a whole container full of toys—Legos, Barbies, baby dolls, Hot Wheels and other brands he didn't recognize.

They loaded as much as they could, the food, clothing and blankets being on the top of the list. There was no way they could take it all, but what they got would help them make it through the winter.

"Should I find some locks?" Gunner asked. "Seal these suckers back up?"

"No." Axel didn't want to be that person. "We could have died if we didn't find this stuff. I wouldn't wish that fate on anyone."

"Fair enough." Gunner closed each of the doors. "Ready? We still need to hit up Tractor Supply?"

"I think we're out of room." Axel studied his list. "We got most everything we needed except the guns. Oh, and the greenhouses." It was the last thing on the list. He'd almost forgotten.

"Greenhouses you said?" Gunner jerked his chin to the garden department behind them where several boxes were stacked along the fence. "God must love us today."

Axel grinned. "It can't be this easy."

Gunner lightly punched his arm. "Don't jinx us. I'll go grab them if you want to bring the truck around."

"Will do." But first Axel needed to load up a few more items.

***

Gunner tilted back and eyed the items Axel had stuffed in the back seat. "Toys, huh? Those a priority?"

"Just do me a favor, okay?" Axel kept his eyes on the road. "Don't say anything about them. Or the books or the wine."

"The wine?" Gunner clutched an overly dramatic hand to his chest. "Why on earth are we not telling the others about the wine? We keeping it all for ourselves, like payment for risking our lives?"

"No, I want to save it. Bring out for a special occasion."

Gunner grinned. "I got you. Saving it for *someone* special."

Axel ignored the innuendo behind Gunner's comment. "Please."

"Your secret is safe with me."

"Thanks." Axel hoped Gunner stayed true to his word. "Now keep your eyes open for the gun shops Britney told us about. Maybe we'll get lucky."

"I think our luck has just about run out." Gunner reached for his gun. "You see that up ahead? On the side of the road?"

The snow had picked up in the last fifteen minutes, making it hard to make out anything, but in the distance Axel could sort of see what Gunner was talking about. "Infected or human?"

"Can't be sure. But they aren't running toward us, and this truck is pretty damn loud." Gunner wiped off the condensation that had formed on the windshield with a dirty handkerchief. "Weird how we haven't really encountered any. In Myrefall they were everywhere."

"The weather was warmer the last time we went into town. We haven't seen any infected since the cold weather blew in late October."

"Slow down as we pass them." Gunner rolled down his window. "I want to get a better look."

"You think that's smart?" Axel asked. The last thing they needed was a horde of infected attacking the truck. It wouldn't take much and they'd be in the cab.

"They're definitely infected." Gunner poked his head outside. "But they aren't moving much. Slow down. I think it'll be okay."

"Think?" Axel didn't agree, but he let off the gas anyway.

Gunner shook his head. "I'll be damned. This cold weather is kicking their ass. Look at them. They can barely move."

Axel felt his heart rate return to normal for the first time since they left that morning. "That's crazy."

"Let's get home. Not only are we bringing a shit ton of stuff back but also good news." Gunner did a little dance in his seat. "Who are the big bad heroes now?"

"Us, I guess." As happy as Axel was to drive by a group of the infected and not be attacked, he didn't share Gunner's enthusiasm. "Can I go faster than ten miles an hour now?"

"Yeah, yeah." Gunner waved him onward. "The sooner we get back the better. Do you think we should unload when we get there, or should we celebrate first?"

"It's going to be dark, so I would say wait to unload until tomorrow. Though people might need the bedding. The last few nights have been damn cold."

Gunner grimaced. "Please don't tell me we stuck those in the far back."

"No, they were the last thing I loaded up." Axel had made sure they were easily accessible.

"Good thinking." Gunner leaned back against the headrest. "It's been a hell of a day. I'm exhausted."

"Get some rest." Axel wouldn't mind some peace. "I'll wake you when we get back."

Axel hadn't even finished his sentence before Gunner was asleep. Silence was better than the entire drive full of small talk and endless teasing by Gunner.

Yes, he had gotten the wine, books and toys for Britney and the kids. And yes, he wanted them to be a surprise, but that meant nothing. Sure as hell didn't mean he had romantic feelings for the woman.

She was great. Probably one of the coolest chicks he'd ever met in his entire life. But she had just buried her husband. Hell, Axel was living in her dead husband's man cave, for God's sake.

Factor in that not once had she ever shown any signs of romantic feelings toward him, and he knew they were just friends. Plain and simple. Which was fine with him. He wasn't even sure if he liked her beyond that.

The wall came into view a while later, and Axel shook Gunner's shoulder. "Hey, wake up. We're here."

Gunner popped his head up and blinked a couple times. "I was out for like five seconds."

"Try near an hour." Axel stopped at the gate. "Mind getting this?"

"Sure, sure," Gunner grumbled as he unlocked the gate. He was still griping when he climbed back in.

From the road Axel could see the faint cloud of smoke rising over the tree line. "You see that?"

"What? The smoke from the fire? Why do you ask?"

"I'm just concerned. Anyone driving by could see that smoke and know someone is here."

Gunner yawned. "And that's a bad thing, right?"

Axel honestly didn't know.

"Remember when we showed up unannounced and Britney held us at gunpoint?" Gunner asked. "Don't you think strolling up here when we weren't supposed to come back until tomorrow might be a little dangerous?"

Axel slowed the truck. "What can we do about it? We either wait here until morning, or we take our chances. She'll recognize the truck and trailer and know it's us."

"She's been a little jumpy lately." Gunner shrugged. "But you're probably right.

The vein in Axel's temple throbbed. He needed a good night's sleep and some time alone. "Are we good? Can I keep going?"

"Yep. Unless you want me to get out and walk the rest of the way, let them know we're back."

Axel pressed on the horn with the heel of his hand. "There. Now they know we're here."

Gunner furrowed his brow. "What the hell, man?"

"You wanted them to know we're here. Now they know." Axel pressed on the gas.

At the house, everyone waited outside, many with guns in hand. Britney must have recognized them, as she was the first to lower her weapon. The others followed.

The closer they got, the more excited everyone became. He could hear them cheering even over the noisy engine.

Axel parked the truck in front of the house and got out.

Britney came racing around the bumper and threw herself into his arms. "You're early!"

"Shit." Axel stumbled, taken aback by her surprise affection. "I wasn't expecting that."

"Sorry." Britney slipped from his arms. "I got a little caught up in the moment."

Axel gave her a lopsided grin. "I'm not complaining."

"Did everything go okay?" She peered over his shoulder. "Wow, you got a ton of stuff."

"It was a rocky start, but we got almost everything on the list."

Her smile slipped. "What didn't you get?"

"Guns and bullets. Walmart had been cleaned out by the time we got there. We're lucky we found this stuff." An unexpected yawn tugged at his lips.

"You must be exhausted. Have you eaten at all since you left?"

Axel hadn't even realized how hungry he was until she mentioned food. "We haven't."

"You want to come in?" Britney offered. "I can heat some leftovers."

"It's late." He knew if he went inside, it would be at least an hour if not more before he made it to bed. "I have some jerky you made in my room. I'll just eat that."

"Okay." She frowned.

"But thank you for the offer. If I weren't so exhausted, I'd be inside in a heartbeat."

She wrapped her arms around herself and shivered. "Well, good night, Axel."

"Good night." Once she was out of sight, Axel grabbed what he could from the back seat and turned to head back to his room.

"Need some help?"

If Axel's hands weren't full, he might have pulled his gun at the unexpected person popping out of the shadows. "Jesus, Gunner. Don't do that."

"Sorry. Didn't mean to scare you." Gunner gathered the rest of the stuff Axel had asked him to keep a secret. "I just thought you might need some help."

"Thanks." Axel headed for his room.

"And I wanted to tell you I saw the way Britney flew into your arms when we got back."

Axel threw back his head and sighed. "Not this again."

"And the way your face lit up—"

"Enough."

Gunner chuckled. "Just promise me one thing."

"What?" Axel snapped.

"Nothing over the top." Gunner followed Axel into his room and placed the couple of boxes he carried on the floor. "Just allow me to say 'I told you so' when it happens."

"Out." Axel jabbed his finger toward the door. "Now."

"Touchy."

Axel slammed the door behind Gunner, still hearing him laughing through the thin walls.

Last thing he needed was to be distracted, and Gunner's words were beyond distracting. They had more important things to worry about, like finishing the wall. Farm security had to be top priority. That and preparing for winter. Nothing else mattered. It couldn't. Not until he was sure they were safe.

CHAPTER TWENTY-ONE

December turned out to be the worst month so far. Not because of the weather—Britney didn't mind the cold—but because of the holiday that engulfed this month.

The kids were old enough to know that after Thanksgiving came Christmas. They hounded her for a week before she gave in and brought out the tree and decorations.

She didn't have the heart to tell them the truth, so she went a different route, explaining that not even Santa Claus, with all his magic, could survive the apocalypse. They didn't buy it and were insistent that, because Santa lived in the North Pole where it was also cold, the infected couldn't get to him.

It didn't help that Rainey encouraged their beliefs by having them create all sorts of crafts and reading them the Christmas books Britney had collected over the years.

Even tonight, on Christmas Eve, she had them bake cookies as a special treat.

"Maybe I should just tell them the truth," Britney said to Axel and Angie, who kept her company at the breakfast table. "It'll break their hearts, but it'll be better than them wakin' up tomorrow with no presents from Santa."

"Christmas isn't just about the presents." Angie and her damn wisdom. "Plus, you've gotten them a couple. That should count for something."

Britney had picked up a few things in the summer on clearance.

"I understand the true meanin' of Christmas." Britney did her best to keep her annoyance in check. "But they're still kids. And the world's gone to shit. They deserve to wake up Christmas mornin' and find presents under the tree."

"It'll work out." Axel patted her hand. "Trust me. Tomorrow will be great."

"Exactly." Angie took Britney's hand. "We'll have a nice dinner like we did on Thanksgiving. Mac promised the kids an epic snowball fight. Everything will work out, and we'll keep them so busy that they'll forget all about presents."

"Look at them." Britney gestured to her three little angels sitting in the living room. "They're addin' last minute items to their Santa list. God only knows what they're puttin' on there. Nothin' I bought them, that's for damn sure."

"Britney," Axel said. "Have a little faith in them. They're young, but they understand the world has changed."

"But Christmas is about magic, not reality." Why couldn't they understand that? "Neither of you has children, so you don't understand."

Angie cleared her throat and looked to Axel. "I'm going to go see what kind of craziness those kids are coming up with."

"What was that all about?" Britney asked.

Axel rested his elbows on the table and propped his chin on his clasped fingers. "I have a daughter—*had* a daughter."

Britney's heart sank. "Oh my God, Axel. Why didn't you say something? You have to be worried sick about what's happened to her."

"I know what happened to her." He sniffled. "She passed away earlier this year. The ride the bikers were on, that was for her."

Tears clogged Britney's throat. "I'm so sorry." She'd remembered the story he told her about the little girl and the cancer that had taken her life. "I can't even imagine."

"We did just about everything we could think of to save her." Axel wet his lips. "Even signed her up for an experimental treatment run by NATO of all people."

"NATO?"

"Yeah. Can you believe it?"

"No." Britney thought back to Thomas and how he had beat pancreatic cancer. "I mean yes. My best friend's father went through the same trials. You saw him, at the fall festival. He was the one who bit… Jesus."

"Britney? What's wrong."

"He's the one who bit John." Britney's voice trembled. "Your daughter…?"

"Sabrina."

"She didn't get violent after the treatment? Bite people?"

"They gave her the placebo."

"Right. But I thought after the first round, they gave all the patients the actual treatment?"

Axel hung his head. "She had already passed away by that time. We were devastated."

Britney scooted closer to him and cupped his cheeks. "Don't be. I think whatever NATO was curin' people with caused this outbreak."

"What?"

"I can't be sure, but it makes sense. When I saw Thomas in church, I noticed his skin had a gray hue to it, just like the infected. Then at the festival he bit someone. And then he bit John, and John became one of the infected."

"Still doesn't mean it originated with the NATO trials." Axel swallowed hard. "But that makes me feel a little better. Her mom and I were heartbroken knowing she could have been cured if we had only gotten the call a few days earlier."

"You and her mom… you guys aren't together?" She had never thought to ask him if there was someone waiting for him back home.

"Our marriage was over before Sabrina got sick. We had filed for divorce a few days before her diagnosis."

"I'm sorry." Britney didn't know what else to say.

"It happens. The love was still there, but we had just grown apart. Became two different people with different ideas on what life should look like."

They sat in silence for a few minutes until Axel stood and stretched. "Probably wasn't the best story to tell on Christmas Eve."

Britney gave him a half smile. "I'm glad you told me."

"I'm going to bed. Unless you need anything?"

"No." Britney looked to her kids. "Just going to put the kids to bed too. I'm sure they'll be up at the crack of dawn."

"It'll be okay. Trust me."

Axel told each of the kids good night and headed out. The rest of the bikers did the same, leaving Britney alone with her kids for the first time in days.

"Okay, guys. Time for bed."

"Yay!" all three of them cheered. It was the only night of the year they didn't fight her on bedtime.

"Can you read *The Night Before Christmas*?" Molly asked as they headed upstairs.

Britney's heart shattered, but how could she say no? "Sure. Is everyone still sleepin' in Carson's room?"

Every night they piled in his small bed and slept together. Britney resisted it at first, didn't think they would get any sleep that way. But, much to her surprise, they didn't fight and went straight to sleep most of the time. She guessed having someone close helped make things not feel so scary.

"That's where we sleep now, Mom," Blake said.

"All right. Well, brush your teeth and get your pajamas. I'll get the book and meet you back in his room." Because no one thought to grab the book before they went upstairs.

She took her time reading the story, enjoying the snuggle time they rarely shared anymore. After a big hug and kiss, she turned off the lamps and headed downstairs to make sure everything else in the house was off. No use wasting the batteries while they slept.

It wouldn't be long before they would need to run the generators to ward off the cold.

Britney paused at the unlit Christmas tree before heading to bed. Maybe she should have said the presents she bought were from Santa? Allow them to hold on to their childhood a little longer.

Maybe a part of her wanted them to know the truth, rip the Band-Aid off before the tooth fairy and Easter bunny came into play.

Or maybe she was just an idiot and didn't think this whole present thing through.

As she lumbered up the stairs and into her room, the tears she'd been holding back most of the day fell. She didn't make a habit of closing her door at night, but she closed it now.

The last thing she wanted was for her kids to hear her ugly cry on Christmas Eve.

***

The sound of Molly shrieking jolted Britney out of bed. She threw open her door, cursing herself for falling asleep with it closed.

Flying down the stairs, gun in hand, she could only imagine all the horrors she might face. If the infected hadn't somehow found their way in, then the lack of a visit from Santa would be crushing their spirits right about now.

"What's wrong?" she yelled when the problem didn't immediately present itself.

"Santa came!" they screamed, shoving Lego sets, Hot Wheels and Barbies in her face.

Britney's mouth fell open. "How?" She shuffled back a few steps until the back of her leg hit the couch.

"Look!" Molly held up the game Trouble. "He brought us each a game too!"

She collapsed on the couch, certain this must be a dream.

"Can we open our presents from you?" Carson asked.

Britney bobbled her head, still unable to form words.

"A princess dress!" Molly shrieked. "I love it so much. Thank you, Mommy."

A knock at the door drew her attention away from the kids and their presents.

Axel popped his head inside. "Merry Christmas. How is everyone this morning?"

"Axel, come see!" Blake waved him in. "Santa came, and he brought us the coolest toys."

Britney watched as he strolled inside and took a seat on the floor, not at all surprised that Santa showed up.

He leaned over and whispered into each of their ears, and they scurried off behind the tree, each retrieving a present.

"These are for you!" Molly handed Britney the first bag. "Here. Open it."

"Presents? For me?" Her eyes darted to Axel, who still sat on the floor grinning from ear to ear.

"What did you get?" Carson asked.

"Let me look." Britney pulled the tissue paper from the bag and lifted out a bottle of red wine.

Molly jumped up and down, clapping. "That's your favorite!"

"Open this one." Blake shoved another present in her lap.

"Ooh," Molly cooed. "Lots of books."

Tears stung Britney's eyes.

Carson handed her the last bag. "One more."

"Bath salts?" Britney cocked her head.

"Santa must know you'll need them again one day."

Britney's entire body shook. Tears ran down her cheeks, and she felt light-headed. "There are no words."

"It's a Christmas miracle." Axel smiled and shot her a wink.

She stared at Axel, her stomach fluttering and heart breaking all at the same time. It was almost as if these feelings that had blossomed for Axel undermined what she'd had with John.

She placed her presents on the floor at her feet and opened her mouth to call Axel over when the door swung open.

"Merry Christmas!" Mac called out. "Ho, ho, ho. Can we join your celebration?"

"Come in! Come in!" Molly shouted.

Mac, Angie, Gus, Gunner, Rainey and Shifter filed in.

Britney had expected the others to come in from the front, but not Rainey since she lived in the basement. But then she saw Gunner's hand brush against Rainey's and understood. Seemed like people were hooking up left and right around here.

"I see Santa came after all?" Angie took a seat next to Britney. "Were you surprised?"

"You aren't?" Britney asked, still unable to take her eyes off Axel.

Angie patted Britney's thigh. "Not in the slightest. He's a good man, you know."

"I know."

"You should have seen him with Sabrina. The love he had for that child. Broke all our hearts when she got sick."

Britney forced herself to look at Angie. "Why didn't he tell me earlier?"

"I don't know. He doesn't like to talk about it with people he doesn't know. You tell people your kid died of some rare disease and they get that look in their eyes. You know the one."

"He was afraid I would feel sorry for him?" Britney rolled her eyes. "Of course I feel sorry for him. He lost a child."

"I'm not going to pretend I know what's going on in that pretty little head of his. But what I know is he cares for you and your babies a whole lot. And after all the shit you four went through, he probably wanted to show you how strong he can be. For you."

"That's crazy." Britney turned her attention back to her kids.

"Like I said"—Angie stood—"that's just my opinion. Now, I think it's about time we work on that Christmas dinner."

"Who wants to help me make the pies?" Rainey asked.

Molly's hand shot up. "Me! I want to help. I can make pies."

"Boys?" Rainey addressed them. "What about you?"

Carson looked to Axel. "Can I help you cook the turkey?"

"Yes, sir."

"I want to build the fire!" Blake, her little firebug, announced. "Let's make a big one, all the way to the sky."

Gunner laughed. "Sure, kid. But first you need to get dressed."

"That's a good idea," Britney said. "All three of you, head upstairs and put on some warm clothes. Don't want to get your pajamas dirty."

Carson jumped to his feet. "Don't start the turkey without me."

"Or the pies!" Molly added.

"You can get the firewood," Blake said as he passed Gunner. "I want to light the matches."

Gunner barked a laugh. “We need to keep a close eye on that kid.”

***

“Did you have a good Christmas?” Britney asked as she tucked the kids into bed.

“The best!” Carson could hardly contain his excitement. “Did you see how Mac fell down when I hit him with that snowball?”

Blake laughed. “That was so funny.”

“Not as funny as Axel hitting Mommy with the snowball.” Molly giggled.

“And Mommy getting him back,” Carson snickered.

Britney gave each of them a kiss. “That was funny. Now get some sleep. I love you.”

“Love you,” they each called out as she left the room.

She headed downstairs to finish cleaning up the new toys the kids had left scattered around the living room. They were so excited, her included, that Santa had come, and she didn’t feel like ruining their excitement by having them clean up.

She tiptoed around the Legos on the floor, careful not to break anything Carson and Axel had already built or step on the others with her bare feet. Those things hurt like a mother.

She picked up the presents she’d never expected to get and took them to the kitchen table to get a better look at the books. And open the wine.

She poured herself a glass and spread the ten books on the table, trying to decide which one she wanted to dive into first. It was a hard decision. All were under the fantasy genre, her favorite. She couldn’t believe Axel remembered.

Or that he thought to bring back toys for her kids. That he played Santa and surprised them all.

She sucked down her glass of wine and poured another, her head spinning. Deep in her heart, she knew there was something between them. Feelings for each other that went beyond friendship. If she were being honest with herself, she'd felt a spark between them when they first met. Not that she'd thought much of it at the time; he was an attractive man, and every woman in town swooned when he came around.

The second glass of wine went down easier than the first. Sitting in the kitchen alone, surrounded by her gifts, she had a sudden urge to find Axel and thank him.

They'd been so busy today that she wasn't even sure if they'd spoken two words to each other. Which was strange because they were always talking.

Another sip of liquid courage and she jumped to her feet. She had to make sure Axel knew how much she appreciated all he'd done for her and her kids today.

Before leaving, she knocked on the basement door to let Gunner and Rainey know she'd be back. She'd made it a point earlier to let them know she didn't have a problem with Gunner staying in the house with Rainey.

Britney slipped on her snow boots and jacket, not bothering to change out of her fleece pajamas, and headed out the door.

"Britney?"

She startled, surprised to find Axel sitting in the swing on her porch. "What are you doin' out here? It's freezin'."

"Trying to get up the nerve to knock."

"What?" His bluntness took her by surprise. "Why? Normally you just knock and barge in without waiting for a reply."

"Barge in?" He grimaced. "Sorry. I didn't mean to intrude."

He got up to leave, but Britney stepped in front of him. "That's not what I meant. Please don't go. I wanted to talk to you."

"About?" Axel's eyes bored into hers.

"Today. What you did for the kids." Butterflies filled her stomach. "And for me."

He took a step closer and her breath hitched. He smelled so good, so manly, it made her insides quiver.

"How do you know it was me?" A hint of mischievousness danced in his eyes.

Britney bit down on her bottom lip. "It was, wasn't it? No one else knew about my love of books and bath stuff."

"Hopefully we can figure out a way for you to use the bath stuff."

Her eyelids fluttered as he leaned closer. Their lips were so close to touching. All she had to do was push up on her tiptoes.

"Thank you," she whispered, unable to break eye contact.

He ran his thumb along her cheekbone and she shuddered. She wanted nothing more in that moment than for him to kiss her.

But he didn't. And she didn't understand why. Couldn't he see the want in her eyes? Was she not giving off the right signals? Maybe he was waiting for her to make the first move?

"Britney," he breathed, "is it okay—"

She was done waiting. Throwing her arms around his neck, she pressed her lips to his.

Axel scooped her up in his arms. She wrapped her legs around his waist as he brought them down on the bench.

Fireworks exploded within her. She felt faint and exhilarated at the same time. Every cliché she'd ever read about in her mother's sappy romance novels became a reality. She'd never experienced anything quite like it. Even with John.

John.

Tears burst from her eyes as she pulled out of Axel's embrace.

He reached out for her. "Brit, what's wrong?"

"I'm sorry." She tried to force the tears away, rubbing her palms across her face. "I had a couple of glasses of wine and got caught up in the moment."

"Oh." Axel stood up, his shoulders drooping. "I didn't mean… I thought… you kissed me."

"I know." Britney couldn't bear to face him. "And I wanted to. So much. But… it's just… I'm not ready."

Axel ran his hand along her arm. "Britney, look at me. Please."

Her body trembled as she rotated around slowly, not wanting to see the anger in his eyes. But there was none. "I'm sorry."

"It's fine." Using his index finger, he lifted her chin. "I understand. It hasn't been that long since John died. You're not ready, and that's okay."

"But everything you've done for us," she sobbed.

"I would have done it anyway, whether you batted your pretty green eyes at me or not."

Her chest ached. "I don't want to lose you."

"Come here." He pulled her into a tight hug and kissed the top of her head. "I'm not going anywhere."

CHAPTER TWENTY-TWO

"Time to add more wood to the fire." Gus wrapped his blanket around himself as he slipped on his shoes. "I'll go get it."

Axel rose from the couch. "I'll go with you."

By the middle of January, it had gotten too cold to stay in the barn. The house didn't have enough rooms for everyone to have their own, but they made do.

Mac and Angie took Molly's room. Gus stayed in Blake's. Gunner and Rainey had the basement. That left Axel and Shifter with the living room, which was proving to be a mistake. The lack of privacy and overall close quarters of the group had taken its toll.

"Maybe we should check the generator while we're at it," Shifter added. "We're going to die from hypothermia if the damn thing keeps freezing up on us."

"What?" Molly gasped. "I don't want to die."

Britney pulled Molly into her arms and glowered at Shifter. "No one is goin' to die. Even if the generator isn't workin', we still have the fireplace. That gives off more than enough heat."

"If we all slept in the living room," Shifter mumbled.

"We'll make sure the generator is up and runnin' before we go to bed," Britney reassured him. "But for now, we have the fireplace goin'. And we're all downstairs. There's no point in wasting gas."

Axel bumped into Shifter as he headed for the door. "Watch what you're saying in front of the kids, won't you?"

"Better watch where you're walking, kid." Shifter got into Axel's face. "I have just as much right as you to say what's on my mind."

"Say what you want," Axel growled, "just not in front of the kids."

Molly snuggled closer into Britney's side. "Don't fight."

Axel and Shifter snapped their heads in her direction. Both men's faces softened at the sight of the scared little girl.

"Sorry." Shifter patted Axel on the back. "No one's fighting. Everyone's just a little grumpy."

Britney could imagine these men had gotten little sleep. "You know what, kids? Why don't we have a slumber party downstairs. That way Shifter can take Carson's room, and Axel can have my room."

"I'm not going to kick you out of your room," Axel said. "I can stay down here with the kids."

"I insist." Britney felt bad that Axel gave up his chance for a real bed. "Please. You shouldn't have to sleep on the couch."

"I'm good. The pullout isn't bad." Axel ran a hand through his hair. "I've slept on worse."

"Then the kids can sleep in my room. That way you'll at least have the livin' room to yourself."

"All four of you will fit on your bed?" Axel asked.

"We'll make do. They can have the bed, and I can sleep on the mat the kids use in our bedroom if they have a nightmare or aren't feelin' well." She had forgotten about that until now. "Which I should have thought about sooner so one of you could have used it."

Shifter waved a dismissive hand. "I doubt it would have done either of us any good."

"Kids, why don't you go upstairs, gather your stuff for bedtime and put it in my room."

"Can't we sleep downstairs?" Carson asked. "Like a real slumber party?"

"No. Axel needs his privacy."

Molly scrunched her little nose. "Why?"

"Because grown-ups like their peace and quiet." Like everyone else, Britney was tired of being cooped up in the house, and it was starting to show.

"That's boring," Blake groaned.

"Just go upstairs," she snapped, then added, "please."

The front door swung open and a blast of cold air swept through the house, chilling Britney to her bone. Gus stumbled in, a stack of firewood in hand. "I have some bad news. We're out of gas."

"What?" Britney jumped to her feet. "That can't be right."

"Must have been the storm last night. All the high winds." Gus dropped the wood next to the fire. "A couple of large limbs broke off the tree. They punctured a hole in the tank and knocked it over. We didn't notice it this morning because of all the snow."

Britney heard the kids' footsteps above them as they dragged their pillows and blankets toward her room. "Change of plan," she yelled up the stairs. "We're all sleepin' down here for a while."

"All of us?" Rainey asked as she snuggled closer to Gunner.

"It'll get cold in this house without central heat." Britney looked to the others. "Freezin'. I hate to say it, but having your own rooms upstairs probably won't happen. I mean you can try, but there's not much insulation left in this old house."

"So we all sleep down here." Axel took a seat in the recliner. "Keep the fire going. That combined with our body heat, we'll be fine. How long does winter typically last here?"

Britney didn't want to say, didn't want to worry anyone. "It should warm up by March. Until then, durin' the days, if we dress warm enough, we can go outside and get some fresh air. We don't have much of a choice anyway. We have to check on the animals and keep them fed."

"Guess we have to suck it up and make it through the winter without killing each other," Mac said. "It's better than the alternative."

***

The days ticked by slower than Britney could ever imagine. By February, the living room looked like a campground. To give everyone their own space, they resorted to pushing her furniture into the dining room to make room for five tents. Axel had brought back four from their first supply run, and Rainey and Gunner took one while Mac and Angie coupled up in another. Gus and Shifter split the other two. Britney dug out a fifth one from a barn for her, the kids and Axel to share.

Axel had refused at first, trying to put everyone else's needs above his own. Again. It was becoming a habit. One she wished he would break. But she wore him down with the kids' help—they gave him their best puppy dog eyes and pleaded until he agreed.

It worked out well. With all of them hidden behind their nylon walls, it gave everyone the illusion of being alone, which kept them all from killing each other, but not from going stir-crazy.

They spent most of their time indoors. This winter had been exceptionally brutal so far, more so than she remembered the past few years. The below-freezing temperatures had always made farm life in the winter difficult, but there was normally a way to warm up after being outside. A heated house and a hot shower did the job nicely.

"Are we sure there's no way to get the generator back up and running?" Angie huddled closer to the fireplace. "This cold is kicking my ass."

"No gas, no generator." Gus threw another log on the fire. "We can light more candles, see if that helps."

Angie rolled her eyes. "Sure, why not? It hasn't helped yet, but maybe it will this time."

"Hey." Mac took a seat beside her and wrapped his arm around her shoulders. "No need for sarcasm. Gus is just trying to help."

"I know." Tears welled in Angie's eyes. "I'm just so cold."

"We all are," Rainey stated. "But the nights aren't too bad. It gets pretty warm in the tent."

The other good thing about setting up the tents was with all the windows and doors zipped tight, they held in heat pretty well.

"We can't just stay in our tents all day." Angie blew out a heavy breath. "It's hard enough not losing my mind being stuck in this house."

"You know what we need?" Axel said. "We need something to take our minds off the cold. You don't see the kids complaining, do you? That's because they stay busy."

Axel was right, the kids hadn't really complained too much about the cold. They kept themselves busy playing with toys or games. Sometimes together, sometimes apart. The times they got bored, one of the adults got them past it. Rainey was the best. She could create a make-believe scenario in a matter of seconds.

“What do you suggest?” Shifter grumbled.

“How about cards?” Axel dug them out of the stack of games Britney kept in the hall closet. “Poker, rummy, blackjack. Something.”

Britney couldn’t remember the last time she’d played card games with adults. “I have the rules for ten-step rummy, and I’m sure we have poker chips around here somewhere.”

Gunner rubbed his hands together. “Sounds like a good way to pass the time. Can’t believe we didn’t think of it before. Let's play on the floor next to the fire.”

“Everybody in?” Britney asked.

They all nodded.

For the first time in a long time, Britney felt a twinge of excitement. “Perfect! What do we want to play?”

CHAPTER TWENTY-THREE

Axel plopped down on the ground next to Gunner, out of breath from chopping firewood. After spending months in the house, he was out of shape.

"Water?" Gunner offered his canteen. "It's not cold, but I'm not complaining."

Axel accepted the bottle and took a long swig. "I'm with you."

"I never thought I'd be so happy to see spring." Gunner sneezed. "Allergies and all."

"I have to admit, when we ran out of fuel for the generator, I wasn't sure we would make it."

"You and me both, brother." Gunner stretched out his legs and rested his head on the barn behind them. "Never thought a flimsy tent could hold in the heat as well as they did. Probably didn't hurt to have a snuggle partner either."

"I wouldn't know about that." Axel took another drink before handing the water back to Gunner.

"What are you talking about? You shared a tent with Britney."

"And the kids," Axel reminded him. "Kind of puts a damper on things."

Gunner cocked an eyebrow. "Is there something going on between the two of you I don't know about?"

"You sound like a teenage girl right now. You know that, right?"

A wide smile tugged at his lips. "Entertainment is lacking these days. How else am I supposed to pass the time?"

"Read a book?" Axel leaned back and closed his eyes, enjoying the warmth of the April sun against his skin.

"Speaking of books—"

Axel already knew where this conversation was heading. "Yes, the ones she spent the winter reading are the ones I got for her."

"Axel!" Molly screeched.

He opened his eyes just in time to catch the five-year-old who dive-bombed his lap.

"Jesus, little girl." Gunner clutched his chest. "You nearly gave me a heart attack. How did you not jump out of your skin, Axel?"

"Because,"—Axel tickled Molly's side—"that was her excited scream, not her scared scream."

"And you can tell the difference?"

"Molly," Carson scolded as he and Blake jogged up. "What did Mom tell you about screaming?"

Over the past six months, Carson had taken being the man-of-the-house seriously. Sometimes a little too seriously. "Carson, remember what we talked about?"

"I'm just reminding her." Carson gestured to Molly. "The infected are attracted to the noise."

"Infected?" Molly hid her face in Axel's chest.

Axel patted her back. "There are no infected. With the wall built and the high fence your dad had installed, we're safe. We haven't seen an infected since before winter, remember?"

"Which is why she needs to stop yelling," Carson said in his best annoyed voice.

"You're not the boss of me," Molly spat.

"That's enough." Axel knew if he didn't put an end to this now, it would only escalate. "Now, did you three come out here for a reason or just to hang out."

Blake threw back his shoulders. "For a reason. It's almost Mom's birthday."

"Is it?" All this time at the farm and they hadn't celebrated a single birthday. "When?"

"Umm." Blake's eyes rolled upward as he thought about it.

"Saturday," Carson hissed. "I already told you."

"Hey." Axel tapped Carson on the nose. "Part of being the man of the house is having patience."

"Daddy was always losing his patience," Molly said. "He told us that all the time."

Axel could imagine. These three, plus Britney, were a handful. "So your mom's birthday is Saturday?"

"Yes!" Molly grabbed Axel's cheeks and squeezed. "What are we going to do? Can we throw her a party?"

"Um." Axel had never thrown a birthday party on his own before. "I guess we can. But don't you think Rainey or Angie might be better at planning a party than me?"

"It has to be you," Molly insisted. "You're Mommy's best friend. And the best friend is in charge of planning surprise parties."

Axel's stomach knotted. "How do you know I'm your mom's best friend?"

"One"—Molly held up a finger—"you always hang out together. And two, she's always laughing at your jokes even when they aren't funny."

Gunner snickered.

"Shut up, man." Axel turned his attention back to Molly. "I think I get it now."

"Good. So, what's the plan?"

Axel drew a blank. "You're her kids. What do you want to do for her?"

"There has to be music," Blake chimed in. "Mom loves to dance."

"Yeah!" Molly clapped excitedly. "A dance party!"

There was an old CD player in Axel's room that might still work with new batteries. And if he could track down some CDs. "Okay. We can probably get some music. What else does your mom like?"

"Wine," Molly said with a big smile on her face. "That's her favorite. And chocolate."

Axel still had a case of wine under the bed in his room. The chocolate might be a problem. "Can you think of anything else we might have missed?"

"Presents. Duh." Molly rolled her eyes.

"Molly," Carson huffed, "we can't just go to the store and buy her something."

Molly frowned. "I know that. We can make her something."

"I think she would love for each of you made her a present. Maybe Rainey can help you."

"What about you?" Molly batted her eyelashes. "What are you going to get her? As her best friend."

Axel massaged his temples. "I don't know… yet."

"Kids!" Britney called out from the front porch. "Come inside and wash up for dinner."

Carson took Molly's hand. "Let's go."

Before Molly let Carson drag her away, she leaned in closer to Axel. "Don't tell Mommy. It has to be a surprise. Do you promise?"

"Promise. Now go before your mom gets mad."

The kids hurried off toward the house, leaving Axel alone with a very smug-looking Gunner. "What?"

"I think it's nice, helping the kids throw their mom—your best friend—a surprise party."

Axel rose to his feet. "I need to finish cutting the firewood."

"What are you going to get her?" Gunner trailed close behind. "Something pretty? Something sparkly? Something to go on her ring finger?"

"Don't you have chores to finish?"

"Nope." Gunner clicked his tongue. "Let's see. You've already given her wine and books for Christmas. Let's not forget the bath set she can't use because of the lack of hot water."

Axel froze. "But we *could* have hot water, if we wanted to."

After the snow melted, Axel and Gunner had made a supply run and stumbled across a gas truck. It took a few hours, but they got the thing running and brought it back to fuel the generator.

"The water heater and all the other nonessentials are not hooked up."

"It wouldn't take much to hook the water heater up for a few hours and run a bath for Britney."

Gunner tilted his head to the side. "You want to give her a bath for her birthday? Isn't that kind of like telling her she stinks?"

"No." Axel swung the axe down, splitting a log. "She loves baths. It's kind of her thing."

"I get that, but let's think about this whole party and gift thing. We've had several birthdays come and go over the past six months. No one had a party thrown for them. There were no presents or cake. Don't you think some might be offended if you do this for Britney and no one else?"

"It's not like I'm the one who decided to throw her a party. That was her kids' idea. Do you really want to be the one to tell them no?"

"Fine. We'll have the party and blame the kids. But the hot bath…."

Axel split another log. "What if everyone took a hot shower? Think about how amazing that would feel."

Gunner thought it over for a minute. "A hot shower, huh? Damn that sounds nice."

Yes it did. "What do you say? Think we can make it happen?"

"Bribe people with a hot shower to help throw a surprise party? Can't imagine anyone would say no to that."

CHAPTER TWENTY-FOUR

"Keep your eyes closed, Mom," Carson ordered as he and the twins led Britney out the front door. "No peeking."

"How am I supposed to peek through a blindfold?" They had tied it on well; she could barely blink, let alone open her eyes. "Just please tell me when to step down."

"I got you," Axel's voice cut through the darkness. "I'm going to take your hand and help you down the stairs."

Britney allowed him to guide her but still wished she could see. "What's goin' on?"

"It's your birthday, Mommy." Molly took hold of Britney's free hand. "And we have a surprise for you."

She wasn't much on surprises, but the kids seemed so excited. She couldn't possibly tell them no. "Great! Can you at least tell me where we're goin'?" It felt like they were headin' in the barn's direction, but she couldn't be sure.

"Be patient, Mom," Carson told her. "We'll be there in a minute."

"Fine." She shuffled on, afraid of tripping on some unseen object.

"Almost there." Axel stayed close by her side. "A few more steps. There you go. What do you think, kids? This a good spot?"

"Yep," Blake said.

Thank goodness. "Can you take off this blindfold now?"

"Remember, keep your eyes closed until we tell you to open them," Carson reminded her.

She thought the eyes closed part was over. "Fine. But hurry."

"I got the blindfold." Axel's strong hands brushed against the back of her head as he undid the knot.

"Ready!" Molly yelled. "Open your eyes."

"Surprise!" multiple voices shouted.

Britney took a step backward shocked to see everyone gathered around. "What is this?"

"Your surprise birthday party!" Molly jumped up and down. "Look, we decorated the barn just for you."

"It looks beautiful." Pink, purple, blue and green streamers hung from the rafters. On a pink plastic-covered table sat an assortment of fruits from their garden, plus a variety of mismatched paper plates and napkins. "Where did you get the decorations?"

"From the box in the basement," Rainey told her. "The one labeled party supplies. The kids said you wouldn't mind."

"Not at all. This is amazin'." Her heart swelled at the thoughtfulness. "But you didn't have to go to all this trouble. We haven't celebrated anyone else's birthday."

"The kids planned it all," Axel explained. "We just helped make their ideas a reality."

"Thank you all so much."

Blake tugged her hand. "Come look outside."

"Okay." Britney followed the kids outside to the back of the barn. She blinked several times before coming to terms with what she saw. "Is that a hog roastin' over a fire?"

Molly shrieked. "Like Hawaii!"

Britney smiled down at her daughter. "How do you know they do this in Hawaii?"

"Mac told me," she said. "He's been to a luau before."

"Has he now?" Britney glanced back at him. "I'm guessin' you told her about this and she wouldn't let it go?"

"Damn girl is persistent." Mac shook his head. "Once she puts her mind to something there is no talking her out of it. She had to have the roasted pig; said you would love it."

"And I do." Britney leaned in and gave each of the kids a big hug. "Thank you so much for my party. It's the best ever."

"You haven't even opened your presents yet." Molly grabbed Britney's hand and dragged her back into the barn.

"You sit here, Mom." Carson pointed to an old wooden chair.

Molly brought over one of her princess tiaras. "And wear this. As the birthday queen."

Britney dipped her head. "I would be honored."

"Now for the presents." Molly went first. "This is from me."

Britney carefully undid the wrapping to find a hand-strung plastic bead bracelet. She slipped it over her hand. "It's beautiful. I'll never take it off."

"Now us!" Carson shoved a present into her lap. "This is from me and Blake. Open it. And you don't have to be careful with the wrapping."

"What could it be?" She ripped the paper away and stared down at the spiral notebook decorated with what appeared to be a dragon. Or maybe a lizard? "What is this?"

Blake puffed out his chest. "Me and Carson wrote you a book."

"A book?" Britney's heart swelled. "You wrote me a book? That's amazin'."

"It's about dragons and wizards and two brothers going on an adventure to save the queen," Carson said with such enthusiasm she nearly cried.

"I love it!" Britney held it tight. "I can't wait to read it."

"You can read it later, Mommy." Molly tugged at the hem of Britney's shirt. "When you take your b—"

"Shh." Axel covered Molly's mouth with his hand. "Why don't we show your mom what else we have?"

"What's goin' on?" Britney crossed her arms. "What was she goin' to say?"

"Only time will tell, but first…." Axel hurried to his room and came back with John's old CD player. "It's time to party!"

He hit Play and Nirvana's "Smells Like Teen Spirit" blasted through the still-decent speakers.

"Oh my God. Where did you find that CD?" She thought John got rid of those ages ago.

"That's not the only one I found." Axel tossed her a small twenty-disk CD case. "There's some good stuff in there. I'm surprised. I thought all you farm folk listened to was country music." He tried his best to add in a country twang to that last sentence but failed. Miserably.

"Please never talk like that again."

"Why not? Do I sound funny?"

Britney scrunched her nose. “Very much so. And it’s weird. Like someone else is talkin’ through you or something.”

“Like a ventriloquist?”

“Yes!” Britney shuddered. “Those dolls give me the creeps.”

“Pig’s ready!” Shifter shouted from the doorway. “I’m cutting it right off the spit, so bring a plate.”

“Go, kids.” Britney handed them each a plate. “Get some dinner. I’ll be right out.”

Axel came up behind her and whispered in her ear. “You know the birthday girl is supposed to go first.”

Britney rotated around. “Thanks for all this. I know the kids couldn’t have done it alone.”

“We all pitched in.”

“That was nice of everybody.” Britney scanned the area. “Where are Gunner and Rainey? I could have sworn they were just here.”

“I’m sure they’ll be back.” Axel guided her outside. “Why don’t you go get some food and I’ll get the wine.”

“Wine? Really?” Britney did a little happy dance inside her head. “Where did that come from?”

“My personal stash.” He shot her a wink. “I’ll be right back.”

***

The party was a blast. Music, dancing, wine and food—Britney couldn’t have asked for a better birthday.

She dropped on the bench next to Axel. “Why aren’t you dancin’?”

“I think you’re doing enough dancing for the both of us.” Axel pointed his wineglass at Molly. “The two of you are.”

"We're not the only ones dancin'. Gus is surprisingly good at two-steppin'. Who would have thought?" Britney snatched his glass from him and took a drink.

Axel reached over and took it back. "Don't you have your own?"

"I do. But then I drank it all. So now I don't." She was pretty sure that made sense.

"And how many glasses have you had?"

She'd lost count. "Plenty and not enough."

"That's deep." Axel handed her his glass back. "Take mine. It is your birthday, after all."

Britney bit down on her bottom lip. There was something bothering her that she couldn't hold in any longer. "I have to tell you somethin'. Today's not my birthday."

Axel's mouth fell open. "What? Are you serious?"

"It's tomorrow. I didn't want to say anythin' because the kids were so excited. I think they were lookin' at last year's calendar."

Axel laughed. "Maybe we should keep this little secret between the two of us."

"We probably should." Britney sipped her wine. "Why do people keep disappearin'?"

"Who's not here?" Axel made a big show of checking the barn.

Britney could tell he was hiding something. "Right now? Shifter's gone."

"Probably went to take a leak." Axel stood up. "I'm going to get another glass of wine since mine has been hijacked."

"Why won't you tell me what's goin' on?" she asked as she followed him to the drink table.

Axel poured himself a glass. "There's nothing to tell."

"Rainey left and came back with wet hair. Why would she do that?"

He turned around and leaned casually on the table. "You'd have to ask her."

"Everyone has left and come back. Everyone but you, me and the kids. Somethin' is goin' on."

"Britney," Rainey interrupted. "Sorry. I just wanted to let you know I'm going to put the kids to bed."

"That's okay." Britney set down her drink on the table. She hadn't even noticed how late it had gotten. "I'll do it."

Rainey's eyes darted to Axel. "Um."

"Britney." Axel poured more wine into her glass. "Let Rainey do it. The kids want her to, right?"

All three nodded. Though none of them looked particularly tired.

"Are you sure you're ready to go to bed? It is my birthday, after all. You can stay up later and hang out."

"We're ready," Carson said a little too quickly. "Plus, Rainey has to finish the story she started reading us last night, so we'll be up a little longer anyway."

"Come on, kids." Rainey maneuvered them out the door. "Let's go finish that book."

Britney scrunched her nose. "What is goin' on around here?"

Axel shrugged. "Guess they're tired. They have been working really hard all week to get everything ready for your party."

"But they never pass up a chance to stay up late."

"Must be one hell of a story." Axel averted his eyes.

Britney rapped her fingers on the table. "You're hidin' somethin', and I want to know what it is."

A sly smile spread across Axel's face. "You were one of those kids who searched for their Christmas presents, weren't you? Couldn't handle the suspense."

She was but didn't want to admit it, not when Axel was acting all smug. "Why do you ask?"

"Not asking. More like an observation."

"You think you know me so well, don't you?" Britney pursed her lips.

Axel laughed. "I'm pretty sure I have a good understanding of who Britney Campbell really is."

His arrogance got on her last nerve. "I'm goin' to tuck my kids in and go to bed." She started to walk off.

"Britney, wait." Axel chased after her. "Don't be angry. Is it really such a bad thing that I know you so well? We're friends, aren't we?

"Friends?" She whirled around. Stupid wine was getting her emotions all jumbled up. "Is that all I am to you?"

Axel peered over at the house and smiled. "No. Come inside with me."

They passed Rainey as they headed in the house. "Where is she goin'?"

"Back to the party, I assume." Axel closed the door behind them. "Want to go tell the kids good night?"

Britney nodded. "It makes me feel better. Reminds me they're safe when I see them in their bed."

"I understand." Axel guided her upstairs and into Carson's room, where the kids were huddled together under the blanket.

"I can't believe they're already asleep." She kissed each of them on the forehead. "They must have been tired."

"Like I said, they've been working hard putting this party together for you."

Britney tiptoed out of the room, careful not to wake them. "I loved it." She sucked in a deep breath and sighed. "What's that smell?"

"Smell?" Axel asked.

"Yeah." Britney took a whiff of the air again. "Smells like lavender and candles. Crap, did someone leave a candle burnin'?"

She followed the scent down the hall and into her room, which was strange because she didn't remember lighting any candles.

"Maybe you should check in the bathroom," Axel said from a few feet behind her.

Britney threw open the bathroom door and gasped at the sight. A dozen lit candles illuminated the room. On the table next to the tub sat a bottle of wine and the book she had started a couple days back. But those things weren't what had her heart racing.

"Is that hot water in the tub?"

"It is."

"How?" Britney spun around. "Did you do this?"

"With some help." Axel pointed to the counter. "There's the bath set you got for Christmas, ready and waiting."

"You hooked up the water heater?" She wasn't sure how she felt about that. On one hand, it had been so long since she'd taken a hot bath that the thought nearly brought her to tears. On the other, it wasn't fair that she was given this luxury when none of the others had.

"It's temporary."

"Do the others know?" She asked.

Axel chuckled. "Where do you think they've been sneaking off to all night?"

That made her feel a whole hell of a lot better. "They all got hot showers?"

"Yep."

Britney turned back to her bath. "All but you? And the kids?"

"Rainey had them take quick showers earlier when you were out checking cattle. As for me, I'm good."

"Take a shower before the hot water is disconnected. I won't take no for an answer."

"Yes, ma'am." Axel lightly shoved her toward the tub. "But right now you need to get in before the water gets cold. I have kid duty, so take your time and try not to worry about anything."

"Thank you, Axel. For everythin'."

"See you soon." He closed the door, leaving her alone.

She stripped off her grungy clothes and climbed in. The hot water felt like heaven, seeping into her skin all the way to the bone. Every muscle in her body relaxed as she settled into the tub. A glass of red sat waiting, and she took a long drink. It might not have been her birthday yet, but it would be soon, and she would soak up as much of this goodness as possible while she had the chance.

***

Britney climbed out of the bath an hour later, the lack of heat left in the water forcing her to leave. She had savored every second of her bath but never did quite relax.

In her head she kept replaying all the wonderful, thoughtful, kind things Axel had done for her and the kids over the past six months. He had been their rock, their shoulder to cry on, their provider and most importantly a friend.

"Best friend," Molly had told her a few days back.

But that wasn't true. They were more than friends. Had been for a while now, at least since Christmas when they'd kissed on the porch. Even though she pulled away, not ready to take the next step, in her heart she knew someday things would progress.

She slipped on a spaghetti strap nightgown and covered up in her fuzzy robe. It might have been spring, but there was still a chill in the air.

After peeking in on the kids, she headed downstairs to find Axel. She had no idea what she wanted to say to him but knew she needed to say something.

She found him asleep on the couch, snoring quietly. He looked so peaceful that she thought twice about waking him. Whatever she wanted to say to him could wait until tomorrow or the next day. Or the day after that.

As she stood there staring at him, her nerve faded away, along with the buzz from the wine. She whirled around, ready to race back upstairs, when he stirred and opened his eyes.

"Hey," he said with a yawn. "Done so soon?"

"The water got cold." Britney averted her eyes. "I was just checkin' on things before I went to bed."

"Everything is good." Axel watched her close. "You okay?"

"Yeah. Good. Fantastic. The bath was amazin'."

He patted the couch beside him. "Do you want to sit?"

Did she? Her body screamed yes while her brain came up with excuses for why she needed to head back upstairs. "Um…."

"You're acting… I don't want to say weird because that's rude, but that's the only word I can think of."

Britney slowly sat down on the couch, as far away from Axel as she possibly could.

Axel gawked at the space between them. "Maybe I should go take a shower. I must smell pretty bad."

"You don't," she blurted. He never did. Even after working outside for days on end, he always had this musky, masculine scent to him that made her insides melt.

"Did I do something wrong?" Axel asked. "Maybe overstepped my boundaries with the whole bath thing?"

"No." She squeezed the top of his hand. "The bath was perfect. The best birthday gift I could have ever hoped for."

"Good." He intertwined their fingers, and their gazes locked.

Every nerve in her body tingled. She wanted him in the worse kind of way but didn't know how to make the first move. Never in her life had she lost the ability to speak until now.

Axel seemed to be having a hard time forming a sentence as well. "I… fuck. Why is this so hard?"

"What is?" Britney didn't know what to make of his wrinkled brow.

He ran his thumb along her wrist but didn't reply.

She sucked in a sharp breath as the want transformed into an unbearable need. What was wrong with her that she just couldn't say what was on her mind? Normally she couldn't stop herself from talking.

He continued to circle her wrist with his thumb, his eyes fixated on her.

"Jesus, Axel." Unable to take it anymore, the words just spilled out. "Can you just make a fuckin' move already?"

"That's all I needed to hear." Her seized her waist and pulled her onto his lap, kissing her neck as he undid her robe.

His lips set fire to her skin as he made his way to her left breast.

"Ahem." Someone cleared their throat

Axel froze and Britney clawed at her camisole in a hurry to cover her exposed chest.

“Sorry to interrupt,” Gunner said. “We were just headed to bed.”

Britney slid off Axel’s lap onto the couch next to him, her cheeks burning.

“How long have you been standing there?” Axel asked through clenched teeth.

Rainey fiddled with her hair, doing her best to avoid eye contact. “We just walked in. And saw nothing.”

Gunner grinned. “Didn’t see much.”

“Oh God.” Britney buried her head in Axel’s chest.

“There’s nothing to be embarrassed about,” Gunner said with a chuckle. “We’ve been rooting for you guys to get together for months.”

“I’m goin’ to bed.” Britney couldn’t believe they had been talking about her love life behind her back.

“Rainey and I’ll keep an eye on the kids.” Gunner took a seat on the recliner. “You two have fun.”

She had no words. Couldn’t even look at Axel. How could they possibly think she was headed upstairs to have sex when people were down here knowing she was having sex?

“Come on.” Axel placed a firm hand on the small of her back.

“I don’t think….” Even through her thick robe, his hand sent a wave of desire racing down her spine.

He leaned in and whispered in her ear, “No more thinking.”

“Good night,” Gunner called as they headed up the stairs.

Britney hurried into her room and closed the door. “I can’t believe they walked in on us.”

“We’re all adults, Britney.” Axel lit the kerosene lamp on her nightstand. “No one’s judging you.”

“If we have sex, everyone will know.”

Axel smirked. "If we don't have sex, they'll think we did. Which way sounds like more fun for us? I, for one, vote we have sex. That way we win."

Her mouth fell open. "First of all, that doesn't make any sense. Second of all, not fifteen minutes ago, you sat there on the couch and refused to make the first more. Now you're flirtin' with me? What the fuck?"

The playfulness dancing in his eyes faded, replaced by something more serious. "On Christmas you told me you weren't ready. I promised myself I wouldn't make a move until you asked me to."

"All this time you've been waitin' on me?" Her heart melted. "Makin' sure I was ready?"

"Hey, like I told you before, I might look like a hardass on the outside, but I do have feelings and have acted on them from time to time."

"Badass," she corrected him.

"What?"

Untying her rode, she let it slip to the floor, along with all her inhibitions. He was right. They'd come upstairs together. Closed the door to her room. They might as well enjoy the alone time while they had it. "You called yourself a badass before, not a hardass."

"That's right." He stalked toward her. "And if I remember correctly, you laughed in my face."

"Me?" She shuffled backward until her back hit the door. "Never."

He paused mere inches from her as his eyes swept over her body. "You are so fucking beautiful."

It was the first time he'd ever said anything like that to her before. Her core quivered, and it took all she had not to jump into his arms.

"I will only ask you this one more time." Axel brushed his lips against hers and her back arched. "Are you sure you're ready?"

"Yes."

He lunged forward, clutching her ass with his strong hands and lifting her off the ground in one fluid motion.

"Bed," she moaned, yanking at his T-shirt, needing to feel his skin against her own. There was a time for foreplay, and this wasn't it.

He laid her on top of the bed, their lips locked except for a brief second to remove an article of clothing. She arched her back, coaxing him inside of her, but he hesitated.

"What's wrong?" she gasped, her unsatisfied arousal growing more painful by the second.

"A condom?" She could see the pain etched across his face.

Britney sucked on her bottom lip as he brushed his arousal over her throbbing clit. "No condoms. Married, remember?"

"Fuck." Axel teased her again, bringing her close to an orgasm already. "Should we stop?"

"No," Britney moaned. "Please don't stop." Why were they even talking about this right now?

The tip of Axel's erection pressed against her burning core. "Get pregnant—"

"Stop right there." She nipped at his bottom lip. "I can't get pregnant. I had my tubes tied."

"Oh thank God." He plunged into her, and she screamed as the most powerful orgasm of her life ripped through her.

Each thrust pushed her further over the edge of pleasure to a place she never remembered going before. Her body convulsed as he explored her. And when she thought she couldn't take any more, he went deeper, filling her to a point that she never dreamed possible.

Hours passed and still she never reached the point of feeling 100 percent satisfied. Not because of anything he did wrong but because of all the things he did right. She felt like an addict, craving his touch, his kiss, his taste. Each hit left her longing for her next fix.

When he wasn't buried inside her, they were wrapped in each other's arms, kissing and caressing until their bodies couldn't take any more.

It wasn't until the sun peeked under the curtains that they collapsed from exhaustion.

As Britney drifted off to sleep, she heard Axel mumble, "Happy birthday, babe."

CHAPTER TWENTY-FIVE

"Good morning, beautiful."

Britney rolled over and snuggled into the crook of Axel's neck. "Good mornin' to you too."

For three months—three glorious months—she'd woken up next to this man happy and even more in love with him than the day before.

She'd never been one to utter the word "love" so quickly, but a week into their relationship, they had both said it. That was the thing about the world they lived in—with death lurking around every corner, the future didn't mean the same thing as it once did. Sure, they still planned for it, but they didn't dwell. Instead, they focused on living in the present and making the most out of what they had in every moment.

And what she had in that moment was the most wonderful man she could ever dream of meeting in conditions such as these.

"So." He threw his leg over her hip and dragged her closer to him. "What's the plan for today? Stay in bed all day, or face the world?"

She planted a big kiss on his lips and nipped at the bottom one. "I'm pretty sure we promised the kids we'd take them to swim in the river today."

Axel groaned. "We did, didn't we?"

"Yep. That was part of the twins' birthday present. We'd take them swimmin' once a week durin' the summer."

"Whose bright idea was that?" Axel ran his hand over her bottom, making her squirm.

"Yours." Britney pressed her bare breasts against Axel's chest. After all this time, he still had the most amazing rock-hard body she'd ever seen.

"Maybe we can take them tomorrow." He pecked at her lips. "After the storms last night, the river might be running a little too fast anyway."

"True." Britney snuggled closer. "But I still think we're goin' to have to get—" She froze. "Did you hear that?"

Axel sat up. "I'm not sure. Did someone scream?"

"Britney!" Gunner's cry ripped through the house. "Hurry!"

They jumped off the bed and threw on some clothes. Britney couldn't get down the stairs fast enough.

"What's wrong?" she yelled, gun in hand as they raced out the open front door.

Everyone was gathered around the steps of the tree house. Carson held Molly as she sobbed.

"Where's Blake?" she screamed as she ran toward them. "Where's Blake!"

This couldn't be happening. He was okay. He had to be okay.

"Britney, wait." Gus moved to block her view.

Her heart shattered. "Please don't tell me he's… he's…."

Gus draped a fatherly arm around her shoulders. "He's not dead. But the fall knocked him out."

"Fall?" Britney trembled.

"He was climbing down from the tree house. The steps must have been wet from last night's rain, and he slipped."

She tried to calm her fried nerves but couldn't. "He's breathin'?"

"Yes."

There was something else, something he wasn't telling her. "What is it?"

"He broke his leg." Gus scratched at his chin. "I want to prepare you for what you're about to see. The bone is sticking out, and he's lost a lot of blood. We were able to tie a tourniquet around his thigh and slow the bleeding, but it's bad."

"Okay." She choked back her tears. "I'm ready."

Britney fell to the ground beside a crying Rainey, who held Blake's head in her lap. "I'm so sorry. This is all my fault."

"It's not. Accidents happen." She took a deep breath before checking Blake's leg. Her stomach rolled at the sight of her little boy's bone protruding from the skin, but she had to be strong for him. And Carson and Molly. By the look of their pale faces, they were taking this hard. "He has a compound fracture of the tibia. We need to get him inside, clean the wound and—" Bile burned her throat. "And set the bone. Then immobilize the entire leg in some kind of splint so he can't move it. That way it'll have a chance to heal."

"Fuck me," Shifter muttered.

Angie placed a comforting hand on Britney's back. "What do you need us to do?"

Jesus, this was bad.

"Get a bed ready," Britney said through her tears. "Clean sheets. And go through the bathrooms and find all the medical supplies you can."

Angie nodded. "Gus, can you come help me?"

"Of course." Gus turned to Molly and Carson. "Can you come inside with us and help find the first aid kits?"

Both nodded.

Gus cupped their cheeks. "Thanks. You're both so brave."

Britney forced a smile. "We'll take good care of Blake, okay?"

"Okay, Mommy." A fresh set of tears trickled down Molly's face.

Carson grabbed hold of her hand. "Come on. They need our help. We have to hurry."

Britney looked to the others. "We need some kind of stretcher to lay him on so we can get him inside. And some boards or something to make a splint for his leg."

"On it." Shifter motioned to Gunner and Mac, and they took off toward the barns.

Axel kneeled beside her. "Do you know what you're doing?"

"I don't know." Britney swallowed hard. "My sister, Sloan, is—*was* a surgeon. I know a little just from listenin' to her talk about the cases she worked over the years. I wish she were here. She could fix him without breakin' a sweat."

"We'll save him, Brit." As Axel kissed the top of her head, she could feel teardrops fall against her scalp. He was crying, which broke her heart even more. "I promise."

Pulling back her shoulders, she wiped away her tears. Crying wasn't going to save her son. "We need to set the bone while he's still unconscious. If he wakes up… I don't want him to have to experience that kind of pain."

"Can we do it now?" Axel asked.

"No. I need to clean the wound first."

Shifter, Gunner and Max came running back with a snow sled and ski poles.

"Will these work?" Shifter huffed, out of breath.

"They're perfect." Britney turned to Rainey. "You get his shoulders. Axel, get on the other side of him. He's not heavy, but we need to keep him as steady as possible."

Blake was taller than he had been a few years back when they'd gotten the sled for Christmas, and Britney didn't like the way he legs hung off the end. She scanned the area looking for something else she might be able to use to place under that leg.

"That skateboard over there on the porch." Britney pointed at it. "Someone grab it. I think it's flat enough that we can prop it under his leg."

"I'll get it." Gunner sprinted to the porch and back faster than she expected. "Here we go. I'll hold it under his leg if the rest of you want to lift the sled."

"Ready!" Angie called from the house.

Britney gave Blake a light kiss on the forehead. "Let's go."

The walk from the tree to the house wasn't far, but they took it slow. The last thing they needed was for Blake to wake up or to cause any more damage to the leg.

In the house, Gus and Angie had the sofa bed pulled out and made.

"I didn't think you wanted to deal with the stairs." Angie re-tucked and smoothed out the sheets. "I hope this okay."

"It's perfect." Britney butted the sled up to the side of the mattress. "We need to get him on the bed. Keep the skateboard under his leg."

"We got him." Angie slid her hands under Blake's armpits while Gus helped move his lower half.

Once they had him on the bed, Britney cleaned the wound with peroxide and readied herself to set the bone. Her touching the area must have hurt, as Blake flinched and groaned.

"Shit." Britney stared down at the leg. "We need to do this now."

"Do you know what you're doing?" Rainey asked.

Britney eyes widened. "Not really, but we don't have much of a choice, do we?"

Blake groaned again.

"Please don't wake up, baby." Britney's hands shook as she reached for his leg.

"Wait." Axel moved in beside her. "I'll do it."

"Have you done this before?"

Axel shook his head. "No, but I've seen it done a couple of times."

She closed her eyes for a second, trying to regain her composure, when Blake screamed.

"What happened? What did you do?"

"I set his leg." Axel waved at Angie. "Did you find any bandages? Gauze, maybe?"

Britney checked his leg for any signs of the bone. "You did it. Why didn't you wait for me to answer you?"

"It was better this way. No time for you to think." Axel cleaned the area with peroxide again, then wrapped gauze around the leg to cover the wound and hold the ski poles in place.

"He's so pale." Britney brushed the hair from his forehead.

"He's probably in shock." Axel ran his hand down her arm. "But he's breathing on his own, and the bleeding has slowed down. Those are good signs."

"That is good." Britney snuggled in bed beside him. "But we're nowhere near in the clear yet."

***

Two days after Blake's fall, the wound was healing nicely. By day three he'd woken up. Even though Britney could tell he was still in a lot of pain, his spirits remained high.

Molly insisted on staying at Blake's side day in and day out. She brought him his food and helped him eat, read him books and told him stories. The perfect little nurse in training.

On day four, Britney finally relaxed a little, thinking the worst had passed. Until she went to change his bandages.

"Shit." Britney ran her hand over Blake's hot and swollen red skin.

"What's wrong, Mommy?" Molly asked trying to get a better look.

Britney pressed on the skin around Blake's wound, and he winced. "Does that hurt?"

He nodded. "Yeah. Is that bad?"

"Molly," Britney said, "can you go get me the thermometer, please?"

Axel moved out of the way as Molly bolted from the room. "Everything okay?"

Britney smiled down at Blake. "I'm goin' to get you some medicine. Do you want me to get you somethin' to eat?"

"No." Blake lay back down. "I'm not hungry."

"Okay, sweetie." She covered him up with his favorite superhero blanket. "I'll be right back."

"We need to talk," Britney whispered as she passed Axel. "In the kitchen."

"What's wrong?" Axel asked.

Rainey looked up from the book she was reading at the breakfast table. "Is Blake okay?"

Tears stung Britney's eyes. "We have a problem. Blake's wound looks like it might be gettin' infected."

"Do we need to clean it more?" Rainey jumped out of her chair. "I'll boil some water."

"Thanks. We're goin' to have to keep a close eye on it." Britney had seen how fast an infection like this could turn sepsis. John had been hospitalized for a week after he sliced his leg on a tree branch and didn't treat it properly. "Molly went to grab a thermometer."

"Mommy!" Molly called from the living room. "It beeped."

"Correction." Britney rolled her eyes. "Molly is takin' his temperature as we speak."

Rainey and Axel followed her into the living room.

"Thanks, baby." Britney reached out to her. "Can I see it, please?"

Molly didn't hand it over but instead read the display out loud. "It says one hundred period eight."

"Give it." Britney snatched it out of her hand, needing to read it for herself. "Where did you take this?"

"Under his tongue," Molly said.

Britney's heart raced. "I need to take it again just in case he moved." She sat on the bed beside Blake. "Hold this under your tongue."

Blake did as he was told. In the past hour, he'd become more lethargic. She thought he was just tired after all he'd been through, but now she worried it might be something worse.

The thermometer beeped. "One hundred point eight. Shit."

"Told you."

"A fever?" Angie asked as she entered the room.

Britney rifled through the medical supplies, grabbing the antibiotic cream and more gauze. "He's developin' an infection."

Axel took a seat next to Blake. "You feeling kind of crummy there, kid?"

Blake nodded.

"It'll be okay." Axel turned to Britney. "Do you have any leftover antibiotics?"

"Nothin' he can use. Stay still." Britney unwrapped Blake's leg and tossed the old bandages in the trash next to the bed. *Poor kid. The swelling must be painful.* "He hasn't been on any in years and is allergic to amoxicillin. So if there was anything lyin' around, he couldn't take it anyway."

"Damn." Axel ran a hand through his hair.

"We have to make sure this wound stays clean. I'm goin' to give him some ibuprofen to help bring down the fever and swellin' around the injury. We need to keep a close eye on him, make sure he doesn't take a turn for the worse."

"And if he does?" Rainey's voice cracked.

Britney didn't want to consider the alternative. "Let's pray he doesn't."

***

The next twenty-four hours were brutal. Britney stayed by Blake's side, watching as her little man fought the infection the best he could. But the infection was winning. In the last two hours, Blake's condition had worsened. He stopped eating, and getting him to take even a sip of water was a struggle.

The look of his wound scared the shit out of her. Red streaks had formed and started to spread outward. Along with the greenish pus and increased swelling, Britney believed he was developing sepsis.

If left untreated, it would probably kill him.

“Mommy,” Blake croaked. “I’m so cold.”

“Here you go, baby.” Britney covered him with a fourth blanket and brushed her fingers along his forehead. As soon as the medication wore off, his fever returned. At this point, the medicine was only masking the fever, not breaking it. “You need anythin’ else?”

Blake yawned and snuggled under the blankets. “I’m tired.”

“Get some rest.” Britney kissed his head. “I’ll be in the dinin’ room if you need me.”

Britney grabbed a notepad and pen before joining the others for breakfast.

“How’s he doing?” Axel asked.

She took a seat beside him and dropped her head. Thank goodness Molly and Carson had eaten earlier; she didn’t want them to hear what she was about to say. “It’s not good. I think the wound is septic. If we can’t get it under control, he’s not goin’ to make it.”

“Fuck.” Axel tossed his fork on the table.

Everyone else stopped eating and started at her with wide glossy eyes.

“What can we do?” Shifter asked. “There has to be something.”

“He needs antibiotics and probably an IV drip since he’s not drinkin’ much.” Britney added both to the list. “Sterile medical supplies, a better splint or materials to cast his leg. I’m sure there’s more, but the antibiotics are the main thing.”

“I’ll go,” Axel volunteered.

“So will I,” Gunner added.

Britney let out a weighted breath. “Thank you. I’ll make sure the list is detailed.”

Axel reached over and took her hand. “Britney, you’ll probably need to go with us on this one.”

“What?” A cold sweat broke out on her forehead. “I can’t leave Blake.”

He patted her hand. “I know you don’t want to leave him, but Gunner and I have no idea how to get to the hospital.”

“I’ll show you on the map,” she blurted. She couldn’t go, wouldn’t leave Blake.

“And if that hospital is destroyed? Or doesn’t have what we need?”

Britney understood his concern, but how could he ask her to leave her baby’s side? What if he got worse and she wasn’t here? What if he… didn’t make it? “I can show you several. Please, Axel, don’t ask me to do this.”

“I wouldn’t ask if I didn’t think it was necessary.” Axel tapped her list. “Plus, you’re the one who knows what all of this stuff is. Without you, it’ll take us twice as long, if not more, to get back. With your help, we can be back tomorrow.”

Britney dropped her head in her hands. He was right, but the thought of walking out that door and leaving Blake—leaving all her kids—made her stomach turn.

“We’ll take good care of Blake.” Angie draped an arm around Britney and squeezed her tight. “Of all of them. But if he’s as sick as you think he is, finding the medicine and getting back as quickly as possible might be the difference between life and death.”

“Fine.” Britney pushed away from the table. “I’ll go. We need to leave now.” Before she changed her mind. “I’m goin’ to go tell my kids bye.”

Blake was asleep, so she headed upstairs. Carson and Molly sat in the middle of his bedroom floor, playing with Legos.

“Is Blake okay?” Molly asked.

Britney sat on the floor between them. “No, he’s not. He needs medicine. Stuff we don’t have here at the house. If he doesn’t get it, he might not make it.”

“He might die?” Legos slipped through Carson’s fingers.

She didn’t want to scare them, but she couldn’t lie. If she was going to leave, they needed to understand the severity of the situation. “He could if he doesn’t get the medication he needs. That’s why I’m goin’ with Axel and Gunner.”

Molly burst into tears. “You’re leaving?”

“I have to. Nobody else knows what Blake needs to get better.”

Carson crossed his arms over his chest. “Can’t you just write it down for them?”

“It’s not that simple.” Britney pulled them both into a tight hug. “Plus, I’m the only one who knows where all the hospitals are. They need me.”

Molly sniffled. “Is Axel going with you?”

“Yes. Him and Gunner.” Britney swept the damp hair away from Molly’s eyes. “We’ll keep each other safe. Promise. Can you two take care of Blake while we’re gone? Rainey and Angie will need a lot of help.”

“We’ll take care of him,” Carson assured her.

“I know this is hard. All of it. But you guys are amazin’. And strong. And brave. I couldn’t ask for better kids.”

“We couldn’t ask for a better mom.” Molly hugged Britney tight.

She cupped each of their little faces and gave them a big kiss. “I love you both. And I’ll see you soon.” Even though they planned on making it back tomorrow, she didn’t want to tell the kids in case something went wrong.

“When are you leaving?” Carson asked.

"Now." Britney pressed her lips together. She promised herself she wouldn't cry in front of the kids about leaving. "The sooner we leave, the sooner we get back."

Molly jumped to her feet. "I have to tell Axel bye."

"Me too." Carson followed her out of the room.

It wasn't until she heard their footsteps pounding the stairs that she let the tears fall. She'd make it back to them. Somehow, someway, she was coming home.

CHAPTER TWENTY-SIX

"You have to be fucking kidding me!" Axel slammed his fists on the steering wheel of the old beat-up Ford. "This is the fourth hospital the fucking military blew the fuck up! What the hell were they thinking!"

They'd been driving from one hospital to another for nearly ten hours without success.

Britney gripped his forearm. "I think they were tryin' to stop this."

He knew she was right, but it still pissed him off all the same. "Yeah, well, they didn't, did they? All they did was screw the people who are still around."

"I think we need to call it a night," Gunner said from the back seat.

Britney squeezed Axel's arm. "I agree. We're all exhausted. There's no point in continuin' tonight and riskin' the darkness. The next hospital is another three hours away. We can head out first thing in the mornin' and still have plenty of time to make it home by dinner."

"If that hospital is there," Axel mumbled through clenched teeth.

"It will be." Britney wiped away a stray tear. "It has to be."

Axel's anger faded. He needed to get his head out of his ass and remember why they were out there in the first place. "Sorry. You're both right. We need some rest. Any suggestions?"

"I saw a library a few streets over," Britney suggested.

"Library." Gunner snorted. "I saw a bar. Let's stay there."

Britney snapped her head in Gunner's direction. "In the library we might find some medical books that might just save my son's life. I think that's more important than spendin' the night in a bar and gettin' shit-faced."

"Simmer down there." Gunner shifted in his seat. "I'm not arguing. I didn't think about there being books there that might help Blake. I change my vote to the library."

Axel snickered. "Library it is."

"Plus," Britney added, even though the decision had been made, "the library is the last place people would have flocked to when the world went to hell. Which means it shouldn't be overrun by the infected."

In the review mirror, Axel could see Gunner was itching to argue. "Let it go."

Britney glared. "Let what go?"

"Nothing." Axel smiled at her. "We're going to the library. And we both agree your reasons are sound."

"Of course they are." Britney rolled her eyes. "The bar is probably overrun with infected. I mean, if you guys didn't come to the farm, where else would you have gone?"

"A bar," Gunner said. "Might as well enjoy the last few days you have."

Axel pulled into the library parking lot. "Should I park in the back so people don't get suspicious or by the door so we can run inside?"

"Door," Britney and Gunner said in unison.

"Who cares if other people know we're here," Gunner continued. "Maybe they can help us."

Axel didn't have near the faith in humanity that Gunner did but didn't want to dampen his optimism. "Door it is."

He killed the engine. "I don't see anything." They had run into quite a few infected during their drive. Not as many as he and Gunner encountered on their first supply run, but enough to make him nervous.

"I'll go check to see if it's unlocked." Gunner swung his door open. "Watch my back. I hate being exposed, especially in the dark. Those fuckers come out of nowhere."

Axel exited the truck too. No way he'd be able to keep Gunner safe from inside the vehicle. "Any luck?"

"Well I'll be damned. The door's open."

Britney climbed out of the passenger seat carrying a small duffel bag. "Doesn't mean it's safe."

"Only one way to find out." Axel locked the truck door. "Let's check the place out."

"Here." Britney handed them each a flashlight. "It'll be dark."

Axel did one final sweep of the parking lot. "We'll take it slow. Aisle by aisle, room by room."

Gunner locked the library door behind them and groaned. "Sounds exciting."

"I hope it's not," Britney said.

"Come on." Axel led them deeper into the dark library. "I want to get this over with."

It took them an hour to search the small library. They found no signs of people—alive or infected—but they noticed several stacks of building materials.

"Maybe it was closed for remodeling when all this shit went down," Gunner suggested as they dug into their rations of dried meat and dried fruit.

Axel reclined against the bookshelf. "Or maybe the place was empty."

"That's so sad." Britney rested her head on Axel's shoulder. "I like the closed-for-remodeling image better."

Axel couldn't remember the last time he stepped foot in a library. "You used to spend a lot of time in the local library, didn't you?"

"Durin' the school year, no. But in the summer, the library used to do all kinds of stuff for the kids. Stories, crafts, movies. We didn't go to everythin', but it was a nice, free way to get out of the house for a few hours when they were goin' a little stir-crazy." Tears laced her voice.

Gunner stood and stretched. "I'm going to get some shut-eye."

"We should stay together," Axel said.

"See those rooms over there?" Gunner gestured toward the right. "They're listening rooms. Soundproof. Added bonus, they have a lock on the door. I suggest you snag one for yourself. Going to make sleep a whole hell of a lot easier. Good night."

Axel wrapped his arm around Britney, who quietly cried to herself. "You okay?"

"If there was ever a time I missed havin' cell phones, this would be it." She sniffled. "I hate not knowin' what's goin' on with Blake."

"He's in good hands." Axel stood and offered his hand to help her up. "I've never been one to put much stock in faith, but all things considering, it might not be a bad thing."

"You're sayin' trust in God? After everything we've been through? Everything we've seen?"

Axel opened the door of a listening room a couple down from Gunner and ushered her inside. "We're alive. The farm is safe. How many people can say that?"

Britney rolled her light jacket into a ball, creating a pillow. "So you're a 'glass half full' kind of guy now?"

Axel settled in next to her and held her close. The carpet didn't have much in the way of cushioning, but he was so exhausted he could have slept anywhere. "What can I say? I have a lot to be grateful for."

***

"Did you find the books you needed?" Axel asked as Britney climbed into the front seat.

She set the stack of books in the floorboard. "I got two medical textbooks, a first aid book and a few survival guides. Can you think of anythin' else we might need?"

Axel started the engine. "Nope."

"Let's get on the road." Gunner smacked the back of Axel's seat. "How far did you say we have?"

"Three hours." Britney pulled out the map.

Gunner leaned between the seats. "I thought you knew where we're going?"

"I do." She shoved him back. "Now stay in your seat, or you'll have to put your seat belt on."

Axel laughed. "You better do what she says. She's got her mom voice going."

"I'll sit right." Gunner tapped his feet and drummed his fingers. "This is going to be the longest damn road trip."

“How can you already be bored?” Axel asked. “It’s been like five minutes.”

“It’s so quiet,” Gunner complained. “I wish we had some music or something.”

“Here.” Britney tossed him a small CD case. “Help yourself.”

Gunner caught it midair. “Where the hell were these yesterday?”

“We were kind of busy.” Britney went back to reading the first aid book.

“Here.” Gunner tossed Garth Brooks’s *The Ultimate Hits* onto the front seat. “Stick this in.”

Axel loaded the CD into the player. “I didn’t know you liked country music.”

“You can’t two-step to rock. And the ladies love a man who can spin them around the dance floor.”

Britney chuckled. “Yes we do.”

“Is that so?” Axel asked. He’d never gotten the hang of slow dancing.

“Don’t worry.” Britney rubbed his arm. “I can teach you.”

“Thanks.” Axel turned his attention back to the road.

A few CDs later, they found themselves parked alongside a high wire fence that surrounded the still-standing hospital.

Axel leaned against the steering wheel and stared out the window. “Well, at least it’s still here.”

“Do you see that sign?” Gunner asked. “It says ‘danger, keep out.’ I’m not much on adhering to the rules, but we might want to take that under consideration.”

“Are there any other hospitals we could try?” Axel asked. He agreed with Gunner. A warning like that was not to be taken lightly.

Britney shook her head. "I don't know of any others. It's this one or we go home empty-handed."

Axel surveyed the area. "I don't see any movement. Several parts of the fence have been either cut or knocked down. That could be a good thing. If there were infected trapped in there, they could have gotten out."

"Or more could have found their way in," Gunner said.

Britney angled herself in the seat so she could look at both of them. "You don't have to go inside if you don't want to. But Blake is my baby, and I have to try."

Axel couldn't believe she'd think for even a second that he would let her go at this alone. "You know I'm going with you. There's no question."

"I came all this way." Gunner rested a hand on Britney's shoulder. "No way am I sitting in the truck. We're going to find what we need to save your little boy or die trying."

Britney wiped her eyes. "Thank you. I just wanted to make sure you knew I would understand if you didn't want to risk your life for him."

"We all love him," Axel told her, and Gunner nodded. "No more talk of going at this alone. We're with you. All the way."

"Thanks." Britney pulled her hair into a ponytail. "Do we need a plan or just go in guns blazin'?"

Good question. "A plan is always good, but we have no idea what we're walking into. Could be empty or overrun with the infected."

Gunner clapped his hands together. "I suggest we keep guns ready and stay together. Shoot first, ask questions later. Stay on the first floor if possible because that's where the exits are. Did I miss anything?"

"Move fast and stay quiet," Axel added.

"Sounds like one hell of a plan to me." Gunner removed his gun from his holster. "Everyone check your weapons and make sure you have plenty of ammo."

Fifteen minutes later, they were out of the truck and inside the fenced area. They moved slow, carefully checking to ensure nothing surprised them.

"Looks like they created a makeshift emergency room here." Axel pointed to the tents. "I bet this is the hospital that couldn't take Queenie because they were over capacity."

"I wonder why they didn't destroy this one like they did the others," Gunner pondered.

"Maybe they ran out of time," Britney said in a hushed tone.

"You see any medical supplies out here we can use?" Gunner asked.

"No." Britney opened the drawers of the rolling supply carts they passed. "I bet someone was already here and took what they could find out here."

Axel figured. "It's what we would have done if we'd gotten here first."

They reached the entrance of the emergency room, and Axel tried the doors. "Locked."

Britney cupped her hands around her eyes and peeked inside. "I don't see any movement, but it's a mess in there."

"What sort of mess are we talking about?" Gunner kept his eye out behind them.

Axel grimaced. "Blood and bodies."

"Dead bodies?" Gunner jerked his head. "Like really dead, not lying in wait for their next victim dead?"

"It's hard to tell if these people were infected." Britney pressed her forehead to the glass. "Their skin doesn't look gray. And most of them have hair. They aren't movin'. I've never seen an infected not movin'."

"We're here." Axel blew out a breath. "I say we go in."

"What about the door?" Gunner yanked on the handle. "Any suggestions?"

"Break it," Britney said. "The sound of the glass shatterin' will draw the inside infected to us. I'd rather know they're coming than be surprised."

Her logic made sense, but Axel didn't know what they would do if they got overrun. "Gunner? What do you think?"

He glanced down at Britney, then back to Axel. "Her kid, her decision."

"Don't put this all on me." Britney crossed her arms over her chest. "All of our lives are at risk. Breakin' the glass was a suggestion. Do you have a better idea?"

Gunner took a few steps back. "I don't think breaking the glass is a bad idea, but maybe do it to a window of a room with the doors closed. That way we know there's nothing in there."

Axel looked to Britney. "It's up to you."

"We should hurry." She peeked over her shoulders. "Bein' out here is makin' me nervous."

"Lead the way, Gunner." Axel gestured him onward.

They ran along the building, Gunner checking in each window as he was the only who could see inside.

"Why are these windows so high off the ground?" Britney asked.

Axel chuckled, feeling her frustration. "To keep people from breaking in."

"Here!" Gunner waved them over. "Find a rock or something so we can break the glass."

Axel ran over to a nearby medical tent and grabbed a metal IV stand. "Try this." He tossed it to Gunner.

Gunner slammed it into the glass until it shattered. "That was easier than I thought it would be."

A ferocious growl ripped through the air.

"Inside! Now!" Axel couldn't tell which way the sound had come from, but it was close.

Gunner climbed through the broken window and reached back for Britney. "Give me your hand. I'll pull you up."

The window was higher than Axel thought. Britney could barely reach the sill.

At another howl, Axel rushed to the struggling Britney. "I'm going to lift you up." It was more like a shove through the window, but it did the trick.

Axel's fingertips scraped against the brick exterior as he jumped for the window. Gunner had made it look so easy. The three inches of height Gunner had over Axel made a world of a difference.

"Man, you need to hurry the fuck up." Gunner extended his hand. "Jump and I'll pull you."

Axel didn't dare look back; he could tell by the panic in Gunner's voice something was coming. "Do I want to know how bad it is?"

"We've seen worse." Gunner seized Axel's forearm and helped him up the wall and inside. "Get down."

Axel dropped next to Britney as they kept themselves pressed against the wall. The shuffling of footsteps just below them twisted his stomach. His fight-or-flight instinct begged him to run, but he kept still. The infected couldn't see the broken window. As long as they couldn't smell or hear the trio, they'd move on.

Gunner tapped Axel on the leg and held up three fingers.

That was how many he saw, but Axel knew there could be more.

Nails scraped against the brick, and Axel dropped his head back to get a better look. If the infected were coming in, they needed to be ready.

Axel readied his gun, as did the others.

They had the upper hand. All that was left to do now was wait.

Wait for them to pass. Or wait for them to enter.

***

"I don't hear them anymore," Axel whispered. After an hour of sitting silently in that office, he was ready to move. "We should get going."

"Maybe we should check outside first," Britney suggested. "Just to be sure."

Gunner uncrossed his ankles and stretched his torso to take a peek. "I don't see anything."

Britney scrunched her nose. "That wasn't very long."

"Long enough." Gunner stood. "We need to go."

Axel helped Britney off the floor and checked outside for himself.

"I told you." Gunner cracked the door open and peered out. "The hallway is clear too. Let's move."

"Are you ready for this?" Axel asked Britney.

She fidgeted with her clothing. "Not really, but I'm ready to get it over with. Where should we go?"

"The pharmacy." Gunner was already out in the hall waiting for them, pointing at a diagram on the wall. "According to this map, if we take a left from here, we'll hit the stairs. Up a flight and it shouldn't be too far down the hall."

"Lead the way." Axel waved him on.

Britney pinched her nose as they made their way down the hall. "The smell is horrendous."

"These people." Gunner dropped his head. "So many dead. And none of them look like they've been infected."

"They were all executed like they were." Axel noticed the chest wounds in each of the bodies they passed.

Britney kept her chin up. "I just can't imagine what happened in here. Do you think the military did this?"

"Afraid so," Gunner said as they reached the enclosed stairwell. "All the bodies down here have military regimentals on."

"These look more like the infected." Axel tried his best not to step on any of them.

Britney held the stairwell door for him. "How can you tell? They're all decaying."

"Teeth and nails are no longer human." Axel closed the door behind him. The sound echoed off the bare walls.

"Maybe try to close the doors a little quieter going forward." Gunner took the stairs two at a time. "We've been lucky so far. No need to call unwanted attention to ourselves."

Axel held his tongue. This wasn't the time or place to argue about such things. "Do you see anything on the second floor?"

"The hall's empty," Gunner called back. "Like *empty* empty. Not a body in sight."

"I'm not sure that's a good thing," Britney mumbled.

Neither did Axel, but he focused on the positive. "Maybe it is. Maybe the military cleared the second floor first, drew the fighting downstairs."

Britney's forehead creased. "When did you become Mr. Optimistic?"

"Shh." Gunner pressed his finger against his lips as he opened the door to the second floor.

They kept quiet as they crept down the hall. Even though Axel couldn't hear anything, something felt off.

Gunner paused at a door in the middle, which Axel could only assume was the pharmacy, and turned the handle. “Don’t hear anything.”

Axel jerked his head. Gunner might not have heard anything inside the pharmacy, but he’d heard something out here. “Get inside. Now.”

“What is it?” Britney switched on her flashlight. The windows from the patient rooms allowed for some light in the halls. The pharmacy didn’t have the same luxury.

“I’m pretty sure I heard something,” Axel whispered. “Grab the stuff we need and let’s get out of here.”

Gunner pulled a small lantern from his duffel bag. “I’ll be your light if you want to focus on getting the stuff.”

“Go.” Axel stayed close to the door. “I need to make sure whatever it is I heard isn’t heading this way. Watch your backs.” They should have taken a few minutes to secure the room, but Axel feared they were running out of time.

With his ear pressed against the door, he listened and waited. He could hear something on the other side—scraping, clawing, dragging—but couldn’t be sure what caused the noise.

“How’s it going?” Axel called out into the darkness. Several minutes had passed since he’d heard their voices.

“Almost done!” Britney answered.

The noise in the hall picked up at the sound.

“Shit,” he mumbled under his breath.

A few minutes later, Gunner and Britney emerged from the darkness, her backpack loaded down.

“I’ll carry that.” Axel slung the heavy bag on his back and tightened the straps. “Got everything we needed?”

“And more.” Her whole face lit up. “Let’s go.”

Axel stepped in front of the door. “We have a problem. There’s something out there.”

Britney’s smile faded, and she turned away. “God.”

Gunner bared his teeth. “How many?”

“I haven’t checked. Didn’t want to get them riled up.”

“Allow me.” Gunner eased the door open and poked his head out before quickly closing it again. “Motherfucker.”

Britney whirled around. “Seriously?”

Gunner seemed taken aback. “Excuse my harsh language, but there are a shit ton of infected out there.”

“I don’t care about the language,” Britney snapped. “I just can’t believe after everything we’ve been through, everything we’ve survived, and yet a broken leg is how my son is goin’ to die. And not because we couldn’t find the stuff he needs to heal him. No, no, no. It’s because we can’t outsmart a bunch of blind, mindless monsters.”

Axel wasn’t sure he agreed with her on the mindless part but kept his opinions to himself. She felt trapped, helpless, just the same as he did, and she needed to get it off her chest. But going off wouldn’t get them out of there. They needed to stay strong if they wanted to survive.

“There has to be a way out.” Axel refused to give up. They’d made it this far. “Gunner, how many did you see? What was their location?”

“It’s not like I took the time to count them all. There’s a handful by the stairs. More scattered about.”

“Take a guess.”

Gunner threw his hands in the air. “Twenty. Thirty. Something like that.”

Britney’s brow furrowed. “No way we can kill them all. They’re too fast.”

“We need a distraction.” Gunner grabbed an IV stand. “This should work. There’s metal railing along the wall. I’ll get their attention and lead them away from the stairs.”

“No.” Axel tried to take the stand away. “That’s suicide.”

Gunner stepped away from Axel and moved closer to the door. “I’ve lived a long and happy life. The kid deserves the same.”

“But—” Britney went to argue, but Gunner stopped her.

“This is my choice. I’m leaving this room and going to Pied Piper these monsters out of here. You need to be ready to go when the hall clears.” Gunner cupped Britney’s wet cheeks. “It’s going to be okay. We’re all going to die. Might as well go out a hero.”

She choked out a laugh. “Isn’t that a line from a movie?”

Gunner kissed her forehead. “Close the door behind me.” Then he burst out of the room, a gun in one hand and the IV stand in another.

The infected growled and rushed for him as he slammed the stand against the metal railing while sprinting down the hall.

As Britney wept silently beside him, Axel waited in agony for the noises to fade. When he was certain he could no longer hear them, he cracked the door open. “Hall is clear. Let's go.”

He took her hand and they rushed toward the stairwell they’d come up. Axel shoved open the door and stumbled inside, hitting the railing so hard it knocked the air from his lungs. Leaning over to catch his breath, he gulped in air.

“Are you okay?” Britney rubbed his back.

Axel caught movement from the bottom of the stairs. He watched in horror as a horde of infected caught a whiff of their scent.

"Go!" Axel pushed Britney up the stairs.

The color drained from Britney face. "Fuck!"

Claws against metal pierced his ears, but he didn't dare look back. Based on the sound, they were gaining at inhuman speeds.

"Door! Now!"

Britney flung it open and took a sharp right, allowing Axel to slam the door behind him. He pressed his back against the door and dug his heels into the rooftop gravel. "We need to lock this door somehow. Do you have anythin' we can stick in the lock?"

"There're some tools in the backpack. A knife. What if we break the tip off inside the lock?"

Axel tossed the bag at her feet. "Find something."

She unzipped a small outside pocket and pulled out a Swiss Army knife. "Can you scoot over just a little so I can get to the lock?"

"Give it to me." Axel opened his palm.

"You can't hold the door and mess with the lock." Britney fell to her knees beside him and stuck the tip of the knife into the small keyhole. "It's too big. It won't turn."

"Use the screwdriver."

Britney stared up at him. "This isn't goin' to work unless we can lock it."

The infected slammed into the door, and Axel's body flung forward. He regained his footing and held his ground. "I don't think I can hold them much longer."

Britney spun around. "There has to be a way off this roof."

"Not going to matter if we don't hold them inside long enough so we can get down."

"Maybe there's something up here we can us." Britney jumped to her feet. "I'll be right back."

"Hurry." Axel could feel the weight of the door pressing against his back. If the infected figured out how to turn the handle, they'd be screwed.

"I found a fire escape!" Britney came running back with a chair in hand. "And this. We can prop it under the door handle."

"I don't know how long it'll hold them." Axel scooted over so she could wedge in the old metal-framed chair.

Britney's eyes locked with his. "There's only one way to find out."

CHAPTER TWENTY-SEVEN

Britney's heart contracted as Axel stepped away from the door. "Should we wait to see if it holds?"

Axel grabbed her arm and wrenched her backward. "No."

"No?" She allowed him to drag her away.

"It's not going to hold." Panic laced his voice. "Where's the fire escape?"

Britney couldn't stop herself from peeking over her shoulder. The door still held, but the way the hinges whined each time the infected rammed into it, it wouldn't be long until they broke through.

"Brit!" Axel tore her attention away from the door. "Where's the fire escape?"

"Follow me." She darted to the right, past the red-and-white helipad and around the solar panels. "This is where I found the chair. I guess they used it while waiting for patients to arrive."

A booming crash had them both looking over their shoulders, but they didn't dare stop until they reached the access point of the fire escape.

"This is just a fucking ladder!" Axel's pupils were huge. "Shit."

"Please don't tell me after everything we've been through, you're afraid of heights?" Britney planted her foot on the first step and pressed against the aluminum. "It's secure. We have to go." She could hear the infected getting closer.

"I'm right behind you."

They started down the stairs at a rapid pace. Above them the infected growled and snapped their teeth, desperately searching for their prey. Thankfully, without the use of their eyes, they had no way of knowing where the pair had gone. As long as Britney and Axel kept quiet, they might make it to the ground undetected.

The infected's constant threat had Britney flying down the stairs. Midway down, she lost her footing. She cried out, wrapping her arms around the ladder. Overwhelming fear washed over her as the reality of how close she'd just come to falling sucker punched her in the stomach.

"Are you okay?" Axel called from the step above her.

She laid her forehead against a rung, out of breath. "I slipped. Oh God. I almost fell."

"Britney," Axel called out to her, but she couldn't move. "Look at me. You're all right now. We're almost down. We got to keep mov—what the hell? Is that Gunner?"

She frantically searched the parking lot until she spotted him sprinting away from the building, close to the same spot they'd entered. "Do we call out to him?"

"I don't know. If the infected hear us…."

"Wait. I think he sees us." Britney flapped her arms the best she could through the spaces between the steps.

"Shit!" Axel gasped. "One's behind him."

“What do we do?” Britney whimpered, pointing and waving, trying to get Gunner to look behind him.

But it was too late. The infected jumped on Gunner’s back, knocking him to the ground.

Axel aimed his gun. “I can’t get a clean shot.”

Britney sobbed as she watched him fight the monster off, but it overtook him in a matter of seconds, biting and clawing at his exposed skin.

“It’s going to turn him.” Axel choked on the words.

Gunner’s head fell to side. He stared up at them, not pleading for help like she would have expected but with sheer determination. As the infected’s teeth ripped into Gunner’s skin, he reached for his gun. A shot rang out, and the infected dropped dead.

“We have to go to him.” Britney started back down the stairs. It wasn’t right, letting him die alone out there.

“Stop,” Axel ordered. “There are more.”

Dozens more came out of nowhere, drawn in by the sound of the gun. “Poor Gunner. Do you think he knows what’s about to happen?”

Another shot rang out. Closer this time.

Britney let out an involuntary scream as she watched blood spill from Gunner’s fresh chest wound.

“I couldn’t let him suffer like that,” Axel muttered. To himself or her, she couldn’t be sure.

The pain in his eyes gutted her, but there would be time to mourn when they got home. “What now?” With the infected on the roof and now on the ground, they were stuck.

He slung his rifle back over his shoulder. “Maybe we can break a window, find somewhere inside to hide until they leave?”

“Axel.” As she listened to his plan, she’d kept her eyes on the infected on the ground. “They’re moving this way.”

"Son of a bitch." Axel hit the ladder. "We're out of time. We need to get inside. Now!"

Britney kicked the window nearest to her to no avail. She lifted her leg to kick again when something slammed against the window. "Shit! Infected inside too. We're trapped."

"Listen, Britney. I want you to take the backpack."

"Why? What's wrong?"

He cocked his chin to the infected on the ground. "We need a distraction. *You* need a distraction."

Britney didn't like where this was going. "Whatever you're thinking, the answer is no. We get out together or not at all."

Axel shifted around to the back of the ladder and climbed down so they were face-to-face. "Get back to Blake. He needs you. They all need you."

"They need you too," Britney pleaded. "Don't do this."

"Take it." Axel shoved the backpack into her hands. "I'm going to lead them away, and then you make a run for the truck."

Britney heaved the backpack onto her shoulders. "You better run like hell, because I'm coming to get you."

Axel kissed her, a kiss that ended too soon. "I love you."

"I love you." This wasn't the end. It couldn't be. "Don't give up."

"Don't look back." Axel made his way down the stairs, slowly this time.

The infected moved closer. If he made too much noise, they'd be there in a matter of seconds and he wouldn't be able to make it the ground.

For a split second, she considered screaming at the top of her lungs, calling attention to their location so

Axel couldn't continue his suicidal plan. But as selfish as she wanted to be, Axel was right. Blake, Molly and Carson needed her to come home. They'd already lost too much. She feared losing her too, losing Blake, would be a blow the other two would never come back from.

Focused on the infected moving in, Britney had forgotten about the ones on the other side of the window. Forgotten how strong they could be when their prey was nearby.

Glass shattered behind her, and she screamed, losing her grip on the ladder. She slid down the slick metal, scrambling to regain her hold.

"Got you." Axel caught hold of her before she hit the ground, and she slammed her forehead into the bottom step.

The world faded in and out as a hot, sticky substance seeped down her face.

"Shit. You're bleeding." Axel set her feet on the ground and wiped the blood from her eye.

Britney's head throbbed. "How bad is it?"

"Nothing a few butterfly bandages can't fix."

"Good." Britney forced her eyes open and her stomach turned. "Now what?"

Her screaming had sent the infected into a frenzy. From all directions—ground, roof and window—they were trying to grasp the ladder.

"Do you think they can climb?" Britney did her best to whisper, but the infected made so much noise she could barely hear her own thoughts.

Axe pulled out his gun and fired, killing one that'd gotten hold of the ladder. "I wouldn't put it past them."

"I'm sorry." Britney was doing her best to hold it together but failing fast.

"We'll find a way out of this." Axel pointed his gun at the first-floor window. "Do you see any movement inside?"

Britney squinted. "We're too far away, and the tint is too dark. I can't be sure."

"The infected on the first floor followed us up the stairwell to the roof." Axel's eyes met hers. "What do you think?"

"I—" A distant sound caught her attention. "Do you hear that?"

"What?"

"That sound." Britney nodded toward the ground. "Look. The infected hear it too. It sounds like a horn."

"A horn? Like a car horn?"

"There it is again. Where is it comin' from?" Britney couldn't see anything, but the sound grew closer. "I see something! Comin' around the building!"

"Holy shit, is that an RV?"

Britney's muscles trembled at the sight of the classic Winnebago truck/camper combo barreling into the infected and stopping next to them.

A man dressed in camo and wielding a shotgun opened the door to the camper. "Come on! Come on! Move it!"

"Thank you." Britney fought the urge to hug their savior as she and Axel climbed in the back. They still needed to get out of there.

"Have a seat at the table," he directed them as the driver took off. "I'm Dale. Is there anyone else?"

"This is Britney, and I'm Axel." He slid into the bench seat next to Britney. "And it's just us. Our friend was killed."

Dale sat across from them, his gun still propped at his side. "Do you mind me asking what you two were doing there? It's a known hotspot for the undead."

"We didn't know that." Britney looked to Axel, who nodded. "But we needed medication for my son. He broke his leg, and it's infected. If we don't get to him soon, he'll die."

"Where you headed?"

Britney swallowed. "Myrefall."

"Give me a second." He left the table with a walkie-talkie in hand and went to speak with the driver, coming back a minute later. "Just sit tight, folks. As soon as we get a safe distance from the hospital, we'll pull over."

"Pull over?" Britney didn't understand. "Why?"

A big smile spread across Dale's face. "You'll see."

***

The thirty-minute drive was agonizing. The worst scenarios played out in Britney's head. Shallow graves. Execution-style murders. Being fed to the infected.

Axel tried to reassure her that everything would work out. If these people wanted to kill them, why risk their lives to save them in the first place?

She knew he had a point, but her brain didn't do rational well. It jumped to the most horrible of conclusions first, then laughed when nothing bad happened.

Dale pulled back the curtain that separated the cab from the camper. "We're pulling over now. Wait here."

"Should we be worried?" Britney had to ask.

Dale chuckled. "You have a hard time trusting people, don't you?"

"You have no idea." Axel nudged her. "It'll be fine. We still have our guns."

"True." And she wouldn't hesitate to use them if it meant getting back to her son.

The back door opened, and Britney sucked in a sharp breath at the sight of the beautiful African American woman climbing inside. “Makayla?”

“Who?” Axel asked.

“Thomas and Patty’s daughter.” Tears blurred Britney’s vision as the women embraced. “My oldest friend in the world.”

“I can’t believe it’s you.” Makayla wiped away her tears. “When Dale said Britney from Myrefall, I wanted to believe it was you, but I just couldn’t. Not until I saw you. And here you are. With Axel, is it?”

“Sorry.” Britney grasped Axel’s hand. “Yes, this is Axel, my….” Funny how they never thought to define their relationship, even though they’d been sharin’ the same bed, same room, for months. Husband didn’t fit. Neither did fiancé. But for some reason boyfriend didn’t feel like a strong enough description.

“We’re together.” Axel shook her hand. “Nice to meet you.”

“You too.” Makayla’s eyes darted to Britney. “Your head looks awful. I need to close that gash.”

“Dale gave us the first aid kit so I could clean it, but there was nothing in there to hold it together.”

Makayla dug around and pulled out a second kit. “I keep all the good stuff in this one. Have a seat.”

“Thank you.”

“I can’t believe you’re here.” Her gaze danced to Axel and back. “What about John? The kids?”

Britney dropped her head. “John didn’t make it. The kids are waiting for us back at the farm. Blake’s hurt. Fell and broke his leg a few days back, and it’s going septic. We have to get back to him as soon as possible.” She lifted her head and looked into her friend’s eyes. “Will you come with us? Please, Makayla. You’re a nurse. You could help him. Stay with us.”

"I'll go back with you and help Blake," Makayla said as she cleaned and bandaged Britney's forehead. "But stay? These people are my family now, and they need me. I can't just abandon them. Plus, Tyler has made several friends within our group. I can't take that away from him."

Britney was thrilled to hear Makayla's son had made it. She already knew the fate of her husband, James. He was the doctor Axel had shot when he tried to steal her truck with her kids still inside. But they would get to that later.

"Bring them all." Britney grasped the hands of the woman she never thought she'd see again. "Are you kidding? It would thrill Carson to have his best friend come live with us."

"There are twenty of us, Brit. Twelve travel trailers."

"We have room. And it's safe. With the fence we already had in place and now the wall in front of the property, we haven't been attacked in months. Rarely ever see the infected. Come stay with us. Please."

Makayla blew out her cheeks. "I have to talk it over with the others."

Britney let go of her hands. "Go. And please hurry. I don't know how much time Blake has left."

***

Makayla let out a low whistle. "When you said a wall, this is not what I expected."

"Axel and the other bikers built it." Britney bounced her leg, ready to be home. They were so close she could hardly stand it. "The infected attacked us. Nobody got hurt, but they killed several animals. We had to make sure it didn't happen again."

Axel had ridden with the lead truck to give directions and let Britney and Makayla have time to catch up.

The women had spent the better part of three hours talking about how they'd survived all this time. Makayla had been at her in-laws' picking up Tyler when it all started. After what James had seen at the hospital, he had insisted they stay put until things got better. A few months later, an attack that killed her in-laws sent them running. They had been lucky enough to hook up with the travel trailer brigade, a group of survivors that had been camping at Glacier National Park when the apocalypse started.

"I'm sure he's fine." Makayla rested a hand on Britney's leg. "It's only been a day, right?"

"Yeah." Britney tapped her fingers on the table. "But it was bad. Fear, redness, pus."

"I have everything I need to get it under control, thanks to you and Axel." Makayla stared out the window. "Are those armed guards at the gate?"

Britney almost laughed at the sight of Gus and Shifter perched up on the wall, guns in hand. "I didn't even realize they had built it to where they had enough room to stand up there."

"I'm going to go out on a limb here and assume these are two of Axel's friends."

Britney smiled. "They are."

"And how did you find yourself in the company of bikers?" The smirk on Makayla's face was priceless. "And in the bed of one boiling-hot biker?"

Heat crept up Britney face. "It's a long story."

"Blushing?" Makayla's hand flew to her chest as she feigned shock. "Well, I never thought I'd see the day."

Britney rolled her eyes. "Hey, Dale, just pull up in the horseshoe driveway and park in front of the house."

"Got it."

"There are more armed people on your front porch, Brit," Makayla stated.

Angie, Rainey and Mac each had a gun pointed at the RV.

"I'll get out first." Britney slowly opened the back door. "It's me. Please don't shoot."

"Lord have mercy!" Angie cried out. "We thought we were being invaded."

Britney jumped down and wrapped the woman in a tight hug. "How's Blake?"

"He's hanging in there." Angie stepped out of her embrace. "Where are Axel and Gunner?"

"Axel's making sure the gate gets locked up right."

"Britney!" Makayla called from the RV. "All clear?"

"Come on!" Britney waved her over. "He's inside on the pullout in the livin' room."

Makayla nodded to the others. "Hi. Excuse me."

"Who the hell is that?" Mac asked. "And all these other people?"

"Makayla is a nurse and my oldest friend in the world." Britney hitched a thumb behind her. "These are her friends. The people who saved her and her son, Tyler. They're goin' to be stayin' here with us."

Angie jutted out her hip. "For how long?"

Britney shrugged. "For as long as they would like."

"Mommy!" Molly screeched as she burst from the house and jumped into Britney's arms. "You're back! I saw Aunt Makayla inside with Blake."

Britney held her daughter close. "She'll take good care of him."

"Hey, Mom." Carson's voice, choked with unshed tears, made her heart ache. "I knew you'd make it back."

"Come here." Britney outstretched her arm and pulled him in for a hug. "I missed you guys so much."

"If Aunt Makayla is here…." Carson trailed off.

Britney shifted her body so they faced the driveway. "Tyler's in the last RV. The black-and-gold one. Why don't you two go find him and the other kids? Show them around, but stay close."

They each squeezed her one more time before running off.

"Slow down there," Axel said as they passed. Carson waved, but Molly stopped to give him a hug.

"They missed you both very much," Angie told her. "Carson really struggled. Molly was more optimistic, but Carson, he's old enough to understand the danger."

Britney pressed her lips together. "Thank you for takin' care of them."

Axel joined them on the porch and gave Britney a quick kiss on the cheek. "Blake doing okay?"

"Yeah. Makayla's in there with him."

"I can't believe you aren't in there yet." Axel ran a hand along her back.

She wanted to be in there, but there was something she needed to do first. "Rainey."

Rainey's chin trembled. "He's not coming back, is he?"

"I'm so sorry." Britney hugged her tight. "We were trapped. Gunner sacrificed himself so we could get out. I tried to talk him out of it, but he wouldn't listen."

"I'm not surprised." Rainey pulled out of Britney's arms. "He couldn't have kids of his own and loved yours so much. He would have done anything to save them."

"He's a hero," Axel added. "Bravest man I've ever known."

Makayla popped her head outside. "Brit, Blake's asking for you."

Axel squeezed her hand. "Go be with him. I'll be right there."

"Okay." As soon as the screen door closed behind Britney, the others broke down and cried along with

Rainey. It killed her to think they'd sacrificed one life for another. It didn't seem fair.

"Hi, Mommy." Blake smiled up at her with tired eyes.

Britney dropped beside him on the bed and held him tight. "Hi, baby. I missed you so much. I was so worried."

"You brought back Aunt Makayla. She said you got all the medicines she needed."

"We did." Britney kissed his forehead. He was burning up. "How are you feelin'?"

Makayla handed Blake a measuring cup of Tylenol. "He'll be just fine. This should break the fever. I have the IV going, and he's already taken the antibiotics. I'll let the wound breathe a little, and then I'll bandage it up. Tomorrow I can work on a better splint for the break."

"Thank you."

Makayla waved her off. "Please. You know I would do anything for you. Now, where can my friends and I set up our trailers?"

Exhaustion swept over Britney. "Um, I don't know. Maybe ask Axel. We don't have electricity."

"Don't need it." Makayla handed Britney two pills and a glass of water.

"What are these?" Britney tossed them in her mouth and swallowed.

Makayla laughed. "You already took them. What does it matter now?"

Britney yawned and snuggled up beside Blake. "True."

"Those painkillers will keep you from waking up with a really nasty headache." Makayla tucked them both in. "Now get some sleep. No talking. No playing. I'll check on you later."

"She's bossy." Britney scrunched her nose at Blake, who giggled. "But she's probably right. Want to take a nap with me?"

Blake's eyes fluttered. "Sure."

"Good, because I'm tired."

"Me too."

Britney gave him a big fat kiss on the lips. "Love you, kiddo."

"Love you too, Mommy."

CHAPTER TWENTY-EIGHT

Axel stared down at the walkie-talkie, confused. He couldn't have possibly heard what he thought he'd heard. "Say that again?"

"It's a damn caravan," Shifter's voice blared through the speaker. "Four Hummers headed this way. They look to be military. The big, troop carrier ones."

"I'll be right there." Axel hooked the walkie-talkie on his jeans and jogged into the house. The cool September air allowed them to leave the windows open most of the day, though at night they always kept them closed. Just in case. The farm hadn't seen an infected in months, but they couldn't be too careful.

"Brit!" Axel called out from the living room.

"Hey." She stared down at him from the top of the stairs. "Everything okay?"

"Yeah. Fine. Want to come down here for a second?" Axel waved at Blake, who poke his head out of the bedroom. His leg had healed nicely over the past few months. "Everything's fine, kiddo. Go play."

"Sure." Britney plodded down the stairs. "What's wrong?"

"I just told you everything's fine."

Britney narrowed her eyes. "Your words might have said that, but the wrinkle in your brow tells a different story. What's goin' on? Did someone see an infected?"

"No. But Shifter just called over the walkie-talkie and said they spotted four military Hummers heading this way."

"Are you kidding me?" Britney lightly scratched at her throat. "The military is heading this way?"

"Or someone with their vehicles. I'm going to check it out." Axel grabbed his rifle from the shelf. "Keep the kids inside."

"You think whoever it is might be dangerous?"

Axel made it a point never to lie to Britney about anything, including his concerns. "I don't know. But it's been a year and we haven't seen a single person drive by this place."

"That we know of." Britney and her optimism. The longer they went without an incident, the more positive she grew. Not that he disliked that side of her, but he didn't want her or anyone else to get too comfortable. Hidden behind their wall, it was easy to forget that monsters waited on the other side.

"Still, we haven't seen anyone. No one has tried to reach out to us. And now suddenly these four vehicles show up. It makes me nervous."

"I get it. I'll grab the house walkie-talkie. What channel are you on?"

Axel checked. "Three."

"Okay. Keep me updated." She rose on her tiptoes and gave him a quick kiss. "Whoever it is, if they stop, just promise me you'll hear them out."

"I promise." Axel left the house, climbed into an old two-door Ford and headed to gate.

Mac, Gus and Shifter waited for him at the top of the gate on the platform they'd built for that very reason.

"Can you believe this shit?" Shifted handed Axel the binoculars.

Axel wouldn't have believed it if he hadn't seen it with his own eyes.

"Do you think it could really be the military?" Mac asked. "Like they're out looking for survivors?"

"I don't know." Axel handed Shifter back the binoculars. "Only one way to find out."

"Let's not get our hopes up." Gus had taken up chewing on some kind of long grass, making him look more like a farmer than any of them.

Except for his leather jacket, which they all still wore. Axel had been forced to cut his at the shoulders after ripping a hole in one side. Considering the cool weather, he normally would have been cold, but after last winter, fifty degrees was nothing.

"Here they come." Shifter reached for his gun.

Axel stopped him. "Britney wants us to play nice."

Shifter crossed his arms over his chest. "That woman and her sentimental heart."

"Let's find out what they want before we hold them at gunpoint, okay?"

"Fine." Shifter took a step behind Axel. "But I'll stand back here, just in case."

"You're a fucking baby, you know that, Shifter?" Axel gave him a gentle shove. "Get over there."

The Hummers stopped in front of the gate, but no one made a move to get out.

"This is stupid." Shifter pointed his gun at the second vehicle. Mac and Gus followed suit with the last two.

"Fine." Axel aimed at the lead Hummer and tried to get a better look inside.

"Out of the truck!" Shifter yelled. "Hands where I can see them."

Axel groaned. "Chill the fuck out, man."

"Someone's getting out on the passenger side," Gus said.

"My name is Dr. Sloan Egan," the redheaded woman said. Her clothes were covered in blood and black goo. She had a bandage wrapped around her wrist, and she looked like someone had beaten the shit out of her. "I grew up here."

"Really?" Britney had mentioned her sister's name was Sloan, but he wasn't going to let some random lady in without proof. "Funny, never seen you before."

Sloan briefly clenched her fists. "Is Britney here?"

"Who?"

"Britney Campbell. She's my sister. What was your name?"

"Axel." And now for a little test. "And you are again?"

The woman pinched her lips together just like Britney did when she tried to keep her cool. "Sloan Egan."

Axel didn't recognize the last name; he only knew Britney's married name. He lifted his chin to Gus, who pulled out his walkie-talkie and tried to reach Britney.

When she didn't answer, he turned his attention back to the woman.

"Now that we're friends, mind telling me how you found us?" Axel knew he was being an ass, but there was something strange about the entire situation.

"Like I said, I grew up here."

"So you said. Got any proof?" He needed something concrete before getting Britney's and the kids' hope up.

"Give me a second."

Axel snorted. "Take all the time you need."

She leaned into the Hummer and returned a minute later with a cell phone in hand. "Proof. In the photos."

"Toss it up."

She hesitated.

"Don't worry." Axel smiled. "I've got the hands of an outfielder on a rainy day."

Shifter chuckled.

She lobbed the phone to Axel, and his mouth fell slack as he flipped through the photos. Static followed by Britney's voice drew his attention away from the phone. He snatched the walkie-talkie from Gus, flustered and irritated. "Brit."

"What's wrong?" The connection was bad. He could barely understand her.

"What's your maiden name?"

Britney paused before answering, "Egan. Why?"

"I'll explain when I get back." He tossed the walkie-talkie back to Gus and mouthed, "Sorry."

"You can enter. But only you."

Sloan cocked her head to the side. "No."

"Excuse me?" Axel would say he couldn't believe the audacity of this woman, but if she was really Britney's sister, it made sense.

"I'm not leaving the rest of my group out here. We've been through so much already."

"So have we," Axel snapped.

"There are only forty-two of us. Six soldiers. The rest are experts in their field of study. We're not here looking for a fight, just a place that's safe."

"Ain't no place safe anymore, lady," Shifter replied.

Sloan ignored him. "Whoever you spoke to knows who I am and that I can be trusted. Please."

Axel stared at her and then the rest of the Humvees and shook his head. "Open the gates. You can follow me."

He led them up to the house and parked in the driveway. "Wait here."

Axel rushed inside and found Britney and the kids in the living room.

"What's going on?"

"I need you and the kids to come outside."

Britney moved toward the door. "What is it?"

The last thing he wanted to do was tell Britney her sister was alive and it not be true. But the pictures spoke for themselves. "It's your sister, Sloan. She's outside."

"That can't be right. There's no way."

Axel handed her Sloan's phone and pointed at the picture of her and the kids. "That woman just showed up at our gate and is waiting outside."

Britney's chest heaved. "Sloan?"

"Come on." Axel guided her out to the porch with the kids close at her heels.

"Oh my God!" Britney cried out, rushing for her sister. "How are you here?"

They collided with such force that they nearly toppled over. Then the twins got into the action. Carson hesitated at first, but Sloan dragged him into their group hug as well.

Axel watched their reunion with awe as he headed over to introduce himself to the man who'd climbed out of the driver side.

"Hey, man. I'm Axel." He extended his hand.

"Lee Archer." He shook Axel's hand. "Thanks for letting us in. You have a hell of place here."

Axel leaned against the Hummer and crossed his legs at the ankles. "How the hell did you get here? Better question, how did you survive all this time on the road?"

"Not on the road." Archer kept his eyes on Sloan. "In a secret government bunker. We got overrun by whatever the hell these things are and lost almost everyone inside—the president, top military leaders. Only forty-two out of nearly two thousand made it out."

"Shit. So you spent a year underground knowing the entire world was being taken over by the infected?"

"They told us an asteroid hit and destroyed everything. Then a few weeks back, me and a few of my men got sent up to the surface to collect soil samples. We were attacked. Everyone was killed but me and a buddy of mine. We got him to the infirmary and Slash—Sloan—patched him up. She thought he was going to be okay." Archer dropped his head. "Then he started biting people. I assume you know the rest."

"All too well."

"I can't believe you all survived this whole time out here with those things running around."

"It hasn't been easy." Axel pushed off the vehicle. "I think Sloan's calling you over. Nice to meet you, man."

Archer slapped Axel on the back as he passed. "Thanks for saving our lives."

CHAPTER TWENTY-NINE

"How's your sister doing?" Axel asked as Britney climbed into bed.

"I can't believe everything they went through." The two had talked for hours, sharing their survival stories. "Did you know they were stayin' in the same place as the president?"

"Archer might have mentioned it."

The excitement of the day had worn Britney out, but there was still so much she wanted to tell Axel. "They know how this all started."

"Really?" Axel shifted to face her. "How?"

"It was what we talked about on Christmas Eve. The NATO drug trials, the one Sabrina and Thomas were a part of. That wasn't a synthetic drug. They found an alien substance in an asteroid, used it on some lab rats and figured out that it cured everything. Then without doin' any more studies, they gave it to people and turned them into monsters. Sloan said it consumes the organs and uses the brain to control the body."

"So people aren't infected, they're infested with an alien organism?" Axel's face paled. "That's fucking nuts."

"It also means there's no chance at a cure. No vaccine."

Axel wiped the sweat beading on his brow. "This isn't a zombie apocalypse, it's an alien apocalypse."

Britney rolled to her back and stared up at the ceiling. "I don't even know how to wrap my mind around that. How do you stop somethin' like this?"

Axel heaved her into his chest. "I don't know if you can."

She lay there for a moment, enjoying the sound of his heartbeat. "Can you believe my sister is alive?"

He chuckled. "It's almost crazier than the body-snatching aliens."

"Ugh." Britney shuddered. "I can't even."

"You know what else I find strange?" Axel ran his hand up and down her back. "The girl you turned into when you saw your sister. All giddy and more country than normal. I'm pretty sure you said 'Y'all.'"

Britney giggled. "Old habits, I guess. I'm so happy she's here, and the kids are over the moon."

"I bet."

As excited as she was to have her sister back, she couldn't help but think of all the other issues that came along with it. "We have a lot more mouths to feed now. I think Sloan said something like forty-two."

"More people to help around here."

Britney glanced up at him. "When did you become Mr. Positive? I thought for sure you'd be the one worryin' about stuff like this."

Axel kissed her forehead. "I just witnessed the miracle of apocalyptic miracles today. Two sisters who lived across the country from each other reunited. It blows my mind."

"How are we goin' to make this work?"

"We're survivors, babe. We'll figure it out. We always do."

Thank you so much for reading. If you enjoyed this book, please consider leaving an honest review.

Follow me on:
Facebook: https://www.facebook.com/mkdawnauthor/
Website: http://mkdawnauthor.com/
Instagram: M.K. Dawn Author

Want a FREE M.K. Dawn Book? Sign up for my Newsletter!

Other Books by M.K. Dawn:

The Decay of Humanity Series (Post-Apocalyptic Thriller)
Dusk of Humanity (Book 1)
Descent of Humanity (Book 2)
Demise of Humanity (Book 2) – Coming 2019
Dawn of Humanity (Book 2) – Coming 2019
There's an untitled spin-off in the works for the Decay of Humanity Series. More information coming soon!!

The Immortal Wars Trilogy
The Immortal Plague (Book 1)
The Immortal Deceit (Book 2)
The Immortal Affliction (Book 3)
There are two spin-offs in the works for the Immortal Wars Trilogy:
A prequel series: The Darrien Barrows Chronicles
A Continuation series about Samantha and the Dhampyr

The Nysian Trilogy (Fantasy)
The Nysian Prophecy (Book 1 is FREE)
The Nysian Prophecy Revealed (Book 2)
The Nysian Prophecy Fulfilled (Book 3)

How We Met Novellas (Contemporary Romance)
Under the Texas Sky

A little about M.K. Dawn

M.K. Dawn was born and raised in San Antonio, Texas. She now lives south of town on a cattle ranch with her husband, two kids, five dogs, and a rabbit. When she's not writing, she can be found driving her kids around to after-school activities, decorating cakes and watching as much Netflix as she can. But her all-time favorite hobby will always and forever be reading.

Made in the USA
Middletown, DE
14 September 2021